# By Their Fruit

Oil, Genocide, and Faith
A Chronicle of the South Sudan

**Gary Moelk**

By Their Fruit

## Contents

By Their Fruit

By Their Fruit

# Acknowledgements:

With thanks to my daughters, Lydia, Sarah, and Yvonne, who read and gave advice on my manuscript. With thanks also to Walt Turner who led me to faith and helped me on my own journey to and from Africa.

I wrote with the continual remembrance of those who died in the conflict in which this book is set. I was heartened when the International Criminal Court (ICC) in the Hague indicted President el Bashir of the Sudan for genocide of the 250,000 souls who died in the Darfur. I am still in shock and angry that the ICC, the United Nations, and the international press corps largely ignored the genocide of the 2,000,000 in southern Sudan. This book does not make up for the disregard of the outside world for the poor and powerless who lost their lives there. I did however write, thinking of them. May they meet glory in the life to come.

It should also be noted that this book is set in the time period just before South Sudan became a nation. It is encouraging that many tribes came together in agreement to make this new nation possible. There is power in agreement. It is my desire that this new nation would continue to find ways to agree and that all peoples and tribes in South Sudan would pull in the same direction.

**Note:** This book is a work of fiction. It should not be taken as an account of the events that inspired it. None of its characters or locations, whether modeled on actual people or places or created out of the writer's imagination, are intended to represent real people and locales.

To contact the author, email: gary.moelk@comcast.net

# Chapter 1

Jerome was on a flight to the Sudan, Africa. He was sitting beside a young Arab man. As an American, he liked Arabs and even spoke some Arabic that he had studied at the university in preparation for his trip. So the thoughts that ran through his mind, like a fantasy almost, surprised him. He imagined himself on a commercial flight the year before, on the morning of September 11, 2001. In the fantasy, shortly after takeoff, a young Arab man sitting beside him rises out of his seat shouting "Allahu akbar". He waves a small hand weapon. He then seizes a young attractive flight attendant and holds a knife to her delicate throat, now joined by 3 compatriots who order everyone to the back of the plane. Jerome rises slowly but deliberately from his seat, 1st class nonetheless. "Why not 1st class?" he thinks. "It's my fantasy." He then acts as if he'll walk obediently to the back of the plane along with the other passengers but just as he passes the terrified flight attendant, he simultaneously grabs the hand holding the knife to her throat and punches swift and true beside her attractive face into that of her bearded captor's while saying in clear and perfect Arabic, "Laisa el yom, ya si Mohammed (Not today, Mohammed.)" As terrorist number one falls unconscious against the bulkhead, his hand releases the knife into Jerome's hand, and he deftly turns and intercepts terrorist number two who is lunging in his direction pushing passengers aside in the crowded aisle. As he dives headlong at Jerome he unwittingly flies into Jerome's up-swinging arm. The knife of terrorist number one is then implanted in the chest of terrorist number two, who drops his own knife as his last breath escapes his lungs. Jerome then picks up the knife dropped by terrorist number two in time to intercept terrorist number three who is tripping over the body of terrorist number two, and likewise with terrorist number four tripping over the bodies of terrorists number two and three … "But that wouldn't be what I'd do," he says to himself. "I can hold my own in a debate, but I've always run from a fight. I wish just once, I could stand and fight, and who knows… maybe even win."

Everyone who knew the Sudan had told him, "Wow, you're in for quite an adventure!" He definitely thought of himself more as a scientist than an adventurer. Most of his acquaintances though thought of him as a geek. He was confident however that this term had not been directed towards him since High School. Sure he was smaller and thinner than average, and he did have thick glasses, but did people really notice those types of things in the adult world?

But now the flight was starting to descend over northern Sudan in preparation for landing in Khartoum. His mind went back 5 months when he was landing on Sakhalin Island, a Russian-owned property off the coast of Siberia where they had discovered gigantuous amounts of oil and gas. He was just starting his summer job with an oil company. The big barrel-bellied man sitting next to him had been drinking Asian beers since the flight had left Seoul and all of a sudden he got talkative, speaking loudly enough for at least 4 rows to the front and back to hear him.

"So what are you going to be doing again, kid?"

"I'll be working on a rig."

"Yeah? How'd a scrawny kid land a job on a rig in Sakhlin Island, for God's sake?"

"Well, when I was studying for my Master's in geology, I helped my professor in a joint university/business partnership. We studied the seismic readings done by the survey crew some time ago and made recommendations on where to drill. As it turns out, we were right."

"Yeah, how's that?"

"Well the rig I'm going to work on sits right in the basin we identified from the readings. So, anyway, I got to know some of the people from the original survey crew and they got me the opening this summer on the rig."

"Yeah? Hmmm. What rig are you working on?"

"The Epsilon drilling rig."

"No kidding? Kid, that's my rig. What're you going to do?"

"I'll be a mud engineer's assistant."

"Yeah? Well I won't hold it against you."

"What to do you do?"

"I'm a roughneck. We roughnecks are the most important guys on the rig. We make it run."

7

He took a long swig of beer burped loudly and exclaimed, "No offense kid, but we could do just fine without the damn mud engineers and their assistants and a whole lot of others, but without the roughnecks, well, you just wouldn't get any oil drilled."

Jerome wasn't sure if a response was anticipated. He sat in awkward silence for a while and then said, "No offense taken."

Jim, now on his 6th or 7th beer, gave Jerome a perplexed look and replied, "No offense taken for what?"

Then after a pause he proclaimed, "These here aint hardly beers at all. They constitute almost the beginning of a beer. Why if you served beer in a can this size back in Louisiana, there'd be things said, and then there'd be fists flyin.'"

In the last hour of the flight Jerome saw 3 more beers consumed and learned more than he wanted about the politics of the rig and found out that the roughneck's name was Jim.

As they got off the plane in a dim, run-down looking airport in Yuzhno-Sakhalinsk there was a man with a sign bearing the name of their rig to meet them. Jerome followed Jim who joined other roughnecks from the flight, who although half-drunk, knew the routine. They got on a bus that took them to a shabby train station where they boarded a run-down train. They were ushered by burly armed guards to a sparse sleeping car, where there was a narrow wooden bunk for everyone. The roughnecks now sobering up were cranky and seemed to want to sleep. The train got started, the lights went out, and Jerome could hear snoring from all directions. By this time, he was wide awake. The train bumped and clattered for 15 hours, through the night and into the next day. Jerome slept fitfully and arrived the next afternoon in the city of Nogliki with a head-ache starting to set in. Nogliki would have looked shabby and colorless even in a postcard. There were Soviet era apartment block buildings, crude wooden structures. Even the new pre-fab buildings were non-descript.

The men started walking toward an ancient-looking bus.

"That's our taxi to Val," Jim said.

"Where's Val," Jerome asked.

"About 30 miles north. That's where we get the boat that'll take us out to the rig."

They got to the bus and were starting to form small groups and make small talk. Once in Val, a boat would take the 20 or so men out to the rig where there would be a short handover meeting, and then 20 men who had been on the rig for the past 28 days would get on the same boat, and head back to Val, take the bus back to Nogliki, take the train back to Yuzhno, then fly off to Korea and then to wherever, come back in 28 days and do the reverse. At this point it all sounded fatiguing to Jerome. Adventures, he thought, should be less fatiguing.

They all got into the bus and each found their own uncomfortable seat. Jerome sat next to Jim. They were all seated, but there seemed to be a hold-up. A better dressed westerner was talking to the bus driver. He was asking him if he spoke English, which he didn't. He made signals with his hands and said very loudly, "Don't leave until I return."

As he walked past the window one of the roughnecks yelled out the window, "What's the hold up, boss?"

He hollered back, "We're waiting for a drilling gear that was supposed to be on the train. We need it and can't leave until we get it."

"So ask if it's on the train," the roughneck hollered.

"I would be doing that if I spoke Russian. Maybe you speak Russian?" he said sarcastically.

"Why hell no," he answered to no one in particular, and for some reason the whole busload broke into laughter. There were loud comments and more laughter.

"They're payin 10 billion dollars for this project an they can't even find a damn translator when they need one."

"Yeah but these people speak English just fine when it suits them."

Jerome pulled his Russian dictionary out of his suitcase. He had been studying Russian for three months, ever since he was offered the job. He knew about 25 verbs and how to conjugate them. He knew at least 200 nouns and hopefully all the common phrases used in normal conversation. He took out his Russian dictionary and looked up 'gear'. He had already learned the word for drilling in advance because he figured he'd need to know it.

"Maybe I can help," he said a bit timidly to Jim.

**9**

"Not unless you can speak Russian, you can't," he barked back
and laughed.

"But I can… at least some.  Do you think I should offer?"

"You don't speak no Russian, kid.  You must be dreamin."

"Seriously, I can speak some."

"This I gotta see.  Hey guys, the kid says he speaks Russian.  I
ain't sure, but anyone wanna bet me he can't?"  Then he leaned over
and said so only Jerome could hear, "I'm countin on you kid.  If you
can't do it, now's the time to say so.  Don't let Jim down."

It seemed that no one in their group spoke Russian, even those
who had been on rotation for a few years. Within 30 seconds, Jim,
Jerome, and 8 roughnecks were off the bus and walking quickly back
towards the train station in search of Graham, the assistant project
manager.

"Ok," Jim announced after thumbing through a fistful of bills, "I
have 100 dollars that says the kid can't do it."  Then he whispered in
Jerome's direction, "Show 'em they're wrong, kid!"

# Chapter 2

She grew up poor, Africa poor, yet she never knew it. There was never a means by which to compare herself with someone noticeably richer. Sure, some families had more cows than others, but they still lived in a tukul like hers. The thought of living in anything but a grass roofed round hut never crossed her mind. The Arabs usually lived in tents, but that was their way of life. This was the Dinka way. The Dinka lived close to the land. The men herded cows and goats, the women grew gardens, and together they survived, usually. The reality of famine was never far from the Dinka. But it wasn't the fear of famine that kept Yandeng Nyeal awake at night. A new terror had entered the Dinka lands, "murahaleen" were on the move.

Yandeng's brother Lual was away at a catechism class the day it happened. She wished they had all been away, but now it was too late. She was at school that morning, sitting under the big tree helping teach the children. An adult nearby heard it first.

"An Antonov, run for cover!"

Yandeng and the others ran to the dry creek bed. There were a few big rocks there and they hid in between them. She looked up and there flying low over the village was a big gray government airplane, what some people called Antonovs, making more noise than she thought possible. As it flew over she saw men at a doorway in the back and they were pushing what looked like barrels out on the village. A few hit some nearby tukuls and they exploded in flames. One hit beside the tree where they had been sitting. There were screams and smoke and a horrible smell. The airplane turned and came back. It still had more barrels to drop. This time a bomb hit her cluster of tukuls. Her sister Alual sat beside her shaking. Yandeng held her hand. Finally, the drone of the airplane engine faded in the distance. They could hear moans and cries for help. Alual got up and ran toward their tukuls. Yandeng was too terrified to face whatever destruction awaited. She crawled into a fetal position and lay there. She didn't know if she had lain there for minutes or hours when she was startled by the sound of hooves and jeep engines. Many hooves and dust, rifle shots, and shouting in Arabic. She knew the murahaleen were upon them. She became still as death. She heard people shouting and begging. She heard the pop of many rifle shots. Then she smelled fire. She smelled burning hair, like when the village men first started cooking a pig on a spit. Men were screaming wildly, like she had never heard men scream before. There were more shots and the agonized screams ended.

She could here muffled voices and the protests of women. She heard Alual screaming, "No, no, please!" She startled from her catatonic state, got up, and peeped around the rocks. Not far away a group of men had gathered around Alual. Some of them were Arabs, some were black men, in white jellabia robes. She recognized the black men by their dress as being from the Darfur. They sometimes came this far from home to herd their flocks on Dinka land. The Dinka were peaceful and usually worked out an agreement with them. She remembered her family offering a meal to some men from the Darfur in front of their tukuls a few years ago.

But now these men had pulled Alual's dress up and were pulling their jellabia up and doing what they said in the village that you should only do when you're married. Alual was screaming and pleading for them not to do it. Yandeng almost cried out loud, "You're hurting her." She couldn't bear to look. Her eyes flooded with tears. She stared at the rock beside her. She pushed her hands over her ears trying to block out Alual's cries. After what seemed like an eternity it stopped. The men took Alual and some other women and boys and tied them together in a line with a rope, then tied the rope to a camel and started walking them away from the burning tukuls and dead bodies. A few of the Arab men rooted through the burning homes for clothing and pots and pans, and whatever remained of value to her people. And then it turned quiet, deathly quiet. The stench of burning flesh hung in the air and sickened her. She lay sobbing and sobbing until she had no sobs left.

She finally stood with what little strength remained in her staggered towards her family's tukuls like she were drunk. She saw in the distance a few men approaching warily. They were Dinka she recognized from Gottong, a nearby village. They carried sticks, as though they were out chasing hyenas. They quickly came to Yandeng's side and led her back in the direction of their village.

"Do you know if any others are left?" they kept asking.

But she was unable to find words to answer. They walked her back to their village about two miles south, sat her in a tukul and gave her some tea to drink. She sat unable to drink or speak or even cry.

The men returned an hour later for their shovels. The reports were grim. No men had survived the attack. They estimated that 30 women, girls, and young boys had been taken captive. They were being marched north, most likely to be sold as slaves in Khartoum. Yandeng's mother was not one of the captives. It appeared that Yandeng was the only remaining survivor. They stayed only long enough to give a quick report and left with the grim task of burying the dead.

In the course of a morning her family was gone, and life as she knew it was over. She sat in disbelief, hoping her nightmare would end and she'd wake up in her own tukul, with the smell of wood smoke and baked sorghum cakes, and the sounds of her parents' voices filling the air. She didn't really feel alive. The only feeling she had was pain. The only thought that encouraged her to remain living was the knowledge that at least her brother had survived. His catechism studies had saved his life. It had caused such strife in the family that he had gone against the shaman's teachings and left the Dinka gods and become a Christian. His father had talked of disowning him. Now, because of this he was alive, somewhere, and her father was dead.

In the days following, she ground sorghum and gathered firewood and helped cook. Her pain began to melt into anger. She hated the murahaleen. She hated Arabs, the government, and even the people of the Darfur who had gone out of their way to help the government army steal and destroy all that was dear to her. But why? Sure, from time immemorial northerners had raided the south to take slaves. But they never came in such numbers and never did such destruction.

Her brother Lual arrived a few days later. He had heard the news on a shortwave radio and started on foot right away. He had already talked to the men who had dug the graves and been to the village. He was also in shock. When he found Yandeng he was shaking badly and sat for a while before the shaking stopped. He held Yandeng.

13

"What did you see?"

"I can't talk about it. But I think Alual is still alive. They took her away, tied like an animal with some of the other young people and women."

"Our herd is gone too."

They were now destitute as well as orphaned.

The people of Gottong told them they could stay and be part of their village. But there was talk of more attacks. That morning an Antonov flew over the village. Everyone fled for cover, but no bombs were dropped.

"They're scouting future targets," one of the elders said.

Yandeng remembered that a plane had circled their village a few days before the attack. Many talked about packing up and leaving. Others said they would never leave. But then two days passed and this time they were bombed. Sentries had been stationed in the area. Shortly after the bombs hit they came running back into the village saying that they saw a cloud of dust to the north. The murahaleen were coming. People quickly grabbed a few scarce belongings and ran on the trails heading south. Yandeng and Lual had nothing to carry and were young and outran the others. Lual knew the trails and neighboring villages from when he herded the family's cows. After three hours they came to another village. Yandeng had never been here before. This village, Giil, was much like her own except bigger. There was a small church here. It was only a large tukul, but she could tell it was a church because it had a cross on it. She didn't know why they put crosses on churches, and she had never been in one before. Lual met an older man near the church. They knew each other from catechism classes. His name was Bodogou. He had a kind face.

"They won't make it this far south yet. You have a home with me for as long as I have one," Bodogou told them.

Lual and Yandeng took over an empty tukul. Bodogou gave them mats to sleep on, a spare mosquito net, and a meal of roast sorghum. A few others from Gottong made their way through Giil later that day and were offered a meal and shelter. Most moved on south the next morning.

The atmosphere in Giil was tense. People were desperate for news. What had happened to Gottong? Had everyone escaped?

Where were the murahaleen? A small SPLA force passed through moving in the opposite direction, marching north to try to engage the murahaleen and stop their forage into Dinka lands. Their weapons were few, what they had managed to steal in raids. They had no uniforms and were all on foot and looked tired. One had a short-wave radio. They picked up a signal and got fresh news. Gottong had been completely burned. Most of the villagers had escaped. There were 5 or 6 deaths reported, older people who could not get away fast enough. The southward move of the murahaleen seemed to have turned east. It was reported though that a second murahaleen band was on the move in the area.

The men of the village came to speak with Yandeng. She was the sole survivor of the raid on her village, Palwung, in Mayom County. With difficulty she recounted, pausing occasionally to weep as she relived the awful day. But was she sure she saw men from the Darfur with the government troops and Arabs? Yes, she assured them, and she described their dress and manner of speech.

Bodogou addressed the whole group.

"Yes, we now have an eyewitness to confirm the rumors that have circulated among us. A greater evil has now been loosed in Dinka lands. It seems our neighbors to the north, who once shared our land and our food, have now joined forces with our enemies. The hungry lion has allied the help of this hyena to help it catch its prey, the unprotected herd of the Dinka. But we all know that the lion will also turn on the hyena to kill it too. Mark my words oh men and women, the Darfur will not be spared from this evil that they have visited on the Dinka. Men of the Darfur have allied with the lion to steal, kill, and destroy in Dinka lands, but the same lion will one day ravage the villages of the Darfur."

By now most of the village had gathered round and men and women were nodding in agreement with sad and stricken expressions at the words of their elder. Others also spoke, some urging a united and immediate retreat further south, while others urged courage.

"It is only a matter of time before the murahaleen arrive here too. We will certainly be attacked. Let us stay and defend our lands. If we run, where will we run to? Our lands are here. Will people give us lands elsewhere? No! We will surely starve if we run. Maybe the rains will come this year before the murahaleen. This will buy us one more year to plant our crops and prepare. But even if they don't come this year, they will come."

It was agreed that for the time being they would not run. They posted permanent sentries to the north of the village during daylight hours to keep watch for the murahaleen. In the meantime, they planted seed and waited for the rains to come.

# Chapter 3

Jerome walked back towards the train station with the others. He looked quite out of place surrounded by a gang of roughnecks. But he didn't notice. He began reciting to himself Russian phrases he had learned from his audio CD course. Once inside the dimly lit station they located Graham. He was talking with, or rather shouting at, a train station employee who was standing behind a counter.

"A package, about this big," and he motioned with his hands. "Do you understand pack... age?" which he pronounced very slowly and loudly.

The man just stared back at him with an steely annoyed look on his face. Graham was even more angry.

Jim led the entourage up to the counter and tugged on Graham's arm and announced, "Graham, we got a kid here on our shift that $100 says he speaks Russian."

Graham turned and looked at Jerome and asked in a distinctly British accent, "Great, but can he speak English?"

"Well yeah, I'm American," Jerome said.

"Well," said Graham, "that hasn't helped your friends any." He had a smug smile as he said it.

There were grunts and comments. Someone asked, "What the hell do you mean?"

"Exactly my point," said Graham. "Anyway, could you be so kind as to communicate to this gentleman, if he's not deaf, that I was assured by a rail employee in Yuzhno, who by the way spoke excellent English, and I want you to mention that point, by phone when we left the station that a package with an important gear was placed on this train and would be turned over to us as soon as the train arrived, and as of yet we have not received it... Now go ahead and tell him all that."

Jerome was stunned. Lots of phrases were racing through his mind, none of which communicated any of the things Graham had mentioned. He seemed unable to get started.

"Hello!" said Graham in an impatient voice. "It must be me. Everyone seems to be going a touch deaf and dumb when I address them."

Jerome turned to the man and said the first thing in Russian that came out. "Hello, my name is Jerome. I am from America. Where are you from?"

The man gave Jerome a long penetrating stare. His eyebrows were knitted tightly as he tried to fathom the question. Then he burst into laughter and answered, "I'm from here."

"It's a pleasure to meet you, Sir."

"Uh huh," he grunted. "You too."

"We need something. It's a ..." and he searched his memory for the word for package.

"I know what you need," he said. "I'm busy right now."

"Oh," said Jerome, and he was trying to figure out how to say, "You don't look busy," when he thought better of it.

"Is there anything I can do to help," he asked, remembering that phrase from his course.

The man snickered and said a word that Jerome didn't know. Then he repeated it more slowly.

"I'm sorry, I don't understand," Jerome said.

"A tip, young man. Let's say 300 rubles," he said leaning forward and speaking softly, even though there were no other Russian speakers within earshot. "And I will only do it because I like you. You speak Russian, although not well. But you speak better than these _ _ _ _," and he motioned towards his group.

This was another word Jerome didn't know. No matter, he got the gist. He turned to Graham and said rather awkwardly, "The gentlemen will get the package but he would appreciate it if uh... he'd like uh ... well, 300 rubles would help things along nicely."

"Well why didn't he say so in the first place," Graham croaked as he pulled a handful of Russian bills out of his wallet. "He'd have saved us all an hour, which will cost us a hell of a lot more than 300 rubles." Then he slapped the bills onto the counter.

The man looked offended and angry and pushed the rubles back in Graham's direction and turned and walked into a back room.

"Well what the hell is that all about?" Graham blurted out.

Jerome thought for a few seconds. He was remembering conversations he had with some of his Middle Eastern friends at college on the subject of giving "tips" to official employees. It was funny that they even had conversations about such things, but in certain parts of the world, there was an art, or at least a protocol, for doing such things. You didn't just hand over a fistful of cash in plain view. This was viewed as insulting by the person on the receiving end. "Tips" of this sort were folded neatly and placed inside of passports, or slipped unobtrusively into pockets. You needed to be intentional, yet indirect at the same time. Jerome thought maybe he could improve on the situation.

"Let me have a try," he said quietly to Graham. He picked the bills off the counter and folded them neatly as he walked into the back room.

The train employee gave him a sinister glare and growled, "What the _ _ _ _ now?"

Another unknown word he could gist the meaning of.

"Sir," he began, "I'm very sorry. I apologize. My friend is, um… rude … We need the box." Jerome was standing in front of him now and put one hand on his elbow and with the other, quickly slipped the rubles into his jacket pocket. "We need it tonight. Please."

The man hesitated, gave a deep sigh, then turned and walked towards a back door which led in the direction of the train tracks. Just before he walked out, Jerome could see in the dim light that he had taken the bills out of his pocket and was counting them.

Within 3 minutes he returned with a box and handed it to Jerome without saying a word. Jerome, who was still in the back room, thanked him, turned and walked out to the waiting entourage in the lobby of the station. As he handed Graham the box, all eyes were fixed on him. There were looks of disbelief, shock, and in one case extreme pleasure.

Jim pretty near shouted, "Well damn, it looks like I just made 100 bucks fellas."

They turned and hurried toward the bus. Graham asked Jerome to sit beside him in the lead bus. In the 45 minutes it took to get to the ferry he drilled Jerome about where he was from, what he was doing in Sakhalin, and whether or not he wanted to change jobs and

By Their Fruit

work with him at the main office, in Yuzhno rather than be a mud engineer's assistant on the rig. By the time the ferry arrived at the rig, Jerome had made a job change, gotten a raise, and was anticipating another night of continuous travel.

After everyone debriefed their incoming counterparts, which was called the "turnaround," Jerome and Graham got back on the ferry with a whole new group of guys, then took the same bus back to Noglicki, then took the same sleeper car in the same train that heaved and bumped for 15 hours back to Yuzhno.

In the morning when most everyone was awake, they served stale fish sandwiches and wretched coffee, obviously leftovers from the trip up which hadn't improved with age. Graham took the opportunity to brief Jerome. There will be lots of packages to pick up, some of which will be in human form, held up in immigration rather than in a train warehouse. We'll have papers that need lots of government stamps… did I mention lots of them, meaning lots of visits to government offices, lots of scraping and bowing, lots of "Red" tape as we call it, and of course lots of "tips." You'll need to use your know-how or whatever means you have to grease the wheels, to keep the machine moving."

"… OK. I'll do what I can. But I also know geology. I'm pretty good at deciphering seismic surveys."

"Yeah? Well don't worry too much about that. We've got lots of geologists and seismic engineers. What we don't have a lot of are people who know English and Russian and can get things done, like find a gear for a drill rig in a small Rusky train station. We needed that gear. I hope to God it's good. Damn Russian quality. We are obliged by contract to buy Russian parts and they're not worth shit. Don't think that's the last time you'll be going to a train station looking for a shipment."

And so the summer began on Sakhalin Island for Jerome. It was filled with visits to dingy cement-block buildings requesting approvals for minor things like the import of a machine, or a part, but sometimes involved papers to bring in people to work the rigs. The rigs needed lots of parts and people and that required lots of approvals. He was kept busy carrying papers from building to building and office to office. He had to find his way around, deal with guards and receptionists and stand in lines waiting to see the right people and ask for approvals in Russian. He did his best to write out a "script" of how to ask to see a government official, then another script to explain what he needed, and another to ask for their help. He didn't have the impression his script helped much but he always had the attention of his Russian hosts who had met few Russian-speaking Americans.

Jerome didn't stay in the expatriate village with the long-term employees and their families. He stayed in town, in a drab building. He didn't mind though. There was a place nearby where he could get a meal. He had only found it through the recommendation and directions of some of the rig workers. There was a weathered wooden sign to the side of a door in a run-down apartment building that read "Bar-Resturant."

"Well, at least they spelled 'bar' right," Jerome said to himself as he walked into a dark doorway, then down a dark hallway as instructed. Then he pushed a door open and walked down a narrow and dimly lit stairway and then down another dark hallway. He then could hear noise through a doorway. He pushed it open and figured it must be the place. It was full of people. In fact, there were lots of people there every time he went. Oil employees seemed to work odd hours, or to be constantly traveling through Yuzhno, and were always coming in and out of the restaurant for a drink or a meal.

"How did they all find this place?" he wondered.

There were roughnecks from America, Australia, and Europe. There were Asians from all different places speaking many different languages. There were native people, who looked like a cross between Japanese and Eskimos. And there were Russians too, men and women. It was the women who caught his eye though. It wasn't just because they were distinctly beautiful, but because they looked so out of place. They definitely didn't dress like they worked in the oil fields, nor did it seem like they had office jobs because they were around at all hours. And in their case, it was always the same women. They didn't rotate in and out like the men.

One evening he was eating alone, as he usually did, he looked around and caught the gaze of one of the beautiful Russian girls. She smiled at him and he awkwardly smiled back and nodded his head. Almost immediately she got up from her table, walked over and sat down across from him.

She had blonde curly hair and blue eyes and seemed so beautiful to Jerome that he felt intimidated.

"Well American boy, you want entertainment?"

"Vy gavarite pa-ruski?" (Do you speak Russian?") Jerome asked.

"Yes, of course," she answered matter-of-factly. "I'm Russian."

She gave him a hard look, almost a scowl. There was an awkward pause, like she was waiting for something.

"Can I get you dinner?"

"No stupid, I get my meals for free. I'm here to do business."

Jerome, not quite sure he understood the response paused and said, "Yes, of course. I too am here to do business."

"Well then, negotiate. I'll give you a special price if you're ready now. 1000 rubles."

It now became evident that Jerome had made a mistake, a huge mistake that looked like it was going to be very embarrassing. His jaw dropped and he sat there speechless.

"All right 750 rubles," she barked, "But I'm worth 1000."

"I'm sure you are, but I… I didn't think… I may be misunderstood…" Jerome was mortified. His face had turned bright red from embarrassment, hers from anger. People at other tables were beginning to look over and he was sure there was about to be a scene.

# Chapter 4

Lual and Yandeng stayed in Bodogou's spare tukul and helped with the chores. Lual pastured Bodogou's herd. Yandeng helped the women grind sorghum flour to make their daily bread cakes and plant their vegetable garden. When she found herself alone, waves of sadness and anger and fear came over her. She feared the bombs, the murahaleen, the thought of losing what little family and companionship she had left. She lived with bouts of inner rage as she came to face the reality of what had happened. Her life would never be the same again. Almost all that she had counted dear had been taken. And for what? Was it oil, was it religion, or was it just pure hatred that had caused the government to do what they had done?

The old president had tried to make them all Muslims. He told everyone they had to where Muslim clothes and learn Arabic and pray Muslim prayers. But the Dinka weren't like that. They had their own way of dressing and talking. Some, it is true, had left the Dinka gods and turned to Jesus, but very few wanted to become Muslims. So when his plan didn't work out well he changed his mind and made war on the Dinka. Now the new president said it was Allah's will to get rid of the Dinka. He said it was a holy war. And on top of all that, now there was oil. It was at school that she first learned of oil. She had heard it mentioned when there had been trucks around the village. Sometimes they leaked it or needed it or smelled of it. Or was that gasoline they smelled of? She didn't really understand it all but she had heard it mentioned. Now in school they said there was a lot of oil and right there in the Dinka land, and of all places, right under their feet. It seemed funny that oil came from under the ground, but they said it was true. And apparently a lot of people wanted it. The president seemed to want it real bad. Some white people wanted it too, but not the same ones that had taught at the school. And they were willing to pay a lot of money, more than she had ever seen, to get it. They bought it by the barrel full. They must have a lot of trucks somewhere and their lands must smell really bad. Anyway, because of the president wanting the Dinka oil, he was now trying even harder to kill them or get them to leave. Imagine him doing such things! Why if he wanted the oil, he'd only have to ask. The Dinka leaders would probably agree to give it to him. But he didn't ask. He sent airplanes to bomb their tukuls, and murahaleen and soldiers to kill them, chase them away, or take them away as slaves, and just so he could fill up his dirty old barrels with Dinka oil.

She was now nearly seventeen, almost full grown as a woman, the age when girls normally married. But times were anything but normal. Eligible men seemed scarce. Survival was more on people's minds than courtship.

Lual and Bodogou and the men of the village planted the sorghum seed in the fields around the village. Then they waited for the rains. The time for rain came. The big African sky filled with dark clouds, and cool breezes came, but the clouds held onto their precious gift. They passed too quickly overhead, spilling only a little here or there. Some seed germinated and sprouted. Other seed stayed untouched in the parched earth. Winds came and scattered dust and seed alike. The seed that sprouted turned yellow then died. The villagers knew what this meant. Famine was never far away from the Dinka. Now it arrived.

With the onset of famine came new choices. Would it be best to try to walk out, to some undefined place, most naturally south, and hope for help from some unknown persons or tribe? Would anyone spare food for dying Dinkas? Would it be best to stay in the village, conserve energy, and wither away? Maybe they could live off roots or grasses, or some had even been known to eat dirt. Some had heard that the United Nations had airlifted food to certain villages. But others argued that these airlifts had ended when the United Nations made a deal with the government in Khartoum not to "intervene." There was also word that the government had set up relief camps, and if you were willing to become a Muslim, learn the Koran, and join the army you'd be fed. The choices were discussed but no decisions were made.

Then there was fresh news that the murahaleen were again on the move. The drought also meant that the army and murahaleen did not have to wait for the wet months to end before moving in again in jeeps, on horseback, camels, and on foot.

People slowly started leaving the village. Bodogou and Lual called everyone together for a meeting in the church. Bodogou called it a prayer meeting. Most of those still in the village showed up. The big tukul that served as the church was full. Bodogou spoke.

"I have often told you of the protection that God has provided. I want to invite you into that protection now. The last words that the Lord Jesus spoke on earth were that he had authority, all authority in heaven and on earth, and that he would be with his children to the end of time. He is inviting us to be part of his village, his people, his family. Only the forgiven can be part of it. On his behalf, I invite you to confess to him that you've been like sheep running from the shepherd, to ask his forgiveness. Then ask him to be your shepherd, father, brother, shama, and Lord. I promise you that no matter whether you stay, head south, or even go to live in the camps run by our enemies, he will be your protector."

Many scoffed and walked out, led by the shama. Some stayed behind. Yandeng stayed too. "What do we need to do?" one asked.

"You speak to Him," Bodogou said. "That is how it begins."

Yandeng was among the group that spoke to God that night. Everyone said something different. They spoke loud enough so that not only God but everyone else in the tukul could hear as well. Yandeng told God she didn't really know much about him, but knew she had never followed him. She was a lost sheep of the Dinka. She confessed her own sin as best she understood it, and asked him to be her father now that she had none, and to be her shepherd, and her God. She sensed as did the rest, that their words had not gone unheard. He had listened. Bodogou said that God had already responded, by visiting their world a long time back and dying a punishing death on their behalf. It was perhaps more than she could really grasp at once, but she nonetheless respectfully held these new beliefs as her own.

Bodogou's last words came from his Bible as he read aloud.

"You will not fear the mouth of the lion. No weapon designed against you will be successful."

There was hugging and weeping and the group departed quietly, each to his or her own tukul.

By Their Fruit

Yandeng slept peacefully for the first time since her world had collapsed around her.  She dreamt of a big scoop in the heavens pouring out sorghum onto the earth in huge piles.  There was more grain than everyone she ever knew would ever need for a whole lifetime.  There was also rain, wonderful abundant rain, enough to bathe in.

The dream was cut short by Lual.  Why was he shaking her?  It was already light out, and the smoke of the morning fire had filled the air.  But it was the sound that disturbed Yandeng, the drone of an Antonov not far away.

"We must run for cover.  Come quickly," Lual was saying as he shook Yandeng by the shoulder.

She struggled to her feet and stumbled out of the dark tukul into the bright morning.  She had slept late for the first time since she could remember.  The Antonov's droning engine sounded close.  The village must be in its sight by now.  She ran with Lual into the thicket toward the dry river bed, arriving just in time to hear the thud of the first bombs hitting the village.  She heard screams and shouting, then more bombs.  The Antonov flew out past the dry, cracking sorghum fields, circled, then flew back over the village.  As it flew low over the dry river bed she could see the men in army uniforms in the opening in the back of the aircraft as they pushed their murderous barrels out onto the undefended huts.

The Antonov made two more passes over the village, which was by now in flames, then turned its nose and headed back to a military base somewhere north of them.

Yandeng, Lual, and the others hurried back to the tukuls when it seemed certain the Antonov would not be returning.  Many tukuls were on fire.  Everyone took a hand to put out the flames.

It was then that a young boy ran into the village screaming, "Murahaleen!  There is dust rising from the north."

The adults nearby relayed the word, shouting over all the other noise.  For a short time confusion reigned.  Then Bodogou spoke, or more shouted, "Follow me, there is no time to get your belongings.  Come now!  Everyone!"

And with that he turned and jogged quickly back into the brush and down into the mostly dry river bed.  Once there he took a quick

By Their Fruit

inventory of those who had followed and said, "We must move quickly.  To the south!  Do not stop until you reach Aberge."

# Chapter 5

Jerome was sitting across the table from one of the ten most beautiful girls he had ever seen and she was talking to him, directly. But, he just realized she was a prostitute and was waiting for his response. And not only her, but half the clientele in the restaurant had stopped their conversations and had turned to watch. A thought came to his mind.

"How much did you say, 750 rubles?"

That works out to less than $30 he thought to himself.

"And I want it in advance."

"For how long?" Jerome asked.

"Half hour," she barked.

"Can I have 40 minutes?" and will you do whatever I ask.

She gave him a hard, sinister look and said in a cold, steely voice, "OK American, but if you cross the line, Boris will cut your balls off." And she glanced towards a large bald, muscular Russian man who was just walking out.

"I'm sure Boris won't need to do that. Here, have a seat beside me," Jerome offered as he pulled out the chair next to him, pushed his plate away, and pulled a notebook out of his backpack.

She didn't move. She stood studying him with a menacing look.

"Oh... yes. Sorry," said Jerome, as he pulled 750 rubles from his wallet and handed them to her. "Now the 40 minutes doesn't start until you sit beside me."

"What exactly do you want?"

"Answers. I have questions."

"About what?"

"Russian, and Russians, and red tape, and getting what you want from people. Can you help me?"

She gave a wry smile and said, "If I can't teach you how to get what you want from Russian men, no one can."

She quickly pocketed the money and took the seat beside Jerome. "Ok American, you have 40 minutes."

In the next 40 minutes Jerome had filled up two pages in his notebook. He learned how to ask for approvals less formally. He had learned his Russian from a language course and he had the impression when he was talking to people that he sounded like a text book.

"How would you ask a government official to sign an import request form?"

"No, not how I would ask. I will tell you how you should ask." She spouted off a phrase. Jerome wrote it down.

"Now say it to me. I want to hear it," she said.

So Jerome repeated it.

"No, say it again, this way. Tell me, don't ask me."

Jerome repeated it.

"No, you sound like you're begging. NEVER BEG! You'll never get what you want from Russians by begging. Now say it again."

Jerome said it 15 then 20 times, but to no avail. She just got more and more impatient and finally said, "You are saying the right words but not the right way. You sound weak. You will not get what you want. Now say it again!"

Jerome realized he was paying almost a dollar per minute to be criticized and insulted, and she was enjoying it.

He lost his temper just a little and said, "Look, I will say it how I want to say it, and this is the way I want to say it. And I'm not saying it again."

He was afraid she'd get up and walk away. But she seemed completely composed and thoughtful.

"Yes, that's pretty good. You can do it after all. Say it just like that. Any other questions, or are we done?" she asked as she pushed her chair away from the table.

"Yes, what's your name?"

"You can call me Nastia."

"Is that your name?"

"No, but it's what you can call me."

Boris was back and was looking at them with a dark look on his face. He caught her eye and she quickly left the table. He barked something at her and looked again over at Jerome and gave him a menacing look.

Jerome returned again the next night to the restaurant. It wasn't just because he wanted to see Nastia. Yuzhno wasn't full of good

places to eat.  There were a few places with better food and more
westerners, but they were expensive, and Jerome figured he'd have
enough westerners to eat around once he returned to America.  This
place was exciting.  There always seemed to be something going on.
Twice fights broke out and he even saw Boris throw someone out
one night.  Boris seemed to have special permission from the owner
to do as he saw fit.

That night Nastia saw him and nodded, then looked quickly at
Boris, then looked away.  Then a few minutes later Boris walked
over to her and she left by the back door with a client.

Jerome said to himself, "Just leave.  Forget her, forget the whole
thing."

He tried a different restaurant the next night, but it was expensive
and boring.

The next night he went back to the "Bar-Resturant".  He looked
around.  Nastia was at a table with the other girls.  Boris wasn't in
sight.  Nastia saw him and walked towards him.

"Oh no!" thought Jerome.  "What should I do?"

Then she was at the table.

"Need any more advice, American?"

"Well uh, no, not really."

"What's the matter?  Are you afraid of me?"

"Of course not.  I just don't have many questions, you answered
them last time.  Do you really want to do it again?"

"I need the money. "How about if I charge you for 10 minutes?
150 rubles."

"Well…" said Jerome, trying to think of something to say.
"What do you do with your money?"  After he said it he felt like it
was the most intrusive and stupid thing to ask.  To Nastia however
this seemed like it was the perfect question and she had the answer
on the tip of her beautiful tongue.

"I send it back to Moscow.  I have 3 sisters, four brothers, a
mother, and a daughter there.  Winter is cold here, but in Moscow
they have little heat or food.  There is no work.  The place is shit.  It
is unbelievably hard to live there now.  I am sometimes the only one
working in my family.  They are all counting on me."

She seemed to be letting down her guard and showing some vulnerability. Then she caught herself and said, "Well do you accept?"

He could spare the money and decided to try to make this work. She was a person who showed little weakness until this moment. Jerome felt sorry for her.

"Hmmm," said Jerome. "How about 125 rubles and I'll talk more often?"

"OK, it's a deal, but on one condition. You must promise me you will not let Boris know you are paying me. And if he asks you must tell him that you're not. Deal?"

"Uh, I don't know. Boris looks mean. I'd hate to cross him." Jerome looked around and still didn't see him. Then he looked into Nastia's rich blue pleading eyes.

"Sure," he said with a smile. "But why don't you want Boris to know?"

"You're not that stupid. And I just told you that I need the money for my family." She was looking angry again.

"OK, fine. I understand," said Jerome, even though he knew he'd have to go back over this conversation in his mind a few times before he'd really understand. She stood looking at him like she was waiting.

"Have a seat," he offered.

"Well, do you have the rubles?" she asked a bit sharply.

"Oh, sorry. Here," he said as he fished some bills out of his wallet and counted them out.

"OK, ask me questions," she said curtly as she sat down.

"Well… I'm not really prepared. I don't have anything written down. Why don't you just tell me about yourself?"

"What? What do you want to know?" she asked as though he were interrogating her.

"I don't know. Whatever you'd like to tell me. Tell me about your family."

"I just told you about my family."

Jerome saw this wasn't working well, but he tried again. It was a question Guadalupe, his Mexican nanny had asked him once.

"Tell me about your happiest memory."

Nastia gave him a hard scowl.

**31**

"Look, Nastia, maybe this isn't a good idea. Maybe we shouldn't do this."

"No," she said with stubborn determination. "If you want a stupid memory, I will think of a stupid memory."

He could tell she was thinking because her hard scowling expression was gone and she seemed lost… somewhere. Then she began.

"This is the last memory of my father... I was six and he was leaving home to go work in Western Siberia. He took the whole family to the park…"

Tears started to appear in her eyes, then she pushed them away.

"We were all happy. He carried me on his shoulders and promised me that next time he saw me he'd have a French doll for me."

She stopped talking as tears began to return.

Jerome didn't know what to say. He felt awkward. "I bet he was a great father."

The mood then seemed to change. She looked up and looked right at Jerome and said, "He was a shit father. He left the next day and never came back. He wrote for a while, then the letters stopped. We learned that he ran off with a younger woman." The steely tone was back in her voice.

"I'm sorry… Well, tell me about your childhood. What is it like growing up in Moscow?"

"I told you. Life in Moscow is shit."

"I see. Could you be more specific?"

"There is not enough food, there is not enough heating fuel, there are not enough apartments, there is not even enough sunlight. There is not enough of anything."

"I see… Well... maybe tell me about your mother."

"No. Don't ask me personal things. Why are you asking me these things?"

Nastia seemed angry and looked at her watch and moaned, "Oh, we have 5 minutes left… You talk. Tell me about your mother. I hardly knew mine."

"Well, my mother died when I was five. I hardly remember her."

"Who raised you? I'm sure your father didn't."

"Guadalupe raised me. She ran the household."

"Who is Guadalupe?"

And so conversation started. Although it was paid conversation, and pretty one-sided, it was more than Jerome had elsewhere. He did most of the talking and Nastia did the correcting, which her stern teacher personality seemed to thoroughly enjoy.

"Who taught you Russian? You make lots of mistakes."

"I taught myself."

"Well that's why. How can you teach yourself, you don't even know Russian."

So, 15 minutes every few nights was what he could afford and usually all he could withstand. He didn't know he had an ego until he felt it getting kicked around in their meetings. And the meetings were problematic. She was sometimes not there, and that bothered Jerome in all kinds of ways. And if she were, they'd have to wait until Boris left the bar. Jerome would signal and she'd come straight over, sit down, hold out her hand for her rubles and then she'd ask the questions.

One night Boris came back while they were still talking. Nastia saw him and immediately jumped up and left the table. Boris had seen them together though and gave them both a dark stare. Then he walked over to Nastia and grabbed her by the arm and said something to her. She pulled her arm away and walked away from him.

The next night when Jerome came in, Nastia had a black eye and looked sullen. She saw Jerome and quickly looked away. Boris saw him and almost ran up to his table with a wild look in his eyes.

He blurted out English as best he could, with a very thick Russian accent. "You cheat me Boy. I hurt you."

## Chapter 6

Aberge was about 2 hours walk south. It seemed the whole village was following Bodogou. Young and old hurried together, one helping another. No murahaleen were seen or heard. The whole village escaped together, leaving everything they owned behind.

Their arrival at Aberge caused quite a stir. Every person in the village assembled within minutes and swarmed around the newcomers. Everyone was talking at once. Then Bodogou motioned for silence and spoke.

"Men and women of Aberge, you know as well as we the situation of the Dinka. We are being killed and chased off the lands our people have lived on since the days of our fathers. The government has sent airplanes to bomb us and murahaleen to burn our villages, kill our people and take our women and children as slaves. Today this evil has befallen us. As a lion attacking a sleeping herd of cows, we were attacked from both Antonovs in the sky and murahaleen on the ground. By God's help we have escaped their hand, but we have escaped without our herds, without our hoes and shovels, without our cooking pots and clothing. We stand before you as you see us today, tired, hungry, and empty-handed. But we are your people and no strangers to you. We are willing and able to work and if you would extend us your hospitality we will do what we can to help you until the day when you may taste the same bitter misfortune that we have tasted today or until we are all freed of this foreign invasion."

After a lot of buzzing and discussion an elder from Aberge spoke.

"Men and women of the Dinka, of both Aberge and Giil, we all know our situation. We are being hunted and killed, village by village. The government has been destroying our homes, stealing our herds and young people, destroying our crops, and taking our land because there is oil underneath it. And now even the rains have been against us. Our crops have failed. We have no food for the coming year to feed our own village. Famine is even now at our door. Some have already left, walking south, hoping for better from the unknown than from what the Dinka lands can give them. And now you come with your hands empty and ask us to fill them. Dinka brothers and sisters, we have nothing to put into your hands. We can only offer that you stay and live the same life or die the same death that we die. We know not which it will be. If the murahaleen have already arrived at Giil, it will not be long before they swarm into our village and crush our tukuls as they have crushed yours."

Even as they spoke they heard the buzz of an Antonov flying high overhead.

The elders of both villages also congregated in front of the largest tukul in the village. There was not much food to be shared, but there was local brewed tea in abundance and people sat in front of various tukuls and spoke of the future. Discussion in all the groups centered on survival. What would they do? Some spoke of the government "Peace Camps." If you became a Muslim and studied the Koran you were given food and shelter. The women were then put to work sewing uniforms or preparing food for the army. Some were then given to the Muslim fighters as wives. Young men, after their Koranic instruction, were conscripted into the ranks of the military to fight against their own people. They were given Muslim names, Arab clothing, and obligated to speak Arabic. Treatment was harsh, but if you gave evidence that you had become a Muslim the men were not killed and the women not often raped.

Another option was to keep walking south and hope you found help before you collapsed along the way. Word had filtered back that some had found work outside of the Dinka lands in Nuer territory pastoring for families fortunate enough to have herds. The most popular alternative was to move in the direction of Nimne, because humanitarian aid in the form of food and shelter was reported to be available. Nimne was about a 60 mile march south through empty territory with few villages between here and there.

The people in Aberge still had their herds and tukuls and decided to stay for the time being. Most of people of Giil decided to walk together and try to reach Nimne in 3 days. Yandeng, Lual, Bodogou and his family waited until the next morning and left with a group of 60 others at dawn. A small packet of sorghum cake wrapped in leaves was provided for each person. Brief farewells were said, and the group marched off.

Before 10 AM the temperatures reached 100 degrees Fahrenheit. Thirst had already become an issue. Crying was heard from children.

By noon it was too hot to continue. The group found cover under some low trees and bushes near the river bed. There were occasionally pools of water found in the riverbed, but was usually too murky to drink. Clean pools had to be located. Some women moved off into the brush to look for roots to eat. For the next 4 or 5 hours people finished their sorghum cake, chewed on roots or leaves, or whatever else they could find and tried to sleep. A snake was spotted, a green mamba. Their bite usually fatal, would certainly be a deadly blow in this forsaken place. Vultures began to gather overhead gliding in low circular patrols.

At about 4 PM Bodogou called the village members to get to their feet and start moving again. They would only have 2 ½ hours before nightfall. Traveling with small children was slow. The estimated march to Nimne was revised to at least 5 days.

# Chapter 7

"I did not cheat you!" Jerome insisted.

"You be with my girl but I know. You both owe me rubles. How many times you be with her. You pay me, I no hurt you."

"You're mistaken Boris. I have never been with her outside of this room."

"You think me stupid? I see you talk. People tell me, he pay her rubles. You meet her later. I no dumb."

"Boris, I'm not saying you're dumb. I think you misunderstand. We talk, but nothing else."

"You liar. Why she talk? Why you give money? To talk?" At this Boris opened his mouth wide and laughed a vicious laugh. The whole room went silent and every eye turned to him.

"She's been helping me with my Russian, Boris."

"You no speak Russian. This is shit!" Boris yelled, and he leaned forward across the table then lunged with both hands for Jerome's throat. Jerome quickly jumped to his feet and stepped to the side and Boris missed and slid facelong across the table, sweeping Jerome's dinner and dishes in all directions onto the concrete floor. Boris fell head first onto the floor right after the dishes. He let out a shriek of rage. Then he yelled all manner of obscenities in Russian, most of which Jerome didn't understand, finishing with the phrase, "I'll kill you, you little ____!"

Jerome wasn't sure of the last word, but at the moment, it didn't matter.

Then even before getting up from the floor Boris lunged at Jerome's legs.

As he lunged, a clarity came over Jerome that cleared his mind. The certainty was that if he didn't move, quickly, he might never move again. He quickly dodged Boris's hulk of a body for a second time. Boris tumbled past him then stopped, turned, fixed his eyes on Jerome and carefully rose to his feet. Jerome was in the awkward position of having Boris between himself and the front door. If not, he would have simply run out. Behind him people were crowding around tight and thick and starting to cheer. They loved a good fight. There was no way out but past Boris. The owner tried to intervene. "Boris, no. He's a good customer."

Boris shoved him to the side, then slowly stepped toward Jerome, careful not to overshoot his prey a third time.

Jerome backed up as Boris stepped forward. Jerome stepped behind another table whose patrons were now part of the crowd behind him. There were 2 half eaten meals and 4 bottles of beer on it. Boris studied the situation for a few seconds, then sneered and again laughed a loud raucous laugh, which sounded almost like a donkey's neigh. He took a few quick steps to the table, swept all the dishes to the floor with his meaty forearm and looked Jerome right in eye. Then he effortlessly lifted the table above his head, leaving Jerome standing alone, very alone, with nothing but empty space between himself and the large angry Russian holding the table over his head, ready to bring it down hard on top of him.

By Their Fruit

## Chapter 8

Bodogou had a plan in mind in case any Antonovs came into range and had passed the word to everyone in the group. Any brightly colored clothing was removed immediately and hidden inside other clothing or under rocks. Some people were nearly naked, but to the Dinka, this was not too out of the ordinary, especially for unusual circumstances such as these.

As they marched along the riverbed, Bodogou began to sing in a loud voice to a tune that everyone knew:

> The Lord is my Shepherd,
> I shall not be in want,
> He makes me lie down in green pastures,
> He leads me beside quiet waters,
> He restores my soul.
> He guides me in paths of righteousness for his name's sake.
> Even if I walk through the valley of the shadow of death,
> I will fear no evil,
> For you are with me.
> Your rod and your staff, they comfort me.
> You prepare a table before me
> In the presence of my enemies.
> Surely goodness and love will follow me all the days of my life,
> And I will dwell in the house of the Lord forever.

Then Lual began to sing. A few others joined in. After a few times through it still others joined. Before long everyone was singing. Yandeng loved hearing all the voices blended together. The Dinka were accustomed to learning long songs and enjoyed singing if the right occasion permitted. This was the right occasion. Their fear seemed to dissolve, their spirits rose, and their energy was renewed. They marched on singing until about noon when they found a nice spot to stop. The river bed took a sharp turn, leaving a large area with ledges and rocks for shade and cover, and a pool of water.

By noon the temperatures was 110 degrees and the air was suffocating. At least 45 miles remained between them and Nimne, which would probably still require at least 3 more days' march. They again took a long rest in the afternoon to avoid the heat. They were also beginning to feel weak.

Most Dinka were used to long marches. Every year they migrated over a hundred miles south on foot during the dry season to be near water. But no one, not even the Dinka could easily bear both hunger and long marches simultaneously. In the best of times the Dinka were a very lean people. Maybe their unusual height added to their lean appearance. They looked to outsiders like dark stick figures. Their long bony bodies stood stiff, proud and tall. Many of the women were nearly 6 feet tall, and the men often reached 6 feet 8 or 10 inches. Yandeng was of normal build for a Dinka woman. She was 5 feet 10 inches tall. She never considered herself thin and had no idea how much she weighed or had given it any thought. But now she and the others were beginning to think about their weight. Sickness and thinness were synonymous to the Dinka. Famine and disease went hand in hand. The best cure for disease was food. They all knew it and were trying their hardest to get to Nimne where, by all reports, there was a better chance of eating.

After 4 or 5 hours' rest they again set out for the last few miles of the day. As they walked, Yandeng stayed as close to Lual and Bodogou as she could. She had questions and didn't exactly know how to ask them. She had never been religious and didn't consider herself religious now. Yet she now was moving into something spiritual and yet more tangible than anything she'd known. The more she yielded to it, the better she felt. She thought of the time she got to swim in a pool of clear water once when her tribe first arrived after their yearly migration to the swampy grazing grounds in the south. She and some other women stripped naked and went in up to their necks. She had never been in that much water before and it was frightening. The water seemed to hold her in its grip, yet it was a good and cleansing grip. She stayed and soaked in the water for over an hour and considered it one of her happiest memories. She sensed something similar now, like she was soaking in something that was powerful and cleansing.

"Bodogou, can I ask you things that are on my mind?" she finally blurted out to him.

"Of course my dear," he answered with his kind black eyes fixed on hers. "Anything you want."

"Well, you said God will protect us. How do you know that?"

"Well I don't know how things will turn out. But I rely on my own history. More times than I can count he protected me. And way before my time, Scripture is full people he protected who trusted in him, and even some who didn't trust him. He's been protecting people for a long time. I don't figure He's going to change all that today or tomorrow, right?"

"Yes, but… a lot of people have died. Some of them I'm sure were trusting in him too."

"That's true. And I don't know for sure I'll survive this war. But what I do know is that this life is not the end. It is the beginning. Jesus died first and was resurrected after. We too who believe in him, even though we die, will be resurrected. Do you believe this Yandeng?"

"I do. But what about the other religions? What about the shama? They believe different. What about the government? They're Muslims and believe that they are making God happy by killing us. Who can say they're wrong? Are all religions right?"

"I think no religions are right."

"What do you mean? What about your religion?"

"God didn't invent Religion, men did. We don't need religion, we need God."

"But… aren't they the same?"

"Religion is what we do, not what God does. I'm interested in what God does. I want God."

"But… what do you mean? What does God do?"

"Part of it he already did. He sent Jesus. He came, died, and rose from the dead for us."

"But how do you know for sure what you say is true? Many don't believe it. Maybe the Jesus way isn't the right way."

"You're not the first one to ask this question. People had the same question in Jesus' day. There were religious people and

**41**

leaders that thought that because they were religious they were right and he was wrong."

What did he say?"

"He said, 'Watch out for false prophets. They come to you in sheep's clothing, but inwardly they are ferocious wolves. By their fruit you will recognize them.' Always remember that Yandeng, it is by their fruit."

# Chapter 9

Jerome was in a seedy underground restaurant/bar with a large mean Russian pimp holding a table over his head and shouting in pained English, "I smash you like little bug, little man."

There was laughter from the clientele on their feet behind Jerome.

All eyes were on Boris who had a wicked grin on his face. He seemed to be savoring the moment. This awakened something from Jerome's past, something not at all pleasant. Most interactions with schoolmates involved defending himself. He remembered continuous arguments with classmates about whether he was a nerd, or a girl, or from another planet. After the interactions often came the challenges to fight and he'd have to back down and hear the ridicule and insults as he walked away. This happened so many times that it seemed to define him. He could argue but he couldn't fight. He wanted so badly to just once beat a bully at his own game. On the other hand, he noticed two important logistical factors. First, the door was straight behind Boris and second, the table was directly above Boris' wide head. So, even though he'd have to run past Boris to get out, Boris's hands were not free to grab him or hit him. Jerome then bolted right past Boris and was through the door about the time the table hit the floor. He ran down the dark hallway, up the dimly lit narrow stairs, through the door, then down the other dark hallway to the front door. He stopped to listen for footsteps behind him, which to his surprise did not follow. He then stepped out the front door. He had again run from a fight. On the one hand he regretted he had run, on the other he was real happy to be still able to run.

The air was cold and damp, not unusual for an August night in Sakhalin. He wondered if Boris would soon come out after him in the street. He began walking in the direction of his apartment. Then he heard footsteps behind him. He turned quickly, the hair rising on the back of his neck.

"Jerome, wait."

It was Nastia.

"Jerome, you are in danger."

"Well you are in danger too."

"Yes, me too. But you more."

"Well, I was in danger. Now, I'm out of danger."

"No, you don't know Boris. He'll be looking for you."

"I'm faster than he is."

"He has a gun and he's used it before."

"I see… What about you?"

"Boris won't hurt me too bad. I make him money, good money."

"When will I see you again?"

"Jerome, you must never come back."

Jerome stood there speechless. Nastia approached him and put her arms around him and gave him a quick kiss.

"Thank you Jerome. I hope … I hope… you do well. I must get back."

With that she turned and was gone. Jerome was left standing with only the smell of her perfume, the feel of her warm lips, and memories of conversations with the most beautiful woman he had ever personally known.

"It could be worse," he thought to himself. "She could have slapped me in the face and said, Get away from me 'Dweeb.' Life is definitely improving."

# Chapter 10

They stopped for the night in a sheltered area near lots of large rocks. It was hoped that in 2 days they'd be eating sorghum cakes in Nimne. The thought encouraged them. There was little but thoughts to encourage. They continued eating what roots and edible leaves they could find. They ate them raw. They didn't want to waste the time or energy starting fires, and they had no cooking utensils anyway.

The next morning they woke early and continued heading south. About 9 AM they heard gunshots in the distance, probably 2 to 3 miles ahead Bodogou estimated. They moved forward cautiously while looking for suitable cover. There was a group of large rocks about ¼ mile ahead.

"Let's try to reach there for cover," Bodogou said, pointing to the rocks.

They started to move more quickly, as quickly as a group of 60 with small children and older people can move. They arrived, finding that the rocks rose out of the river bank at odd angles, forming odd shapes. They began to climb onto them, going up the east side of the river bank. The progress was very slow. Some with shorter legs had to be pushed, pulled, and carried. The older members had to be helped along too. It was hot and everyone was tired. Yandeng was carrying one of the young children when she slipped and fell down into a crevice. She fell badly. She felt a very sharp pain in her right ankle. The child began to cry and Yandeng groaned in pain. Slowly people assembled above her. Lual's face appeared staring down on her from above.

"Are you OK Yandeng?" he shouted with panic in his voice.

"No, help me! My leg hurts, and I'm stuck" she cried.

Lual lowered himself into the tight crevice and tried to pull her out.

"Soldiers!" someone shouted.

Around a bend in the river bed about 100 yards away soldiers began appearing. They were marching in single file. They were coming straight towards them. They were in clear view of each other and knew there was no escaping. It was clear from their rag-tag appearance that they were SPLA, the local militia group. They jogged up the river bed to the spot right below the group.

"Who are you and what are you doing here?" one of the men shouted. He was wearing a military shirt, but all the other wore t-shirts and shorts. No one had a pair of boots. Some had plastic sandals, some had worn-out leather shoes with no socks, and a few were barefoot. They had an assortment of pistols and rifles.

"We're on our way to Nimne to find food and shelter. Our villages have been destroyed," answered Bodogou. "We need some help. We have someone stuck in the rocks. Can you help us pull her out?"

A few of the men climbed up and looked the situation over. They called for a rope which one of the men pulled out of a backpack. They climbed down into the crevice wrapped the rope under Yandeng's armpits and indelicately pulled her out, writhing in pain. As she sat wincing on the rock Lual and Bodogou examined her leg. The man in the military shirt climbed up to have a look.

"First," he said, "my men are all hungry. They have been ambushing the GOS (Government of Sudan) army and the murahaleen. We need all the food you have and we need it now. We don't have much time. The murahaleen may organize a counter-attack and if they do we will need to move quickly."

"But… look at us," Bodogou said a little sharply. "We have lost everything. We have no food. We are weak with hunger. We have nothing to offer you."

The commander scrutinized the group, looking from person to person for food or belongings that could serve them. Seeing none, he fixed his eyes on Yandeng.

"I'll take her. I need a wife. She is a little young, but she'll do."

Lual stepped forward as if he'd attack the ragtag commander. Bodogou intervened, moving in front of Lual. "Look at her condition," he barked. "She can't even walk! Give us some help! Do you have a medical person in your group?"

There was a round of laughter from all in his group. Someone produced some sticks of wood and a rag and said, "The ankle should be braced. It is probably just sprained. If it's broken, use the same brace until it heals."

At that point, one of the men pointed downstream and shouted, "Murahaleen!"

Everyone looked. No riders were in sight, but a distinct cloud of dust had risen not far from where they were standing.

The commander looked at Bodogou and said, "I'll be back for her. Make sure she's fit to travel."

Then he turned to his men and shouted, "Single file, and on the double."

Within seconds they were back in the river bed and jogging upstream.

Bodogou quickly saw the seriousness of the situation and he too gave orders. "Everyone, quick, down into the crevice before we're seen!"

The younger and stronger got down in first and then helped the less able. Everyone was in when they heard the deafening sound of hoof beats in the riverbed below. Dust rose thick in the stifling air creating partial shade, but making them gasp.

"Don't be afraid," Bodogou's voice reassured them all. "The rocks have hidden us. We are safe here."

"It is ironic," thought Yandeng, "the same rocks that had caused my injury, are now protecting me from harm."

In a few minutes it grew silent again. Lual slowly climbed out of the crevice and peeped over the edge. The cloud of dust had moved upstream, where they had been only a half an hour ago.

"I think it is clear out here. What should we do?"

There was a buzz of discussion in the hollow of the rocks. Some wanted to keep hiding. Others wanted to flee downstream.

"I believe we should wait in the rocks," Bodogou said. "The SPLA will certainly not beat the murahaleen. We don't have to worry about them returning first. The murahaleen will likely return this way to continue to wherever it was they were raiding. Let us wait a spell. It is getting too hot to march anyway. But bring in the sticks and rags and let's put a brace on Yandeng's leg."

Before long they heard the popping of gunshots about a mile upstream.

"The SPLA must have set up an ambush on the murahaleen as they raced up the riverbed," Bodogou postulated.

"The gunshots are continuing, they must be doing well," another conjectured.

They found a spot where they could sit Yandeng. They placed the sticks on either side of her leg and wrapped it tightly with the rag.

About that time the gunshots ended.

"It didn't last too long," said Bodogou. "Let us wait and see. If the murahaleen come past celebrating, we'll know the SPLA are all dead. If not, we'll know they are still out there."

Within 10 minutes they heard the first hoof beats. No one looked out but they could see the dust rising around them again. They heard an occasional voice, from riders not 20 yards from where they lay hiding. There were orders being given from commanders. It sounded like they were being told to keep up the pace. There was no celebrating.

"They have not beaten the SPLA," Bodogou whispered. "We will need to move quickly. They will certainly return before long and they'll be looking for Yandeng. We don't want to be here when they return."

# Chapter 11

When Jerome returned to the office at the end of the next day, his boss jumped up, looked around behind him, ushered him into a chair and shut the door.

"Jerome, your life may be in danger. What are you thinking?" he said in a very concerned tone in his voice. "Was she worth it? By the way, I never thought you were the type to hang out with... uh, well, anyway, it's none of my business. You're free to do what you want in your spare time."

"Graham, what are you talking about?"

"Jerome, he looked mad, real mad. Plus, he's one of the meanest looking Russians I've ever laid eyes on. Word in the office is that he's a loose cannon, and a loaded one, so don't try to make light of it. By the way, what were you doing in that ... anyway it doesn't matter. I've made up my mind."

"About what? Wait, when did you see him?"

"A decision about your job. Him? I saw him a half hour ago. He came looking for you. There was a buzz in the office when he left and someone had heard what happened last night. I like you Jerome. I have from the start. You're a smart kid. I want to keep you alive and return you to your mother."

"Well, that would be hard, she died over 15 years ago."

"Oh... sorry. Look, I don't want any fatalities in my department. The company has already had a number of these non work-related fatalities this year. I'm taking actions to make sure you're not the next."

"What kind of actions?"

"I know you only have two weeks left but I've arranged for a job transfer. It's an opportunity for you that I think you'll like. Our seismic group could use a support person. Now that doesn't mean you'll be making decisions on where to drill. I'm talking more about corresponding with the field, keeping up on the group's communications and such. This should be a good opportunity to learn new things. Well, what do you think?"

"Great, when do I start?"

"Immediately! And oh, I've also arranged for you to live inside the gate. You'll have to leave your apartment in town, tonight. You'll be getting all your meals at the company cafeteria. No more muscle-bound Russian pimps and pretty call girls with meals. I hope you don't mind. Here's your key and new apartment number."

"I appreciate the concern, but I don't think it's necessary to go to…"

"Jerome, this is a non-negotiable. You can't stay under my responsibility if you can't agree to all this."

"OK... I'll move."

From that point on he worked in a cement block building with few windows and had little conversation with anyone. His office mates were geologists who spent most of their time reading reports from the field and studying maps. The only breaks in the monotony were mealtimes.

The two weeks in the geology department were actually the longest two weeks of the summer. He was so close to what he loved, yet it was so far from what he thought it would be like. All he really got to do was check the department's email and phone messages and make sure the flow of communication between the office and the field didn't lapse. He was the office communication police. He knew that when he graduated from the university he didn't want to get a job badgering field technicians about readings, but even so, he wasn't sure he'd really want to sit in a dark office all day either. His father worked in a research lab for decades without any noticeable change in the landscape. He never asked for more. Jerome knew he was not wired to repeat his father's life. He wanted more variety, or adventure, or something.

He broached the topic at lunch with his fellow office mates. They seemed a little offended that he implied that they led boring lives. "You call Sakhalin Island boring? You of all people! You've had more excitement in 3 months than we've had as a group in three years. Why we've only been to those kind of bars a few times, and…"

"No. You're misunderstanding my point. I'm not sure I'm cut out for a desk job, that's all. I'd like to be outside somewhere, talking with people."

"Maybe you should get into sales, car sales in particular. People always need to buy new cars."

"Funny! I like geology. I love it in fact. I just don't think I'd be happy if I never left the office."

"Ah, well, if it's excitement you want, maybe you should try somewhere like the Sudan," he said mocking.

"What kind of excitement do you mean?"

"Ah, I don't know. The kind that comes with civil war and hoping no one attacks your office that week, and such like."

"I didn't know there was a civil war going on in Sudan. I haven't heard anything about it in the news."

"That doesn't mean anything. I've talked to people who have been there and it's happening."

"Well, I've never heard of it. It must not be a real civil war."

There was laughter at the table.

"So, if you've never heard of it, it can't be happening?"

"Well, I mean if it were significant, it would be in the news, right?"

Wow! So the fact that the Associated Press covers it makes it real? Neither the press nor the United Nations is interested. They've turned a deaf ear to it. Anyway, if you're interested in some adventure, I have some contacts with a Canadian oil company there. I've heard they need adventuresome geologists out in the field. Problem is, your Russian wouldn't help you there. They speak Arabic, a God-awful impossible language."

"Really? Hmmm. Pass along the information."

# Chapter 12

They started to climb out from the rocks in response to Bodogou's call to start up their march again.

"But what about the murahaleen?" someone asked.

"They're moving faster than we can. We won't catch them. Unfortunately, the SPLA can move faster than us too. Let us pray they are delayed and that we can move quickly," Bodogou responded.

Then he prayed out loud to God, as though he were talking to one of the members of the group, asking his protection and speed, and if he saw fit, to give blind eyes to the murahaleen and slow legs to the SPLA, until they could escape. They climbed back down to the riverbed. Bodogou and Lual got on each side of Yandeng and acted as her crutches as she stepped as best as she could with her good leg. Two lookouts were assigned to march up on top of the bank of the river and to keep a watch in both directions. It was about 2 in the afternoon. The heat was oppressive. Their hunger and fatigue were only matched by their fear of being caught by either the SPLA or the murahaleen. Capture by the SPLA would mean the loss of Yandeng, whereas capture by the murahaleen would mean the loss of all.

Bodogou started singing again, softly but clearly.

*"The Lord is my shepherd I shall not be in need..."*

At first only Lual joined him, but when Yandeng's voice blended with theirs, the others followed.

*"Even though I walk through the valley of the shadow of death, I will fear no evil."*

After they finished a verse, Bodogou called up to the sentries, "What do you see now?"

"The cloud of dust is about 3 miles ahead and still moving."

"And behind us?"

"Still nothing."

They sang another verse and another. The murahaleen seemed to be staying in the riverbed and gaining distance between them. The cloud of dust was almost out of sight. A good 5 miles now separated them. The group was hungry and in need of rest. Yandeng was in more pain and getting weaker. Bodogou and Lual were bone tired too. Even though Yandeng was not heavy, carrying her thin frame in the 110 degree heat had sapped their remaining strength.

"We must stop," people were complaining. "We are thirsty and weak. Please, let us stop!"

"We must go further," Bodogou insisted. "If we stop now, the SPLA may catch up to us. Besides, we need to keep moving anyway. We need to get to Nimne."

They continued for another 15 minutes and finally half the group rebelled.

"No, Bodogou. We can go no further. Maybe we can continue further later today, but not now."

They gathered round a pool of water and began to drink. Then certain ones split off to go look for roots or edible plants. Others found shade and lay down. Yandeng was carried to a shady spot where she collapsed in pain. Her foot had swollen to nearly twice its size. Her dark ebony face looked pale. She was soaked in sweat.

After a short rest the sentry called down into the riverbed from a small tree above, "The soldiers, I spotted them."

"Where, how far off?" Bodogou called up.

"About 2 miles upstream," he answered back.

"Have they spotted you?"

"I don't think so. They are walking not running."

"We must move," Bodogou commanded. "Those who choose not to come with us will be left to the will of the militia."

And with that he fought to his feet, motioned to Lual, and again pulled Yandeng up to her one good foot, put her arms over their shoulders, and resumed their march downstream. The others followed.

"Keep us posted," Bodogou said to the sentry, as they marched along in parallel.

They could only go as fast as Bodogou and Lual could carry Yandeng. She winced in pain with each step.

Within a half an hour the sentry announced that the militia was about a mile behind them. Darkness would come within 2 hours, but by then it would be too late.

Bodogou started to sing again, but in a low voice. The others joined in, careful to keep their voices down. "Even though I walk through the valley of the shadow of death, I will fear no evil."

Before long the sentry announced that only a half mile separated them. He was sure they were now following their trail.

"Your rod and your staff they comfort me."

They tried to walk faster and Bodogou slipped and fell dropping Yandeng awkwardly forward. She shrieked with pain and lay on the ground in tears.

"No, I can't do it anymore," she wept. "Let the soldiers have me. I can't go on."

"No," said Bodogou firmly, but kindly. "We are not defeated yet."

With his last strength he picked her up and carried her in his arms. The others stood staring, knowing that he couldn't carry her for long.

"More bad news," the sentry called down.

"What now?" Bodogou said under his breath, exasperated.

"A cloud of dust from the other direction."

"The murahaleen have turned back on us?"

"No, I don't think so. It's not coming from the riverbed.

"From where then?" Bodogou insisted.

"I'm not sure. It's from out on the plain to the west."

"What? That's … that's not possible… unless…"

Bodogou gently set Yandeng down and found a place to climb up the 10 foot wall of the riverbed. He looked out to the west and he too saw a small cloud of dust. He watched for a minute and was assured that it was moving, and in their direction.

"Yes," he said, "I think I know what it is. There is a road running to Bentiu. That is a vehicle on the road. It must cross the riverbed somewhere ahead of us."

"It could be government troops," the sentry warned.

"True, the government has a post in Bentiu. Or it may not be. In any case, we need to move ahead. Keep us posted."

Bodogou climbed back down into the riverbed with renewed energy. He lifted Yandeng and began carrying her again. Lual was at his side and the two of them took turns.

"Surely goodness and mercy will follow me all the days of my life," Bodogou sang, "And I will dwell in the house of the Lord forever."

"What do you see?" Bodogou called out.

"It is a vehicle, a lone vehicle, and it looks big."

"And the militia?

"Still closing on us, but they must have taken a break when we stopped. Still over a quarter mile back."

And then they came to a spot where they could see straight down the riverbed for about a half mile. And there in front of them, crossing the bed, was a cement bridge. It was quite a novelty in a land of dirt roads.

"Let us hurry, please, everyone, do your best," Bodogou pleaded.

They plodded on, now walking in the evening shadows.

"It's a bus," the sentry called. "And it is close."

"Run ahead and stop the bus," Bodogou ordered Lual. "Lie down in the road if you have to, but don't let it pass until we get there."

Lual ran on ahead.

"The militia is only 300 yards behind," the sentry called down softly.

"They're almost within earshot," Bodogou thought.

The last quarter mile to the bridge took all the remaining strength anyone could muster, especially Bodogou, who was carrying Yandeng.

When they were fifty yards away the bus crossed the low bridge. They all watched as it drove right over without stopping. But then just as it passed, it skidded to a halt. They heard the horn honk. Then they could see the driver talking to someone, then looking their way, then waving at them to hurry. They climbed the embankment to the road and Lual confirmed, "You were right. It is going to Bentiu. And no soldiers on the bus, only civilians, mostly Dinkas and Nuer. The driver is a Dinka. He says he can take people to Bentiu but he only has 1 seat left and he needs 2000 dinars. And he's in a hurry!"

Bodogou sighed. "Does anyone have any money?" he asked.

"I do," said Lual. "My dad had some buried beneath our tukul. The fire didn't destroy it. I dug it up before we left.

**55**

"Wait," Yandeng cried out. "I can't leave you! I don't want to go to Bentiu! Not alone!"

"There is only one seat," Bodogou said, nodding his head. "This is the right decision. We can no longer help you. If you stay with us, we'll lose you to the SPLA. Bentiu is the best we can do."

Lual then emptied his pocket, put a fistful of cash in Yandeng's hand carried her onto the bus, put her in the empty seat and kissed her on the top of the head. He looked at the people around her on the bus, and said in a pleading voice, "Will you please look after her? She's my sister."

Lual stepped off the bus and waved as the bus rolled away in a cloud of red dust.

# Chapter 13

A week after his discussion about the Sudan, Jerome left Sakhalin and returned home to begin his doctoral program. He called his advisor within hours after arriving.

"So, how was it? Did you meet any young Russian women? Are Russian women pretty?"

"Well, uh, I guess 'yes' to both questions."

"Jerome, you met a Russian girl? Now you're surprising me. Did she work there with you?"

"Well she worked there, yes. But no, not with me, or I mean... not with my company."

"Tell me more, Jerome. Come to think of it, I've heard the only women on that island are prostitutes. I'm sure that wasn't your case. So how did you meet?"

"Oh, uh, well... first, don't believe everything you hear. I just met her at a restaurant, and I struck up conversation, and well, that's how we met."

"Hmmm. You'll have to tell me about it sometime. Listen, the reason I wanted to get hold of you was because the government has decided to send their funding to another university. Ouch. I know you were counting heavily on this for your doctoral studies. We'll need to rethink all that. Don't worry. We still need you. It's just that we'll have to work on another project."

"How will that affect my program? Will I need more time?"

"Well you know how these things go. I'm sure a little more time will be needed. Just a quick year or so. Don't worry about it. We'll figure something out. Ooops. Got another call. Let's talk again soon. Got to go."

This left Jerome stunned. Another "quick year?" Yes, he did know how things went. First, there were no "quick years." Projects, even when they went well usually dragged a year or so beyond what was estimated. After having been out working for a few months and liking it for the most part, the idea of more school, and then adding another year on top of that sounded about as exciting as watching rocks stratify.

Then, his father, who had been battling cancer, took a sudden turn for the worse and died. Jerome felt like his life had fallen apart. He had no more living relatives. He made funeral arrangements, contacted the few friends his father had, and put announcements in the local newspapers.

Not only was he having a hard time coming to grips with the fact that he had just lost his last remaining relative, his own father, whom he didn't feel like he had gotten to know, but he also felt he had no appetite for life as it was now presenting itself. He didn't want to study for 4 more years. He didn't know what he wanted but it wasn't that. And now, there was nothing, or no one, preventing him from doing or going somewhere else. But what or where? Those were questions for which he had no answers.

# Chapter 14

Yandeng tossed and turned all night. The bus bumped and jerked and rattled. Her whole leg was in such pain it was all she could do to keep from crying out. Some of the people around her put clothing and sacks underneath her foot to pad it from the rough ride. She tried to thank them, at least she thought she thanked them, but couldn't remember. She was weak from hunger and felt like she was passing in and out of consciousness. The words of the song they had been singing kept passing through her mind. "Though I walk through the shadow of the valley, or green pastures…" Her mind was not lucid. Her thoughts jumbled with fatigue and pain. Shortly before dawn she either passed out or fell asleep. She had a dream, or a vision, of a man in shining white robes. He said, "Yandeng, don't be afraid. I will protect you from death." She saw herself fainting, and he picked her up and carried her to her home where her mother and father were waiting for her with a big batch of sorghum cakes on the fire outside of their tukul. Her brother and sister were there too. Then she felt herself being shaken and she found herself again on the bus, feverish and with a hideously swollen foot. The bus was arriving in Bentiu. Yandeng began to think about what she would do next.

"Excuse me. Does anyone know where I can stay in Bentiu? I have no family here," she said to no one in particular, yet loud enough for many to hear.

"There is a government camp. They will take you," a man said.

"Yes, but you must become a Muslim," another interjected.

"I've heard there is a church that takes people in," said another.

"How can I find it?" Yandeng asked.

"I don't know. I'm not from Bentiu either."

The bus pulled into a dusty lot filled with other buses and lots of people. The door opened and the passengers started getting off. Finally, Yandeng was left on the bus with the driver.

He said to her, "There are some French doctors in Bentiu. They have a hospital."

"But I don't know the French. And how would I pay them? Do I need French money?" she asked.

He chuckled. "No, I think they may help you for free. I know where their hospital is. If you can walk, I can take you."

"But I can't walk. I don't think I can even get off the bus without help."

He helped her off the bus and had her sit down on the dusty ground.

"Now, let me see if I can find some help," he said looking around the lot. He walked over to a group of young men on motor scooters and spoke a few words to one of them and pointed to Yandeng. Then the driver handed the young man something and he pulled his scooter over beside her. The two of them lifted her onto the back seat and then the driver accelerated out of the dusty lot away from the buses. She looked back and waved to the driver and wondered why he had been so nice to her.

Yandeng had never been to a big town like Bentiu. Much of it wasn't too different from her village except that it was far bigger. There was one group of tukuls after another. But there were also makeshift shelters made out of sticks, bits of wood and many colors of plastic sheets, and cement block buildings. Her senses were overloaded seeing so many new sights. She tried to drink it all in and keep her mind on protecting her leg from the bumps. They crossed a bridge over a swampy area. Then in a half mile or so they came to a sign that read "Médécins sans Frontières / Doctors without Borders." There were about 20 buildings of various sizes ringed inside a small fence. One area had a secondary fence around it. There was a small sign outside of it in French, English, and Arabic. She understood the English "TB isolation unit - face mask is needed when in this area."

The scooter driver pulled up to the door of a cement block building, helped her into a reception area and onto a bench, then left. She had rarely been in buildings that had wooden or tin roofs, or anything other than a grass roof. She looked around and tried to take it all in, but she felt very light headed and feverish. She sat for what was probably a short time and the next thing she remembered was looking up into the face of a white man who was asking her in a funny accent in English, "When was the last time you ate?"

Yandeng had to think back to remember. She then started to tell him her story. He listened, asking a few questions. Before she finished a woman came with a cup of a runny yoghurt drink and some bread. Yandeng sat up and started to quickly devour it.

"Slow down Miss. You should eat slowly."

She knew he was right but was unable to do so.

The man and the woman spoke. They were speaking in a language that Yandeng didn't know. It didn't sound like an African language, at least none she'd ever heard. She continued to eat until there was no longer any bread or yoghurt left. He finished his conversation and gave Yandeng his attention again.

"We will take care of your ankle," he said.

Yandeng was in extreme pain but at least had eaten real food for the first time in days and was starting to feel optimistic. He examined her leg and made a disapproving grimace. He and the woman took her to another room and lifted her onto a shiny metal bed with long metal legs, higher than her waist. It looked so odd that she almost laughed. Why would anyone make a metal bed she wondered? The doctor unwrapped her brace and squeezed and pulled her ankle.

"Well, it doesn't seem to be broken, Miss. We can only give you a better brace and send you on your way."

"But I have nowhere to go," she protested.

"Do you have any family in the area?"

Yandeng began to cry and said she had no family anymore. The white doctor frowned. His face betrayed tiredness and sadness.

"There is a government camp in town where you can go. They will take you, give you work, food, and a place to live," the attendant recommended.

"But I'm not a Muslim. I am a Christian now. I was told I would be mistreated if I went to the camp."

"Don't believe everything you hear," the attendant said. "And why not become a Muslim, at least for a while, until things improve. It can't be that bad being a Muslim."

"But I can't pretend to be something I'm not."

"Sure you can. If you're hungry enough you can. You can do a lot of things when you're hungry. Don't be stubborn. You don't have choices, just a decision. Do you want to survive or not?"

The whole idea went against all Yandeng's inclinations and convictions. She heard a voice inside of her that kept repeating, "Don't go there, trust me."

The attendant continued to pressure her.

"Miss, if you refuse to go there, you still need to leave. We can't help you. It is the only choice you have."

She brushed off the warning voice in the back of her mind and told the attendant she'd go to the camp and become a Muslim, albeit temporarily. From the moment she made this decision she felt like it was the wrong one, but the attendant praised her and said, "You've made the right decision. You'll thank yourself for doing this."

## Chapter 15

That night was the showing at the funeral home. Jerome decided on just one night. His father only knew a few people. Right at seven a handful of friends and associates of his father showed up, almost as a group. They seemed awkward, like they wanted to say something but weren't quite sure what to say. He shared their awkwardness. They didn't stay long. Then his advisor and a few classmates from school showed up. They made their stay brief as well. And then Jerome was alone. He sat beside his father's body and tried unsuccessfully to fight off the ever encroaching darkness coming over him. He would have left but he had nowhere in particular to go. He figured he'd stay until nine, since the room was rented until then anyhow. Everyone he could imagine coming had already come. It seemed almost fitting that his last moments with his father would be spent in absolute and deathly silence.

He reflected on his childhood. His mother had died before he could really remember. His dad seemed married to the research lab and was never around. One thing his father did right though was to hire Guadalupe to take care of him when he was young. She provided as much of a home life as Jerome ever knew. Had it not been for her, he wouldn't have known that passion, sentiment, and conversation existed. She was kind to him. He grew to admire and love Guadalupe and her ways. She wasn't smart, or particularly attractive, or wealthy… far from it. But she was as happy as she was kind and considerate. She had her own family and sacrificed all she could for them. She even sacrificed for her surrogate family of an unappreciative skinny introverted white kid with thick glasses. She always seemed content, always smiling and saying kind things.

At about 8:45 Jerome was startled out of his deep thoughts by some movement and the sound of rustling near the doorway. He looked and at first thought he was dreaming that he was looking at Guadalupe. But when she walked over and kissed him on the top of his head, he knew it was her. She sat down beside him and took his hands in hers and looked deep into his eyes.

"Jerome, mi hijo. I am so sorry for you." There were tears in her eyes. "I am so, so sorry."

Then Jerome's eyes started to water.

"You poor boy," she said.

"No, no, I'm fine," he lied. "Death comes to all of us at one time or another."

"First you lose your poor mother, who must have loved you so much. And now your only parent and family member leaves you all alone. How hard!"

He wished she hadn't mentioned his mother. His eyes completely blurred with tears. He felt her hand on his shoulder.

"What are your plans now Hijo?"

"I'm not sure. I guess I'll just continue with what I've been doing."

"Are you happy with what you're doing?"

"Happy? Well, I don't know. I guess I am."

"You're not sure if you're happy?"

"Well, I guess I'm sure that I'm not really happy. But there's nothing I can do about it."

"I would think you're the only one who can do something about it?"

"Like what?"

"Well, if what you're doing isn't making you happy, maybe you're doing the wrong thing."

Jerome was silent.

"Do you like studying rocks, Jerome?"

"Well yeah, or at least I used to like it."

"You don't like it anymore?"

"Well, I'd like to do something with rocks, not just study them. But I have at least four more years of study before I can work."

"Really? Four more years of study? Well, I only went to school for 6 years and it hasn't stopped me from doing things. I just decided to do what I wanted."

"You wanted to be a maid... I mean, a... uh... housekeeper?"

"No, I wanted to come to America and start a new life. And being a housekeeper allowed me to do that."

"That must have been hard."

"Sure, there were hard times. But it wasn't so bad. I got to meet people. I met you, right?"

"Yes... But what about leaving your family?"

"Sure it was hard. But eventually they all followed me and I was able to help them start a new life too. But you don't have a family anymore, Jerome. You can start a new life if you want to, whatever life you want, wherever you want. Are there things you'd like to do? Any adventures you've thought about?"

"Yes, I suppose. It's funny you should mention adventures. I've thought about one, but I don't know if I'm really cut out to be an adventurer."

"Well, if you've thought about an adventure, you probably are an adventurer. Anyway, life has its problems whether you decide to go on an adventure or do nothing. I'd just as soon have my problems while on an adventure. But, you do as you think best."

"Really? How will I know?"

"You'll know what's best. Vaya con Dios mi Hijo."

"You too, Guadalupe. I'll never forget you."

Jerome went home and slept a deep peaceful sleep, lost in dreams, although he couldn't quite remember them when he awoke the next morning.

## Chapter 16

The attendant gave Yandeng a pair of wooden crutches and an envelope and had someone from the clinic drive her to the government camp on the back of a motor scooter.

At the camp she was dropped off at the front door to a building. A man in a white robe and skull cap gave her a hard stare as she struggled off the scooter. He did not smile, nor offer a greeting. She handed him her envelope. He read it and continued to examine her, inspecting her, much like the men in the village inspected their cows. He looked stern and disapproving. Then he spoke to her in Arabic. She understood enough to follow what he was saying.

"It says in this letter that you are a Muslim. Is this true?"

"Yes," Yandeng said sadly as tears came to her eyes. She felt like somehow she had just betrayed a close friend.

"Well you're not dressed like a Muslim," he barked.

"I don't have any other clothes," she managed.

He left and came back with an armful of clothes and pushed them at her.

"Ash ismik? (What is your name?)" he demanded.

"Yandeng, Sir."

"From now on your name is Miriam, not Yandeng," he croaked.

"Ok," she said.

"La la," came a stern rebuke in Arabic. "Ittikillim bil Arabi. Qul mutafaqqa, laisa 'OK.'"

She understood that she was no longer to speak Dinka, or English, but only Arabic. Another man joined them and told them to come into the front room.

"What are we going to do with you?" he asked. He seemed to be in charge. The other man just stood shaking his head in negative agreement.

"Look at your leg," he shouted.

Miriam looked at her leg, although she already knew what it looked like.

"You can't do chores like the other girls! Not in a brace! Do you know how to sow?"

"No, but I can learn."

"Oh listen Ali, she can't even sow, but she can learn. And who should teach you? If we had enough people around to teach you, we could very well do without you, couldn't we?"

Miriam was not sure if he was waiting for an answer. Then the other man answered.

"Yes we sure wouldn't need her then."

"Do you have any skills?"

"I can cook, but I can't walk, so I can't cook right now sir."

There was a phone in the room, one of the first Miriam had seen, and the first time she had heard one ring. When it rang, the man in charge answered it and said, "Ay na'am, Director Ali here." There was a pause and then he said to his assistant, "Mohammed, take this. It's an English speaker. Why don't these people learn Arabic!" Ali handed him the phone.

Mohammed reluctantly held the phone to his ear and then said in very halting English, "I help you ... please."

It sounded like the caller was seeking information about the camp. Mohammed told them, "Visit to his camp some time. You come. We teach you Islam, the Koran, and Arabic."

The caller seemed to have unanswered questions, but all Mohammed could say was, "You come. You come." He handed the phone back to Ali who abruptly hung it up.

Then they turned to Miriam again and seemed to be groping to try to remember what they had been talking about.

"I speak English," Miriam said.

"So, what is your point?" Ali barked back.

"Well maybe you could use help answering the phone in English."

The idea didn't immediately translate to their line of thought. But then Ali said slowly and deliberately, like he had just thought of the idea himself, "You speak English. Hmmm. Maybe you could answer the phone in English and help some of these stupid people who keep calling."

"Yes," said Miriam wisely. "That sounds like an excellent idea."

"But can she type?" Mohammed asked. "We need help typing."

Miriam thought for a few seconds and said, "No, but I'd really like to learn how. My parents and teachers always said I learn quickly."

"We don't care about what your parents and teachers say. We'll be the judges. You start tomorrow morning here in the office, and if you don't learn quickly you'll be sent to the kitchen whether you have a brace or not. Understood?"

"Yes sir."

Ali motioned with his hand for Mohammed to get Miriam out of the office and went into an adjoining office and shut the door. Mohammed brushed past her, motioning for her to follow, barely giving her time to put her crutches in place, and walked quickly to the women's tent area. There were two large tents with cots and mosquito netting where the women slept. He turned Miriam over to an Arab woman named Laila. Then he quickly left.

"Marhabban," Laila said to her. "Welcome."

Laila was kind, and patient. She immediately put Miriam at ease. Laila helped Miriam put on her new clothing, a traditional long Muslim taub, which consisted of about 10 yards of semitransparent black cloth that wrapped around her body, with an accompanying head scarf and veil to cover her face in public. She wrapped the long black taub over her thin body and dirty, worn, and faded dress that she had worn for weeks. She saw other girls around, all wearing the Arab garb, like her own. It was hot and uncomfortable, but she was glad to finally have new clean clothes. The girls were all doing chores of some sort. Some sowed while other did laundry or prepared food. Laila asked her name and introduced her to the other girls. They all stared at her brace. Laila then explained. "Miriam has an injured leg and won't be able to join you for chores until her leg is better. In the meantime, the Director said she will be doing office work."

The other girls looked envious, but were otherwise hospitable. They assigned Miriam a cot and mosquito netting and let her rest until mealtime when they took her to another tent where other girls were working dishing up bowls of sorghum mash. It wasn't terribly special, but it was plentiful. And so Miriam's new life at the camp began.

By Their Fruit

Miriam spent her afternoons in formal study of Islam and Arabic in a classroom in one of the buildings at the camp. They sat crowded together on wooden benches. There was a male and female teacher. There was a black board in the front of the room that the teachers screeched and scratched on with chalk. They sternly shouted the lessons like they were teaching a lesson to a naughty child. Arabic was almost as important as the study of Islam itself.

"Arabic is the language spoken in heaven by angels," the male teacher said, "so I will not tolerate mistakes."

He was humorless and strict. The female teacher seemed his equal in both respects. The girls would often make mistakes, which they found funny, but learned to keep their laughter hidden. If not, they would certainly get evil looks, or even raps on the shoulders or hands with a stick. Miriam loved to learn but there was such a heavy mood surrounding the learning that it seemed to suck all the joy out of it. There was first of all the fear of the stick. And secondly there was the fear of a more lasting punishment that permeated the atmosphere. The teachers were quick to remind them of how undeserving they all were of the good hospitality of the camp and how deserving they were of God's wrath, especially those who weren't good Muslims.

Yandeng was actually good at Arabic. Learning came more easily to her than it seemed for the others. She loved to learn anything. She wasn't particularly fond of Arabic, but loved the challenge of trying to learn to speak another language. She found herself trying to remember how to say things in Arabic even in her free time and would ask Laila questions. She quickly became the top Arabic student in her group.

Islamic studies were another question altogether. She just didn't understand it. As the teachers communicated it, God was all knowing and all powerful, yet not particularly interested in the everyday comings and goings of his slaves. He was so far removed from humanity he wasn't very interested in their sufferings or concerns. Yet, if they displeased him, he could quickly become involved to punish them. This seemed contradictory. What was God like, she wondered. Was He really like her teachers? If so, what would the ramifications be? She would certainly not want to get close to God. But she would have no way to escape him either,

**69**

without getting whacked hard and often. It seemed a no-win proposition.

After class one day she went back and lay on her cot in the tent. The girls were supposed to be helping get dinner ready, but she was in such a dark mood she couldn't bear to be with the other girls. Laila found her on the cot.

"Are you sick Miriam?"

"No, I'm fine really."

"Then why aren't you helping get dinner ready?"

"I don't know. I just don't feel like being around anyone."

"Well you know the rules. If you don't help get dinner ready, you don't eat."

"Yes, I know the rules," she snapped at Laila, in a way that surprised both of them.

"What's the matter? You don't sound like yourself."

"I don't know. I just … I don't know."

"OK. I'll let you alone. May Allah help you," she said, parting with a common phrase.

"I don't think he's really interested in helping me," she stated darkly. Laila paused, but could find no words to reply, then turned and left.

Recurring nightmares began in which a healthy fruit tree, with ripe and delicious fruit growing on its branches, came under the force of a strong and vicious storm. The storm blew off the fruit and then blew the leaves from the tree with violent gusts, and then uprooted the tree itself and blew it away. She would awaken terrified and covered in sweat. She would cry out in the night after waking from the terrifying visions.

"God, is the wind you? Are you against me?"

There seemed no answer from him. She prayed less and less, seeming to have lost her desire to talk to God. She felt so alone, so utterly alone. She felt like ever since she arrived at the camp, she had started walking down a long dark tunnel with no light at the end.

When her brace came off she still had pain in her leg and limped badly. By this time, she was doing a lot of work in the office. Ali had her answering correspondence. He told her he wanted her to type the letters. She had once seen a typewriter that one of the missionaries had brought to her village. None of the children were allowed to use it but had seen some of the white adults using it. Now she got to use it herself. She used only her two index fingers but quickly learned where all the letters were and could type almost as fast as she wrote by hand. There was a lot of work to do and little rest. So, even though her brace was off, Ali said she was needed too badly to leave the office and would continue there.

There was a local army garrison attached to the camp. The women at the camp did constant food prep, sewing, and laundry in support of the camp in between Islamic and Arabic studies. Miriam was also volunteered by Ali to serve as a secretary for some of the officers at the camp. She typed letters and reports having to do with their maneuvers in the area. At times Miriam pondered the fact that she was supporting those who went raiding through Dinka territory, destroying ancestral homes and killing the inhabitants. She tried not to think too much about these things.

Weeks stretched into months. Miriam became even more morose and moody. She felt like she had betrayed her new faith in Jesus by claiming to be a Muslim. But maybe now she was a Muslim. She wore Muslim clothes, said Muslim prayers, and spoke Arabic. Maybe this is what a Muslim was. She felt so conflicted and unhappy. She hated her environment and what she had become, but could see no way out.

## Chapter 17

The first thing that Jerome noticed when he awoke the morning after his father's wake was that he had a plan now, or maybe a part of a plan. He didn't want to drag his studies on indefinitely. He wanted change, maybe even some adventure. That day he found Alfred, his advisor and had a long talk about the long road ahead for his doctoral studies. He mentioned his interest in actually doing something, even if it meant putting his studies on hold. Alfred seemed surprised and less than supportive. He asked if Jerome had any ideas.

"Well, not really. I have a lead or two. One would be quite an adventure, and I don't know if I'm cut out for it. But anyway, I don't have anything definite."

"I used to think about adventures. You're better off to keep your feet firmly planted in academia. Adventures are usually overrated."

"Have you ever done anything outside of academia?"

"Like what?"

"I don't know. Worked in industry?"

"Well we have our joint projects with industry, but I've never been employed outside the university... maybe I wish I had."

"Why's that?"

"Just because I could have. Just to see what's out there. It's a little late for me now. I don't see me making any changes between now and retirement."

"But you won't retire for 15 more years!"

"Well, it comes sooner that you think."

That day Jerome visited the career center of the university to see what companies would be visiting in the near future.

"It's not really the time of year we get recruiters," he was told. "Come back in four months."

"Four months," groaned Jerome. He went back to his apartment and found the name of the Canadian company working in the Sudan. Tallman Oil Inc. had a web page, and sure enough they mentioned exploration opportunities in Africa. Jerome filled in an online application and attached a letter mentioning the name of his referral on Sakhalin Island.

It all seemed so far away, a Canadian company, doing work in a remote area on a distant continent. He had to keep looking. He spent the rest of the day and into the wee hours of the next day creating resumes and introductory letters online. There were so many options. You could pay $75 to have your resume put at the top of the list, or $150 to have your resume put on a special list, or $300 to have a professional post your resume on a private list, or on and on and on. There were government jobs. The US government described itself as the largest employer in the non-communist world. That sounded promising, since he'd always been a non-communist. Then of course there were private jobs, and jobs you couldn't tell who they were with, seemingly hundreds of thousands of jobs. Jerome finally fell asleep at 3 AM and awoke the next day exhausted. He figured he had probably put his name in the hat for hundreds of jobs and decided he'd take some time off from job hunting until he heard back from at least a few.

Three weeks passed before he heard anything. He received an electronic rejection for a job he didn't remember applying for. It was impersonal and matter-of-fact. "You unfortunately don't have the skills and/or experience that match the current position or assignment. We wish you the best in your professional endeavors."

Jerome wondered about putting in another day or night, or both, and sowing the employment field with fresh seed. The thought didn't excite him. In fact, he dreaded the idea. He was sending his resume, which felt like a part of his own soul, out willy-nilly into the ether world for who-knows-who to step in and reject him. Or, even worse, for someone to accept him and have him move to who-knows-where to work at a job he didn't like.

More weeks passed and depression started to set in. He had never felt desperate about his future, but now for the first time he did. He was not a God believer, far from it. His professors had discipled him well in a somewhat open-stanced agnosticism. They weren't openly hostile to God-believers but certainly viewed them as a mentally weak and generally steered clear of them.

He thought to himself, "If I were a God-believer, I'd probably pray right now. I'd ask for a great job, an adventure and a woman

73

that loves me. But, truth be told, I don't believe there's anyone out there listening. Too bad. I could use the help.

Later in the week he stopped in to see if Alfred had received any fresh news on a new research grant. "Yes, we received good news," he said enthusiastically. "We were told we should know within weeks… probably."

"Well, didn't they tell you that weeks ago?"

"Yes, but this time it sounds more definite."

Even though Jerome somehow couldn't rise to the same level of enthusiasm as his advisor, he congratulated him on the news. In Jerome's mind though, more weeks of waiting was not good news, and in fact seemed like a lack of news.

As he turned to go, the administrative assistant asked him, "Jerome, what do you know about Tallman Oil Company?

# Chapter 18

At the government camp, Yandeng focused on something that had never left the back of her mind, finding out what happened to her sister Alual. She began by asking Laila questions. She trusted Laila. She was the one soft spot in an otherwise hard and unforgiving environment. Yandeng knew that the tribe who had taken the villagers away as slaves were Bagarra from the Darfur. This she had learned from the neighbors in Gottong on that horrible day. She asked Laila about the Bagarra. Laila thought this was funny and asked if she wanted to become a nomad like them.

"No, it's just that I've met some Bagarra and I want to know more about them."

"Well, they come from the north. They are one of the tribes from the Darfur area. They are Arabs. They move around a lot, herding their camels and flocks, and buying and selling."

"Do they ever sell people?" Miriam asked?

"Whatever do you mean?" Laila was shocked.

Miriam's lip began to tremble and she began to cry.

Laila put her arm on Miriam's shoulder.

"What is it? You can tell me."

Miriam decided to trust Laila all the way and blurted out her story, or at least the part concerning Alual.

"I'm sorry for you my dear. If the Bagarra took her, it was certainly to sell her. They likely won't keep her. I have heard that people that this happens to end up in Khartoum, but I have no evidence."

"What happens in Khartoum?"

"They would be bought by people with money, like… maybe government people."

"But how can I find her?"

"Find her? My dear… It's in God's hands. You can do nothing for her, unfortunately."

"No, I must find her. People must know where they took her. She wasn't the only one. There were 30 of them! And more from other villages. Someone must know where they went."

"Child, don't talk to anyone else about this. If the wrong people know you are asking about it, you could get into a lot of trouble."

Laila had always been kind to her, but after that, she seemed to take even more of an interest in helping her.

"So, you were from Palwung, in Mayom County?"

"Yes, have you heard of it?"

"Well, I've heard people speak of the area."

"Really? What do they speak of?"

"Well, an oil company has moved into the area. They're building a pipeline from there all the way up to the Red Sea and they'll soon be pumping oil into it."

"Yes, I know. That's why they wanted our land. We'd have given them the oil if they'd have let us stay on our land. The land is worth far more than the oil you know."

"Yes. I'm sure. I'm sorry for what happened. Do you have any interest in going back there?" Laila asked.

"What do you mean?"

"Well, I hear that the oil company is hiring people. They're trying to find Dinka who know Arabic and English."

"Why do they want us to return? They chased us away."

"They think that if they hire Dinka, the SPLA won't attack their camps."

"Well, I don't think hiring Dinka will stop anyone from attacking, especially the SPLA. The SPLA is not all Dinka you know. There are even many SPLA who don't like the Dinka."

"So you wouldn't be interested then? I'd give a good recommendation for you. I think you'd be good. You speak English, Arabic, and Dinka, and you're smart and learn quickly."

Miriam had received few compliments in her life and was uncomfortable.

"Thank you Laila," she said after a long pause. "But I couldn't do that. I couldn't work for people who have taken our homes and our land and who are now taking our oil. Sometimes I get so angry about it I think I could kill, just like they have done."

"I understand my dear, but you mustn't say these things in public. You could be punished for it. Remember, you are now supposed to be part of the new Sudan, a Muslim who speaks Arabic, and who is loyal first to the government. The Dinka can no longer help you."

Miriam had a sinking feeling that Laila was right. The Dinka could no longer help her.

A week or so later, Laila came into the tent in the morning looking for Miriam.

"I need to talk to you," she said, "alone."

Miriam left her cot and followed Laila into an empty area.

"What is it? Do you have news of my sister?"

"No, no, dear. I just heard some of the camp leaders talking. They have taken notice of you and think it is time for you to be married."

"Married...?" Miriam was stunned. "To whom? When?"

"To one of the officers, and soon. Probably within 2 weeks."

Miriam eyes started to tear up. "But I can't, I won't. You've got to help me."

"I assumed you wouldn't be happy. Maybe I can help. You limp still. Muslim men do not want to marry a woman with defects. You could make it seem worse than it is."

"You mean act like I'm crippled?"

"Well... sort of. You could pretend to be in more pain than you are. No officer is going to put up with a young bride with medical problems."

Miriam had never faked pain in her life. To the contrary, she was used to putting up with a lot of pain and acting like it didn't bother her.

"Well, OK I guess. How do I do it?"

"My poor dear. You aren't the sneaky type, are you? Here's my advice. Tomorrow morning stay in bed and complain about pain in your leg and cry some. Say that your leg hurts too much to stand on it. Do the same thing the next day. By the 3rd day Ali will approve for you to see a doctor. When you see him tell him that the pain is getting constantly worse and that you are no longer able to walk. Do you understand?"

"Yes, I'll try."

The next day, Miriam did as Laila prescribed. And by the third day, Ali ordered her to see the camp doctor. Her old crutches were found and she made her way to his office.

"Hmm. Does it hurt here? And here? And here too?" he asked as he examined her. "It can't hurt everywhere!"

In truth she still had a lot of pain in different parts of her leg. She had been trying to ignore it and be brave. Now she just let herself relish her pain. The thought of marrying a Muslim soldier whose task it was to empty her land of her people caused her to feel her pain in far deeper places. The doctor prescribed daily massage and exercise until the pain lessened. So a new daily routine began in which Miriam got up, ate, and then went for a leg massage and exercise. She had never had a massage before. It made her giggle even though parts of it were painful. Then she strapped on leg weights and did various types of leg lifts. Then she only had an hour or so left of office work before lunch, and then afternoon classes.

She liked her routine. She felt like she was being pampered. Her masseuse, Ajak, a big Nuer woman, was nice to her and wasn't in a hurry to get through the massage. She too was at the camp for reasons similar to Miriam's. She preferred giving massages to cooking and cleaning, and if there was no one to massage, she cooked and cleaned. So she took her time. She liked to talk and seemed to know everything going on around camp. She wanted to know Miriam's story. It was therapeutic for Miriam to talk.

"My dear, my dear. How we have suffered! Where is your brother now?"

"I don't know. The last I saw him he was headed for Nimne in search of food."

"Nimne, hmmm. Hope he found what he needed. You know our "government boys" bombed it a while back. Took helicopter gunships in and opened fire on people standing in line for food. I hope to God he wasn't there when it happened."

"I sense that Lual is OK. I know God takes care of us. I came to know him shortly before I came to the camp. The camp has been hard though. I felt like I knew him better before I got here. Now, well I don't pray much anymore. I pray the Muslim prayers. Five times a day... it's just that I don't talk to God anymore."

"I know child. I know exactly what you mean. I do the same?"

Miriam knew that this conversation, if overheard, had the potential of getting them in serious trouble. She lay speechless on the massage table.

"It's Ok child. I came to know Jesus when I was a bitty little girl. I'm here like you, to survive. I'm learning Arabic and bowing to Mecca five times a day too, but in my heart, I know who takes care of me."

"I don't know," Miriam confessed. "I've felt like I denied him by coming here. I felt like I heard him say he'd take care of me, and I didn't listen."

"Where would you have gone?"

"I don't know. Someone mentioned a church in town and they might help me there."

"I've heard that too, but I've never been there. Could get us in a lot of trouble by visiting."

Over the weeks Miriam and Ajak became bosom friends. Miriam shared her marriage dilemma with Ajak, who agreed to help in whatever way. She had to report to the camp doctor on a regular basis on Miriam's condition. She said that she was making some progress, but very slow, and that she still experienced pain while walking. While this was true, the massage and physical exercise were doing wonders for Miriam. Her limp was disappearing.

Miriam shared her plan to find her sister Alual with Ajak. She told her all she knew.

"Yes, I've heard that the Bagarra are involved in this. The government invited them to join the troops in the raids and part of their payment is that they get to keep whomever they decide not to kill, to sell or do what they want with them. I hear that most of them end up in Khartoum."

"I've never been to Khartoum. How can I ever find her?"

"I don't know child. I'll see if I can learn anything from my Bagarra contacts. I sometimes work with military people who are Bagarra."

The next day Ajak told her she had bad news. The camp doctor was getting impatient and wanted to examine Miriam himself. She had to go that day to see him. Ajak coached her on playing up her pain and trying to limp more than normal.

"I am under pressure by the camp authorities to see my patients get healed, Miss," the camp doctor told Miriam. "And although you are not 100% better you have definitely recovered quite a bit from when you came to me. The authorities are eager to have you return to a full schedule. It seems they are suspicious of your symptoms since it took you so long to complain of them. In any case, I think they have something uh … new in mind for you. I am giving them my recommendation that you return to a normal schedule."

That same day Laila told Miriam that Ali and Muhammed asked to see her in the office as soon as possible.

# Chapter 19

"What? Why do you ask if I know of Tallman Oil?"

"They called here today asking about you. They asked some strange questions."

"Really? Like what?"

"Well, they asked if you knew Arabic. Do you?"

"Well, not real well. What did you tell them?"

"I didn't know. You're not an Arab are you? Well I shouldn't be asking. Anyway, I told them you probably did. What with all the other languages you speak, why not Arabic? And Russian, Jerome, Alfred told me you speak Russian. Really?"

"What else did they ask?"

"They asked if you were connected with any radical political or religious groups. Imagine that!"

"Wow, that is an odd question. What did you tell them?"

"Sorry Jerome. I told them the truth. I told them you're not political at all because you're not even registered to vote. I know that because you told me that on election day last year. And I let them know you're an atheist. I told them if they needed religious or political people in their oil company, for God knows what reason, they'd have to look somewhere else. Besides, I told them that Alfred would never let anyone hire you away. Then they asked me who Alfred was. So I told them and they hung up. Who are those people anyway? I should have just told them I didn't appreciate them snooping around and hung up on them."

"No, thanks Sandra, you did the right thing. I appreciate you letting me know."

"Well, you be careful Jerome. Now you know they're out there asking about you. Be careful."

"I'll be careful Sandra. Thanks again."

He could hardly sleep that night. "Sure, I can understand asking if I know Arabic, but being religious or political? Why do they want to know that?"

He didn't have long to wait. The next day while he was in class his cell phone vibrated. He looked at the number and it was from an outside area code. When he got out of class he had a message to call Rose, a recruiter for Tallman Oil Company from Canada. He called, got put on hold, then got put through.

"Jerome, thanks for calling back. Is this a good time to talk?"

"Sure."

"Good. We received your application and had to check into some things before getting back to you. I see you're interested in our exploration in Africa, the Sudan in particular. We do have an opening there, but why the interest?"

"Well, I've been studying and researching for a number of years, and I have a desire to do some field work. The Sudan sounds like it would be a good place for field work."

"Well... yes it certainly is that, but what about the personal risk?"

Jerome was taken aback. He was not at all sure what she was referring to.

"Oh, the risk. Yeah, well, you can't expect to accomplish anything if you're afraid of risk."

"Sure, but not all risks are equal."

"True, but not all endeavors are equally worthy of risk."

He had no idea why he was arguing for risk. He didn't even know what risks she was referring to.

"Are you ready for that level of adventure?"

They were falling further into abstraction.

"I wouldn't have contacted you if I weren't ready for some level of adventure."

"Well that's what I needed to know. If you would be willing to sign waivers saying you know what you're getting yourself into, I can set up an interview with our Upstream Director of Exploration."

Jerome paused and asked himself almost out loud, "What the hell are we referring to here?"

She waited and then interjected, "The waivers usually sober people up. I know the money is attractive, but when if comes down to it, most of us prefer the security and safety we've come to appreciate..."

Jerome cut her off. "Consider me willing to sign the waivers. How soon can we meet?"

There was a pause. Well, let's see, he's free the day after tomorrow, which would mean you'd need to fly up here tomorrow."

"That wouldn't be a problem if I had a plane ticket. But at this late date the ticket would probably cost a fortune."

Another pause. She sounded offended. "If you're free to fly up tomorrow, I'll get you a ticket. We don't expect you to come here at your own expense."

"Oh… sure. Yeah, of course. I meant, uh, well, sure I can be there."

"Window or aisle?"

"Window."

"Of course, you geologists are all alike. Probably spend the whole flight staring out the window instead of watching the movie."

Jerome wondered how she knew.

"Anyway Jerome, I have your email address. I'll make the reservation and email the details. Call if you have questions. Thanks for your time. Hope to see you day after tomorrow." Click.

# Chapter 20

Miriam knew why Ali and Muhammed wanted to see her. She walked slowly to the office. When she got there Ali looked at her in his disdainful way and told her to have a seat. He left and came back with Muhammed and two soldiers. One an older Arab soldier and the second a younger black soldier, from the Nuba mountains judging by the way he spoke.

"That's her," Ali said pointing at her. "Look her over good. Once you choose, you must take her. There is no renegotiation. If you choose and then turn her down, you will not be offered another later. Lieutenant, you have first choice."

The older Arab walked over to her and pulled her to her feet by her arm. He then walked around her, looking at her body in particular.

"She's very thin," he said disapprovingly to the administrator. "Don't you feed these girls?"

"I told you, she is a Dinka. The Dinka are all thin. But they work hard. This one can read and write and even type."

"Hmff," he snorted disapprovingly. "They should be taught to cook, not type." He walked around 2 more times and then said, "Call me again when you get some others. I prefer lighter skin, more meat... and less typing," he said and walked out.

The administrator nodded for the Nuban to take his turn. He also walked in circles around Miriam. He seemed to like what he saw but he also spoke harshly to Ali.

"She is thin. Maybe she has a disease."

"I told you, she is healthy. I just had her examined by the doctor. The Dinka are strong people."

"Yes, but I already have a wife and they may fight."

"You told me she hadn't born any children. This one is young and will bear many children. Now do you want her or not?"

"I am open to discussing it further."

"There is no discussing. I could ask for twice as much and still have offers. I have only made the offer I made to you because I know you serve God and our country. I am making a great sacrifice for you."

"You know our salaries in the military. What you are asking is a fortune."

"Then you should only have one wife. Now do you want her or do I offer her to your superiors, who will be happy to pay twice what I'm asking?"

"She is not an officer's wife. I am sure none would have her. But I am willing to take her from you. Let us discuss the terms further."

"Well my brother, there is little to discuss. God knows the price I mentioned to you is only because I love our country and our troops and I'm willing to donate much of my profits to you. And now you are insulting my generosity and asking to discuss it further?"

They left the room together still disagreeing yet hand in hand, two seemingly incongruous behaviors. Miriam had seen Arab men take the hand of men in her village while haggling for cows. Miriam knew from these signals that a deal would soon be struck. She would have days, a week at the most, before her ceremony and then move to her new quarters, wherever they were. What little she had gleaned of her husband-to-be was not to her liking. She began to cry. 45 minutes later Ali and Muhammed came back into the room.

"We have good news," Ali said without enthusiasm. "You will be married very shortly to an honorable Muslim, the very man who just met you and generously agreed to take you into his home as his wife."

Miriam sat stone-faced, as if being read her sentence in a courtroom. Then what she said surprised not only the two camp administrators, but herself as well.

"I will not marry him. I will leave your camp, but I will never marry this man."

"What do you mean you won't marry him? After all we have done for you, you ungrateful girl! It is your duty as a Muslim."

"I am not a Muslim. I have studied your religion, but I am more convinced than ever that I am not a Muslim."

"What do you mean you are not a Muslim! You say your prayers, you speak Arabic, you wear Muslim dress. How can you dare say you are not a Muslim?"

"I do these things from hunger, not conviction," she spat back.

"You have not only lied to us, you have lied to God," Ali pronounced angrily.

"It is true, I have lied to God. If I had listened to him, I would have never set foot here."

"Listened to God?" Ali shouted incredulously. "You dare to say God speaks to you?"

"I do hear his voice," Miriam said, almost defensively.

"How dare you speak like this! It is true you have never 'submitted,'" Ali concluded, using the word which was also used to mean becoming a Muslim.

"But there you are wrong, Sir" Miriam said boldly. "I had submitted myself to the Lord, but since coming here I have turned a deaf ear to him."

Upon hearing this statement, the two men gave each other dark stares.

"Get out and never return. You are no longer welcome."

Ali then took her by the arm and pushed her out the door. She went back to the dormitory tent and found Laila.

With tears still in her eyes she said, "Laila, thank you for all your help. I have to leave the camp. Can you please give me the address of the office where they are looking for Dinkas to work with foreign oil companies? Can I please get it now? I must leave immediately."

"Of course. Why so suddenly? What has happened?"

"I was told I must leave, immediately."

"God help you my dear one," she said. Then she went into a file, fished through some papers, copied down an address and handed it to Miriam.

Fighting back tears, Miriam took the paper and gave Laila a hug.

"You have been kind to me. I will never forget you. May God bless you," she said.

Then she turned and walked quickly out. Next she headed over to the other women's dorm tent and asked for Ajak.

"If you find information about my sister, please find a way to bring it to the church we spoke about. I must go now. Thank you for all your help."

"Don't be afraid, child. God will care for you."

"I know that. I have been afraid to let him care for me. But now I am ready."

They hugged and Miriam left the camp with nothing but the black taub on her back. The clothes were only one of the things she planned to change now that she was leaving.

She walked in the direction she had been told there was a church. She asked a few women who looked like Dinkas. She asked them in Dinka and they explained where it was. In a short time, she was there. It was not a stone cathedral, but a thatched tukul, bigger than the one in Bodogou's village. But as she approached, thoughts rushed into her mind. "What if no one is there? Or if they don't accept me? What can I do then? I have nowhere to go back to."

An older man, a Nuer judging by the pattern of the tribal scars on his face, came to the doorway as she approached. The Nuer and Dinka were not often at odds with each other, and even more often enemies, being at odds over land ownership and leadership in the area. The SPLA itself was split over Dinka and Nuer loyalties. He gave her a long hard look and asked, "What brings you here?"

She noticed him looking at her Muslim taub.

"Yes, God bless you, Sir. I am in need. Can you help me?"

"It might be arranged," he said softly. "We don't have many Muslims showing up at the church asking for help."

"Well, sir, I am a Christian. I heard that I might find help here."

"A Christian you say? And what type of Christian are you?" he asked suspiciously.

Miriam was taken aback by the question.

"Why sir, I'm a convinced Christian. I wasn't one by birth. I became one when I became convinced."

"Yes, that's nice, but are you Orthodox or Evangelical or Catholic, or what?"

"Well sir, I'm not at all sure. But I'm sure that if they are friends of Jesus, they are friends of mine."

"I see…. And the Muslim taub? It's a bit… unusual for Christians to dress this way, is it not?"

"Well you see, I have spent the past months at the government camp. I had nowhere to go. I was afraid I'd starve. I made the decision at that time to… anyway Sir, it's a long story. I left the

**87**

camp only an hour ago. I am never going back. I'm sorry if my clothes are not acceptable. I have no others."

His face softened and he asked, "What is your name, and where are you from?"

"My name is Miriam... I mean, Yandeng. I come from Palwung in Mayom County. My village is gone. It was destroyed by government troops and murahaleen over a year ago. My parents were killed and my sister taken as a slave. My brother remains alive, God willing, but I don't know where he is."

His face softened even more and said, "Come in child. As you say, 'Any friend of Jesus is a friend of mine also.' Forgive my suspicions and questions. We are willing to share our bread with you, scant as it is, if you are willing to share our hardship as well, although it sounds as though you already have. By the way, my name is Gatwech."

She received his acceptance of her as a gift. In this country and at this time, acceptance and hospitality were not taken for granted.

The large one-room tukul was occupied by 15 – 20 mostly women and children. There were also a few men, one of whom was missing a leg and part of an arm. They huddled together in small groups on the floor, on temporary bedding of mats, blankets, and cardboard. They looked somber but safe. They nodded their welcome to her.

"Make yourself at home," Gatwech said.

She found a spot not occupied, along the wall near a water bucket and cup and sat down.

As she sat, different conversations started. They wanted to know who she was and what brought her here. They too shared their stories which were similar to hers. They had lost homes, loved ones and limbs due to bombings, shootings, and raiding. They were all trying to somehow restart their lives.

Movement near the door caught everyone's attention. Some arms set a sack of round loaves of coarse barley bread inside the doorway. She wasn't sure who had brought it, but it seemed to be awaited expectantly. Everyone got up and took their share. She also took a small loaf and thankfully ate it. It was today's bread, probably baked early that morning. It would not be fit to sell in the market tomorrow but was not yet stale. She was thankful to have something to eat, and especially thankful to be away from the camp. She had a roof over her head and was in a safer place than she had been in for quite a while. She helped a mother rock one of her children to sleep. The mother then lent her a blanket to sleep on and she lay down and slept.

# Chapter 21

It happened so quick Jerome was left wondering if he'd imagined the conversation with Tallman Oil. He checked his caller ID and sure enough, there was a record of a long distance call that had lasted four minutes and 48 seconds, although it seemed shorter. And sure enough, an email arrived within an hour with a flight itinerary and hotel reservation in Calgary, Alberta. He looked two, then three times at the flight reservation. It said "1$^{st}$ Class" and the price was listed at $1012.48.

"Wow!" Jerome crowed. "Unbelievable! They could have had the interview over the phone for under $10. I wonder what they want from me?"

Jerome left a message with his advisor saying that something had come up and he'd be taking the next two days off from classes, but that he could be reached by cell if needed.

That night he hardly slept. Thoughts of adventures and wild African animals and people dressed in safari clothes danced through his mind. His mind raced all the next day as he traveled to Alberta.

"What was he getting himself into? Was he insane to be considering leaving his secure life in academia to charge off into who knows what? On the other hand, why not take some risks? Why not leave the mundane in the hopes of an adventure? What was the Sudan like? Would they actually consider him for a job there? Wow, wasn't flying first-class cool! Today the only questions he had to answer were whether he'd like something else to drink. Tomorrow, who knew what he'd be asked?"

When he got to his hotel, he found a note and a fruit basked from Tallman Oil Company waiting for him in his room.

"Jerome, I'm looking forward to meeting you tomorrow. Someone will be around to pick you up about 9. Relax and enjoy the evening. Regards, Herbert Austin, Director of Exploration, Tallman Oil Co."

"Wow," I'm not used to people making a big deal of me. If they're just trying to impress me… it's working."

90

Sure enough, the next morning the hotel reception called his room at 8:55 to let him know that a driver was waiting for him. He was politely whisked away to the main offices of Tallman Oil. He was greeted in the lobby by name where he was given coffee and some company brochures. Then he was ushered into a large and handsomely furnished office. Even the university deans didn't have offices like this. There were handmade carpets, knick-knacks, and paintings from all over the world. There were leather couches and arm chairs, and more coffee was served.

Mr. Austin, although he insisted Jerome call him Herb, seemed very friendly. He was a Texan by birth, who joked he had been in the oil business for "just about as long as there's been oil."

He sat down at his desk and offered Jerome a seat in a very comfortable swivel chair facing him.

"Well, ya'll tell me 'bout yourself. Tell me 'bout your experience in oil."

"Well, sir, my experience is in geology more than oil. I've been at the university for 6 years now and I'm starting on my doctoral..."

"Oh hell, I know all that. Let's talk about the Sakhalin project. I don't want to hear about yer damn classes."

And with that Herb pulled out and slapped a copy of a report he and his professor had published together onto the desk in front of him.

So, Jerome simply recounted what he had done to help his advisor in the Sakhalin report, citing page numbers and nearly direct quotes, and then backing up the recommendations made in the report with updates he had learned while in Sakhalin the past summer. Herb seemed to be scrutinizing his every word, yet spellbound at the same time.

"Well, hell, that's quite a fine story for a geology student now isn't it. Why isn't your name in this report?"

"Well sir, it's not because... well, you see, uh... my advisor's name is there."

"Yes, but that isn't your name now is it."

"No sir, but it is enough mention for me that his name is in it. I didn't do it to get my name in the report. I did it because I like it."

Herb stroked his chin and studied Jerome for what seemed like an awkward length of time.

"I see…" was all he said. He then put the report in a basket on his desk, stood up, walked over and sat down in one of the leather sofas. He put his boots up on a glass table in front of him and invited Jerome to join him.

"Sit over here. We spend enough time sitting in front of those damned desks and computers. We may as well be comfortable when we can."

He pulled out 2 cigars, lit one and offered the other to Jerome.

"No thank you, Sir…"

"Don't call me Sir. Hell, call me Herb, please!"

"Ok, Herb… I'm not much of a smoker."

"Well good for you."

As he puffed, he seemed to be putting some things straight in his own mind.

"Jerome, there seems like there's really just one question left. Why the Sudan? What causes an American like yourself to be interested in Africa, and for God's sake, the Sudan?"

Jerome was prepared for this question.

"Well Sir… I mean Herb, as you were saying, we spend a lot of time behind desks and computers. I'm about ready for something else."

The answer seemed to resonate with Herb. He seemed to inhale it and let it back out again with a look of satisfaction.

"Yes, indeed we do spend a lot of time behind desks. But, the Sudan, now what do you make of all that?"

Jerome was completely unprepared for this question. All what?

"Well, to be honest, I'm still formulating my opinions. What do you make of it, Herb?" he answered.

"I don't know. It's a hell of a situation. I don't know what to say about all the killing. I ain't never been there so I have no first-hand knowledge of it."

The killing? What killing?

"Yes, the killing," Jerome said. "What is Tallman doing to try to protect its people there?"

"Good question, Jerome. I'm relieved you've asked. Well, we're doing all we know to do. We try to collaborate as best we can with the government."

"Well it's good to know you have a good relationship with the government there."

"Yeah, I guess, but hell, it is the government that's accused of doing most of the killing. I guess they haven't aimed at oil workers yet. As long as we're making them money I suppose we're safe. But I only suppose. Why I remember raising cattle back on my grandpappy's ranch in Amarillo. We had cows and steers and a couple of bulls. For the most part the bulls didn't act too much different than the steers. They came when you fed them and didn't break down the fences. But every once in a while, why one of 'em would just get it in his head that you were the devil. You always had to watch your back. You know what I mean, Jerome?"

"Yeah, I do," he said, although he wasn't sure if you should really compare the Sudanese government to Texas longhorns.

"If we send you over there, we do it at a risk. We need to make sure you're going to keep the risk as low as possible. You're not involved in politics, nor radical Islamic hooplah, are you? Neither for it nor against it, I mean. Because if you're against it you'll get yerself in trouble just as easily as if you're for it. We'd want you to stay completely uninvolved. If the Sudanese Muslims are killing the poor black folk in the south, and I don't know that they are, understand me, you need to stay neutral and unattached."

"Well I can assure you that I'm uninvolved. I'm not a radical. I don't even believe in God," Jerome blurted out. Then he felt like maybe he had said too much.

Herb looked a little surprised at Jerome's confession of faith, or lack of faith. Then he specified, "Just so I know you don't have a horse in the race, and that you can assure me you won't even be sitting in the grandstands and rooting for one side or the other, I can consider sending you to the Sudan."

Jerome stammered, "Of course. I assure you, I have no horse in the race."

"You'll also need to sign papers for you and your family not holding us responsible for loss of life or dismemberment resulting from civil war and the like."

"That won't be a problem. I don't have any family. I'm all that's left. I don't mind signing the papers."

Well that sure went smoother than stockings at Silky's Saloon."

Jerome was happy that Herb seemed content.

"Yeah, I guess that was smooth," Jerome responded, although deep down there was a sick, anxious feeling starting to brew. Civil war, loss of life, dismemberment? He decided that it wasn't worth worrying over things for which he had no control. Or did he have control and should he be worrying?

"The rebels have no beef with us in particular," he assured Jerome a week later over the phone. "It's just that they don't like what the Sudanese government is doing with the oil revenue."

Jerome hesitated to show his ignorance, but decided to ask anyway. "What are they doing with it?"

"Buying bigger and better guns to fight the rebels with. You know, helicopter gunships and the like."

"Have you had any problem with the rebels?" Jerome asked hesitantly.

"Oh hell yes! I mean, sure. Why you must know that."

"Well yeah, but no one ever mentioned any specifics."

"Mostly tearing up the place, stealing stuff and wrecking the pipeline. They've never gotten really rough with our people. Some of our people are their people anyway."

"Some of our people are rebels?

"Well sort of. They're not Arabs from the north. We hire as many locals as possible. I'm told it helps with the SPLA."

Jerome decided not to ask any more questions. He didn't want Herb to know how little he knew about the Sudan and the SPLA rebels, whoever they were. He'd find out some other way.

In his last days at the university, he researched the Sudan over the internet. He was spellbound by the stories he read. He doubted half of it could even be true. Could 2 million people have been systematically killed without the world being in an uproar over it? Could members of one religion attack members of another without there being an international outcry? Could members of one race be committing genocide of those of another without someone raising an alarm? And the taking of human slaves in grand proportions... could this even happen in this day and age? Surely there was some mistake. The Arabs he knew did not seem to be racially prejudiced against the black race. The Muslims he knew did not seem to want to kill Christians or non-Muslims. This must be a case of gross exaggeration.

"Again," he told himself, "I will not worry about what I can't control. And besides, I have to see for myself before I form my opinions."

Jerome's studies ended anticlimactically. He had thought he'd be leaving the university with a doctoral degree and much acclaim and fanfare, with numerous companies clamoring for his attention. Instead, he left with a master's degree, no fanfare, and only one company desiring his expertise, and they were starting to worry him.

# Chapter 22

The first night at the church Yandeng had a dream that seemed real. She saw a stone wall. In the wall was an old heavy rusted metal door that looked like it had been closed and locked forever. It seemed impossible to open. Yet as she stepped up to it and put her hand on the large rusted iron latch and pushed, the door opened. She could tell that it wasn't her that actually opened it, although it opened at the same time that she had pushed. It had been pulled open from the inside by a strong hand. She only caught a glimpse of the hand. It was a strong, weathered hand that reached out of a long white sleeve. The back of the hand showed evidence of some sort of deep injury.

It was early, still before dawn. She heard whispering and sat up. She saw a man kneeling in the front of the church, in front of the cross, with his head bowed. It was Gatwech, the man who had questioned her when she arrived. He was speaking softly to an unseen person. She approached and also knelt and prayed.

She hadn't prayed for months.

"God, I want to be on talking terms again. I know I'm the one that hasn't wanted to talk."

It was like a dam beginning to burst.

"I'm sorry, real sorry I haven't spoken to you or listened to you."

She had started softly but now was speaking out loud.

"I thought I knew best. I was afraid you wouldn't help me, so I went to the camp. It was a mistake. I didn't do a good job of taking care of myself. I want you to take care of me."

Now she was weeping.

"Please Father, I want you to take care of me. And oh, I really liked the dream. I know you are going to open a door for me. Thanks Father."

Her praying had awakened others. Some of them approached and began praying out loud too. Then everyone was awake, even the children. Loud voices seemed to harmonize with soft pleading voices. After a time, the room quieted down and people went back to their mats. Some had saved bread from the night before and pulled it out to eat. Gatwech, who was the caretaker of the group, approached Yandeng and said, "You really started something this morning! We haven't prayed like that since I can remember!"

"Well, it's been a long time for me too. But it won't be that long before I pray the next time."

"Well may the Lord answer you," he said. "Let me know if you need any help."

Yandeng pulled the piece of paper with the address Laila had given her. "Yes," she said. "There is something I need help with. Do you know how to get to this address?"

He read it over and said, "It's not in town. It's about 3 kilometers outside the other side of town. I can walk there with you."

An hour later they were standing with a group 30 or 40 people, both men and women, crowded around the doorway of the main trailer in a group of temporary trailer offices. Some were Arabs, some were Dinka, others Nuer, and Shillick, judging by their dress and speech.

"Yet, who would know me as a Dinka in my Muslim taub?" thought Yandeng.

There was a guard at the doorway who kept them from entering. Gatwech tried to get through the crowd to talk to the guard but people jealously held their positions.

"Excuse me," Yandeng said to a woman standing in front of her, "How do you get inside the office?"

"You need an appointment," the woman said wearily.

"But how do you get an appointment?"

"You have to get in the office and ask for one," she answered, with no further explanation.

It was nearly unbearable standing in the hot sun in a crowd. And it seemed like a fruitless waste of time. Finally, at about two in the afternoon the guard announced that the office was now closed for the day and would reopen again the next day.

"But if you don't have an appointment, don't bother returning," he said brusquely. There were protests from the crowd. Someone shouted that they'd been waiting for three days. The guard disappeared inside the door and locked it from the inside. The crowd slowly dispersed. Yandeng considered her situation. She thought of her dream and of the confidence she felt that she was being taken care of.

"Let's go, Dear," Gatwech said. "I'm sorry it didn't work out."

"No, let's wait," Yandeng answered. "Let's sit over there in the shade."

"But why? You heard the man say that they're closed. And besides, you don't have an appointment," he said as they walked over and sat down under a tree.

"But I feel like I do have an appointment. You can go. I want to stay."

"I'll stay as long as you do."

They didn't have long to wait. After the crowd had completely gone, the guard was seen coming out the door with a woman. She was an Arab and very well-dressed. Yandeng quickly got to her feet and caught up to the woman as she was getting into a white land rover with a driver. She came up from behind her and addressed her in Arabic.

"Excuse me Ma'am. I've been trying to get an appointment with you. I was sent here by a person you may know."

The woman stopped and studied Yandeng from head to toe, and then asked, "And who is this person that I may know?"

"Laila Asharrifa from the government women's camp."

"Ah yes, Laila. I just got a phone call from her telling me to expect someone. And what is your name?"

"Yandeng Nyeal, Ma'am."

"No, I'm sorry. That wasn't the name I was given," she said and she turned to get into the land rover.

Then Yandeng called after her "Miriam, Ma'am. Miriam Nyeal. I'm known in the camp as Miriam."

The woman stopped, turned, and said, "Yes, Miriam. That sounds like the name I was given.

# Chapter 23

"But why me Herb? Surely you could have found someone in the Sudan to hire," Jerome said candidly over the phone.

"I like you. You've been in on a big find, namely the oil and gas fields in Sakhalin Island. That was an important find in a difficult place. We're looking for oil and gas in difficult places. I think you can help us. Plus, you're young enough to be open to live in the kinds of, uh … conditions that the Sudan will require. You know the language, which beats me all to hell. I never did ask you how you learned Arabic. Anyway, I'm off the subject. Also, and very importantly, you don't seem to have an axe to grind in the whole civil war thing going on over there. We can't afford to have our people get mixed up in it. You understand that, don't you?"

"Yes, I've told you, I have no interest in religion. I know and like Arabs, and am not racially prejudiced, and… well, I guess that should cover the spectrum of possibilities."

"Well, to be honest, we have had people get too involved there. We need to leave the Sudanese to their problems and their way of handling their problems. I know it is brutal there, and I don't have much stomach for it, but I'm going to be the last one to take sides. And I hope you'll be second to the last."

"Sure Herb. I can't imagine myself taking sides."

"I would ask one thing of you that would sure satisfy my curiosity."

"Sure, what's that?"

"Keep your eyes and ears open, without letting on that you're looking or listening. I sure as hell would like to know if things are as bad as I sometimes hear. I've heard the damndest stories about slave trade and genocide and scorched earth policies that I cannot believe hold much weight. I know there's a civil war, but people exaggerate for their own ends and get away with it. Can you help me out there?"

"Yes. I actually had in mind to do the same for myself. I'm not convinced either that some of the stories I've read about could have possibly taken place."

"Good, we're agreed then."

And that is how it was left.

There were 2 weeks of scheduled orientation in Calgary, which included some field trips to interesting places, one of which took Jerome to the Yukon for 3 days to familiarize himself with the seismic equipment he'd be using in the Sudan.

Now he was on the flight bound for Khartoum. The aircraft felt like it was a kind of womb from which he would very shortly emerge to start a new life.

# Chapter 24

"See me tomorrow," the woman at the oil office told Yandeng. "The guard will announce your name. I'll see you then." And she disappeared in the vehicle with dark tinted windows and drove away.

Yandeng and Gatwech watched as the land rover disappeared in a cloud of red dust. They turned and looked at each other with huge smiles on their faces and without saying a word walked back towards town.

They returned to the church about the time the evening bread was dropped off. Yandeng was hungry. After they had eaten Gatwech stood to his feet and turned and asked everyone to gather around.

"Brothers and sisters," he said, "I was reminded of something today that we all will do well to remember. First, God is for us. If we trust him, he'll prove in some way that he is for us, maybe not the way expect, but he will prove it. Yandeng showed me that. Second, what I just said is not apparent. It's more likely that people will believe the contrary. The enemy we have to fear is not the government of Sudan, it is not the army of Sudan, it is not Islam, it is not the Arabs, nor the murahaleen. It is not even hunger or death. Our enemy is the enemy of our souls, who would sow disbelief and doubt and cause discouragement and fear to grow."

Gatwech encouraged the small flock then he prayed for each one individually, putting his hand on each one's head and asking God's blessing on them. They sang a quiet song together, a simple song that some sang in Dinka and others sang in Nuer."

After the get-together, there was a very peaceful atmosphere in the room. The young mother got her two children to sleep with no fuss and handed Yandeng a blanket, gave her a hug, and went to sleep. Yandeng then lay down and was asleep within minutes. She had another dream that night that she remembered vividly in the morning. She told it to Gatwech as they walked to the oil company's offices.

"You have a gift for dreams," he told Yandeng.

"What do you mean a gift for dreams?"

"You see, God speaks to us all differently. To you he speaks in dreams. He never speaks to me that way. I wish he would, but he doesn't."

"It's true. I have had many dreams. But this one was special."

"Tell it to me again."

"I saw myself back in the Sudd. My village took our herds there during the dry season because there is always water there. I had been walking a long time and was tired. I felt very, very dirty and wanted to get clean but there was no water anywhere around. So I took some dust and started to rub dust on my dirty arms and legs. I rubbed and rubbed. But the more I rubbed, the dirtier I became. Finally, I gave up. As soon as I stood up to continue on my way I noticed that right beside me was a pool of water. 'Why didn't I see this before?' I asked myself. I saw a bowl with some soap in it and a towel sitting beside the pool. 'Who put this here?' I asked. A large hand then took my hand and led me into the pool. As I stepped in I found myself naked and clean, really clean from head to foot. Then I awoke."

At that moment a white land rover drove past, stirring up red dust. Then it slowed, stopped, went into reverse and stopped beside them. A tinted window lowered and the Muslim woman from the office the day before peeked out and said, "You're Miriam, aren't you?"

"Yes Ma'am, I am."

"I assume you're on your way to see me. Is that right?"

"Yes Ma'am it is."

"Why don't I save you the walk? Do you mind riding?"

"We'd appreciate it," Yandeng answered.

The door opened, and the woman moved to the other side.

"Well where are you coming from?" she asked. "This isn't exactly the direction from the government camp."

"Oh yes, you're right. You see I moved out recently."

"Ah, I'm glad to hear it. I hear it's a dreadful place. Good for you. Are you staying with family or friends?"

"Well yes. I'm staying with friends near town who are almost like family. This is one of them, Mr. Gatwech. He's agreed to keep me company on my way to your office."

"Well that is wise. The roads aren't safe as I'm sure you know. He must be a very good friend. Well it seems our interview has already begun. Laila said you spoke very good Arabic. She was right. This is one of the things I needed to be sure of. Can you type as well as you speak?"

"Well actually no. I can speak much more quickly than I type."

The woman seemed to find this statement hilarious and said that she had never met anyone, especially a woman, and she winked at Yandeng when she said it, that could type as fast as she spoke.

At the office Yandeng demonstrated her typing abilities in Arabic and English. The woman seemed impressed.

"The only thing I can't test you on is Dinka. I assume you speak well. You are Dinka aren't you?"

"Yes, I am Dinka. And I speak Dinka."

"Well I'll take your word for it. Where are you from?"

"I was from Palwung, in Mayom County."

"... I see." There was an awkward silence and then she continued.

"I'm sorry about your village. Would you be interested in returning to that area to work there?"

"Yes. I think so. I mean, I need the work, and I think I could go back..."

"I understand. I'm sure it would not be easy to return. Our company you understand had nothing to do with the um, well you know, the ah, well the unfortunate circumstances of the Dinka."

"I don't blame your company, Ma'am. But why would you want to hire Dinka, since so much time and effort were spent to remove us. Why not hire Bagarra or other Arabs?"

"Well, we do that as well. But we like to have people who know the land and might be able to help us... well let's say communicate for us with the SPLA. They do blame us for their circumstances."

"I see. Well I would not be a good one to communicate with the SPLA. I don't think they'd listen. If you want me to be a spokesperson, I don't think I can do it."

"No, no, don't get me wrong. We don't expect you to communicate formally with them. Your mere presence will communicate some good will. We believe they will view us differently, maybe treat us differently, if they know that some of their own are among us."

"Well, I can't really speak for the SPLA but, if you are offering me a job, Ma'am, I'll take it. I've survived attacks by government air raids, hordes of murahaleen, and roving bands of the SPLA. I am willing to go back to Dinka land and will hope for the best. May God's hand guard me in the future as it has in the past."

Speaking so frankly was not the custom in these interviews and it took some seconds for the interviewer to collect her thoughts. At last she said, "Well I suppose, yes, I am ready to offer you a job. You'll need to sign papers saying that the company is not responsible for any injury or death that may result from civil war or attacks by private or government militias, that sort of thing. Would you be willing to do that?"

"Yes. Why do I need to sign papers? I'm sure the company would not take responsibility if I were injured anyway. Right?"

The woman had a stern look on her face, and said, "Well yes, or I mean no. I'm not sure you understand. The important point is that we are not responsible."

"No, I am agreeing with you. I'm saying your company is not responsible."

"Well, I wouldn't put it in those words."

"But I was only repeating your words."

"Yes, well… anyway, we are a responsible company. We just have no responsibility to people, who… well, when… well, you know, like yourself. Maybe that doesn't sound right. But would you sign the papers?"

"Yes, I said I would. When can I sign them, and when can I start?" Yandeng asked eagerly.

"Well we don't normally jump into things. It could be weeks, maybe even months."

"If you want me," Yandeng said innocently but firmly, "you must take me now. I cannot wait weeks or months. I can sign papers and start right away or I'm afraid I will leave the area and not return."

There was a long silence. The woman didn't seem angry or speechless, but lost in thought. "Forgive me, Miriam. We do need someone right away. I had hope to give some time to training before starting. We could get you in, but I think you'd have to start tomorrow, with no training. You see we have a land rover leaving in the morning, and if you're not on it..."

"I'll be here. What time does it leave?" Yandeng cut in.

"Well just after dawn."

"OK. Can you get the papers for me to sign? And oh, will I be paid?"

The woman's mouth dropped. "Of course you'll be paid. At the end of every month. We haven't talked over details at all. You'll have a company room to stay in. You'll work every other week at the camp. When you work, you'll work long hours. Then you'll get a week off."

Yandeng signed some papers, shook hands and agreed to return in the morning.

Gatwech insisted on walking with her to the offices just after dawn the next day. A caravan of vehicles was to assemble to drive a whole shift of people back up to the oil camp. Apparently they did this every week. Yandeng felt an array of emotions pulling at her. She was anxious about her new job, but even more anxious to be going back into Mayom County for the first time since "it" happened. She also felt torn about whether or not it was right that she should work for an oil company who was in some way involved with the loss of her life as she had known it.

She spoke to Gatwech along the way.

"Gatwech, there is something that worries me. A new emotion has come to me, like a lion attacking an antelope, and feels like it is taking me over."

"What emotion, Child?"

"Anger, Gatwech. I am so angry I feel like I could kill."

"Anger about what, child?"

"I get angry at men, especially Arab men. I feel like I hate them."

Gatwech nodded and walked along thoughtfully.

"We have all been hurt by the war, some more deeply than others. We really have only 2 choices in the end. One is vengeance, the other is forgiveness."

"Yes, I think Jesus would want me to forgive, but I want vengeance. What's wrong with vengeance if the people you take

**105**

vengeance on deserve it? After all, won't God bring judgement on the world one day?"

"Yes, that is a good point. God will bring judgement on the world. This is God's task. He actually is slow to bring judgement because he is patient, wanting all to come to know him and change."

"So, what's the problem with taking vengeance?"

"Well... are your smarter than God?"

"Of course not!"

"If we take vengeance, we are taking the role of God. We are pushing him aside and taking his responsibility. Another problem with taking vengeance is that we become like what we hate."

"How do you mean?"

"If you were to kill a man because he is a soldier of the government, how are you any better than the soldier that killed people in your village? If you do what they do, you become like them. If you hate them because they're murderers, and you have murderous thoughts, are you any different?"

"I guess not. But how do I change my thoughts?"

You can start by admitting you have the problem. In the end only God can help you."

"How?"

"Why don't you pray like this? Dear God..."

"Dear God," she repeated.

"I confess being angry at men, especially Arab men, and being so angry I feel like I could kill some of them."

Yandeng repeated slowly but deliberately.

"Vengeance is for you to take and in your time, and not me. I trust you to do what is right."

Yandeng shook her head in agreement and repeated.

"I now choose to forgive the men who destroyed my village, killed my parents, took my sister as a slave, and ruined my home."

Yandeng began to weep.

"I can't pray that. How can I forgive them? They don't deserve it."

"No, they don't deserve it. Let me ask, are you sure God has forgiven you for all your sins?"

"Yes, I'm sure."

"How much do you deserve it?"

"Well I've never killed anyone."

"Uh huh. And if God asked you why he should forgive you, would you tell Him that's your reason, because you never killed anyone?"

"No, that would be a bad answer."

"Yes, it would be."

"But what would be a good answer?"

"That's just it, there is no good answer except that he forgives those who confess to Him and ask for forgiveness in Jesus' name. It isn't that we're deserving. It's that He is forgiving."

"Yeah. But still, I just can't overlook what has been done to me."

"No. You can't overlook it. But you can choose not to take revenge for it."

"Yes, I guess I could do that."

"Well, that's a good place to start. You see, you have evil thoughts and God has forgiven you. Me too. Don't think I haven't already faced the same thing you're talking about, and every time I remember the loss of my own family, I go through it again."

"I'm sorry Gatwech, you never mentioned losing your family."

"No, and I won't mention it right now either, except to say that if we really want to be a friend of God, we must put our revenge aside, like an old piece of clothing that we toss out in the bush and decide not to use anymore. We need to commit to loving our enemies, just like God loves his enemies."

"I won't ever forget what you've said to me, Gatwech. I pray God helps me to forgive, somehow."

They arrived at the offices and could see land-rovers sitting in a line and people standing around them.

She hugged Gatwech and said a tearful good-bye. He had taken on a father role and although she had known him only a few days, he had been a great encouragement. Then the harder emotions began. She climbed into a land rover and headed back towards what had been home. She passed a few burned out villages, each one reminding her anew of her own losses. Her mind wandered as they drove on. Where were all the people who had lived here? Were they dead? Had they been carried off as slaves? Were they roaming

**107**

miles south looking for food and shelter?  How could the land be emptied of its people?

# Chapter 25

As Jerome stepped out of the baggage claim area into the small, dingy airport, he found no one with a "Jerome Schultz" sign waiting for him amidst the crowds of people. He was immediately besieged by young men saying, "Taxi? Taxi? Great price for you. Taxi? Taxi?"

One of the taxi piranhas moved in. "American man need help. I help you. I take you to hotel, yes? You trust me. I am Ahmed."

Jerome spoke to him in Arabic and told him to give him some space. He backed off only slightly but continued to prattle his virtues to a distracted and tired Jerome. It was now Saturday at 5 in the afternoon. He had been traveling for over 24 hours and he was exhausted and his thinking was not the clearest. He checked an email he had printed out before he left.

"OK Ahmed, take me to the Hilton Hotel."

And so Jerome was out into the crowded and less than organized streets of Khartoum. Whatever he expected, this wasn't it. Khartoum, although bright and sunny, was drab. He saw street after street of non-descript low-rise dirt colored stucco buildings broken up only by the occasional run-down warehouse.

At the hotel Jerome took a lukewarm shower, which was the hottest he could make it, and fell into bed. It was about 6 PM. He slept until 8 the next morning. After a hotel breakfast, he went to the front desk.

"I know it's Sunday, but is there any way you can try to contact the Tallman Oil office here in Khartoum?"

"Yes, we can give them a call. They should be open by now."

"But, are they open on Sunday?"

"Sure. Why not?"

"Isn't it the weekend?"

"No, the weekend is over. It ended on Friday."

"Ok. I'm looking for an AbdelKader Rahman."

Within minutes he was handed the phone.

"Where are you Jerome? We thought you were getting in yesterday."

"I did get in yesterday. I looked around at the airport and didn't see anyone waiting for me so I got a cab and came to the hotel."

"I see," he responded in a very unconcerned tone. "Well we can send someone over to pick you up if you like."

"Yes, of course. How soon?"

"Oh, we'll send someone right away."

"Great, I'll be waiting in the lobby."

An hour later, Jerome was still reading the local newspaper in the lobby. A local leader called Al Mahdi was calling for political solutions to the crisis of Darfur to avoid a confrontation with the international community. Then he noticed a related article saying that a local oil company, Tallman Oil of Canada, had been receiving increased pressure from its shareholders over its involvement in the Sudan and was considering abandoning its operations here.

"What? Herb never mentioned anything to me. How can this be?"

Then the driver arrived.

"Mr. Jerome?"

"Yes. Did you have a hard time finding the hotel?"

"No, I have lived in Khartoum all my life."

"Ah I see. It's just that I thought you would be here sooner."

The driver gave Jerome a shrug. With that, he was driven to the office a short distance away. He was taken past a receptionist into the office area where he met AbdelKader, the acting director. He was having tea with a number of colleagues. He welcomed Jerome and introduced him to the others in English. Then he said in Arabic, "Anta titikillum alarabi, el huqq?" (You speak Arabic, right?) as he offered him some tea.

"Ey, na'am ya sidi, shawaya." (Yes sir, a little.)

There were approving nods and smiles around the circle. Jerome took his tea and thanked his host.

Then Jerome took away the awkward silence by asking, also in Arabic, "And you sir, do you speak a little Arabic as well?"

There was laughter and nodding as he said, "Yes, a little also."

AbdelKader asked the driver to take Jerome's luggage to the guest apartment, and the group stood and talked for at least a half hour, mostly in Arabic, about the flight, the weather in Calgary, which seemed to fascinate his Sudanese hosts, and what news he had of the company. Jerome produced the newspaper and said this was the only news he had. They all shook their heads and said that they had seen the same in the local news. No one seemed sure what would happen. Yes, they had heard that shareholders had been kicking up a fuss, but over what? So maybe some of the "abid" in the south had been moved to other areas, but that was in the best interests of the Sudan.

"The "abid," asked Jerome, "who are the abid?"

There was some nervous laughter, and then someone finally answered, "Oh that is the Arabic name for the people who live near the oil."

"I see. But isn't abid plural for Abd (slave)?" asked Jerome.

There was more nervous laughter.

Then AbdelKader responded for the group. "It is an old word in Arabic with many meanings. It is just a name we use for southern people. There is nothing negative meant by using the word."

"I see," said Jerome and then he answered innocently enough, "It appears that some of the shareholders believe there have been human rights abuses."

The atmosphere changed and all eyes fixed on Jerome, none of which communicated warmth.

"You are new here. You don't know anything about our ways. We are a very generous people. We Arabs let the abid live where they wish as long as they stay away from our wells. It is they who will not let us get on with our work. It is they who fight us. We have no choice but to return the fight. We are defending our oil. We have been very patient with them. We are a very patient and generous people."

Jerome felt like the skunk at a garden party. He knew he had not made a good first impression and wanted to make it up.

"Of course, of course! Your generosity is known the world over," he answered, trying to sound as sincere as he could. The conversation ended with dark looks and shaking heads on the part of his colleagues. Abdelkader invited Jerome to come into his office.

"Well it seems like it would be best to get you to the field as soon as you are ready. We have flights leaving early in the morning every Monday and Thursday that can take you down to the Ligheg camp. That is where your team is stationed. There is housing there

**111**

and you come out to Khartoum every third week. Now, the next flight you'll probably want to take is on Thursday which is only 3 days from now, so I suggest you rest up and spend what time you can reading procedure ..."

Jerome interrupted, "Is there a flight leaving tomorrow?"

Abdelkader paused in his diatribe and said "Yes, tomorrow is Monday," and took up where he left off, "... reading procedure manuals and safety instructions to prepare you for..."

"Can I leave in the morning?" Jerome asked.

Abdelkader paused what he was talking about.

"Are you saying you want to leave tomorrow?"

"Yes, I mean if possible. I can read the procedure manuals when I get there. I'm eager to get started."

Abdelkader scratched his chin, thought for a few seconds, picked up the phone and dialed.

"Do you have a seat on tomorrow's flight to Ligheg? ... No, just one. He's the new Drilling Engineer... I know, I thought so too. He said he wants to get down there as soon as possible... "I don't understand either, but do you have a seat?... Ok, I'll tell him."

"Mutaffaq. Agreed, my friend," he said sternly. "You are on tomorrow's flight. Your pilot is also in the guest house. He's a Russian, Mikhail. He'll wake you at 5, have a quick breakfast, and should get you to Ligheg by lunchtime."

Over breakfast the next day Jerome satisfied the curiosity of the Russian pilot and also his own curiosity as to why a Russian pilot would be working for a Canadian company in the Sudan. To hear Mikhail tell it, you'd think it was the most natural of career moves. Lots of Russian pilots were flying in the Sudan. He had worked for the Sudanese government before starting his own career as a contract pilot on a long-term contract with Tallman. Most of the aircraft flown by the Russian government were Russian Antonovs which he had been trained on. He had then trained Sudanese Air Force pilots how to fly them and then started his own business contracting out to the government, and whoever else would pay him, such as Tallman Oil. He ran regular supply runs down to the oil camp and took on passengers on these runs whenever there were any. He still occasionally ran runs for the government he said. Breakfast seemed to end at that point and they headed to the hangar, on the edge of the main Khartoum airport. Jerome climbed into the Antonov and took a fold down seat behind Mikhail's. There were crates and equipment strapped down all around him. Some of the equipment he recognized as being used in seismic testing.

Jerome watched the landscape pass by below. It was every bit as interesting as a movie. He saw the dry flat plains around Khartoum turn to mountains further south, which he figured were the Nuba from his quick study of Sudanese geography. He could see lots of dry river beds and a few rivers lined with green vegetation for a short distance that quickly petered out into dusty desert. The landscape did seem greener the further south they went. After a few hours they flew over a group of shiny metal buildings and landed on a dirt runway just to the south of the camp, which was surrounded by a mixture of low-growing trees and scrubby landscape.

When they got off the plane a military land rover met them. Mikhail was handed an envelope and he gave the soldiers some packages. Jerome saw a few oil derricks in operation and a group of 1 story metal roofed pre-fab buildings where some other late model trucks and land rovers were parked. They walked the quarter mile from the airstrip to the buildings.

"This is the office," Mikhail said, pointing to a small pre-fab building. "That is your dormitory," he said, pointing to another.

"You eat in that building," he said, pointing to the largest pre-fab type structure that had smoke rising out of a metal chimney. There were 2 women in colorful local dress washing pots and hanging things to dry around the side of it. They waved at the two men. Jerome was starting to feel the heat. At 11 AM the temperature had already reached 95 degrees.

He headed across the open area towards the building he was told was the office.

# Chapter 26

Yandeng wasn't exactly sure where she was because the road was new. She was probably within less than a day's walk of Palwung. She could feel it and the more she felt it the more she felt like she would just burst into tears.

When they arrived at the camp her mood changed quickly. She just couldn't take it all in. The camp was made up of buildings, not tukuls. Buildings were rare in these parts. They were similar to the ones where she had her interview and typing test. They were called "pre-fab" buildings, which was a new concept for Yandeng. She had never been in one before yesterday. There were also trailers, which weren't too different from the pre-fab buildings. And inside all of them was furniture, all types of desks and chairs and computers. She had only just yesterday typed on her first computer during her typing test. Now she saw 3 in one room. Then when she thought she had seen it all, she was taken to the dorm to "drop her things off," even though she thought it should seem obvious she didn't have any "things." She was told this was her room. It was just a small room, but it was full of things she had never really seen before. The mattress for sleeping was extremely soft. It was on some sort of bouncy platform which had legs and was 6 inches off the ground!

"Why would anyone put legs on a mattress?" she chuckled to herself.

And the room was cool! Then she noticed the cause for the coolness. There was a machine sitting right in the middle of the window that was blowing cold air! There was also a chair beside the bed that had soft padding on it and a place to rest your arms as you sat in it! There was a light stand that held a light bulb right over the chair. She noticed a button near the light bulb and tried it to see if it worked. It did! As you pushed the button, it turned the light on and then off! Then there was a little bathroom connected to her room that had a modern toilet that you could sit on, and there was running water! She had heard of such things, but now she was standing and seeing them with her own eyes. She stood and stared at it all for a while. Then she went into the bathroom and turned the water on and off, and on and off, then flushed the toilet twice, then turned the light bulb on and off 5 or 6 times. Then she bounced on the springy mattress. It all seemed like a dream.

"This must be what hotels are like in big cities," she thought. She had never seen one, but had met a few people who had worked in them and had mentioned such things. Until now she had not fully believed them. There was a knock at the door. Another woman, an Arab, was there.

"Do you need more time or are you coming back to the office?" she asked. "We have a lot to cover in a short time."

"Yes, yes. I'm coming. I'm sorry I didn't know you were waiting."

"Hi, I'm Fatima," she said holding out her hand. Then she said a bit impatiently, "I need to brief you on running the office before the land rovers leave, right? You do want to learn how to run the office don't you?"

"Run the office? No, I'm not supposed to be running the office. I am supposed to be giving administrative support."

"Yes, but that means running the office. Believe me, you'll be running it."

By the time they got back to the office there were men all around waiting for Fatima.

"Oh yes," she said, "you're probably waiting for these."

She opened a large bag that had been delivered with the land rover and started handing out envelopes. One man opened his and complained loudly, "Fatima, my overtime pay wasn't included again. Are you sure you sent the office my hours?"

"Yes, of course I did. Give this new girl your information. She'll follow up on it. What's your name dear?"

"It's Yandeng."

"That's a funny name," Fatima blurted out. "What kind of a name is Yandeng?"

"It's a Dinka name," she said, as now all eyes in the room were on her.

"Oh... I'm sorry," she said awkwardly. "So you're a Dinka?"

"Yes, I am."

"Are you from Bentiu?"

"No, I'm from Palwung, in Mayom County."

"Is that where you live?"

"No, Palwung isn't... well it isn't there anymore."

There was an awkward silence that could be felt by everyone in the room.

"Do you live in Bentiu then?"

"No, not really."

"Well where do you live?"

"Here. I live here at the camp." she pronounced.

"Where will you go on your week off then?"

"I won't go anywhere. I'll stay."

"But... there's no room for you."

"Yes, I have a room."

"Well that's my room too... Look, this isn't the time to talk about this. The land rover leaves in 30 minutes. We have work to do. Ok men, everybody out."

The men all turned and shuffled out.

"My God," said Fatima. "Where do I begin? I guess first, I'll say, stay close to the computer. Your email is your lifeline to the outside world, outside of this God-forsaken place. Also stay close to the phone. The seismic guys are always calling or emailing from the field asking for this or that."

She went over to the computer and typed quickly on the keys and moved a plastic device to the right of the computer that had a wire connecting it to the computer. The computer Yandeng had used didn't have one of these plastic devices wired to it.

"Here's the spreadsheet where you keep track of everyone's hours. I have a folder for it here, see? I keep it on the desktop."

Yandeng looked on the top of the desk but didn't see anything.

"Are you paying attention Dingding?"

"My name is Yandeng."

"Sorry, it's just that you don't seem to be looking at what I'm showing you and you have a blank look on your face."

"I'm sorry. I learn quick. I just need someone to teach me I think."

"Well, sorry honey. That isn't going to happen. It's time for me to leave, thank God! I'll see you in a week. Don't let the place fall apart."

And with that she got up, picked up a large travel bag near the front door and walked out.

Yandeng sat dazed. She looked at the computer for a while, then moved the plastic device with the wire, like she had seen Fatima do. She noticed that when she moved it, a small arrow on the computer screen also moved. This seemed impossible, but sure enough, after several tests she confirmed it was the case. She practiced moving it to the right, then the left. She noticed there were buttons on it and she pushed them a few times. When she pushed one of them a small drop-down box appeared on the computer screen that had words written on it that made no sense to her.

"My my. What will I do?" she said out loud.

The man who had complained about his overtime being forgotten stuck his head in the door. He was holding his plastic helmet and his bald black head was glistening with sweat.

"You will check with Khartoum on my overtime, won't you?" he insisted.

"Yes, I hope so. I'll do what I can."

"Make it happen for me dear. That Fatima doesn't give a damn. Try to help me out. My name is Taban. Here is my employee number." And he stepped in and handed a wrinkled, hand-scribbled piece of paper to Yandeng.

"I'll do what I can," she said, not having the faintest idea on how to actually do anything.

She sat for a few minutes alone, hearing outside sounds of car doors closing, engines starting, and vehicles driving away. Then there was silence. She was startled by a phone ringing. She hadn't noticed it, but there was a phone on her desk. She had never answered a phone by herself. At the government camp the administrators always called her to the phone when they needed help. She picked it up uncertain of whether she should say something or wait for the caller to speak. She held the phone to her ear. She heard a voice repeating, "Allo, allo, is anyone there?"

"Yes, I am."

"Fatima? Is that you?"

"No, this is Yandeng."

"Who? Where is Fatima?"

"She just rode away in a land rover.  She'll be back in a week, I think."

"Who are you?  What did you say your name was?"

"I'm Yandeng."

There was a pause.

"But... what are you doing in the office?  Do you work there?"

"Yes, I do.  I live here too."

"Uh huh.  I see... When did you start?"

"About 10 minutes ago."

"Really!  Well anyway, I'm calling from Khartoum.  I wanted to let you know that there's a new employee, a Canadian, starting tomorrow.  We're flying him down on the morning flight.  He'll be heading up the seismic crew.  So, can you give him all the support he'll need?"

Yandeng had just answered her first phone call, and it was from the capital of the country, from Khartoum itself.  The caller was giving her what sounded like an important assignment.  She was to provide support for an important foreigner, who was going to arrive on an airplane from another country!

"Sure, I can give him support... What does he need?"

"Well, make sure he has a room ready and that the crew knows he's coming."

"OK.  How do I let the crew know he's coming?"

"Are they in camp or out in the field?  If they're out in the field, you'll need to call them."

"I'll need to find out.  Is there a certain number I need to dial to talk to them on the telephone?"

"You're being sarcastic.  Great!  Well it's better than being rude. Fatima has everyone beat in that department.  Did she give you their number or email address?

"No."

"Oh great!  Never mind.  I'll contact them myself.  Just make sure the camp staff knows he's coming.  And oh, did I mention he's a foreigner.  The Canadians have sent us another one, if you know what I mean.  Doesn't know a damn thing about the Sudan, but he's supposed to be a good geologist.  Anyway, take care of him."  Click.

"Hello.  Are you still there?  Hello?"  There was no answer.

Yandeng put the phone back on the hook like she was returning fine china to a china closet.

She got up and went outside to look for the "camp staff," the caller had referred to. She found a woman with an apron walking into a larger building that smelled like food. This reminded her that she was getting hungry. Yandeng walked up and introduced herself and said proudly that she had received a phone call from a man in Khartoum saying that a foreigner would be arriving tomorrow on an airplane, as though this mere news would cause her to stop her daily routine and marvel with her.

"So?" was all she said.

"Well, he said we need to make sure the camp is ready for him."

"That's not my concern. Talk to housekeeping." And she walked in the door and closed it behind her.

Yandeng opened the door and followed her. She found herself in a kitchen full of stainless steel tables and bowls and pots and pans. This too was almost more than she could take in. The government camp had a kitchen, but much of it was open air and didn't have shiny stainless steel equipment.

"Excuse me, can you help me find this housekeeping?"

The woman gave her a hard stare and said, "Next building to your left." Then she turned away and put her hands into a sink. Yandeng stood for a few seconds then walked out. She turned left, saw the next building and walked up to the front door. It seemed odd that all the doors were shut. Back in the village, doorways were open and people stayed out in front most of the day. She didn't know if she should walk in or knock. She decided to knock, but very softly. There was no answer. She knocked again, a little harder. Still no answer. She knocked again, waited and then started to walk away. The door opened. A Shillick woman, judging by her clothing, stood in the doorway.

"Yes? What do you want?"

Yandeng told her story again, but with less enthusiasm.

"OK dear, we'll make sure a room is ready."

Yandeng went back to the office. She played some more with the computer mouse then tried to type. But she had no idea how to make letters appear on the screen. She typed hard on the keys but no letters appeared. There was just a blue screen with little square pictures on the left hand side of it with odd words under it them: "Word," and "Outlook," and "Workhour Worksheet." Frustrated, she sat and stared for a long while.

Then she walked back to her room. She tried the shower in the room, not fully understanding all the knobs and which way to turn them but eventually figured out how to make water come out of a spout above her head that sprayed all over her as if she were standing out in the rain. If all this wasn't enough, she discovered that if she turned the left knob, hot water came out of the spout. She stood under the water for a long time. She found a towel hanging to the side of the glass door of the shower stall. And why a glass door? Who thought of such things? It was all very overwhelming. She lay down, and fell asleep.

Awakening the next morning at dawn she realized she was now very hungry. She hadn't really eaten the day before. She had seen a kitchen at the camp. "There must be food available," she thought. "I still don't have any money, though. I hope I get paid soon. I'll need to eat."

She meandered over to the office. She found the computer screen still staring blankly at the empty chair in front of it. She sat down in front of it. She moved the mouse. It still moved like she had seen it do the previous afternoon. She again tried to type, but still with no luck. The more she looked at it the more lost she felt. She walked around the office looking in drawers. She opened a metal file cabinet. She had used a file cabinet at the camp. She leafed through the papers for a while and closed the drawer. She found a folder of maps. She opened the one on top. It showed various "blocks" and the location of the camp she was in. She had no idea what a "block" referred to. She had never seen a map of her county so she had no idea where her village had been located. It seemed amazing that she could be so close to home, or what had been home, and yet still have no idea of how to get there.

A man entered the office, introduced himself and set a sheet of paper on her desk. "Can you please email or fax this supply order up to Khartoum for the next shipment, hopefully by plane?"

Yandeng hesitated. She didn't really understand what he wanted.

"Well? Can you do it or not?"

"Yes, I'll do my best to get it done as soon as I can," she answered sincerely, although a feeling of anxiety was beginning to stir inside.

"Ok. We need this stuff within a week or we won't be doing any drilling. Understand?"

"Yes, yes."

The door slammed shut and she again sat in silence. As the morning went on, others came by with requests. She kept notes on scraps of paper and piled them as neatly as possible. With each new request came a feeling of being out of her depth. What would she do? People wanted faxes, print-outs, electronic file transfers, emails, and such. These were terms that were beginning to become familiar but she still didn't have a clue what they were. What was an electronic file anyway?

About that time she heard a plane overhead. She immediately shuddered and wondered if she should run into the bush and hide. It it sounded like the plane landed somewhere close. Then she remembered that a plane was due to arrive from Khartoum with an important foreigner.

# Chapter 27

Jerome walked up to the office door and knocked, then thought better of it and opened the door. It seemed dark inside after being in the direct African sunlight.

Yandeng was sitting at her desk when the door opened slowly. The white man that walked in seemed quite young to be so important, from her point of view. He didn't take charge like most men she knew. He just stood there looking at her like he didn't know what to say.

When his eyes had adjusted he saw two desks. Someone was sitting at one of them and was looking at him. It was a girl, or a young woman. He didn't see anyone else in the room. He awkwardly walked in her direction. She was thin and attractive. Her skin was as black as he'd ever seen, yet was it his imagination or did she seem to glow? He didn't know what the customs were here. Should he address her? Should he try to shake her hand?

Yandeng broke the silence and said, "You must be the Canadian engineer."

"Yes, I am. I mean, no I'm not, at least not entirely."

"What do you mean? What are you not... entirely."

"Sorry. I mean I'm not Canadian. I'm American. Nice to meet you." And he extended his hand.

She stood to take his hand. Not only was she thin, but also tall. She was at least 2 inches taller than him.

She looked down into his eyes and said, "I am Dinka, nice to meet you."

Her voice had a warmth to it that Jerome also found attractive.

"Well Dinka, it's nice to meet you."

She laughed. "My name is not Dinka."

"But I thought you just said you were Dinka."

"Yes, I am Dinka. But my name is Yandeng."

"I see," said Jerome, although he didn't see at all. "Nice to meet you Yandeng."

"You don't understand what is Dinka," she said bluntly.

"Well, I uh... I... hmmm. No I don't."

She seemed like she needed to clear the air on the subject and stated, "I am Dinka like you are American. The Dinka are my people. This land is Dinka land," she said proudly.

"Dinka. Oh, I understand. I hadn't heard of the Dinka. You are the first Dinka I have met."

"I have heard of America," she said proudly.

"I see... Umm. What have you heard about it?"

"Not much. It is a big country, bigger than all the lands of the Dinka, and no one walks, they all drive motor vehicles."

"Yes, well, uh, I suppose you heard right. I actually don't own a motor vehicle anymore. So there is at least one American that doesn't drive."

Jerome laughed at his own joke but noticed that either Yandeng didn't understand it or didn't think it was funny. No matter, it was her face that caught his attention. It was an unusual face. He couldn't get over the fact that she had dark black smooth skin that looked like it shone. In fact, she looked like she shone from somewhere deep within. And her face looked both happy and sad at the same time. She was also attractive.

"So this is Dinka land you say. Well, you must be rich with all the oil here."

Yandeng wondered if he were joking. Was he trying to make fun of her? She didn't answer.

Jerome was taken aback. She seemed offended. She was so thin, almost frail, yet she seemed to have the heart of a tiger.

"Yes, ah well now that we've been introduced, could I ask you to show me around? Where can a hungry guy get something to eat? I had a light breakfast and am half starved."

Yandeng looked him deep in the eyes to try to get a read on him. He didn't look half starved. If he had breakfast, why did he even say he was hungry? It wasn't yet noon. He looked smart enough, but he didn't say smart things. Were conversations with foreigners always this strange?

"I'm sure there is food here. I don't know much about it. If you have money you should try the big building in front of us."

"That's funny... Thanks. Your name is Yandeng, right?"

"Yes."

"Well good-bye then."

**123**

He walked out thinking, "My, that was an awkward conversation. I wonder if all African girls are that difficult?"

Jerome met his new seismic team over a big bowl of beef stew. They told him about the survey they were preparing for. They hoped to leave the next day or the day after. There were still some repairs to be made to the equipment and then they'd be out in the bush again. They spoke of constant danger, but the way they laughed and joked about it, he couldn't take them seriously. They'd be a team of 13, counting himself. There would be 3 juggers, the men who carried and set the geophones, or listening devices, on the ground. There were 3 men that drove the vibrator buggies that were maneuvered to various spots and then activated, at which point the jugs picked up the vibrations and sent signals back through the wires to the recording truck. Here an observer, Jerome, would sit and take the readings to make sure they were collecting good information. He would be helped by Osman, an Arab from Khartoum who was the party manager and number two in charge after Jerome. There were also 2 mechanics to keep all the landrovers and equipment running, one electronic technician, and two cooks to make sure they all ate well. They ate and joked and bragged about adventures in the bush, about coming face to face with lions, or cobras, or packs of hyenas, or SPLA rebels, or any number of dangers. They spoke of it all as great sport, like they couldn't wait to get started again. Others in the camp sat around them and listened to their stories, envious of them.

Meanwhile, Yandeng was faced with another dilemma. What should she do? She had no money, and she knew not to expect a "free meal." She didn't consider it a good thing to beg food from her new colleagues, so she decided to take a walk into the bush and try to find her own lunch. There were some trees in fruit at this time of year and she knew which ones were. After a 10 minute walk she found one but the fruit was out of reach. She decided to remove her Muslim taub and head scarf and sandals and climb it like the boys did back in Palwung. She still had her old ripped dress on underneath. She climbed the tree and reached the low fruit and started picking and dropping them to the ground. She saw riper fruit higher in the tree and reached above trying to pick as high as possible. As she reached, she noticed movement in the branch above her. It was a snake, a green mamba, the most poisonous snake in the area. She startled, lost her balance, and began to fall. She grabbed onto various branches on her quick descent to the ground. She had no broken bones, but had bleeding scrapes on her knees and elbows.

Back in the office she found paper towels and some water and cleaned herself up as best as possible. She ate her fruit and started to feel a bit revived. But then the phone rang.

"Ma'ak Yandeng min sharikat Tallman (This is Yandeng with Tallman Company)," she answered in Arabic.

"Yo, this is Herb, from Tallman in Canada. Do you speak English?"

"Yes sir. This is Yandeng."

"Hey, has my man Jerome landed?"

"Yes sir, he just arrived."

"I'm emailing you some information. Can you give it to him right away? It is very important, and confidential. What is your email address?"

There was a pause.

"Ma'am, are you there? What is your email address? I need to get him some information as soon as possible."

"Sir, I'm new here. I don't know the answer to your question. I am sorry."

"You don't know... well, uh... tell him to call me first chance he gets! Tell him to call me on my cell. OK?"

"Yes sir."

The weight of her situation came home to her. She was hungry, she was in way over her head and knew there was no way to hide her shortfallings. Besides, her body stung all over and the bleeding hadn't completely stopped. And now, she was going to have to go find the young white man and give him the message and somehow let people know she didn't know how to work on a computer or send an email, nor did she even know what an email was. She began to cry. She had held too many tears back for too long, and now they came in a torrent.

## Chapter 28

Tears begot more tears. Yandeng sat weeping at her desk, contemplating her situation. As she sat weeping, she heard a soft voice say, "Excuse me? Is everything OK?"

It was the young white man. What was he doing back in the office? As if reading her mind, he said, "I'm sorry, I forgot my bag here and just came back to pick it up."

She nodded, unable to speak.

"Is there anything I can do to help?" he asked.

"No, please go."

"Sure. Sorry, Yandeng." He felt horrible. He was certain there was something he could do to help if she would only let him know what it was. At this moment seeing this girl who only a short time ago seemed like a tiger, was now helplessly in tears. A sense of bewilderment overcame him. He turned to go.

"Wait."

"Yes?" he said with hope in his voice. Was she going to confide in him and ask for his help?

"You have a message." She handed him one of her scraps of paper with nearly unintelligible scribble on it.

"It says I need to call her? Who is her?"

"It was a man, from Canada," she said, finding enough of a voice to answer.

"Oh, Herb. Was it Herb?"

"Yes probably."

"But he's not in the office now."

"Oh, he said to call him on his cell. I think that is a wireless telephone."

Jerome wondered if she was joking. She sure didn't look like she was joking.

"Thanks. Can I use the office phone?"

"I don't know? Can you call Canada with this phone?"

Again, Jerome didn't know how to take the remark. He walked over to her desk. He noticed there were bloody paper towels in her trash can, there was blood on her dress, and there was half eaten and

**126**

strange looking fruit sitting on her desk. He picked up the phone receiver.

"May I?" he asked.

"Sure."

He dialed and got a busy signal.

"What number do you dial to get out of Sudan?" he asked.

"I don't know."

"Well, what number do you use?"

"I've never done it... Sorry."

"I see. Well what number do you dial to get Khartoum?"

"I've never called anyone in Khartoum."

"Hmm. I'll tell you what. Can I borrow your Ethernet cable to hook my laptop up? I'll can call him on Skype."

She knew he had asked her a specific question but she wasn't sure what it was.

"Go ahead. I'll watch. But whatever you borrow from me you need to return it as soon as you're done with it," she answered.

"Sure. I won't keep your Ethernet cable," he said defensively.

Jerome opened his bag, took out a small black case and opened it up. The top half was a computer screen and the bottom was a keyboard. He plugged it in and typed on the keys. Within less than 3 minutes total he stopped and said, "Ok, let's see if Herb is there."

She heard ringing and then a voice came through the computer.

"Hello, Jerome is that you?"

"Herb, how are you?"

"Not too good. I wanted to let you know of some news."

"Shoot."

"Our shareholders, they're kicking up a fuss about the Sudan. They claim we shouldn't be involved in a civil war. They're throwing words around like genocide. I can't believe it though. The Sudanese government would never just open fire on their own people. It's ludicrous. Anyway, they're threatening to pull out funds if we don't leave the Sudan. God damn it! What a bunch of wimps and wusses. You can't cook if you don't stir the God-damned pot. Anyway, it's not final. I just wanted you to know what's going on. Let me email more information to you. I talked to a woman there who didn't know the office email address. What the sam hell is your office like? I know they have email."

Yandeng was listening to the whole conversation. Jerome was embarrassed for her.

"Don't worry Herb. The office is doing fine. Just email it to my personal address. And thanks for keeping me in the loop."

"Sure. And Jerome, keep your eyes open, keep out of trouble, and keep me in the loop."

"Ok. I'll look around. Take care."

There was no further answer and Jerome did some more typing and then said, "Good, here's the info from Herb. I hope you weren't offended. He's really a nice guy. He means well."

"Did he just send you something?"

"Yeah, I just got it. Your line is pretty good for a satellite connection."

Yandeng pondered this.

"Did he send an email?"

Jerome looked up at her to see if he understood her question. There were certain things that she had said that added together, didn't add up.

"Sure did," he said, chuckling at her. She didn't seem to find this funny although she was no longer crying.

"Well I'm glad to see you're feeling better. I need to find my room, get set up, and then go spend time with the team. Again, if there's anything I can do to help, let me know," he said as he headed for the door.

Yandeng took a deep breath and a big chance. Just as he opened the door, she said, "Yes, there is something I'd like to ask you to help me with."

"Sure, what is it?"

"Can you teach me how to make an email?"

"How to 'make' an email?" Jerome asked.

"Yes," she said very resolutely. And then she added in a rather hushed voice, "I've never made one."

"I see… I think, I see…" He walked slowly over to her desk. He almost asked 3 different questions but thought better of it. Then he asked one he regretted afterwards.

"Now tell me how you got this job?"

Yandeng hung her head. She was visibly choked up and there were tears in her eyes. "Someone said yesterday that they want to

**128**

hire Dinkas so the SPLA won't attack. But they're wrong. They'll still attack. I'm no safer from being attacked by them than I am from the government."

Jerome was speechless. This was certainly not the answer he expected and he saw there was a lot more to this country, and this girl, than he could understand.

"Look, I'm sorry for my comment. It's none of my business. Uh… let me show you how to create emails."

He pulled up a chair beside hers.

"Ok, tell me where to start. What do you know already?"

"Why don't you teach me from the start?"

"OK. Let's say you just logged on. Now, the first thing…"

"Excuse me. Why don't we start with logging. I don't know much about logging."

"I see. Hmmm. Yes, let's start at the beginning. Let's reboot the computer. You know the logon password?"

"What's that?"

"Wow. Well it's a…"

There was a quick knock and the door opened. It was Osman the party manager. He gave the 2 of them a hard look, made an attempt at a hello and said, "Let's go Jerome. I thought you were just collecting your bag."

"Yes, I am. I was just checking some email issues. I'll be right over."

"We need to get moving. Let the abida take care of the email issues. That's what they hire them for."

The hair rose on the back of Jerome's neck.

"You said what?"

"You heard me. Come on. We have a trip to prepare and you have a lot to learn before we leave."

"I'll be over soon. Thank you very much," he said as bluntly as he thought necessary. Osman took the hint, gave them a last almost menacing glance and pulled the door hard behind him.

"Let me make a suggestion," Jerome said. "I think this may take some time, and I don't mind giving it to you. But I don't have the time right now. Why don't we meet after dinner and spend as much time as we need?"

"You will come back after dinner?" she said, looking at him suspiciously.

"Yes, I promise."

Yandeng gave him a hard stare as if to say, "I'll believe it when I see it."

"Honest," he said as he walked out. "I'll be back."

# Chapter 29

As Yandeng sat in the office, she thought about Jerome. He seemed nice, but not real smart. He had told her, "Honest, I'll be back." In her world, the only people who chimed on about their own honesty were those you didn't trust. Now it was 6:30 at night, dark outside, and he hadn't showed up. She was getting weak from hunger. She thought about the shower in her little room. She got up and opened the door to leave and almost walked right into Jerome. He had a plate full of something in his hand and it almost spilled.

"Woa! You're not leaving are you? I thought we were going to meet tonight after dinner."

"Yes, we were…"

"Well, let's meet. By the way, where were you at dinner? Everyone is asking about you. You don't leave the office and they said you haven't eaten since you've been here? Are you sick?"

"No, thank God."

"Well then, I guess you're just trying to keep your thin figure," Jerome said and chuckled. She gave him a look that had no hint of laughter in it. Jerome immediately knew he had made a faux pas, a big one, but wasn't even sure what it was.

"Uh… I brought you this peach cobbler they made special for me, but I guess you don't want it."

He set it on top of the filing cabinet.

Yandeng stared at him, then the cobbler.

"What is peach gobble?"

"Cobbler," Jerome laughed. "It's kind of like peach pie."

Yandeng had a blank look on her face at this explanation.

"Do you eat it?"

"Yes, it's great. I had as much as I could eat. If I had another bite I think I'd burst. I'll throw it away on my way out."

"Let me have it," Yandeng said, almost sharply.

"Sure, take it." Jerome was sinking further into bewilderment. He just didn't seem to be on the same page, or even in the same chapter as this Dinka girl. At least he knew now that the Dinka were a tribe. She had picked up the plate and was staring at the peach cobbler. She reached into it with her hand and took a small taste.

"Oh, I forgot to bring a fork. I'm sorry. Do you have one here?"

Yandeng had seen forks before, although she wasn't used to using one. Village Dinka were accustomed to using spoons, but never forks. They most often ate with their hands.

"This has sugar in it!" she exclaimed.

"Yes, it's dessert."

"Dessert? Do you eat this often in Canada?" She had rarely tasted food sweetened with sugar and the concept of dessert was unknown to her.

"Well yes, or no, or I don't know. As I said, I'm not from Canada. We eat it sometimes in America."

"Hmm," she said as she devoured the plateful using her bare hand, then licking it off. Jerome found this terribly funny but decided not to say a single word. He was sure anything he said at this point would not be taken as it was meant.

"I'm glad you like it. Can I go back and get some more?"

"Is there anymore?"

"Well… I can find out."

"Sure. Thank you Jerome," she said with great emotion.

On his way back to the kitchen he pondered the facts. She didn't seem to eat at all, ignoring meal times at the mess hall, giving the impression she worked all the time. Then she devours a plate of peach cobbler with her bare hands and asks for seconds. He asked the cook for more cobbler, which was provided with a surprised smile.

"You like it too much, no?" she said.

"Yes," Jerome answered, hoping "Yes" was the right response to the question "No?"

He took it back and there was a genuine look of gratitude on her face. This time he handed her a spoon, which she used, and devoured the second plate of cobbler, leaving the plate and spoon clean as a whistle.

Then she said, "Thank you very much, Jerome. Now can you teach me everything about making emails?"

And so the evening began. He found that in fact, she knew nothing of computers or the software packages they ran, or of the concepts behind basic things like electronic files, or even what a spreadsheet was and why they were used. The only redeeming point was that she was very eager to learn and learned quickly enough for someone coming from such a deficit. The only break came about ½ hour into the evening when Yandeng looked to be in great pain and was clutching her stomach and bending over.

"Maybe it was something you ate," Jerome offered.

"Yes, it certainly was," she answered.

"What did you eat?" he asked innocently enough.

She gave him one of her angry stares. It then started to dawn on him that it had to have been the peach cobbler. He also put the other data he had about her into his own mental spreadsheet. She hadn't yet appeared at the mess hall. She was thin as a bone, and the only thing he had seen her eat, besides the peach cobbler, was a small piece of local fruit. She must not be eating. He wanted to collect further data but thought he'd go slowly and indirectly. She recovered to a point that she insisted they continue, although she still clutched her stomach over the next hour and had to run out and come back somewhere in that time.

It was about 1 AM that the lesson was ending and she decided to put some of it into practice. She thumbed through her pile of odd shaped scraps of paper and put one in front of her. "Let's work on this," she said.

"What is it?" asked Jerome squinting and holding the small scrap of paper at different angles trying to make sense of it.

"It's a note I wrote to myself, to remind myself to ask Khartoum to make sure one of our men gets credit for extra time he worked. He mentioned overtime. What is overtime? Does everyone get paid more if they work more?"

"Well yes, sort of, or sometimes. He must get paid by the hour. So if he works more than so many hours per week, he gets paid extra."

"Really! That's great. How about you? Will you get overtime for working tonight?"

"No, no, see I'm not hourly. I'm paid the same no matter how much I work."

"That's too bad. It's OK though. I'm sure once they see how well you work they'll pay you hourly like the others."

Jerome chuckled and decided not to try to explain.

"OK. Let's send the Khartoum office an email. You know their address. Let's see if you can send it."

So she opened her email, put the address in, and typed:

My dearest Khartoum Offise. Your kindness is needed in a most urgent matter. One of our dear workers, Mr. AbouBakr, has done us a great service by working overtime. He has..."

"Wait a minute, Yandeng. I don't mean to offend, but I think the tone of the email is wrong."

"Wrong? In what way?"

"Hmmm. You see writing an email is not like writing a letter."

"What's it like?"

"Well it's more like sending quick notes, or bits of letters, or just thoughts. You say what you need to say in as few of words as possible."

"Why? If you are going to send a letter to important people in a far away office, you should write them wonderful letters. No?"

"No. Or yes, you shouldn't!" Why did people use "No" to ask questions? "If you were working and very busy, would you want to get a long letter from someone that took 5 sentences to say what could have been said in one?"

"Sure I would. Wouldn't you?"

"No. No I wouldn't. What I'm trying to say is that you need to keep your emails short, like these little notes you've written. You don't write yourself long notes do you? You write short ones."

This explanation seemed to turn the light on for her.

"Yes, you are right. We need to save emails and not waste them. It is better not to waste them."

Jerome decided not to argue the reasons. He was beginning to feel weary although she seemed energized.

"I can't read your note, but write enough in your email so they'll understand."

Her next attempt read:

Mr. AbouBakr – Needs paid for overtime – was missed 2X.
Yandeng

"Hmm. Yeah. Hit the send button. They'll get the idea. If they don't, they'll ask."

They then went through the stack of hand scribbled notes until they were all dealt with. Jerome noticed a pattern with the notes. The scrap of paper was always just big enough for the note. It wasn't bigger, nor smaller, and the scraps were hand torn, usually all the way around. Since the notes were varying lengths, the scraps were all different sizes, but neatly stacked. When she finished with them she created another stack. When they finished with the last scrap, Jerome picked up the whole pile and threw them in the trash can. She watched him with her brows tightly knitted and stood to look where he had thrown them. She looked down into the trash can and back at him. There was some problem here and he didn't know what it was, but he was too tired to pursue it.

"Well, I think we've covered as much as we planned. I think I'll call it a night," Jerome announced. It was 2 AM.

"We haven't read the emails yet. I have a lot here and some you said have files attached."

"Oh, that's right. Can we work on those tomorrow night?"

She clearly wanted to do it now.

"You are tired. I am fine. I will try to find the files that attached and pile them somewhere on my driver."

"No, I'm not tired," Jerome insisted. If this thin Dinka girl who apparently hadn't been eating for days could continue, surely he could too. They worked 3 more hours cleaning out the inbox, creating new folders for files, printing out files and making copies for people, and so on.

At 5 AM Jerome realized the night's sleep was about over. "Is there anything else you need before we stop?"

"No, thank you so much. Except, there is the faxes machine. People want me to send them faxes. What are faxes?"

For the next half hour he explained faxes.

"But why don't people just send emails?"

"Because you can't email a picture."

"But we already emailed pictures."

"Yes, you're right, but you can't email a hard copy picture, only electronic pictures."

This for some reason caused Yandeng to laugh and laugh. Jerome, although he was quite short on humor finally got the bug and the two of them laughed hysterically.

"If my brother and sister could see me! Sending pictures by a machine to other parts of the world where it would take you weeks to walk!" She laughed even harder.

"It would take more than weeks. In fact, you'd drown if you tried to walk to Canada."

They laughed even more.

She finally settled from spasms of laughter and Jerome asked, "Where is your family? Maybe we can send them a picture?"

He saw immediately that he had done it again. By the time he blinked, the mood had changed.

"They're gone," was all she said as she fought back tears.

"I'm sorry Yandeng. I didn't mean to pry."

After an awkward silence he interjected, "Look, we both need to shower and change before the new day starts, and we probably don't want everyone to know we were up all night working. Let's go back to our rooms, shower and change, and meet for breakfast."

"No, you go ahead. I just ate."

"Yes, you ate almost 10 hours ago. I'd like to see you at the mess hall."

"Mess hall?"

"The cafeteria, the meal room. Why haven't you been there? Everyone is asking about you and saying 'What does she eat?'"

"But I haven't received any payments for my work yet."

"You haven't … what do you mean? Do you think you have to pay to eat there?"

"Of course. Don't you?"

"Yandeng, don't be silly. The food is part of our pay, just like the room. You mean you haven't been eating because you thought you had to pay for it?"

"Well, yes."

"No! You come over this morning. They open in a half hour. Go back to your room, freshen up, put on clean clothes, and come over. If you're not there I'm going to come and get you. Understand?"

"Yes, I'll be there."

She looked relieved.

## Chapter 30

Yandeng felt better than she had felt for a long time. Just over a week ago she was at the government camp under a heavy black fog. Then she went to the church, met Gatwech, had a dream about an old difficult door opening and had an interview with a foreign oil company. Now she had a job back in Dinka lands. She had her own room with things she had never had, or really even seen before. And in the course of a night she learned the mysteries of emails, and electronic files and folders, and faxes and really felt like she understood it, at least far beyond what she had 12 hours previously. And to think there was food available and all she had to do was walk next door and eat it. It was strange food to be sure, sweet and sticky, but apparently in abundance. This small white guy with the thick glasses seemed like a genuine friend, of which she could name few right now. Although he sometimes said stupid things, he was on her side. What a difference a week could bring.

"Thank you God. You have rescued me from many traps. Well I best tidy up the office then go back and stand in the shower in my room. That will feel wonderful."

She was standing in the shower, letting water run over her hair, then onto her back and down her legs when was a knock at the door.

"Oh my. Who could it be?" she wondered.

"Wait, whoever you are."

The knocking continued. She picked up a towel and held it in front of her and went to the door. Dinkas didn't walk around naked, but they weren't unaccustomed to not wearing much on certain occasions. She opened the door to find Jerome standing there. He looked at her and his mouth dropped. It seemed his face turned a reddish color.

"Yes, do you want something?"

"No. I mean yes. I ... just came to get you for breakfast."

"I'll be over soon."

He looked at the ground and turned and walked quickly away. This seemed like odd behavior to Yandeng. She dressed, putting back on the same black taub she had been wearing for months.  How she'd like to get rid of it.

When she walked into the cafeteria she had the impression that everyone stopped talking and looked at her.  Jerome pointed to the beginning of the food line.  She walked over to where he had pointed, somewhat unsure of what to do.  Fortunately, someone came in behind her and passed in front, picked up a plate and started heaping servings from several different pans.  She did likewise.  There seemed to be no limit to the amount of food you could take, and there was meat.  She hadn't eaten meat for weeks.  They rarely served it at the government camp, and she had hardly had a real meal since she left the camp.  Jerome motioned for her to sit at his table with the seismic guys, causing a few of them to whistle and cat call.  Jerome found this very annoying but offered her the chair in front of him.  She sat down and just as Jerome leaned forward to ask her why she hadn't changed her clothes, she bowed her head to pray.  His jaw dropped.  Did they pray in Africa?  He thought this more an American custom, and only the custom of a very few.  Although this sort of situation usually made him look down on the other person, he felt a strange softness for her.

When she looked up he gave her a few seconds to reorient to the non-spiritual world and again leaned forward and whispered, being careful that no one else could hear.

"Yandeng, why didn't you change your clothes?"

"Oh no," he thought.  "It just happened again.  I meant well.  But I just got that angry look.…  What could I have said wrong?"

"Oh my," she thought.  "How can he be so kind and helpful and then say such insensitive things?  He doesn't seem stupid, but he says stupid things."

Meanwhile the seismic guys were acting like complete grade school kids.  They were nudging Jerome and making noises and saying, "Do you two know each other?"

As Yandeng began to unstiffen and eat and take account of her surroundings, she noticed there were very few other women here, and the few present were all eating together and shooting glances at her.

"Why did I even sit here?  This was a mistake," she thought.  "Jerome has helped me, but he doesn't know our ways."

As Jerome sat there pondering the situation he thought, "Look at this place. There are 4 girls and 40 guys and the girls all sit together. And all the Arabs are sitting together. People criticize Americans for being segregated, but look at this. I sure don't understand the African ways."

Later that morning after breakfast, Jerome and his team made final preparations for their seismic exploration trip. The equipment had all been prepared and tested. They decided to leave and have a late lunch on the road. He decided to check into the office to let Yandeng know of their plans and see how she was doing, since they didn't speak to each other at breakfast.

As he entered the office he noticed she was typing. He walked over to the desk and noticed that all the little hand scribbled notes that he had thrown in the trash were stacked on her desk again. He almost commented on them, but congratulated himself when he stopped short.

"Thank you for helping me make emails last night. You see, I am making one now and have made many already today. It is easy. I am making many new friends in faraway places."

"Really? That's great. Where are the emails going?"

"To Khartoum and Canada."

It's funny she would think Khartoum a faraway place. He thought so. But why should she?

"Have you ever been to Khartoum?"

"Oh no!" she laughed. "Never! Have you?"

"Yes, on my way here."

"What was it like? I hear it is a gigantic city, all modern and new with gigantic buildings and some touch the sky. And there are buses and trucks and cars everywhere. So many you sometimes have to wait to cross a street!" With that statement she laughed in disbelief.

Jerome wasn't quite sure how to answer. Khartoum was sure not his picture of a bustling modern city full of tall buildings, but he again felt it prudent to hold his tongue.

"Well, what did you think of Khartoum?" she asked again.

"Yes, you're right. There are tall buildings. My hotel was 5 stories tall and had an elevator."

"See, it's as I said!" Yandeng exclaimed excitedly.

**140**

"Yes… It is as you said. Anyway, Yandeng, I just wanted to let you know that we're leaving… I mean we the seismic testing team, we're leaving on an exploration trip. We should be back in 5 days, barring any unforeseen problems. I just wanted to make sure you were OK here… you know, that you're able to keep up with the emails, calls, faxes, and all that."

"Yes. I hope so. And thank you. I don't think I thanked you enough. You helped me too much."

Relieved, he said, "No, it was nothing. I'm glad I could help. You just needed a few pointers."

"Yes, it's true. I did need points. You helped me with lots of them. And where are you going?"

"Oh, south somewhere. Not too far away. The military will be with us and doesn't want us exploring too far from here."

"Oh?" she said, although her look told him she wasn't really following. "What are you exploring for?"

"Well, … oil. We are an oil company."

"Yes, but you already found it, didn't you? They say it's under the ground, right underneath us."

"Yes. Uh… yes it is."

"Well then why are you exploring for it if you already found it?"

"Well, it is hoped that we'll find more."

The words seemed to hang in the air. He could tell she was pondering them, deeply. But why? What was so hard to understand about oil exploration?

"Anyway, I'll see you when I get back. Here's my email address."

And he pulled over the notebook on her desk and jotted down his email address.

"What do you mean your email address? I thought this address I am using was everyone's email address? You have an address? It is your own?"

"Yes, well the whole seismic team can use this one, and here is my personal one." And he jotted a second address down on the pad. She stared at them and he could immediately tell he had opened up another area where a few pointers, or "points" as she called them, were needed. But he was in a hurry.

"Yes, just type in either address, like you do for your new friends in Khartoum, and I'll get it."

He noticed she was ripping the paper he had jotted his address on. She ripped an oval shaped hole in the paper leaving his address right in the middle of the oval. Then she set the oval right on top of her stack of scraps.

"OK. I will make you an email. But how will you get it? Do you have a wire to plug into your little computer I saw you using?"

"Well, I have wireless and we'll have a satellite hookup out in the field just like you do here."

"Hmm. I really don't think you will get it until you come back here," she said with conviction.

"Uh, OK. You'll see."

# Chapter 31

Jerome and the seismic crew left camp in a caravan of 10 vehicles. There were 3 company landrovers, the recording truck, 3 vibrator buggies which were large trucks that only seated 1 person, the mobile kitchen truck, and 2 army landrovers that came along "for protection," although the team said they only came along for the food because in case of attack the soldiers were sure to bail quickly. They made a cloud of red dust ½ mile long on the road that Jerome was told had only been carved out of the raw Sudan landscape months ago. It was cut by the oil company through the bush and went all the way south to Bentiu a government-controlled city. After a two hour drive they stopped to eat a lunch of fried Nile perch that had been cooked back at camp that morning, kisra, a thin corn flour bread, and hoshab, a cold sweet made from a mixture of chopped bananas, figs and raisins.

Shortly after lunch the dusty red road passed by a group of blackened shells of tukuls. Jerome was riding in the lead landrover with Osman.

"What's that?" Jerome gasped.

"What's what?" Osman asked, trying to act like he didn't notice.

"These burned huts!" Jerome croaked. "What happened?"

"Oh, the huts. Don't know. They must have had a fire."

"Yeah, I'll say. Where are the people?"

"What does it matter?"

"Well… I don't know. I mean, it looks like something happened. I don't think the huts just all caught fire by accident and the people walked away. Right?"

"We really don't need to know. We need to find oil, not ask questions about fires."

Jerome didn't like the tone, but didn't have much choice but to drop the subject. But then 20 minutes later he saw a similar sight about 100 yards off to the right of the caravan.

"Look, another burned out village!" he said, while pointing out the window.

"Hmmm, maybe. It's hard to tell," was all Osman said.

Before they stopped about 3 that afternoon Jerome saw another village that had fallen to the same fate. When he asked some of the crew about it while setting up camp, everyone changed the subject or said they didn't know.

There was a whole routine to go through in setting up camp. There were tents and mosquito nets to put up, generators to start, equipment to check out, food to cook and eat, everything had to be done before it got dark at about 6:30. After dark there was a VCR that was hooked up and everyone watched together. The first night they watched "The Princess Bride." Jerome had already seen it but watched anyway. Then they all went to bed early. Jerome woke numerous times during the night to the sound of snarling and growling that seemed nearby. Then at dawn they had breakfast and set out immediately after.

"Why are we leaving the tents and equipment?" Jerome asked Osman.

"We'll be surveying near here. We'll be back tonight. One of the army landrovers will stay here to watch the camp."

They drove only a few miles when Osman announced, "This is where we start."

He directed the whole team. He sent the vibrator trucks to their starting spots, told the juggers where to set up the geophones to get the readings back to the reading truck where he stationed himself with a big glass of hot tea. He ignored Jerome who followed him around. Jerome could tell the rest of the team was watching to see who was really in charge. He was new and so let Osman direct operations. By 9 AM they were already recording readings. Jerome kept his eye on them and started studying them. Meanwhile, Osman ordered to move the trucks.

"There has been some interference. We need a better read in this area here," Jerome said. "We can't move the vibrators yet."

"We need to keep moving," Osman answered Jerome curtly, and spoke into the radio. "Ok, start moving the equipment south south east."

"We need to redo this section," Jerome said again. "The readings here are useless."

"If they want it done again, they'll ask us to do it. They are in charge, not us," Osman retorted. He then continued ordering the crew to relocate to the next position.

Jerome could see this was an obvious power play. He thought about pulling out all the stops and standing his ground. Osman had been with the crew from the first survey. They'd surely side with him in a showdown. In the end, he just let Osman continue to direct traffic.

The surveying continued moving south south east throughout the day. They made it back to camp that night just before dark. The cooks had dinner waiting. After dinner they all gathered round the VCR and again put on "The Princess Bride."

"Why are we watching the same movie again tonight?" Jerome asked. "Didn't we bring any others?"

Mahjoub, one of the electronic technicians, said, "We have some others, but we've seen them all a lot of times. And besides, Osman likes this one."

That decided the issue for Jerome. He went into the reading truck where they had their email set up. No emails were in his inbox, so he decided to send an email to Herb.

"Herb:

Hard to believe, I left Calgary only a little over a week ago and here I am surveying in the African bush. You'd think it would be a lot wilder and more exciting than surveying in the Canadian wilderness, but it's not much different. Except for the heat. It hit 110 degrees F here today, in the shade, although there was only enough shade for the thermometer. A first glance of the readings show a lot potential drill sites. This place is amazing, so big, so empty, almost eerily empty. Some army guys follow us around for protection, but we haven't seen a soul since we left camp. (Jerome considered putting in a line about Osman taking command of the team. He didn't want to highlight his weakness though and decided against it.)

One more thing, you told me to keep my eyes open about things here. Well, I saw the remains of 3 villages on our way here, all within our blocks. They appear to have been burned and not a soul was around. Creepy.

Talk later.

Jerome"

Then he chuckled and decided to send Yandeng an email.

"Yandeng:

Hello. How are things in the office? Are you keeping up? How is camp? (Here, Jerome sat for 3 or 4 minutes trying to think of something to say. He knew he could easily say the wrong thing, even without knowing it, and also knew that he had little in common with her, and so could think of nothing to say.)

Now do you believe me Yandeng, that email can be sent via satellite from the bush? See you in a few days.

Jerome."

Hopefully he had said nothing offensive or inflammatory. If he did, he wouldn't be there to see that fire in her eyes.

The next day went much like the first, with Osman deciding when to relocate the team and equipment. Jerome decided to take a long-term view and not get discouraged. Worst possible scenario, his situation wouldn't change much, but within a year or so, he'd know as much as anyone about doing seismic surveys in rural Africa, or rural anywhere. At that point, he'd at least be more marketable. It didn't help his ego at all though, having Osman order everyone around in front of him and even shout orders at him on occasion. Jerome knew this was posturing on his part. He was showing everyone on the team, and the military "observers" that he was the boss. He was the alpha male and anyone that wanted his spot would have to challenge him openly. Jerome was used to arguing, but not challenging people openly. He had never won a fight in his life.

The third day of surveying looked like it would go pretty much like the previous two until they relocated to the second survey point. As they drove through some tall brush and low trees not far from the new road they ran right up into a village, or an ex-village as was the case. The same fiery fate that had befallen the other villages Jerome had seen had befallen this one also. The mud walls of the huts were still standing but the grass roofs had burned off.

"Look at this!" Jerome exclaimed, as the team got out of their vehicles and gathered around Osman for instructions. "What do you think happened here?" Jerome asked in a loud voice to no one in particular.

"Nothing happened here," Osman pronounced in a loud and condescending voice.

"What do you mean nothing happened?" Jerome was incredulous. "This was once a village. And it looks like there was a fire that wiped the whole place out. Just like the villages we saw the other day."

Some on the team members were smiling, or maybe laughing, at him. It felt like he was on the outside of an inside joke.

"All right, what's up?" Jerome asked. "You all know what happened, but no one wants to say. Why?"

"Are you accusing us of something?" Osman said very loudly and defensively.

"All right, forget it. I'll find out on my own. Let's get on with the surveying," he said.

"Thank you!" Osman said. And he proceeded to give instructions to set up geophones and vibrator trucks right in the midst of the one-time village. People scurried to their stations and set up as though the charred structures were not there. He tried to act like he was tending to things, but was really having a hard look around. Then as the team got into their groove, he tried to stay out of sight, and investigated as much as he could in the time he had. He noticed that the village had been divided into groups of 4 or 5 huts circled closely together. Who had lived here? What had happened to them? He heard the vibrator trucks starting up and spied a group of huts in the opposite direction, on the outskirts of what had been the village. He walked quickly over and walked into one of the huts. There were charred remains of clothing and mats.

"My goodness, the people who lived here didn't even get their belongings out. The fire must have surprised them."

He walked out of that hut and into another. The same situation there. One of the trucks was coming closer. He left that hut and into another whose open doorway faced opposite the trucks. Just inside he saw it, part of an arm with a hand attached, but not attached to a body. He noticed many dark objects on the floor. Was it what he thought they were? Yes, charred bodies strewn all over the hut. He noticed that three of them had belonged to children. He also saw a burned skull with a huge slice in the forehead. There was still charred flesh on the bones and their mouths were locked in an open position as though they died screaming.  Whatever happened had occurred in the not too distant past.  It was also clear that the fate that befell these people was no accident.  They appeared to have been burned alive, or mostly alive.

"Who would do this?" he gasped almost out loud.

"What are you doing here?" a sharp voice spoke startling him temporarily out of his horror.

# Chapter 32

Jerome turned to see Osman at the entrance to the death trap that had once been a tukul.

"We are supposed to be working. You are not to be here!" Osman barked.

"Look... Look at ... this!" Jerome was gasping, almost unable to speak.

"It is nothing of interest to you!"

"Nothing of interest? These people were killed! Someone needs to be notified! I'm getting my camera," Jerome sputtered as he started past Osman with the intention of getting his digital camera from his bag in the recording truck.

"Oh no you're not! Remember I told you last night that if you were to communicate that all was not going well, there could be trouble for someone, and it would probably be you? And, if you were to go talking to people about this, I'm sure there would be trouble."

Jerome took in what Osman was saying and he became incredulous.

"You mean that you're saying that a whole village of human beings was hacked and burnt to death, right in their own homes, and you think it best to just not say anything, even though we may be the only ones who know?"

"You are naïve. Many know. Truth be told, the whole world knows and doesn't care."

"What the hell are you talking about? The whole world? No one knows about this. There are lots of villages like this one aren't there? And you knew and you wanted to keep me from knowing. Why?"

"I don't care if you know," Osman said defiantly. "There, now you know. You are one of the many that know. You're not alone. You're like the rest of us now."

"Like hell I am. I'm going to take pictures and let lots of other people know and do whatever I can to make sure those who did this are held responsible!"

Osman opened his mouth and laughed like a hyena.

"Oh, so you're going to start a crusade against the Sudanese government, who is here protecting you, and helping to pay your high salary!"

Then just that quickly he stopped laughing and gave Jerome a hard stare.

Jerome was stunned. "The Sudanese government? ... they did this?"

"This is not as bad as it looks. These people were subversives, rebels, working against the government. It was war. They lost. The government won."

"War? Look at the skeletons. There are children buried in that pile. Were they at war with the government?"

"You don't understand. These are abid. They are born ignorant and have fought against all plans at developing the south and making their world better. They are merely casualties of war."

Jerome was feeling sick to his stomach and angry. He pushed past Osman and said loudly and disdainfully, "Casualties of war, my ass!"

He walked quickly back to the reading truck, found his backpack and dug out his digital camera. When he stepped out of the dark room with all the monitors and back into the bright African sunlight, Osman was waiting for him and handed him the satellite phone.

"It's for you," he said with a hint of a smirk. "It's AbdelKader. He's calling from Khartoum. He wants to talk with you. Take the phone."

Jerome grabbed the phone put it to his ear and said, "Yeah? Who is this?"

"Jerome, it's AbdelKader. I haven't heard much from you since you left Khartoum. I was hoping we'd stay in closer contact. How are things going there?"

Jerome knew Osman had called him and would have already explained the situation. He figured he'd play hard to get.

"I'm great AbdelKader. How are you? How are things in Khartoum?"

"Good Jerome. Osman and I just had a conversation. He said you're working around one of the abid villages and the sights have gotten you pretty upset. Is that true?"

The cool, collected tone of AbdelKader asking such leading questions caused Jerome to hit the flash point, "Slightly upset? I just came upon the bodies of murdered children and adults, who look like they were hacked and burned to death. Yeah! I'm upset. Are you upset hearing about it? Osman isn't. He says they are the natural casualties of war."

"Jerome, this is hard. War is difficult. Many have suffered. We too have suffered. But you mustn't do anything that would draw attention to yourself or our work. You know we had nothing to do with this unfortunate confusion."

"Confusion? AbdelKader, I didn't say confusion. I said murder. They were murdered, in their homes and then left there."

"Yes, how unfortunate for them," he said, betraying no sense of sympathy in his voice. "Well, let's just try to forget about these awful things and move on. Osman needs your help, so make sure you help keep the team's morale positive. I've heard that the readings from this trip are very promising."

Jerome was incredulous. "Sure, AbdelKader. I'll keep smiling and trying to tell myself that a village full of children's skeletons is Ok. Is that right?"

AbdelKader caught the sarcasm and finally got to the point. "Jerome, there is a lot at stake here, for the company and for you personally. Don't get caught up in this. And above all, no pictures. You will do well to keep this matter to yourself. There are many who wouldn't want these things talked about. If you do, it may be hard to protect you. Your safety is very important to us. We can't do anything for those who have died, but we can take precautions for ourselves, to make sure we don't join them. Understand?"

Jerome now added the sensation of being threatened to his emotions of anger and disbelief.

"Jerome?" he repeated. "Do you understand?"

The old enemy of fear was knocking on his door. He again felt the old sensation of being bullied. He hated it more than anything else he knew, yet he was used to it, and did what he had done so many times when faced by bullies.

"Yes, I understand."

"And no pictures, right?"

Sigh. "Right."

"That's a wise decision. Put Osman back on the phone please."

Jerome handed Osman the phone. Osman put it to his ear but his eye was on Jerome's camera. Jerome turned and went back into the reading truck. He put his camera back in his pack and sat down in front of the reading monitors. A short while later he felt the truck shift gears and start moving. In 15 minutes he was back in the bush, the village out of sight and seemingly out of everyone's mind. But, he would never forget what he saw that day. Camera or not, the pictures were etched in his memory.

Jerome didn't say a word to anyone for the rest of the day. He stared at monitors and tried to get the scenes and the situation out of his mind.

At camp that night they put on "The Princess Bride" for the third night in a row. Jerome sat with the group but could generate no interest for the film, the event, or even the company he was with. He got up and walked out to relieve himself in the bush. One of the technicians followed him out for the same reason.

"Great movie isn't it!"

"Yeah, I liked it the first 10 times I saw it," Jerome answered, not trying to hide his sarcasm.

"Yes, me too," he answered, oblivious to the cynicism.

"Tell me, what do you know about the village we were in today? Why doesn't anyone want to talk about what happened there?"

He looked around to see if anyone else was in earshot. Satisfied that they were alone, he whispered, "The government killed them."

"Why!?" Jerome almost shouted.

"Shh. These things should not be talked about."

"But why did they kill them? There were bodies of children in that village."

"They lived too close to the oil. And they aren't Muslims. And they're black like me."

Jerome tried to understand all this. "So what if they live close to the oil. What difference does that make?"

"The government wanted their land. Now they have it."

Jerome felt sickened and even guilty. Why did he feel guilty? He surely had no part in this. He was only here doing a job.

"Who were these people?"

"The Dinka," he said as he zippered his pants.

"The Dinka? But Yandeng, the girl that works in the office, she's a Dinka."

"Yes. She's from around here."

"How do you know?"

"I heard her tell a group of people in the office the other day that she was from Mayom County and that her village wasn't there anymore. And well, we're in Mayom County."

They had arrived back into the lights of the camp and the conversation ended. Jerome all of a sudden felt like he now understood Yandeng a lot better. And yet at the same time questions popped up and he felt like maybe he didn't understand her at all. Why did she of all people come to work with an oil company that was implicitly involved with the government that destroyed her village? It was understandable why she didn't know anything about computers and electronic equipment. She must have grown up in a hut like the ones he had seen. But why come back? And why did she wear a Muslim dress if the Dinka were not Muslims? Maybe he didn't really understand her, but one thing was for sure, he greatly admired her. She had a lot of backbone for someone so skinny and vulnerable.

The next day they continued taking readings in a south easterly direction, very close to the new dirt road. They didn't see a soul all day. Once though 2 military helicopters flew overhead at low altitude. The military escorts got out of their landrover and waved to them.

"What are military helicopters doing way out here?" Jerome asked out loud.

"Just making sure we're safe," Osman answered.

"Safe from whom? It seems they're the ones we need to be afraid of!" Jerome snapped back, still feeling raw from what he had witnessed the day before.

Osman shot him a dark look but said nothing.

## Chapter 33

Back at camp Yandeng was beginning to feel good. It was amazing to eat 3 meals a day, and as much as you wanted! There were stews, roast meat, potatoes, bread, mountains of vegetables, and cakes. Yes cakes! Why back in the village, cake was only eaten on very rare occasions, such as the wedding of someone important, like the village chief or his brother or son. But here they served cake after lunch and dinner! Then for breakfast they served toast with sweet fruit preserves that came in a jar. What things people had thought of! She usually was so full after a bowl of stew or a plate of roast chicken and vegetables that it was impossible to fit a bite of cake, but it sure was fun trying. And cola in cans, now that was another thing! Yes, she had tasted it, but only rarely. Now it was available every day, all the time. It didn't really taste good. It made your nose burn if you took more than a small sip, and it made you burp. Then if you drank a whole can, it made you fell jittery. But oh, just the thought of it was fun.

And as it turned out, Jerome was right, you could make emails even out in the bush with nothing but a computer. What a satellite really was or what it had to do with the process wasn't clear, but it seemed to work. The emails were there as proof. They had just emailed to ask if Mikhail had brought any extra fuel from Khartoum. Yes indeed. A short reply, so it didn't use up as much of whatever it took to make an email. It was good not to be wasteful. That's what the village elders, and adults had always said, and practiced. Resources were scarce. You never knew how long they would last, so you learned to use as little as possible. It was a wonder why the rest of the people at camp wasted as they did? Why some people even left meat on their plates and dumped it into the garbage on their way out of the cafeteria. They certainly weren't Dinkas.

Anyway, the office work seemed under control. Emails were coming and going. Making phone calls was still quite hard, with so many numbers, and then sometimes getting odd sounds but no voices on the other end. And then sometimes voices answered the call but it turned out to be only a recording of the real voice asking you to speak, but no one answered when you did.

Then there were the nights. After dinner, people hung around the cafeteria and watched movies on a TV screen. There was a different movie every night! Some had singing and dancing, some had men on horses with pistols and big hats. They weren't like the murahaleen though. They never attacked women, only other men, and didn't even do that very often and when they did it was usually for good reasons. The best movie though they said was about a princess who had to marry a man who didn't love her. That seemed normal enough, but there was apparently a giant in it too that would be really fun to see. But they said the men always took this movie with them when they went out surveying. Jerome must be enjoying it.

The women at camp were starting to become more sociable. They seemed interested in finding out about the happenings in Dinka land. They said they had seen burned Dinka villages and were sorry for what had happened but they seemed afraid to let others know they were talking about it. It seemed odd that others knew what had happened to Dinka villages. Or was it odd. Surely those horrible things couldn't have taken place with nobody ever finding out. Maybe it seemed more odd that people knew but hadn't tried to help? Anyway, life had turned a corner. There was food, shelter, and even kindness around her. And to top it all, there would also apparently be pay coming at some point. Now if only she could locate her brother and sister and somehow begin to share the bounty with them.

## Chapter 34

Five days on the road had passed and they were getting short on gasoline, food, water, and other provisions. So, they wrapped up at noon and started the drive back. It had taken them 4 hours to get to where they had started. Their surveying progressed more or less four miles per day. So each five-day trip put them 20 miles or so further from camp. They returned to Leghig before dark. Yandeng had been notified by email that they were coming and had alerted the kitchen staff, so extra food was prepared. They created a lot of commotion when they arrived. Not much happened in camp, so commotion happened over almost nothing at all. Everyone filed over to watch them unload the trucks and then they were followed into the cafeteria. Jerome looked around for Yandeng but didn't see her.

"She must be the only one at camp at that moment not crowded into the cafeteria," he thought.

He decided to check the office under the guise that he needed to see if there was any news from Canada. He knew there was none because he and Herb communicated directly. When he got to the office Yandeng seemed engrossed in the computer screen.

"Well it looks like you've made peace with the computer."

"Oh Jerome! Welcome. I have never been at war with my computer."

"I'm glad to hear it. Are you still sending emails?"

"Oh no. Emails are done."

"Dinner is ready. What are you doing?"

"I am swimming the web."

"Swimming? Oh, you mean surfing the web."

"Yes, that is what I meant. I asked one of the girls what surfing meant. She said it was sort of like swimming."

"Fine with me. Anyway, dinner is ready. I'll walk over with you if you like."

Yandeng looked up at Jerome and stared at him.

"No! You don't need to walk me over."

"Ok," he said, now feeling silly for asking. As he turned to go a thought came to mind and he stopped and turned around again and asked, "What are you surfing, or swimming, for?"

She got her stern and serious look that Jerome had almost forgotten about and now knew that he had overstepped his bounds.

"It is personal!" she said abruptly.

"Of course. You're right. Sorry I asked." And he hurried over to the cafeteria.

He was halfway through dinner when she came in. She looked his way and half nodded to him then got a small plate of chicken and vegetables and sat down with the handful of women at the women's table. After a while she got up and went over to look at desert. She was looking at it like she was observing an exhibit in an art gallery.

"Do you like banana pudding?" Jerome asked after he approached.

"Well I think so. What is it made of?"

"Hmm. You're asking the wrong guy. I just know it's made of pudding and bananas."

"I see. Well bananas are good, so I guess I'll try it... Jerome, I want to thank you."

"Really? What for?"

"You helped me, you really helped me."

"Oh, you mean with the emails and stuff?"

"Of course. I can now make many emails quickly. I have also made pages in Excel and Word. I can save them and then use them again."

"Well I am glad I could help you." And he felt this sincerely. To think she had grown up in a grass roofed hut and he was the first person to teach her how to use a computer. He felt very proud of this and hoped he could do more.

"If there is anything else I can help you with, let me know."

"Well OK. You know, I have a question."

"What's that?"

"Well AbdelKader from Khartoum sent me an email and asked me to copy some lines from the big Excel of all the employees' hours. Is that possible, to copy things and then put them somewhere else?"

"Why yes, it is. Can I show you how?"

"Oh yes, I'd be very thankful if you could."

"How about tonight, right after we finish dessert?"

"Well… I'd really like to see the movie. They say that you watch it every night, but I've never seen it. I've never actually seen a giant before, in a movie or walking around. Is he as big as they say?"

"Oh the movie, the Princess Bride. Yes, I see." Disappointment rose in him. Two reasons came to mind for his disappointment. First, he wanted to spend more time with her. And secondly, the last thing he wanted to do tonight was watch The Princess Bride yet again. But he could see that she was reading his disappointment and seemed possibly ready to make another one of her stern faces.

"Well yes he's big, even for a giant. Gigantic, you might say." Now he was sounding really stupid.

"If you want to watch the movie, then you can show me how to copy words. I'm so looking forward to the movie."

Jerome tried his best to look cheerful.

Jerome sat beside Yandeng when the movie started, which caused the men to snicker and guffaw out loud. She seemed awkward as well. What was with them all? They acted more like grade-schoolers in this regards than adults.

The movie started and everyone became very serious and attentive. They remained attentive up until the moment when André the Giant appeared. Gasps, shrieks, and cheering came from all sections of the room. Yandeng put her hands over her mouth, let out a little scream, and then started to laugh. "Look, look at him!" she was saying. "He's so big!"

The excitement was contagious. Seeing André for the 30th time evoked no emotion, positive or negative, but seeing all these people going crazy was a different story. When André got into a wrestling duel there was rooting and cheering around the room, but then conflict with the storyline of the movie. The crowd was quite disappointed when he lost the match.

"He should have won!" Yandeng lamented out loud. "He could have beaten the best wrestlers in my village."

When the heroes of the film had ridden off into freedom on horseback and the lights came back on, there was a new buzz about the giant. Why did they ask each other if they had seen him? Could they have possibly missed him?  In some ways people here seemed basically the same as people back home in their needs and aspirations.  But in other ways, such as what caught their attention, and how they reacted, was so different that he had to try hard relate to them."

Finally, Jerome approached Yandeng as tea and cookies were served.

"Can I walk you over to the office?"

She gave a conflicted look, began to speak, stopped, and said, "Maybe come over after I leave."

Jerome thought about this response and using the line from the movie answered, "As you wish."

## Chapter 35

He noticed she seemed awkward when he entered the office. He walked over to the desk and noticed it was well organized and clean, yet there was the stack of little odd scraps of paper with scribble on them still stacked to the side of her keyboard. And if he wasn't mistaken, some of them were the same ones he had wrinkled up and thrown into the trash can a week before. As he formulated different questions he could use to broach the subject, she spoke.

"You will make everyone talk about us. Do you want that?" she said matter-of-factly.

"Talk about what? In any case, I don't care what any of them says."

"I don't know what people do in Canada, but here a man does not spend time alone with a woman ... except for, well if he and she..."

"Hold on. First of all, I told you, I'm not Canadian. But, you asked me to help you with copying files. Didn't you?"

"Yes. I know. But if people know we are alone, they will talk. Do you want that?"

"I don't care. Do you?"

"No, but I don't want to get fired."

"Fired? Why would they fire you for working with me in your office after hours?"

"You don't know how it is here."

"How it is here? Look, I don't care how it is. If anyone tries to fire you, they'll have a fight me. I promise it."

This obviously touched Yandeng. Then she said quietly, "Teach me how to make words and files copy each other."

And he did. In far less time than it took to teach the essentials of email, he went through the basics of cutting, pasting, and copying. At about 11 PM when she was satisfied that these amazing functions could be repeated without Jerome's intervention, she turned the computer off. Jerome knew he had gotten back into Yandeng's favor, so he thought he'd take the opportunity to bring up another matter.

"Yandeng, we were surveying south east of here this week. We followed the new dirt road. You must have come in on the same road."

"Yes, I did. It's a wonderful road, isn't it?"

"The road? Yes, I guess it's wonderful. Anyway, we road past, or actually through, a village... But it wasn't a village anymore. It had been destroyed. Burned. Huts were burned ... with people still inside them. Honest. I saw bodies."

Tears welled up in Yandeng's eyes. He realized he had hit a very sensitive nerve. She began to sob softly.

"I'm sorry Yandeng. I shouldn't have brought it up. I'm just trying to understand exactly what happened."

"It is as you said. The village was burned and the people killed or captured or chased away."

"Who did it? And why?"

"The murahaleen."

"The murahaleen? Who are they?"

"Horsemen, from the Bagarra tribe, from the Darfur, from lots of places, along with government troops."

"The government allowed this?"

"They did it. They invited the other tribes to come and help them."

"Help them do what? Burn villages?"

"Help them get rid of the Dinka, and anyone else living on these lands. They want to get rid of us and take our land."

"So that was a Dinka village I saw. Where is your village?"

"I have no more village."

"Was it your village?"

"No."

"How do you know?"

"Our dead were buried, thank God. Did you bury them?"

"Well... no, I ... I mean I probably should have but..."

"It's not your problem. Our people need to do it."

"But your family...what happened to them?"

Yandeng again clammed up and tears came back to her eyes. She started to sob softly, then harder, then sobbed uncontrollably. She hadn't talked about that day for quite some time.

Jerome stood there helpless, wishing he could do something, and especially that he could take back his question. He was at least beginning to understand why their conversations had so many "land-mines." He never wanted to defend a woman more than this simple yet complex, fragile yet incredibly strong, Dinka girl.

"Yandeng, I'm so sorry. I had no idea. Forgive me for asking."

She tried to answer but couldn't. She just kept weeping, her head in her hands. The scene brought back his own memories, sitting in a funeral home, feeling completely and utterly alone in the world. Anyway, he took a chance and stepped up beside Yandeng and put his hand on her shoulder.

"Go ahead and cry. It'll do you good."

She reached her long thin, yet strong arm around and touched his hand with her bony wet fingers, in a show of gratitude for his support.

"You're not alone, Yandeng."

She shook her head in acknowledgement, and her weeping seemed to lessen.

"I lost my family too. It was really hard for me."

She now wrapped her long black fingers around his hand.

"You probably feel like you're all alone in the universe, like your dreams have all been ruined and there is no future."

The sobbing stopped. Her hand stiffened, then pulled away from his. Her voice croaked out, "I do NOT feel like that. I'm NOT all alone in the world. God is close to me. I have a future. Is that what you think Jerome? That you're all alone in the world?"

The moment was gone. The bond that was so evident only seconds ago had disappeared. He was now on the defense. And he found himself in the awkward position of trying to defend himself.

"Well, no, I believe I have a future … and you too. And it is possible there is a god."

"A god! What does that mean? There is only one, the one who created us."

"Yes, sure. I'm sure there is only one."

"Why would you think I feel all alone? He is so close to me. I don't know what I'd do without him. He has saved me lots of times and given me everything that I have!"

How could he be having this conversation? He was on her side. He wasn't the enemy. But, he had done it again. He had somehow turned sweet into bitter. How did he keep doing this?

"Look, Yandeng, I'm sorry. I only meant to make you feel better."

"Make me feel better? Well, saying I must feel like I'm alone in the world does not make me feel better."

"Ok. I said the wrong thing. It just seemed to me that you are down and out and not much has been going your way."

Her mouth dropped and she fell momentarily speechless from anger.

"Oh no!" he thought. "Whatever it is that gets her worked up, I just did again, but worse than usual. I need to figure out what it is I'm doing or saying."

When she finally spoke her voice was steady but icy.

"You think I am down and out. You are talking to me like I am a poor refugee. You have no idea. I am far better off than hundreds, if not thousands, that I have known. I don't know what life is like where you come from, but where I come from I am blessed beyond what I can describe. And you are not going to change my happiness."

Wow! So that was it. They obviously saw the same world in a different light.

"Actually Yandeng, I don't want to change your way of thinking. Honest. I'm just trying to understand what it is that you think."

"Well that is what I think. Hmph!"

Jerome could think of little to say. It was a rare moment.

"Well, anyway, thanks for sharing what you think. I don't think of you as a poor refugee. I think of you as a ..." and then the worst happened. He could think of nothing to say.

"... uh, what I mean is... I don't think of you like that at all, like a ... poor refugee. No, I don't."

Her hard stare was stuck on his face, seeing right through him.

"Ok, well maybe I do think of you that way," he finally blurted out.

"Uh huh!" she exclaimed, triumphantly.

"Well, I mean, I know you've had a hard time. Life must have been difficult living in your village and..."

**163**

"You know nothing of life in my village! Life was quite fine actually, until the day when…" Then she stopped and there was anger and hurt in her voice and Jerome knew he was going in the wrong direction.

"Yandeng, you don't have to talk about it. Look. I'm sorry I brought it up. I need to be going. I'll see you tomorrow."

She didn't put up any argument about his leaving so he quietly closed the door behind him, went back to his room and tried to sleep, but the conversation kept repeating over and over in his mind.

# Chapter 36

The next morning he saw Yandeng leaving the cafeteria as he was coming in. He said hello and she responded very properly,

"Good morning, Jerome." Then she walked quickly away.

People were buzzing in camp because it was change of shift day. Jerome had been there a week already and the next shift was due in today. A few landrovers arrived just before lunch. Most of the people he had worked with met with their incoming counterparts, had lunch, and left. He followed them to the waiting caravan of landrovers and trucks and saw that a small scene was developing. A woman in Arab garb was talking very loudly, almost shouting, at Yandeng. A small crowd had gathered round.

"You can't stay. There is no room for you. Pack your things and get in the truck!"

"No. I was told I could stay here."

"Yes, you can stay every other week. Now you need to leave!"

"No I plan to stay. I will keep working."

The woman then laughed rudely and said, "You have nowhere to go! You have no home."

"That's not true!" Yandeng protested weakly.

"Well, if it's not true, then go home!"

Jerome wanted badly to intervene. He blurted out, "I think there has been a misunderstanding."

All eyes were then on him.

"She was never given instructions about being on a seven-day shift. This is completely unexpected."

Osman joined in.

"So how do you know what she was told Jerome? Are you two intimate?"

There was laughter.

"We discussed it!" he lied, staring Osman defiantly in the face.

"You are the only one on a two week shift, everyone else is one week. She must leave, and now! She's holding us all up. We're in a hurry to leave."

Everyone around shook their heads in agreement and murmured their discontent in the direction of Yandeng. Jerome could see his argument didn't have a leg to stand on.

"OK. Give her a minute to get her things," he said. "Yandeng, let me give you a hand."

More laughter and rude noises arose from the small crowd.

"Make it fast! We're not being paid for our time anymore." Osman ordered.

Jerome signaled to Yandeng to follow him. She did so slowly and reluctantly.

"Do you have anywhere to go?" he asked cautiously, not wanting to start a blow up.

"Yes, and no. God will provide for me. I have no doubt."

"Do you have any money?"

"They haven't paid me yet."

This made Jerome choke up a little. Was she naïve, crazy, thinking that God was on her side? The Sudan didn't seem like it would make the top 100 list of countries you'd want to be homeless in and without money. He knew she didn't have any belongings to collect. He stopped in front of his room and told her to wait just a second. He ran in, found a small sports bag, quickly pulled his wallet out and put all the cash he had in the bag. He figured there was almost $100 worth of Sudanese dinars. He threw in a towel and a bar of soap and quickly returned to her.

"Yandeng, please take this. It should help you until you return. You will return in a week?"

"What is it?"

"Just a bag, with a towel and a few things. Keep it. I don't want it back."

She took the bag, apparently resolved to go without any more fight, turned and walked back to the waiting caravan. Within minutes, all that was left of her was a cloud of red dust, and her picture etched in Jerome's memory.

She didn't find the money until she unpacked the belongings of the bag that night at the church. Gatwech was very happy to see her return although he seemed stressed. More people had arrived and there was almost no room for everyone to lie down at night now. The bread rations barely made it around.

"I don't need to eat much. I have been eating all the time at the camp. I'll have to tell you about the feasts we have had, like being at a wedding every single day. Can you tell I'm getting fat again?" she asked enthusiastically.

"Yes, indeed. You are looking good." Gatwech insisted.

There weren't enough blankets to go around either. She remembered that Jerome had said he had packed her a towel. She could use that to lie down on. That was when she found the money. At first she thought she had the wrong bag. She checked around on the floor. There were no others like this one. And she recognized the towel as being from camp. The soap too was the type issued at camp. But how did the money get here? Did Jerome know it was there? The reality sank in. He had put it there. Why? It looked like a fortune. She tried to count it without anyone seeing her. She kept her hands in the bag and counted. She had never held so much money. She felt nervous. There could possibly be, she thought, as much as 20,000 Sudanese dinars! How did he get so much money? How could she ever repay it? What did he mean when he said, "Keep it, I don't want it back." Was he talking about the money? Well it looked like the money was badly needed now. She wouldn't worry tonight about paying it back. When the time came, she'd find a way to pay it back.

She picked up her bag, held it close, and found Gatwech talking with someone outside the front door where the men sat.

"Can I talk to you for a second?"

"Sure. I was looking for you too. I have something for you." The man speaking with Gatwech gave him a pat on the shoulder and left.

"First, my child, tell me what you have to say, then I'll tell you."

"Ok. I see that you are in need of many things here, food, blankets, clothing."

"It is true, Yandeng. The situation has not gotten better since I last saw you. In fact, there are more here now than a week ago. So many without homes."

"Maybe I can help, at least for the moment."

"I have been praying that God would supply. How can you help?"

She handed the bag to him and said, "Open it and look inside. I think there are 20,000 dinars. They are yours to buy food and blankets, and whatever else is needed."

He slowly took the bag while looking into Yandeng's eyes. He unzipped it and looked inside. He reached in and like Yandeng did not wish to count such an amount of cash in the open, and thumbed through it.

"So it's true. The oil companies pay well."

"Well I hope so. But this isn't my pay. It was a … well sort of a gift."

"A gift?" Gatwech whistled. "20,000 dinars? That's quite a gift!"

"Well you see, I haven't been paid yet," Yandeng quickly interjected, trying to divert the conversation. "But, I plan to pay this money back, every dinar."

"Yandeng, this is a lot of money. I can't take it from you."

"No, but I can give it to you!" she said quickly.

Gatwech scrutinized her. He knew her well enough to see that she had made up her mind and she could be a very determined young woman.

"I will accept this on behalf of the church and everyone housed here, but on one condition."

"What is that?"

"That the first thing I buy with this money is a new dress for you. Something more Dinka," he said and he winked at her.

She looked at her dress and then laughed. Yes, he was right. She had worn the same Muslim taub for months, that was now worn, dirty, and most of all reminded her of her experience at the government camp. How glad she would be to be rid of the dress.

"Agreed, Gatwech! First thing tomorrow we will go shopping." They laughed and shook hands.

"Oh, you said you had something to give me. What is it?"

"Yes, just a number and a note. It was brought here the day after you left, by a Nuer woman. Her name was Ajak. She said if I ever saw you again, and I didn't know if I would, to give this to you."

He opened his Bible and pulled out a small piece of paper he had tucked away inside it. She took it, and in the dim light strained to read it. It said:

*Miriam, this is the name and phone number of a Bagarra that may have news of your sister. Ali - 824-992-561. God bless.*
*Ajak*

Yandeng stared at the note for a long time. The note evoked the worst memories of her life, yet it also gave new hope. Was her sister still alive? If so, would it be possible to locate her and buy her freedom? The possibility caused her to go deep in thought, praying that God would intervene in these plans and give them success.

"Is it good news?"

Gatwech startled her from her thoughts.

"Oh yes, very good news. It is the phone number of a man who may have information about my sister."

"But I thought she was taken up north as a slave."

"She was. At least I assume she was. Anyway, he's a Bagarra, and it was the Bagarra who took her."

"And he knows of her?"

"I don't know. But if anyone knows, it would be a Bagarra."

"Well child, I hope you aren't taken advantage of."

"I know I can't trust someone like this. But what else can I do? I have to try. She is my only sister. I need to try to find my brother too. I can't understand why he never found me at the government camp. If he had come looking for me he would have checked there."

"Hmm. I know people are putting up notices at the post office, trying to reconnect with loved ones."

"Really? Well tomorrow we have two important things to do then."

## Chapter 37

Jerome spent his first afternoon with the new team trying to act interested. They wanted to find out more about him but his mind wasn't on conversation. His mind was on Yandeng.

"Yes, of course I like it here in the Sudan."

Was she going to try to go back to her burned out village? Did she have any friends anywhere? Not having a home or family or friends, boy does that sound familiar. Maybe she's more like me than anyone I know.

"Yes we had a good survey trip."

But then again, I sure don't understand her. I can get her madder than a hornet just by saying the most caring, thoughtful things.

"Yes, yes. I'm listening. Sure, I'm ready to go out surveying again."

She's not the prettiest girl I've known. She's so skinny. Yet she's certainly attractive. There's no one I'd rather be looking at right now. She seems to glow. I know I'm not imagining it. She looks like she has a light bulb under her skin and she glows. I've never seen anyone glow before.

"No, I like living out on the road. No, I'm not rich and didn't grow up in a mansion."

I'm not in love. No way. This would just never work. We're almost from different planets. Why can't I get her out of my mind?

"Well, I think we could be ready to leave tomorrow if we work hard today. We have to pack and do maintenance on the machinery. There's a lot to prepare before we can leave."

I wish there was some way I could help her. She seems to think God is taking care of her. That's the real kicker! Her village is burned out. She loses her family and is forced to flee homeless and half starved, and she believes God has her back! Man, she sure is a "Cup is half full" type of person, even when her cup is mostly empty. Guadalupe had that same way about her.

"Osman? Yes, he's a good guy. Sure we got along OK."

I like her. It's a fact. I really like her.

"OK then! Let's get started. You two, start the pre-trip maintenance checklist on the vibrator buggies. Don't assume the other team did anything. And you two, run through the inspection on all the equipment in the reader truck."

The afternoon was busy and disorganized. Maybe it was just the way he felt, like he was being pulled in two directions. He thought continually about Yandeng while being pulled from one half-finished task to another.

The following day they left on another survey trip. They picked up where the previous trip had finished, cutting another swath in the map about 4 miles long every day. They worked for almost a week and returned to camp in time to unpack the trucks before the turnaround meeting. There would be the usual one-hour overlap when both shifts were present to hand off vital information as best they could in hurried discussions before leaving in a caravan of vehicles creating a cloud of red dust all the way to Bentiu. Having finished his two-week rotation, he would fly up to Khartoum on the bi-weekly flight with Mikhail the following day. He'd at least have almost a day to see Yandeng, if she indeed returned. What he wouldn't give to have news of her.

The caravan arrived at about noon, in time for lunch. Jerome stood near the office, waiting to see if Yandeng was with the crowd of people climbing out of the dusty landrovers. There was the usual whooping and hollering that the sub-Saharan Africans were fond of. The Arabs also greeted their counterparts, but in a much more reserved manner. Osman spotted Jerome and walked over.

"Salaamu alaik, ya Jerome," he mechanically spouted off.

"And peace upon you," answered Jerome equally unenthusiastically. He had so looked forward to seeing Yandeng that he forgot that the new shift also brought Osman with it.

"What are you standing here for?"

It was uncanny. Jerome wondered if he could read his mind.

"Just waiting for the dust to clear."

"Yes, of course. Well, you need to call your team together and make sure there is a good handoff before the other shift leaves. That's what it means to be in charge."

"Thank you Osman. I was about to call everyone together."

Osman turned and walked back towards the crowd. Jerome almost didn't notice that a young woman had walked in his direction towards the office. He had been looking for a thin girl in a black taub with a head scarf. But up walked a thin beautiful African girl, with her hair in braids and beads and a colorful purple African dress, with bare arms and legs showing. She was much thinner than he had remembered, but she glowed, absolutely, he could see it. She seemed to float as graceful as a gazelle. She was carrying the bag he had given her. This was a good sign.

"Yandeng, you look… great. I like the hair that way. Nice, really nice. And what happened to your black dress? I hardly recognize you."

"Jerome, you left something in your bag."

"Oh that. It wasn't much. I didn't know if you had any … well, money."

She studied his face.

"What? Why are you looking at me like that?"

She didn't seem to have words to speak. He wondered if he was about to see the "look" and he braced himself for a tongue-lashing. She approached him, slowly and stood right beside him. She leaned forward like she wanted to hug him, but just touched his hand and said, "Thank you Jerome. I'll never forget."

He wanted to answer, but could not find words. He was still trying to find words to answer after she shut the office door behind her when he heard his name being called. It was Osman. Had he been watching them? He walked over in Osman's direction and before Osman could have the pleasure of giving him another order Jerome raised his voice and hollered, "Hey team, let's get together in a group over here and have a quick meeting before lunch."

He gave brief, yet authoritative instructions about what they needed to do in the next hour, beginning with sitting together at lunch with their counterpart. They could socialize while exchanging information, an idea that seemed odd, yet was apparently accepted. Men began pairing up and heading into the cafeteria. Osman gave him a look that said, "OK, maybe you look good for the moment, but I'm watching you." Then he approached and said with a smile that was definitely contrived, "Will you take your own advice and sit with me? You need to fill me in as I'll be in charge this week."

"Of course, I want to make sure you're up to speed. We made a lot of progress while you were gone."

Yandeng was late to lunch. Jerome kept looking in the direction of the door to see if she'd show up. She finally came in about the time the men were heading over to the equipment area. Jerome was not planning on trying to talk to her, although he was dying to know where she'd been and what she'd done. She walked past him on her way to the food line and stopped and asked, "Jerome, are you going to Khartoum tomorrow?"

"Yes. I plan to. I'll be going back on the company plane. It's due before lunch tomorrow."

"I see…" she said. He could see there was something on her mind.

"Do you need something in Khartoum?" he offered.

She seemed very relieved that he asked.

"Yes. Well maybe yes. Or, I hope so… Can I talk to you later?"

"Sure. Tonight after work, I'll come over to the office."

"Ok. Thanks Jerome," she said, sounding very relieved and marched over to get some lunch before the food was taken away.

Jerome turned to leave and caught Osman with a smirk on his face. He had caught every word and seemed to be amused and disapproving at the same time. But why care? She had asked for help again, which gave him a chance to spend more time with her. What could she possibly need in Khartoum?

That night at dinner Jerome sat with the men. There was talk of new movies that people had brought back with them from home. There were 3 Bollywood movies. Jerome had only seen a few Indian movies and they all seemed identical in plot and script. Poor boy meets rich girl or rich boy meets poor girl, they want to marry but face social resentment and family antagonism. There is a lot of singing, choreographed dancing and a corny but happy ending, but without the final kiss. Strange that Indian movies would not show kissing. But anyway, he hoped Yandeng would head to the office as soon as dinner ended. No. She was enthralled with the movie. She even seemed to have tears in her eyes and even laughed at the funny parts, which frankly, were far from funny. Oh well, it wasn't that late. People finally started leaving at about 8:30. He left the dining hall five minutes after her, under the ever watchful eye of Osman.

**173**

## By Their Fruit

He found her at her desk, rearranging things.
"So, what's up?"

## Chapter 38

Yandeng was staring at one of her scraps of paper. In fact, there again by her desk was her ever-present stack of paper scraps. Curiosity got the best of Jerome.

"Yandeng, why do you keep this stack of paper scraps beside your desk? What is it?"

"It's my work notes."

"Ok... but why on little scraps?"

"What do you mean?"

"Well, why not write them in a tablet, or in a notebook?"

"Why would I do that?" she answered accusingly.

"Well... why not? I do. A lot of people do."

"Well that's not my problem."

"What problem?"

"Exactly! There is no problem."

Jerome didn't know if they were in fact agreeing or disagreeing.

"My question is why you don't use a notebook."

"We Dinka don't waste things, important things, like water, or food, or paper."

"I see. But Yandeng, we have lots of paper here. You can take a whole notebook and use a whole sheet instead of a little scrap if you want."

She looked Jerome square in the face and said, "I've never done it like that. I don't waste paper."

He could tell the discussion was over.

"... Ok, so what was it that you needed in Khartoum? By the way, I like your dress. Do you need more clothes?"

"No I don't need new clothes. And if I did, I wouldn't need someone to go to Khartoum to get them. If you really liked my dress, you wouldn't ask if I needed a new one from Khartoum!"

"I'm sorry." Then he decided to just be quiet and wait.

"Jerome, I have a sister."

"You had mentioned that. I sometimes wish I had a sister."

She continued as if he hadn't even spoken.

**175**

"When the murahaleen took our village they killed most of the people. But some of the women and children they tied together and marched away north. My sister was with them. Some died during the long march, some were killed. But some survived. Those who survived were probably sold as a slave to rich people in Khartoum and other places. I have a phone number of a Bagarra. He lives in Khartoum. I spoke with him today when I got back. He said he might be able to find out where my sister is if she survived, and might be able to help me find her, but he wants money first. A lot of it."

Jerome was shocked speechless.

"Are you sure?" was all he could say.

"Sure? I'm not sure about anything. But I have no choice. He's the only one I know who says he might be able to help. I have to try."

"But slaves? Yandeng are you sure there are slaves in the Sudan? I mean, wouldn't the government stop it?"

Now Yandeng was speechless. First she just sputtered. Then she said very clearly, "Jerome, you are one of the smartest men I've ever met. Yet you are also the most stupid. How can that be?"

"Stupid? Why do you think I'm stupid?"

"How can you question whether there are slaves in the Sudan? That is stupid!"

"Well if there are, why would the government allow it to take place?"

"Jerome, people from the north have been taking slaves from the south forever. And this time it was the government who invited others to do it."

"Wow! Well if that is the case, then you are negotiating with someone who may himself be involved in the slave trade!"

"Of course I am. Why would I want to negotiate with him if he weren't? If she is alive, she is a slave."

About the only times in his life Jerome could ever remember losing arguments were in conversations with Yandeng. Yet he didn't dislike her for it.

"I need your help Jerome. I need a favor and I have no one else to ask."

He'd always remember the words that came out of his mouth next.

"Anything! Ask me anything Yandeng."

The tension in her face eased and her body relaxed.

"Thank you so much Jerome. You are my friend."

She sat back at her desk and started writing on a small scrap of paper with no further explanation.

"Well, what is it? What do you want me to do for you?"

"I want you to meet with this Bagarra in Khartoum and find my sister."

"… Ok, but…."

"Well, what's the matter?"

"Hmm. This Bagarra, can he be trusted?"

"Of course not!"

"Could he be dangerous?"

"Sure."

"You don't see a problem with that?"

"Sure I do. Don't you?"

He was at least relieved that they agreed he'd be dealing with a potentially dangerous slave trader.

"Well how do I find Mr. Bagarra?"

"He has a phone that he carries in his pocket. It is like your walkie-talkie that you use on seismic surveys, but it is a telephone. I've seen them before. They're no bigger than your fist and …"

"OK. He has a cell phone."

"Yes. I have written the number for this phone on this piece of paper."

Then she handed him a second piece of paper and said, "And this is his name."

In Arabic it said "Ali."

"You say he probably wants a fortune. What are your plans? How do we pay him?"

"I need to ask another favor."

Jerome braced himself. "OK. Ask."

"Can I pay you back? I haven't been paid yet. But, I will pay you back."

"Great. I appreciate that," he said, realizing that she'd never in 10 lifetimes be able to pay the kinds of ransoms he'd heard kidnappers asked.

"But Yandeng, how much is he asking?"

"He said he wants 5000 dinars now and another 5000 when he finds her."

Jerome did the math. 10,000 dinars amounted to about $50.

"That can't be right. Are you sure he said 5000 dinars?"

"I'm sure. I asked him twice and begged him to lower the price, but he wouldn't."

"But that is an insulting amount of money!"

"You're right. That is why he can afford a phone that he carries in his pocket. But I will pay it, every dinar."

Tears were coming to her eyes and her lip was quivering.

"Ok, listen, the money is not a problem. I thought he'd be asking 1000 times that much. 5000 dinars we can handle. But can he find your sister?"

She tried to speak but couldn't.

"I know. You're not sure. That's Ok. I'll contact this guy and see what we can do. Give me all the information you have. His name, number, your sister's name, photo, anything you have."

In the end he received a scrap of paper that said:

*Ali 824-992-561*
*Alual Nyeal*
*28 May, 2000*
*Palwung, Mayom County*

"What's the date?" Jerome asked.

"The day they took her."

Jerome took a notebook out of his backpack and copied the information, although he didn't think he could now forget it.

"Can you keep me informed?"

"Of course. Stay close to your email. Oh, one other thing. Let me take your picture."

"Why?" Yandeng asked.

"In case I need to show it to anyone."

He pulled out his digital camera and told her to smile. She gave her big contagious smile that seemed so magnetic. It was a smile that was truly happy. It expressed real joy and made him want to be part of it. When she wasn't angry, she did seem to be truly happy.

"OK, now one of both of us."

"Hmm. Why is that?" she said with a mischievous grin.

"In case I need to prove I know you."

He set the camera on a chair, moved Yandeng back while looking in the LCD screen, then said, "Perfect. Don't move."

He clicked the button, then ran to Yandeng's side. He put his arm around her, which she didn't seem to mind. Then he heard the shutter click and reluctantly removed his arm.

"Did it take a picture? Show me my picture! I thought there had to be a flash of light to take pictures. Are you sure there is a picture?"

"Let me show you."

Jerome then totally amazed Yandeng as he downloaded the pictures to her computer. She stared at them laughing.

"When was the last time you had your picture taken?"

"When I was a girl. A white person, who taught us English, took a picture of our class. It made a flash, and the picture came right out of the camera."

"Must have been a Polaroid."

"If I get a camera, I will get a 'Poler' one."

"But digital cameras are better."

"No, the picture doesn't come right out of the camera like with the poler ones."

"Sure it does. Just in a different way. You saw that I downloaded it to a computer and now you're looking at it."

"Yes, but with a poler camera I don't need a computer, just a camera. And I like the bright flash. It's better."

He doubted they were even made anymore but he wanted to keep the pleasant atmosphere.

"Ok. I hope you get a poler camera one day. Anyway, I'll leave tomorrow as soon as the plane from Khartoum arrives. Should be before lunch. So I should be in Khartoum by early afternoon. When is he expecting a call?"

"Call him as soon as you can."

"Ok. Why not call him now?"

"No! He told me not to keep calling. He said 'Don't call until you get to Khartoum.'"

"Ok. I will. I promise."

Yandeng looked very appreciative. She looked like she wanted to hug him or something. In the end she held out both her hands, took his and squeezed them.

He felt honored to have won her respect, yet he was fearful. Dealing with a slave trader in a foreign country for the life of Yandeng's dear sister put him in a precarious situation in general, and with her in particular. What if he failed?

# Chapter 39

Jerome landed in Khartoum in the early afternoon. He visited the office and found Abdelkader who had left Mikhail a message saying he needed to see Jerome.

"Ettfaddel ya Jerome!" he said, motioning with his hand for Jerome to have a seat in a wooden chair on a carpet in front of his desk. Jerome sat down.

"We took some good readings down there Abdelkader. I bet the geophysicists are salivating. From what I saw, there's enough oil for a long time waiting for us at about 5000 feet."

"Yes, yes. Lots of oil. In fact, the reason I wanted to talk to you was another subject."

Jerome had suspected what was coming.

"About our conversation a few weeks back…"

Jerome played dumb.

"Which conversation, AbdelKader?"

He gave Jerome a hard, penetrating stare.

"About the … unfortunate discovery you were contemplating taking photos of."

"Oh, the burned village."

"Yes, that. I was wondering if any further discussion is needed."

"No. I don't believe so."

"I just want to ensure that this delicate matter is left at rest. It is after all a matter for others and not ourselves."

"I understand."

"But, what I want to know is whether any of what you have seen has been communicated outside of the camp? We like to manage any information that might not be seen in the best light."

Jerome was liking this conversation less and less.

"Abdelkader, I'm not trying to make Tallman look bad. If, as you say, we had nothing to do with it, what harm is there in bringing it to light?"

"Perception!" Abdelkader snapped. "It has to do with how others perceive us. It doesn't matter what happened. What is important is what people may think happened. If you have a daughter and she is raped and becomes pregnant, would you publicize this fact?"

Jerome saw no connection from this example to the present conversation.

"Abdelkader, those people, or those bodies, I saw, had been brutally murdered. And they hadn't even been given a mass burial. Their village was destroyed, and from what I've heard some of the villagers were even taken away as slaves. Is it right to turn a blind eye and pretend it didn't happen? No, I wouldn't publicize my daughter's pregnancy, but I'd sure try to find who raped her and see justice done."

"You're either not listening, or you're slow to understand! What you saw is very different from what you think you saw. There was an uprising of rebels that needed to be stopped. Nothing more. And this idea of slaves is a vicious rumor of people trying to discredit our government."

"That's interesting because I never said it was the government who took the slaves."

"Enough Jerome. This conversation is over. I never want to have to bring it up again. And if any pictures or stories of this get out beyond our camp, you will be considered to be working against us. You will be biting the hand that feeds you. Understood?"

"Yes," Jerome gritted through his teeth.

Jerome walked back to the apartment, and although he had never had the experience in person, he felt like a small boy who had just left the principal's office after a lecture and a spanking. His mission to make contact with Ali the slave trader and find Yandeng's sister was now even more delicate than ever.

Jerome decided to try to call Ali on Skype via his computer. It couldn't be traced that way. He logged on, keyed in Ali's number and clicked the call button on the screen. He heard the phone ring and then a short message and a beep. Unsure of what to say, he hesitated, then hung up. What kind of message do you leave in a case like this? "Ali, I'm the money guy and want you to buy a slave for me?" After some minutes of thought and deliberation he wrote down in Arabic what he wanted to say. He then clicked on the number, now in his saved list, and clicked the dial button again. This time Ali answered. "Ay, na'am (Yes)."

Jerome hesitated again.

"Na'am?"

Jerome decided to deliver his message as written.

"Na'am ya sidi. Yes sir, you received a call from a friend, a Miss Yandeng Nyeal, concerning her sister.

There was now hesitation on the other end.

"Who are you?"

"I am a friend of Miss Nyeal. I am in Khartoum and would like to meet you to discuss her matter with you."

"OK. Are you a foreigner? You don't sound like you are from here."

"Yes. I am from America."

There was a long pause.

"America?"

"Yes, Mr. Ali, America."

"Well now, that could be problematic."

"Problematic? Why?"

"Well these matters are very delicate and require local sensitivities. Dealing with outsiders, well that is out of the question."

"Wait. What are you talking about? You told her you would help her. She said she would send someone to Khartoum. She sent me."

After another long pause he spoke.

"Well sir, you will understand that the previous arrangement that may have been agreed with the young lady would have to be renegotiated in light of the new circumstances."

"But that is dishonest! You made an agreement."

"That's Ok. I'm dishonest. You can find someone else."

There was a click on the other end and Jerome saw on his screen that the call had ended.

"No! What do I do now?"

He considered trying to find someone local to help him but the only locals he knew worked at the office. Involving any of them was out of the question. He could ask Mikhail, a man of the world certainly, who would be a tough negotiator, but it was again risky to involve anyone at Tallman. And, would a Russian be accepted any better than an American?"

**183**

Jerome chose the number again and clicked the call button. Ali let the phone ring 5 times then answered, "Na'am."

"Ali, let's say I was interested in renegotiating. How much would the new price be?"

"Let's not talk like that. We're talking about families and lives. They are worth far more than money."

"Very true Ali. How much more?"

"I can't think of costs. I am thinking of trying to reunite loved ones, and the risk of having an American seen with me. I could maybe take all these risks, but at what cost personally?"

Jerome decided to join in with his own hyperbole.

"Ali, you will not recognize me as an American. I am dark and many mistake me for Sudanese."

"Really! Well there are many other risks you know. My work is dangerous. Many would like to stop me from finding and freeing these poor people. My enemies lurk everywhere."

Jerome didn't laugh, although there was a temptation to do so.

"Ok Ali. Tell me, how much will it cost for you to help me out?"

"In dinars or American dollars?" There seemed a glint of expectation in his voice.

Jerome knew he was already in trouble and if he mentioned dollars, he'd be classed in a different category.

"Oh dinars! I don't have dollars. You see I live in the Sudan. When I said I was American, it's that my parents were born there. I live here."

"Uh huh."

Jerome wasn't sure by the tone if he bought it, but he could tell there was some quick readjustment of thinking going on.

"Well, Mr. American, and what is your name?"

Jerome thought quickly and said, "Yusef." He knew this was an Arab name but was also used by non-Arabs.

"Well Mr. Yusef, my services for any preliminary investigations will be only slightly higher than mentioned earlier. Let's say an extra 5000 dinars."

"But you were asking for 5000 dinars. You are doubling the price!"

"My work is difficult and dangerous. I am an artist at what I do. If you don't want my services, well… wait one second, I have another call."

Jerome waited a full 5 minutes and realized he was being played with. He disconnected and sat and thought for a long time. He really didn't have a choice. How many slave traders did he know? And still, the opening price was just $50. If this was a complete fraud, he wouldn't lose a fortune. If he could find her, he certainly wouldn't think twice about paying far larger amounts. He decided though to let Mr. Ali sit tight for a while and try not to let him know that he felt desperate. He fought with himself to set a target to wait until the next morning at 9 AM to call Ali back. He found Mikhail and went out for dinner.

At dinner Mikhail asked him what he'd do with his one-week leave. Jerome actually wasn't at all sure beyond the immediate project of negotiating with someone to buy back the enslaved sister of a girl he was beginning to think a lot about. He of course didn't want to mention this to Mikhail, so he said he had no plans. This sparked a reaction from Mikhail.

"Get a woman, travel, go to Egypt, Dubai, have fun. You're young!"

"Sure, sure. Maybe I will another time. I think I'll just get to know Khartoum this time."

"Khartoum is shit!"

Jerome wondered whether Russians were able to converse in English without this expletive.

"Well, I've never really seen it. So, it will be nice to look around."

It was true. He was beginning to wonder what in the world he'd find to do in Khartoum for 6 days. After dinner he watched TV, or what there was of it. 1 channel of government sponsored programming, such as Koranic reading, censored news, and speeches of the president, a friendly looking man who did such harsh and hateful things it seemed incongruous.

# Chapter 40

The next morning at 9 AM, Jerome had Skype open and was clicking the call button. Ali answered after 3 rings.

"Ay, na'am."

"Ali, it's me."

"Who?"

Jerome tried to remember the name he had given Ali but couldn't remember.

"We spoke last night."

"Ah, Mr. Yusef."

"I don't think we finished our discussion."

"You hung up."

"No Ali. I think you hung up."

"Of course I didn't."

"In any case, I thought about your offer of 10,000 dinars. It would be difficult for me to find that much money right now. I can give you 7,500 and the remaining 2,500 when you deliver the girl."

"Oh no, I don't like this. You are changing the price on me. I thought we had agreed on 10,000, and that was a very special price."

"No, Ali, we hadn't agreed. As I say, I can pay you 10,000, but only 7,500 now."

"Impossible. My work is difficult. I need time and money to do my job well. I'll accept 9,000 now and another 9,000 when I deliver."

"Hmmm. If I pay you, when will you deliver the girl?"

"It depends how long it takes me to find her. These things can take time."

"What do you mean by 'finding her.' Wasn't it your people sold her into slavery to start with?"

"You're insulting me. I don't know who did this. I only help to free them from their unfortunate situations."

He was sharp and almost shouting. Jerome was afraid he might hang up again.

"Ok, Ok. Look, what kind of guarantee do I have that you will find her?"

"There is no guarantee. I can only promise you I will try."

Jerome was feeling worse and worse about the whole deal. He wanted so much to just hang up and forget it, but he remembered Yandeng's face and how thankful and hopeful she was. He figured he could waste $45 to stay on her good side. After all, a date with a girl in America was easily that much. This was a far cry from a date though, even though he was only doing it because he liked her and wanted her to like him. And, as an added bonus, this guy might actually find her sister. Who knew?

"Well Mr. Yusef, what is your decision. I am a busy man."

"Ok Mr. Ali, agreed. I will pay you 9000 dinars to find the girl, and then 5000 more when you find her."

"Mr. Yusef, I thought you understood, I need another 9000 when I find her."

Jerome started to argue, but then thought to himself, "If he ever finds her, I'd pay 10 times the price."

"Ok Mr. Ali. Ok. Find the girl please."

"When will you pay me? I need to get started and need the money now."

"Ok. Where do we meet?"

"Are you really dark? I don't want to be seen talking to a white man. It attracts attention."

"I'm … well, don't worry about it."

"I was afraid of that… Let's meet at the Café Suez. Do you know it? There are a lot of foreigners there."

"I'll find it. When do you want to meet?"

"Tomorrow morning at 10."

"How will I find you?"

"Do you know the Sharq el Awsat newspaper?"

"The one printed on green paper? Yes. Why?"

"Buy one and sit alone. I will find you."

"Ok."

"Don't be late!"

The screen showed that the call had ended. Jerome sat a little dazed. It seemed to have gone well, although where it would lead was anyone's guess. Then he remembered he had no more cash. Oh well, he'd stop at the bank, use the ATM machine, one of the few in the city, and make a withdrawal. He'd also need to find the Café

Suez. He went next door and knocked on Mikhail's door. He came to the door with a drink in his hand. By the smell on his breath, he'd already put down a couple.

"Sorry Mikhail, just a quick question, do you know the Café Suez?"

"Sure, don't you? It's across the street from the office. Haven't you seen it before?"

"Oh… Sure. Dumb me… Thanks."

He turned and hurried back to his room and shut it about the time he heard Mikhail asking loudly, "Why? When are you going there?"

But he didn't feel like talking, and especially not about this subject. Oh well. He'd have to hope for the best. He emailed Yandeng and said, "Meeting Ali tomorrow morning at 10. He raised the price, but it's Ok. I will send news when I have more."

Then he went to bed.

The next day he was out the door of the apartment by eight and went to the bank. He saw the ATM machine by the front door, put in his card and PIN and got a message. "Card refused. See bank for more details."

The sign on the door said hours were 9 AM – 4 PM. Ok, so it was a bank. He'd wait. He walked by the café and saw some clientele but no one sitting alone. He wondered if Ali would be there with someone else.

At nine o'clock he was standing at the bank's front door which was still locked. He saw someone inside. He knocked on the window. The person inside motioned for him to go away. He assumed he was saying that the bank was closed. Jerome pointed to the sign on the front door. The person again motioned him away. Jerome had no option but to wait. At 9:12 the man inside came and unlocked the door with a very stern and bothered expression on his face.

"I'm sorry," Jerome said very unapologetically, "I thought the bank opened at 9 AM."

Equally unapologetically the man answered, "Young man, the bank is open. What is your business?"

Jerome decided not to argue. He needed all his senses and abilities for this one. Within the hour he hoped to be meeting with a middleman to buy a human being out of slavery.

"You're right, sir. I must have arrived early. My business is that I need a little cash. The ATM machine refused my card and gave me a message to see someone for details. So, I'm sure you must be able to solve this problem."

There he had turned a negative to a positive.

"Let me see your card."

"Sure. Here it is," Jerome said handing him the card.

"Well, that's the problem."

"What?"

"It's issued by a foreign bank."

"Is that a problem?"

"I just said it was a problem."

"I see. I'm sure you can help though, right?"

Jerome could see the battle going on in the man's mind. Finally, he said, "Yes, give me a minute. I'll run the card from in here. You'll have to sign for it though and we charge a fee, 100 dinars."

Jerome chuckled to himself because the fee amounted to about 50 cents which was undoubtedly less than the fee for using the machine.

"Yes sir. Of course."

"How much money do you need?"

"Jerome knew he needed money for Ali, and he'd better have cash on hand if Ali called him with news, and he needed to have cash on hand anyway, so he figured he'd need about 400 dollars' worth of dinars.

"I'd like about 80,000 dinars."

The man whistled and looked Jerome up and down.

"80,000 dinars! What does a young man need with 80,000 dinars?"

"Oh, I need it just in case… You never know when you'll need money. You can do so much with it, you know?"

He continued shaking his head and clicking his tongue disapprovingly.

"Why it takes me months to earn 80,000 dinars, young man, and I support a family of 6!"

"Yes, but that's different. You're local. I'm a foreigner. You see when I buy things, people charge me 2 or 3 times as much as you, so I spend it quicker."

Jerome saw he had stumped him with this answer, and it somehow also seemed to put him in his good graces.

"Young man, I know what you're talking about. There are many dishonest people out there. But don't let them cheat you. If you ever need someone to bargain for you, come and see me. I know the value of money. I will help you."

Jerome was touched by his change of tone. He was also feeling a sense of urgency.

"Thank you so much sir. Actually, there is a merchant waiting to see me at 10 AM. He is overcharging me, yet he says that if I am not there at 10 he won't do business with me at all. Imagine!"

"May God help you! I will hurry."

He returned in 5 minutes with papers to sign, then disappeared again, this time with the card. By this time, others were arriving at the bank and were now in line behind Jerome. When the man came out and saw other customers present he did a dead stop, turned around and disappeared again. He then returned and asked Jerome to follow him into a back room.

"I don't want to give you this much money in front of strangers. You know, just to be safe."

He counted out 79,900 dinars.

"I have deducted the 100 dinars for the withdrawal fee," he announced.

Jerome handed him another 100 dinars.

"Here, this is for your quick work."

"Oh, you don't need to," he said as he pocketed the money.

"I appreciate the way you do business," Jerome said honestly, and knew he now had a friend at the bank. "And by the way, could you do something so that the next time I can use your ATM machine?"

They shook hands and Jerome left in a hurry.

# Chapter 41

On the way to Café Suez, Jerome found a news stand and bought a *Sharq al Awsat* newspaper, probably the only green newspaper in the world. By 9:50 AM he was seated in the back of the café surrounded by empty tables, away from the street where office colleagues might notice him. He ordered a coffee and pulled out the cash he had just withdrawn, holding it under the table where no one could see it. He counted out 9,000 dinars and put them in his right pocket. The rest he wrapped in a piece of the newspaper and tucked it down into his pants. He then tried to read Al Sharq al Awsat newspaper. Classical Arabic was more difficult than the spoken dialect, and very different. It seemed odd that a society could have a written language that was so different from the spoken language. He could understand some of the headlines but not the details.

His coffee came. It was 10:03. He drank it slowly. At 10:15 he ordered another. It came at 10:20. He let it sit. At 10:25 he was wondering if he had been stood up, when a man in a white jellabia robe and sunglasses sat down 2 tables away. He looked as weathered as the desert itself. In his leathery hand he carried a cell phone and when he sat down and put his elbows on the table, his loose white sleeves gave way to a very expensive glittering watch, somehow looking out of place on his bronzed and bony wrist. Jerome looked back at his paper wondering if this could be Ali.

"Ismik Yusuf?" his coarse voice croaked, trying to talk softly.

"Yes, I'm Yusuf. And you are Ali."

Ali's hard face put on a big smile which somehow also looked out of place. It was not a face that looked like it smiled much. Three gold teeth glittered for just a second, then the smile disappeared.

"I see you are alone."

"Yes."

"I also see you are as white as snow. I am glad we met here."

"I'm not that white," Jerome protested.

"No bother. But what is a white man doing buying an abida? I dedicate my tireless work to freeing people. Are you now going to undo my hard work?"

"Do you mean that I'm buying her for a… Absolutely not! I told you, I'm helping her sister. Her sister cannot make it to Khartoum. How else could I get the name and date she was taken if I didn't know her?!"

Ali looked satisfied that he had returned Jerome's insult of him being a slave trader.

"Do you have what I asked you to bring?"

"Of course. 9,000 dinars. Here it is."

"Don't take it out you fool. Besides, I looked over my expenses and I'm going to have to ask you for 11,000 dinars."

"But I went to the bank and got 9,000."

"Look at you. You are a white American. You are rich. What is 2,000 dinars to you? We are poor in the Sudan. So anyway, the price has gone up to 11,000."

Jerome was furious. What should he do? He felt like he could almost take this guy in a fight. But that wouldn't solve the problem. Should he walk away? Should he bargain? He felt like the longer this dragged on the more it would cost him.

"Wait a few minutes," Jerome said, and went to the restroom. It was a dark little Turkish toilet stall that reeked of human filth. He transferred money around and returned to the table. Ali was contentedly sipping a bottle of Perrier like he didn't have a care in the world.

"Ok! I found some extra," Jerome snapped.

"Shh. Quiet Yusef! Keep our business to ourselves. Now go back to the toilet, wrap the money in your newspaper and leave it on the table beside me."

Jerome fought back all urges to attack this vendor of human souls. He returned to the foul stall, wrapped the 11,000 dinars in the paper and then walked passed Ali, laid the paper on the table beside him and said, "I'll be calling you, Ali." He then paid for his 2 coffees and left.

Many emotions flooded his senses. Outrage at Ali surfaced first. Then came the regretful feeling that he had just thrown good money into the wind. But then came the thought that maybe, just maybe, he had done one of the most significant acts of his entire life and that he was directly involved with changing the life of a young woman he had never met. He let this thought linger. He thought about Yandeng. He thought about her faith. Then he made a very emotional and spontaneous decision. One that he had never made before. He decided to pray.

"God, I don't really know if you exist or if you do are you even listening and do you care... Well, if you really are God, you must care... so, uh, I know we've never spoken before, but I'd like to ask if you could help us, or her, or I guess even Ali, if you help people like him. I don't think I need to give you the details because, like I was saying, if you are God, you heard the whole conversation." He didn't know if he needed to say amen, but he didn't even know why he had decided to pray either. So he decided not to say amen. "Hmmm. Do you need me to say amen when I'm finished? I think you know I was finished. Right?" Funny, it felt cathartic to talk to God, even if he was completely out of his depth. Yandeng prayed, he knew. "I wonder how she prays, or if she says 'amen'?"

That gave him the idea to return to his room and email Yandeng. He wished he could see her face when she got the news. She was so hopeful. He wished he were more hopeful.

He opened his email and wrote Yandeng a quick note:

"I just met Ali. He..." Jerome didn't know if he should mention what a complete thief Ali seemed. This might cause Yandeng to be discouraged. He decided not to paint him as he was, but just to tell the facts.

"... negotiated for more money. He says his work is dangerous. Don't worry about the money. Your sister is all that matters here. I prayed that Ali will come through. I don't pray often. I'll keep in touch with Ali by phone. I'll keep in touch with God by private conversations. I'll contact you by email. Take care.

Jerome"

He then also emailed Herb. He hadn't communicated with Herb about what he had seen at the burned out village for fear of being discovered. He now decided to tell him everything, the burned out village, the recently charred bodies he had come across within their survey blocks, and the reaction of Osman and AbdelKader. He knew it was significant that the village was located within their blocks. The blocks were sectors of land that Tallman had paid good money to the Sudanese government for the right to survey, drill, and pump oil out of. The government of course would get their cut of anything pumped. The fact that the government had "cleared" the land for them before they started exploration as a favor made him feel implicated in what they had done. He told Herb as much. He also told Herb about Yandeng and her sister, and that he had just met with a "real live trader of human souls, who for the sum of $55 dollars, and an inflated foreign rate at that, claimed he could find a slave as long as he knew the slave's name, village of origin, and date captured. You asked me to keep my eyes open. You asked me if slavery exists in the Sudan? Well Herb, if it doesn't exist, a lot of people are involved in a huge charade to make it look like it exists." And he ended by saying, "And frankly Herb, I'm getting more and more uncomfortable because the company line here is that nothing bad has happened. When you point out the fact that indeed something bad has happened, you're told to turn a blind eye and act like nothing happened. I've been made to feel like I've dropped a turd on the dinner table by saying I don't want to pretend that nothing happened."

Just then he got a message back from Yandeng.

"Oh Jerome. I am so happy. Thank you so much. I want you to get to know my sister. She will be so thankful, as I am. Let me know as soon as you have news!"

She was setting herself up for great disappointment. Finding her sister would be like finding a needle in a haystack that had been blown to the four corners by the desert wind. He would have to try to manage her expectations. He sent the message off to Herb then thought of ways to answer Yandeng. He couldn't bring himself to say anything to discourage her positive outlook. This was in fact something in her that really attracted him. She had no home, no family, only 1 dress, unless she had also kept her old one, so ok, maybe 2 dresses, 1 pair of sandals, and not so much as a small bag of possessions. If she had a friend, he hadn't met her, or him. Yet she was so positive and saw herself as having so much. Her dark black face usually shone like she had an inner light inside her. She did get angry too, but most of the time she radiated with joy from another world. How could he rain on her parade? He felt he would rather die than attempt to take away her hope. No, if Ali didn't come through, and it was more than likely he wouldn't, then reality would be her teacher. He wouldn't try to prepare her for it. He decided not to answer her message.

## Chapter 42

Jerome set his mind to the immediate. He now had 5 more days in Khartoum. What could he possibly do with his time? He realized his life pretty much revolved around work. He had no friends, no family, no hobbies. He wished he could be as cheery about life as Yandeng.

He went out for a walk. His short look around told him there wasn't much to see or do. On his walk he noticed a karate school near the apartment. It was in a non-descript one-story stucco building, like most in Khartoum. It said only "Karate" in English and Arabic above the door. He had told himself back in college that he would try to do something with his non athletic body. He also knew he needed some life outside of work. He returned to the building and peeped in the open doorway. An Arab and a black man were sweating profusely as they sparred. As Jerome darkened the doorway they stopped and stared at him. He realized they probably had few skinny white guys joining their school.

"Do you need something?" one asked.

"Yes, I was wondering what it would take to join your karate school."

The guys seemed stunned.

"You will need to pay first."

"I assumed as much. How much is it per week?"

They looked at each other and the Arab spoke up.

"2000 dinars per week."

Jerome knew he had just been given a "special" price.

"Ok. But I want you to know I'll be here every day for the next 5 days."

"That's fine. Do you know any karate?"

"No. Can you teach me?"

"If you can learn, we can teach you."

And so for the first time in his life, Jerome began exercising his body, voluntarily. He spent most of the next 5 days in the dojo, as they called it. He learned several forms, or series of martial arts movements. He worked out. And best of all, he sparred. He never seemed to get ahead, but he was learning to defend himself physically. His body ached, but he loved it. He couldn't wait for the next day to start all over again. He told himself that if he could push his body to learn self-defense the way he pushed his mind to learn geology, he'd succeed.

He visited the office every day at about the time AbdelKader arrived, had tea with the group, caught up on news, and then headed to the dojo. He also called Ali every day. Ali always growled at him and told him he was working hard but had no news. He kept asking Jerome not to call. He asked for a phone number where he could be reached if he had news. He didn't know what Skype was, and couldn't understand why Jerome couldn't receive calls if he could make them.

After 5 days, he told his new friends at the dojo he'd be back in two weeks and then headed back down to the Ligheg drilling camp on the morning flight with Mikhail. He arrived a few hours before the survey team was due back. He knew he'd be under Osman's scrutiny as soon as the team returned, so he went straight to the office to make sure he got to tell Yandeng everything. She was so happy to see him, and again looked like she wanted to hug him, but instead took his hands and squeezed them.

"I am so happy to see you, Jerome. The camp is not the same without you. What news do you have?"

"I'm happy to see you too, Yandeng. I wish I had news to share, but I don't really. Ali says he has no news. I will continue to call him."

She looked disappointed but still so full of hope.

"Yes, we must continue to call him. I'm sure he will find her. How much did he make you pay?"

"Don't worry about it. I have it covered."

"No, I was paid finally. Mikhail brought money this week. I have lots of money now. Look!"

She pulled a purse out from somewhere near her slender breasts tied to a shoestring. She popped it open and showed a wad of bills.

"There's 20,000 dinars here!" she said proudly.

"Is that what you get paid for 1 month?" Jerome asked, trying not to sound surprised.

"Yes! Can you imagine? In 5 months I'll have 100,000 dinars! I will pay Ali." she bubbled.

That amounted to $100 a month. Jerome was shocked at the difference in pay scale. He didn't want to take away her joy. He wanted more than ever to help her.

"Don't worry about it yet. That's your first pay check. Save it. Ali is covered for the time being."

"Jerome, I'm paying everything back, even all those dinars you already gave me. I'm serious!"

She got that "I'm serious" look as she said it and he didn't want to get into one of those discussions.

"Once you get money saved up, we'll talk about it. Don't worry about it now. Ok?"

"Well, all right," she said reluctantly and dropped her purse down inside her dress again.

"Look, you'll be leaving soon. If I hear from Ali while you're gone, how should we communicate?"

"We can have him put her on a bus to Bentiu," Yandeng suggested.

"Ali won't do anything if we don't pay him first."

"I see. I can take the bus to Khartoum and pay," she offered.

"That might work, but how can I communicate with you if you're in Bentiu?"

"I could call you every two days."

"Can you call me?"

"I think I can find a telephone to use. There are phones at one of the post offices. You can stand in line and pay them to use a telephone."

"Ok. Oh, you'll need to call me on my field phone. Remember, sometimes the phone is shared, so someone else may answer it."

"I know."

"And I think it would be best if we don't let others in the company know what we're doing. Do you agree?"

"Yes, I agree."

"When you call, just ask me if we struck oil. If I say, 'Not yet,' it means I don't have any news."

"What if you have news?"

"Well, I'll say we struck oil."

"But you're not drilling for oil."

"I know. It's just a way to communicate. Understand?"

"Of course. I hope you strike oil."

"Me too. But be patient. This may take a while. You never know."

"I think he'll find her soon."

Jerome saw that hope in her eyes and the glow in her face.

"Yeah, I hope so too."

Jerome went to his room, unpacked and waited for the survey crew to get back to camp.

When they arrived, Osman greeted Jerome with a scowl and an insincere "Salaamu alaik (Peace upon you)."

"Wa alaik salaam (And peace upon you)," Jerome responded. "And how was the trip? Did you get good readings?"

"Good enough," Osman grumbled.

But Jerome had heard some of the guys in the office saying they thought this trip's readings weren't very good. There was trouble with one of the vibrator buggies which was down for 2 days. They had had to send a land rover back to camp for parts. And then the vibration recorder went out. Then after they fixed the recorder, it didn't seem to be calibrated. So in the end, they had made little progress and the readings they got were suspect. Jerome read over the results. He realized the readings were not reliable and was convinced that the entire section should be redone. Osman was already furious about the problems he had, but now when Jerome mentioned his decision, he focused all his anger on Jerome.

"Don't tell me about the readings! If you think you can do better, go right ahead. You think you're smarter than the rest of us?" he said loudly in the presence of the team. They watched to see what Jerome would do.

"That's enough Osman," he replied so everyone could hear. "It has nothing to do with being smart or dumb. You know what good readings are as well as me, as well as the geologists back in the office. What do you think they'll say? I'm not blaming anyone. I'm just saying we'll need to go back and redo this area."

"That's not your decision. Khartoum makes these decisions, not some little Canadian."

There it was again. He was being challenged because of his size.

"OK, you're right, they decide. I'll contact Khartoum. I think we already know what their decision will be."

"Don't try to make us look bad little man!" he shouted and stormed out.

All eyes were on Jerome. He hadn't won the fight, but he hadn't ducked his tail and run either.

"Look, guys, mistakes happen. None of you are being blamed. It could have happened to the other team too. It's just that if mistakes are made, we need to correct them. Understand?"

Some grunted a sort of approval. Others just turned and walked away. Jerome knew this team was closely allied with Osman and he'd have a hard time ever winning their trust. He made his way into the makeshift office area and fired off an email to the geological team in Khartoum asking them what they wanted done about the current week's readings.

Jerome thought about Osman. He had often backed down in these types of confrontations. He had never won a physical contest of any sort for the duration of his life. But his fortunes seemed to be changing. He had recently surprised himself by enjoying the sparring in the dojo. He had never won there either, but he wasn't losing as badly as he did at first.

The response came from Khartoum within an hour. The geological group recommended going back over the survey area and start retesting. If initial results were identical, they could assume Osman's readings were reliable. If they were different, they could assume the readings were skewed and they'd need to redo the whole area. Osman was copied on the communication.

"Don't you dare try to make me look bad you little turd," Osman growled at him in front of one of the buggy drivers.

"You're taking this personally Osman," Jerome answered. "It has nothing to do with you. I'm just doing what's best for the project. You'd do the same in my position."

"Don't tell me what I'd do! I'll be waiting to hear how this all turns out. Don't cross me!"

# Chapter 43

Jerome waited for the next shift to arrive. They were late. He went to the office and asked Yandeng if he could join her.

"Of course," she smiled. "You don't need to ask."

Jerome sat down and looked around.

"I just called. Ali," she said. "I think he's getting close."

"Wait, why did you call Ali? And why do you think he's getting close?"

"I called him because I wanted to talk to him. I won't have a telephone next week."

"Ok. But he gets cranky if he gets too many calls."

"So?"

Jerome thought to himself, "Good answer! She's has grit. I shouldn't let Osman intimidate me either."

"Then why do you think he's getting close?" he asked her.

"When I pray about it I hear the Lord telling me not to worry. My wait is almost over."

"You... hear the Lord?"

"Uh huh."

"... He talks to you?"

"Sort of, sometimes."

"What does he say?"

"What I just told you."

"Yes, well, when he... or how does he... how do you... Hmmm. I've never met anyone who hears from God," he said in a tone that expressed almost shock.

"You haven't?" she answered in an almost equally surprised tone.

"Well no! How can anyone hear from God?"

"Usually by listening. But sometimes he just speaks, even when you're not praying or listening. Have you never heard him?"

"Well no! I mean I wouldn't know what he sounded like anyway. I mean how can you hear him?"

"We have ears inside of us that we hear him with. Before I knew him I couldn't hear him. It's like I was deaf. You do know God, don't you?"

Jerome was feeling quite uncomfortable. This was getting way to deep or personal or something.

"Look I told you, I prayed."

She seemed unaware of his discomfort.

"I didn't used to know him. I found him when I wasn't even looking for him. You could say he found me," Yandeng said.

"He found you?"

"Well yeah, because I wasn't looking for him. And at a good time too. It was right before I fled from Giil. Right before I hurt my leg."

"You hurt a leg?"

"Yes, you didn't notice I limp?"

"Not really."

"Well it probably ended up saving me from worse harm."

"Like what?"

"Like being forced to be the temporary wife of an SPLA soldier."

"Being forced to... Yandeng, what have you been through?"

She laughed lightheartedly and then looked Jerome right in the eyes and said in dead seriousness, "I've been through a lot. It's what I'm telling you, having God speak to me is what has allowed me to survive and have everything I have today."

Jerome wouldn't dare contradict her about what she had.

"Well I'm glad God is helping you."

"Yes, me too. I'm not sure how people get by without his help. Although, I think he helps everyone. They just don't know it."

The conversation between them ended, but it continued in Jerome's mind.

The landrovers arrived late for lunch, the turnaround meetings took place quickly and then the cloud of red dust carried away Osman, his team, and a thin Dinka who was now at the center of Jerome's thoughts.

That night an email came back from Herb.

"Jerome: What you bring up scares me. The shareholders have been bringing these kinds of things up and pressuring us to get out. I know we're in this business for the money, but frankly I don't have the stomach for the kind of stuff you're talking about. What, slavery and genocide? If it's really happening, I'd be the first to get the hell out of the Sudan. We need evidence though. Is there any way you can get some kind of proof, pictures or something, that this happened in our blocks?"

Jerome thought for a while, lost in thought himself, then he answered.

"Herb: Yeah, I'll try to get you some evidence. But I told you, if they find me taking pictures or snooping around, I may not be there to email them to you. I'm willing to try though. I'm actually not joking when I say that if I don't make it out can I give you the name of a beneficiary? I know I told you I don't have any family, and I don't, but I'm thinking about naming someone else. Anyway, I leave tomorrow on another survey trip and I'll do what I can."

They left the next morning heading south on the dirt road, the same one Yandeng had left on the day before. He thought about the burned out village and wondered how he could maneuver stopping there and getting pictures. It would be easier without Osman around, but still, how could he do it without the others finding out? He had made a note of the gps coordinates of the site after he first found it, and kept track as they got near. He thought about causing an intentional breakdown in one of the vibrator buggies, which were fickle enough anyway. This would be difficult to time, and he hated sabotaging his own equipment. In the end he stopped the caravan about 200 yds. past the site and announced they'd all take a stretch break and eat since they'd been traveling about 3 hours already. This was unusual but no one argued. Jerome got his backpack and told his assistant in the recorder truck he'd be back in a few minutes. He grabbed some toilet paper to make it look like he was going off in the bush for other reasons and made a beeline for the burned out tukuls.

He got to the edge of the village and sensed an eerie feeling. It was still, as still as death. Maybe it was his imagination. He hurried in the direction of the tukul with the charred bodies. He set his backpack beside the doorway and walked in slowly. He looked around and saw it all over again. About 15 charred bodies, 3 of them children's and the others indistinguishable as men or women. There was no hair left and only deformed sections of burned flesh. He almost vomited and stepped outside to get his camera. As he knelt down to pulled his camera out of his backpack he saw feet. It was one of the juggers. His name was Mustapha, from Khartoum.

"What are you doing, Jerome?"

"Nothing. Why are you following me?"

"Osman asked me to keep an eye on you so you didn't get yourself in trouble."

"I'm fine. I'm just looking at this village. I've never been in a village like this. I thought I'd take a few pictures. People at home would love to see them."

"Not a good idea. Some things you don't take pictures of."

Jerome could see he had been caught. So he tried to make light of it.

"Sure. No pictures have been taken. Don't worry. Let's go."

Jerome dropped his camera back in his backpack, got up, and walked back towards the caravan. Mustapha followed. The team had gathered together off the dirt road and was already huddled around lunch. Jerome joined them while Mustapha went into the recording truck where they kept the internet connection for email and Skype calls. There was no other reason a jugger would need to be in the recording truck at this time unless it was to use the computer for personal reasons. There was nothing Jerome could do about it. He especially didn't want to draw any more attention to his interest in pictures of the nearby village. Mustapha came out 10 minutes later. One of the other juggers asked where he had been and he just said, "Sending emails."

They got back on the road and reached their destination about 3 hours later. They set up camp and made plans for an early start the following morning and called it an early quit that day. There were still a few hours of sunlight left which was unusual for a day on the road with the team. So Jerome decided to practice his karate forms. He went outside of camp, but not too far for fear of lions, hyenas and the like and started working through his forms from memory. Two of the guys noticed and joined him.

"Jerome, we didn't know you knew karate."

"Well I'm new at it. Why, do you do karate?"

"Yes, we've been taking karate for over a year."

They said they were in a Korean school. Jerome said he didn't think his had a "nationality." They laughed and asked if he liked to spar.

"Love it. It's the best part."

"We agree. Would it be Ok if we sparred here at camp?"

"Sure. Why not? Since I'm in charge, I'll say that it is definitely OK."

And so camp sparring began. They made makeshift pads out of clothing and duct tape. It became a spectator event every night after work for the rest of the week, just before the evening video was shown. This was actually very close to the Sudanese pastime of village wrestling events. The sub Saharans especially seemed to love wrestling. A few of them tried to take on the "karate kids" as they were now called, but they got their butts kicked, literally, and figuratively.

"Hey Jerome, you surprise us. How long have you been taking karate?" they asked.

He actually surprised himself. He was really enjoying sparring.

"About a week," he answered truthfully. "I started studying it on my break."

His esteem grew in their eyes. His confidence in himself also grew as he got better at sparring. "It's just like having an argument," he thought, "but instead of using your tongue, you use your arms and legs." He noticed that he needed to use his head in sparring as much as he did in arguments.

The next day he needed his head again for some verbal sparring. When they started to take the readings, a disagreement broke out about whether the numbers were significantly different from the previous survey or not. Jerome could see that they were. Mustapha, whose job it was to lay out the jugs so they could pick up the vibrations from the vibrator buggy, saw fit to walk into the recording truck and demand to look at the readings. He had somehow gotten hold of a copy of the previous readings and began to compare.

"They look close enough to me," he announced.

"Close enough for what?" Jerome asked.

"Close enough to not need to redo them!"

"And on what basis do you figure that?"

"What do you mean on what basis?"

"Well, I didn't know you were an expert at deciphering seismic readings. Did you take courses in geology?"

"Courses! What good are courses? I've been working in this business for 6 months. That's longer than you've been in it."

"Good. Sounds like you're pretty nearly an expert. Tell me Mustapha, what is the standard deviation for seismic readings?"

"What are you talking about?"

"I'm talking about probability, statistics, and the likelihood of being accurate. The same thing the geologists in Khartoum are going to be looking at. And I'll save you embarrassing yourself. I'm certain they'll want them redone. But if you want, I can give you the phone, here it is, and you can give them a call and tell them why, from your 6 months' experience as a jugger, you see fit to contradict me and insist we shouldn't redo these readings."

Mustapha looked at Jerome, looked at the phone, stared at the floor, then turned and slammed the door behind him.

Jerome knew now for certain that Osman had his team in place to lobby for his interests, and he now knew who was on that team. Jerome had finally won a battle.

"Good for me! I not only did the right thing for the company, but for me too. So, good job, me!"

Testing continued and the team redid what the previous team had done the week before. Nights were now spent sparring, eating, and watching videos, and in that order. Every 2 days Jerome made calls to Ali who continued to complain that the work was difficult and dangerous and that he was still working on it.

"Kull shay fiyid Allah (Everything is in God's hand)," was Ali's response du jour.

Yandeng would call the following morning, before 8 AM, always eager and hopeful. After 5 days they returned to the Ligheg camp.

The following day Yandeng, and Osman arrived in the usual cloud of red dust, just before lunchtime. Jerome waved to Yandeng at a distance but had a face to face with Osman.

"Jerome, my friend," he said through gritted teeth, "you have been taking more pictures I hear. I thought we had an agreement."

"You must have been given bad information Osman. I didn't take any pictures."

"I think you're mistaken Jerome. I think I'd like to check your computer."

"Like hell you will. I told you I didn't take any pictures. If I had, whatever it is you're afraid of, and I'm not sure what it is you're afraid of, would have already been done by now. But it wasn't, because, like I said, I didn't take any pictures. Now, I think we should get our turnaround meeting started. The caravan heads back in less than 2 hours."

Osman gave Jerome a hard piercing stare. Jerome knew he was weighing his options. If he called Jerome's bluff and insisted on checking his computer, he'd have a fight on his hands and in the end maybe not find anything. At last he turned and walked away.

He then had to sit with Osman in the lunch room because they were paired up for the turnaround meeting. Jerome had the task of informing him of the progress made the previous week, namely that they had completely redone what had been done the week prior. Osman sat and seethed. Jerome almost felt sorry for him. It hit him as a sudden realization that at least part of the reason Osman hated him was because he had been hired to improve the quality of the seismic findings, a sign to him the he himself had failed as the previous survey lead.

# Chapter 44

The afternoon went slowly. Jerome couldn't get his mind off of Yandeng. Now that they were both at camp he wanted to see her and catch up with her. He'd have to find a context to do so. Maybe she needed computer coaching, or maybe he needed to catch up on office work. He knew nothing could long go unnoticed in a community as small as theirs, and when things were noticed, tongues wagged. Should he even pursue a relationship with Yandeng? Could it ever be possible? They were so different, and from different worlds.

At dinner he passed her as she was serving herself a bowl of stew.

"Will you be in the office tonight?"

"No, no. There is a movie tonight. A funny one, about a Chinese man and a black man in America. 'The Ruch Hour.'"

"Oh, 'Rush Hour.' Yes, I've seen it. It is sort of funny."

"Oh, you've seen all the movies Jerome. And what is a 'ruch hour?'"

"'Rush hour,' oh it's when traffic is really bad, you know, like at 5 in the afternoon."

She had that look on her face like she didn't have a clue what he was talking about. Then her face brightened and she said, "Good, I can't wait to see it!"

"Of course you dummy," he thought to himself. "She's probably never been in city with a rush hour!"

Everyone loved the video. Will Smith was a big hit. They didn't laugh in the right spots but seemed to enjoy it more than audiences in the US. And of course they loved Jackie Chan. Most people in the south had never seen an Asian although there was talk that the Chinese oil company was leasing blocks in the Sudanese oil fields. Jerome had even heard that the Sudanese government was allowing the Chinese to bring military personnel with them from China to "protect" their blocks from their enemies. He had never seen "the enemy" although there were reports that small SPLA battalions had attacked various military outposts and damaged the new oil pipeline that ran from the nearby wells 500 miles up to the Red Sea. This would now be the aorta through which liquid cash would be pumped into the government's pockets. Any break in the pipeline got immediate attention and was about the only thing in the country that got fixed quickly.

Jerome wanted to talk to Yandeng but could find no pretext to do so. He left when everyone else did after the video and went to bed. The next day he stopped in the office after breakfast to have a quick word. There were people there so all he could say was that they would be communicating from their camp out on the survey.

"Ok," Yandeng smiled. "Be careful for hyenas."

It was true they often encountered hyenas. He knew he had to watch his back, but it was not the hyenas he was concerned about.

They left after breakfast for his 4$^{th}$ survey trip. It went much like the others except that he didn't find any sparring partners on this team. He asked if anyone knew karate. They found this funny for some reason. They found it even funnier when he practiced his forms on his own.

"Are you showing off Jerome, or trying to intimidate us?" Osman asked him in front of the whole team.

"Actually, neither," he answered. "Just trying to keep in practice. You never know when you'll need to defend yourself."

Osman sneered and imitated something that sort of resembled a karate move and the rest of the team snickered.

The situation was getting worse and he knew he'd have to stand up to Osman sometime, and better sooner than later. He just didn't feel like he could do it now. It was the old feeling that told him he was powerless and couldn't possibly win.

Jerome called Ali faithfully every two nights. He had to do it during the video time when he knew no one else would be in the recording truck wanting to use the computer and satellite connection. The last night on the survey trip Ali asked Jerome to repeat Alual's name, village of origin, and date taken.

"Alual Nyeal, from Palwung, Mayom County, 28 May, 2000. Why Ali? What have you found out?"

"Just wait. I will tell you when I have found her." And he hung up.

"Boy," thought Jerome, "don't ever ask me for a referral!"

He then emailed Herb from his own computer using his personal email account and told him that he felt he was being watched closely by the team, and especially Osman, whom he felt sure was reporting back to the Khartoum office. They definitely did not want him taking pictures in their blocks. Somehow he'd try to get photos.

The next day the caravan returned to Ligheg camp, their readings already emailed off to the Khartoum office via the satellite connection. Jerome was sure they were happy about the readings in the Khartoum office. A few people had told him as much. On the last flight down, Mikhail the pilot told Jerome he had heard positive reports about him.

"Yes, I overheard them say in the office that it's hard to find a technical person with the balls to go out on survey trips. Technical people don't like to leave the office. But they say it's even harder to find field people who can be taught the technical side of surveying. So I think they like you Jerome."

"What else did they say?"

"About what?"

"You know what I'm asking. About me."

"Oh nothing."

"Don't lie, Mikhail. You're a bad liar."

"All right. They said you need to stick to technical things and not mix with local affairs."

"Anything else?"

"No. That's it. And I don't even know what they meant. What did they mean?"

"Just what they said. They don't want me digging in their garbage. This place has a lot of secrets that they don't want outsiders to know about."

"Yeah, like what?"

"Like the fact that the government bombed out the villages all in and around our blocks and either killed the people, sent them away homeless, or took them as slaves."

"That's no secret. Hell, I knew that."

"How did you know?"

"I used to fly Antonov's for the government, and I taught their pilots how to fly them."

Jerome was stunned.

"You mean you dropped bombs on villages?" he said in horror. Mikhail picked up immediately on his tone.

"Of course I didn't drop bombs. Look, I was just the pilot," he said with an expression of purity and innocence dripping from his tongue.

"But did you fly the plane when they dropped the bombs?"

"Look, I was paid to do a job. If they dropped bombs from the plane while I was flying it, it was not my business. I was only doing what I was paid to do."

Jerome liked Mikhail, but now saw a new side to him, one he did not like.

Back at camp he made it to the mess hall in time for dinner. Yandeng waved to him. She was now enjoying eating and even talking with the girls at the "girls' table." It made Jerome feel better that she had some friends. He wondered what she talked about with them. He couldn't imagine her talking about her hair, how she liked it or didn't like it, or which boys she thought were cute. He especially couldn't imagine her talking about whether or not they thought she was too fat or needed to exercise. He liked the way she looked. He still couldn't get over that most of the time she was so genuinely happy her face seemed to glow. She had a deep down kind of happiness, even if she didn't smile all the time. She seemed to have a sense of what she wanted, and seemed to have it, which was the oddest part of it. Anyway, he found just about everything about her attractive. She could use a new dress though. She wore the same one day after day, which at least was different from the long black dress he had first seen her in.

"I wonder how she ever started wearing a Muslim dress? I'll have to ask her one day, but I'm sure I'll have to ask carefully."

That night after dinner they watched "Rush Hour" again. Judging by the reactions, he would have thought it was the first time they had seen it. They laughed and laughed, but again at odd times. He was tired and decided to retire early. He went to his room, and made his call to Ali.

"I may have news. Call me tomorrow," Ali said and hung up.

Jerome had planned to go to bed but wondered if he should tell Yandeng. He was looking for an excuse to talk to her anyway. He found his way over to Yandeng's side as the video ended and people were getting up to leave.

"I just made a phone call," he said under his breath, so no one else could hear.

"What did he say" she said in a much louder voice than he wanted.

"Let's talk outside," he again said in a very low voice.

"Ok," she said as she started to the door.

As soon as they got outside she turned and said very anxiously, "So what did he say?"

"Now don't get your hopes up. He just said he may have news and asked me to call tomorrow."

"What else did he say?"

"Well nothing. Uh, he actually hung up on me after he said that."

"You didn't ask him what news he had?"

"I would have, but as I said, he hung up on me."

"He just hung up?" she said in a testy voice.

"Yes, Yandeng. He does that. He just said what he had to say, then hung up."

She stood there shaking her head. He could tell she was upset and agitated. He wasn't sure if she was mad at him or at Ali.

"Look, Yandeng, I'll call him as soon as I get to Khartoum. It is good timing. I'll try to see him."

"Yes," she said slowly. He could tell thoughts were racing through her mind but she didn't voice them.

"Is there any way I can get in touch with you this week? I mean, if I get news."

"Yes. I'll call. I'll call you when I get to Bentiu. I'll call tomorrow from the post office."

"Ok. Don't worry Yandeng."

"I'm not worried!" she said with that fire in her eyes. "This is my sister. I am very concerned!"

# Chapter 45

Back in Khartoum his new karate friends were eager to see him.
"Jerome, we thought you wouldn't return."
"I told you I'd return."
He realized he had actually improved out on the survey trail. He
was really starting to feel proud of himself. This was after all the
first physical achievement he could ever remember. If only his gym
teachers could see him now.
That night he called Ali.
"Yes, I am working hard. I may have something soon. You
keep in touch."
"Well I'm in touch now Ali. What have you found? Do you
have news of her?"
"Yes, maybe."
"Yes, maybe? Do you mean yes, or maybe?"
"I mean maybe. Yes."
"I don't know. Do you mean maybe?"
"Yes. I said I did! Listen to me."
Jerome listened and waited.
"Are you there Yusuf?"
"Yes, of course."
"Why are you silent?"
This conversation seemed lost.
"Ali, what is the next step?"
"Call me."
"When?"
"This time tomorrow."
"Ok. I'll call about 7 PM tomorrow... Hello? Ali? Are you
there?"
Jerome realized he had already hung up.
The next day Yandeng called at 8 AM.
"Well Jerome, what news does Ali have?"
"He didn't say. He just said he may have news soon."
"I'm so excited. I know he is getting close."

Jerome tried to end the call quickly because he sure didn't feel overly optimistic and didn't want to conjecture on what Ali may or may not know. After the call, he checked in at the office and had tea with AbdelKader and colleagues. There was excitement from the geophysical team on the readings they were receiving from the survey trips.

"Very promising signs," they said. "Good work, Jerome."

AbdelKader seemed less positive. When the team members started to head back to their offices AbdelKader asked Jerome to come into his office. He shut the door behind them and gravely took his seat behind his desk.

"So, I've been told you haven't taken me seriously about digging up the past. I think I've already made myself clear. And I see you've made up your mind to try to bring shame on us. I'll give you a last warning… beware! That's all I have to say."

The two stared at each other for at least 15 seconds, but it seemed like an eternity. Jerome could see in AbdelKader's face the cold determined look of a man whose mind was beyond being changed. He nodded his good-bye, turned and walked out.

Jerome spent the rest of the day in the dojo but his mind wasn't in it. He took 2 hard kicks to his ribs that he should have blocked. He realized he needed to focus and protect himself, or leave. In the past, he would have left, but today he decided to focus and fight back. He sparred his opponents to a draw for the rest of the day.

As part of his new confidence in fighting back, he decided not to avoid AbdelKader. In the past he would have gone out of his way to stay away from him. But he continued to visit the office every morning he was in Khartoum, except Friday, when they were closed for the Muslim holy day. He decided not to act any differently around him. After all, he hadn't done anything to be ashamed of. So he was cheerful and sociable at the office. Was it his imagination or did this seem to make AbdelKader even madder? No matter. If he was angry, that was his problem.

Jerome kept to his schedule, office, dojo, dinner, phone call to Ali, and emails to Herb to keep him abreast. Herb told Jerome he could bail out of his gig in the Sudan if ever he felt he was in danger.

Jerome didn't sense any imminent danger and had no intention of throwing in the towel.

For the first time in his life he was getting a fire in his belly, like a war horse getting the scent of battle in his nostrils. This was a new experience and it was exhilarating.

He called Ali at 7 PM.

"Ma'ak Yusuf. Ash khabarik? (This is Yusuf. What news do you have?)"

"Alual Nyeal, you said, no?"

"Yes."

"From Palwung in Mayom County, no?"

"Yes. Why?"

"I think I've found her."

Jerome was stunned. He could think of nothing to say.

"Yusuf? Are you there?"

"Yes, I'm here. You found her? Where?"

"Don't worry where. That is my business. I think I can get her back."

"Ok... Good. Why wouldn't you be able to get her back?"

"There are ... complications."

"What do you mean by complications?"

"Her ... owner doesn't want to part with her. I think it will take a lot more money than we thought to compensate him for his loss."

"What do you mean he doesn't want to part with her? He bought her. We're buying her back. We're paying him more than he paid for her in the first place and he's already had her for more than a year."

"Ah. That's the problem."

"What's the problem?"

"He's had her for a year."

"And?"

"He says he thinks of her almost like one of his wives now. He doesn't want to part with her unless I, or you, make it very interesting for him."

Jerome could have predicted this. He decided to fight.

"You gave me a price Ali. And you gave me your word."

"Yes, but this is beyond my control. This is a complicated situation."

Jerome had no idea if the "situation" Ali was describing had any basis in reality. He suspected it was a fabrication.

"I don't think I believe you Ali."

"What don't you believe? If you think I'd lie, you are an ignorant bastard. I am the most honest person I know."

Jerome wondered if this last statement could unfortunately be true.

"Look Ali, we made a deal. I am still agreed to keep my end of the deal. Are you in agreement to keep your end?"

"I told you, I am telling you the truth. The man wants more money. There is nothing I can do about it. I don't get the extra money. This evil man does. He is hurting both of us. I want to get your friend back and end this horrible ordeal."

This sounded far too patronizing for Jerome's liking.

"Look Ali, we agreed I would pay you 9000 dinars when you found her. I can pay you 9000 dinars, no more!"

There was a click on the other end of the line. Jerome was furious. Did he even have Alual? Was this whole affair a scam? What could he do? He knew Ali had no way of contacting him. He also knew he couldn't go back to Yandeng and tell her he had the opportunity but decided not to pay more for her sister. He gritted his teeth and clicked the redial icon on the screen. The phone rang and Ali answered.

"Aiwa? (Well?)"

"All right, Ali. Tell me, how much more does this evil man want?"

"He said he wants 60,000 dinars."

"60,000 dinars! That's almost 7 times what we agreed!"

"Unfortunately this is true. And this amount only includes the money that evil man wants. I also need to be paid."

"And how much do you want to be paid after we pay THAT EVIL MAN?"

Jerome was now almost shouting.

"Well since the money needed for the evil man has risen, so have my fees."

Jerome knew he was losing his temper.

"Ok Ali, I'll pay you 65,000 dinars. And that is my final price."

"Ok 67,000. She is in good health, God be praised."

There was a pause. Jerome was thinking. 67,000 dinars was still only just over $300.

This was by comparison an order of magnitude more than the "local price" yet several orders of magnitude less than what he would expect in dealing with kidnappers in any other part of the world.

"Ok Ali. Where and how do we make the exchange?"

"Meet me in 2 days at the same café and have the money ready."

Jerome quickly thought of all that could go wrong.

"Wait Ali. When do I see Alual?"

"After I get the money I will send her to you."

"No. Unacceptable. Sorry Ali, I don't trust you. I will pay you when I see her."

Now there was a pause on the other end and Jerome thought maybe he had hung up, but the computer screen showed that they were still connected. So Jerome waited. He knew this time Ali had to compromise. Finally, he spoke.

"This makes a difficult situation even more difficult."

"Why?"

"How do I pay this… evil man… if I don't have the money in advance?"

"Don't know. But how do I know if I pay you, this evil man will honor his end of the agreement?"

"I guarantee it 1000%."

"No. I told you Ali, I don't trust you."

This didn't seem to offend Ali. It only made him go into a problem solving mode.

"If you could give me ½ in advance, I could probably get the evil man to agree to it."

Now Jerome knew that Ali was making at least ½ of what he was asking.

"How about if you and I both visit the evil man and when I see Alual I pay you."

"No! No, I don't think the evil man would respond well. As soon as he sees a white man trying to buy an abida, his price will go up."

Jerome was thinking and wondering how he would even know if the girl Ali was proposing to sell to him was indeed Alual. He had never met her and didn't even have a photograph of her. He had a last thought.

"Ali, before I pay you, I need to have a short conversation with Alual."

"Why?"

"Trust me. I need to."

"You're making this impossible."

"I have an idea. Bring her and the evil man to the café. I'll be there but you won't talk to me. I'll find a Sudanese man to talk with her, a Dinka. If I'm satisfied, I'll have the Dinka pay you."

"Hmm. I don't know. Women don't go to cafés."

"Then somewhere else. How about the post office?"

"No. There are too many police there."

"How about the bus station?"

"Ok. If God wills. Call me tomorrow."

Before Jerome could agree he saw on his computer screen that the call had ended.

# Chapter 46

If Ali was not lying, and Jerome decided he had to act as if he wasn't, the exchange would need to take place within the next 3 days before he headed back to camp.

Who could he get to work with him? The next day at the dojo, he broached the subject with Taban, his sparring partner.

"I have a huge favor to ask you Taban."

"What is it?"

"Well it's an unusual situation, and I prefer if we keep this between just you and me."

"Ok."

"I have a friend. She is a Dinka."

"Jerome, are you messing with Dinka girls?"

"No. She is a good friend. I work with her. She needs me to help her, but for me to help her, I need someone to help me."

"Uh huh. What help do you need?"

"Well, her village was attacked. Her parents were killed and her sister was sold as a slave here in Khartoum."

Taban was now staring hard at Jerome studying his face with a surprised look on his own face.

"So, what do you want from me?"

"Well, she found someone who said he could find her sister, a Bagarra who lives here in Khartoum. I've been in contact with him and he said he found her."

"Hmm. You have to be very careful with the Bagarra. They'll say anything to trick a white man out of his money."

"Yes, uh, well that's why I need you. So this tricky Bagarra doesn't cheat me."

"You need a black man to act like he's buying back his sister. Is that it?"

"Well, sort of. This person will need to let her know he is acting on her sister's part and find out for sure if she is the sister of my friend."

"And how will he do that?"

"I'll have some questions he will ask her. If she can't answer them, we know she isn't the right person."

"Hmm. Ok. You know that buying slaves is illegal. You can get in trouble for it. Big trouble."

"But I'm not buying a slave. I'm freeing one."

"Yeah. Tell that to the police if this deal goes bad."

"Well will you help me find someone?"

"Maybe. How did you get involved in this? How important is this Dinka girl?"

"I said she was a friend."

"A friend? Jerome, you are risking a lot here. She must be more than a friend."

Jerome had no answer. It was true. He had to admit it first to himself. He was risking a lot here, maybe not his life, but certainly his career as he knew it. But he did it willingly. His thoughts returned to Yandeng as they often did. What was she doing? What did she think about this or that? What made her tick?

"Ok Taban. I like her. She's more than a friend. I really want to help her."

"Interesting, Jerome. I'll help you. Did you know I'm a Dinka?"

That night he called Ali again.

Ali seemed cranky.

"I'm trying to convince that man of our plan to come to the bus station."

"And, is he willing?"

"Not yet. He's afraid it might be a trap. If he's caught it could mean embarrassment for him."

Jerome thought to himself, "Too damn bad. It should mean imprisonment." But he only said, "Listen, he can stand off at a distance and watch. I'll be standing at a distance watching too. If anyone tries to catch us, they'll only catch you… I mean of course they can't catch you. You're not buying or selling here. You're just observing."

"I'm taking a great risk. I am worth a lot more than I am asking."

Jerome knew what was coming so he changed the subject quickly.

"Anyway, Ali, I have a problem. I leave Khartoum in 2 days."

"What do you mean you leave in 2 days? You didn't tell me that!"

"Well I'm telling you now. Can you make this happen in the next 2 days?"

"Oh. This is difficult. More difficult than I thought."

"Ok, talk to the evil man and let me know tomorrow."

This time Jerome hung up and felt really good about it. The last thing he wanted was more negotiating on price and hearing Ali yammer on about his difficulties.

The next morning Yandeng called. Jerome chose his words carefully.

"Listen Yandeng, I don't know if I can trust this Ali, but he says he thinks he located your sister."

"Oh really? Oh Jerome, I'm sooo happy! Oh thank you God! I am soooo happy!"

"But Yandeng. Listen, I don't know if I trust him. If he hands a girl, or woman, over to me, I need a way to determine if she is really your sister."

"Well you need to make sure it is my sister!"

"Yes, well that is what I'm getting at. What question can I ask her that only she would know how to answer?"

"Like what do you mean?"

"Well, like... what was your father's name, and your mother's name?"

There was a pause on the line. Then in a voice that sounded like it was on the verge of cracking, Jerome heard in a whisper, "Vivian and Yona."

Jerome wasn't sure which was her father's name and which was her mother's, but he figured it didn't matter. He jotted them down.

"Thanks Yandeng. Also, the schedule is starting to work against us. If he does have your sister and brings her within the next two days, it's Ok because I'm here. But if he doesn't, I'll have to return to camp and we'll have to wait 2 more weeks."

"Yes, I pray he brings her in the next two days." She was now sobbing.

"Yes, me too. But if he does, I'm wondering how to get her back to you. You'll be at camp. I can't bring her on the plane with me, because if I did, you'd get in trouble if she were at camp. And I don't think we want anyone at camp knowing about this."

Yandeng had no reply. Jerome could still hear an occasional sob.

"Listen, Yandeng. This is what we'll have to do. Do you have an address in Bentiu where she can go? I can put her on a bus with an address and you can find her there the next time you get back there."

"Yes," she said softly. "There's a church in Bentiu and a man there who will take care of her."

"Ok, good. Does the church have a name?"

"It's called the Good Shepherd Anglican church, and it is south of the bus station, on the other side of the river. People here know of it. All she has to do is ask around for it. There is a man here named Gatwech. He will help her. I will let him know."

"Can Gatwech find her a place to stay?"

"Yes. Here at the church."

"At the church? Are you calling from the church?"

"No. We have no phone. But there is room for her."

"I see... Is that where you stay? At a church?"

"Yes."

Jerome was a bit shocked. But then again he knew she had no home.

"Ok, I wrote down the name of the church, and Gatwech. Call me tomorrow if you can."

"I will. Thank you Jerome. I don't know what I'd do if you weren't helping me."

"... sure Yandeng. I hope this works."

Jerome felt good. He was beginning to hope too. He knew Yandeng was probably praying at this minute. He decided he'd pray too.

"God, again, I'm asking you to help us. Help this Ali find Yandeng's sister and help this 'evil man' whoever he is, if he even exists, part with her. Personally, if he is real, I hope you hurt him somehow... but that's your business. Also, while we're talking, I'd like to be on better speaking terms with you, like Yandeng seems to be. I no longer have a father, and never had much of a connection with him anyway. So I guess what I'm saying is I need a ... father

**222**

figure, you know. Anyway, I'm rambling and probably not being very clear. Hope you can figure it out, being God and all. So... well, that's it for now."

He got his karate outfit and left for the dojo.

# Chapter 47

Taban arrived at the dojo late. They went off in a corner to spar.

"So, when do you need me to help you?"

"I don't know. I need to call the Bagarra again tonight. I hope he'll be ready tomorrow, because I fly back down to my camp the next day a 7 AM."

Taban threw his right leg in the direction of Jerome's left arm. He easily blocked it with his left hand and threw a right side kick of his own that was also blocked.

"What if he isn't ready tomorrow?"

"I don't know. I haven't figured out a plan yet."

This time a front kick came in the direction of Jerome's chest. He side stepped and kicked low, catching Taban's quad with a snapping sound. He pulled back so it wasn't full force, as was the practice at the dojo. He had never kicked anyone as hard as he could and wondered what effect it would have.

"Lucky kick. Ok. Let me know as soon as you can."

"All right. How late will you be here today?"

"I leave at four, but then may return at six to work out for an hour or so."

Taban then stepped forward with a stiff arm punch towards Jerome's head. He again blocked it with a forearm chop and came quickly back with a punch of his own that landed in Taban's solar plexus.

"Good, I'll call the Bagarra early tonight and come back and look for you if I have news."

"Ok. You know, you're getting better at this Jerome."

"I know. I've had good 'sensais'."

"Thanks."

Jerome was back at the apartment by four and called Ali. He had never called him this early, but felt he had to do what he could to push for closure.

"Ay na'am."

"Ali, any news? It's Yusuf."

"You're calling early."

"I know. I told you I am leaving Khartoum the day after tomorrow. I wanted to see if we could conclude this before I leave."

"What if we can't?"

Jerome could sense some anger, maybe even panic, in Ali's voice. He felt a sense of payback. It would be good for Ali to get a taste of frustration, anger, and panic. Jerome knew he was anxious to get paid.

"I don't know Ali. I just don't know."

"Well I'll tell you. You'll lose the girl, for good."

Jerome knew he was bluffing.

"Well Ali, you'll have to make it happen tomorrow then."

"This is difficult. You don't have any idea how delicate and dangerous this is."

"Well Ali, what do you propose? Can you bring her to the bus station like you said?"

"I'll try, God willing. But I don't want to see you. I must not be seen handing a Dinka over to a white man. It would be bad for both of us."

Jerome was sure Ali was only thinking of himself.

"All right. I'll arrange to have a Dinka there. You can hand her over to him. But Ali…"

"Na'am?"

"Before he pays you she has to answer 3 questions."

"What questions?"

"Questions only she knows the answers to."

"Tell me the questions."

"No Ali. If she is Alual Nyeal from Palwung, she'll know the answers."

"This is wrong! Don't try to double-cross me. You won't get the girl without paying!"

"Ali, if she answers my questions, you get your money. If she can't, I'm not taking her. She'll return with you."

"But what if she forgets, or doesn't want to answer?"

"If she is who you say she is, she'll answer."

Ali didn't say anything for at least 10 seconds. Then he barked, "Call me tomorrow at noon."

As was his habit, Ali hung up without saying goodbye, or asking if there were any questions. Jerome went back to the dojo, found

**225**

Taban and told him what he knew. They agreed to meet again at the dojo at 1 PM the next day. They'd both be there anyway.

The next day Jerome got up early, walked around Khartoum until it was time for the office to open, then made his daily visit. He drank tea and said his goodbyes. AbdelKader was no less antagonistic than he had been but Jerome did his best to ignore it. He picked up some mail to take back to camp. Jerome had downloaded the photograph he had taken of Yandeng and himself standing side by side in the office onto a thumb drive and needed to print it. He found a computer not being used, plugged in his thumb drive, opened the photo and sent it to the color printer. He then quickly closed out of the computer and ran to the printer. He was there as it printed and saw that no one else had seen him. He folded it longwise and put it with the camp mail.

He went back to the apartment, picked up his karate uniform and made a last check of his money. He had 100,000 dinars, roughly $500, in cash on hand. Surely Ali wouldn't ask for more than this? He then sent an email to Herb.

"This guy claims to have somehow found Yandeng's sister. She was taken captive from within our blocks over a year ago. I wonder what you're like after being a slave for over a year? I have no idea if he has found her, but he claims to have done so. I'll let you know how it turns out.

Jerome"

Then off to the dojo. He practiced his forms and started sparring. Taban came in about 11.

"Well?"

"I'll call again in an hour. I should have news. I hope we'll be able to do it this afternoon. You haven't decided to back down have you?"

"Never. I'll look at it like a sparring match. Only it isn't practice."

"Yeah. I feel the same."

They sparred, rested, and sparred some more. Then Jerome left, with an anxious knot in the pit of his stomach. Would the "deal" really take place?

At 12 sharp he clicked the call button on his computer screen. Ali answered by saying, "What's taken you so long to call. I've been waiting."

"You said to call at noon."

"I have the girl. We need to meet as soon as possible. Be at the bus station in a half an hour."

"Wait, Ali, don't hang up. I need more than a half an hour. I have to get my Dinka friend."

"Get him and be there no later than 1."

"Ok…"

Jerome hoped this would be their last phone call.

"How will I recognize him?" Ali asked.

"He will be near the front entrance. He'll have a green Sharq el Awsat newspaper in his left hand."

"Are you stupid? Dinkas don't read Arabic newspapers."

"It doesn't matter! He'll have one. He'll also have the money."

"About the money, we agreed on 67,000 dinars, but the price has changed due to the changing circumstances."

"Ali, we agreed on 65,000 dinars. And what circumstances have changed?"

"You, you are leaving and I had to pay extra to get my client to part with his girl quickly. These special arrangements cost extra money."

"Ok, Ali. If she can answer the questions, I'll have 67,000 dinars inside the newspaper."

"No, 70,000!"

"No, 67, 000!"

"Do you want the girl or not?"

"I'll give you 67,000 which is more than we agreed."

"You are rich and greedy."

"Good for me. I'll be nearby, watching. My friend will not pay unless all the questions are answered correctly."

"I also will have friends nearby, and you won't know who they are. If you try to trick me, they'll even the score. Be there at 1 sharp."

# Chapter 48

Jerome was in shock. Did Ali really have Alual? Would she be free and in his company within an hour or so? He knew he'd have time to get to the bus station if Taban were still in the dojo. He hurried over and was relieved to find him there. He gave him the photo, which was folded in half so that the half showing Jerome was folded underneath and only Yandeng's picture was visible. He also had him repeat the three questions.

"Within 20 minutes they were at the bus station entrance. Jerome bought one of the green Arabic newspapers at the newsstand. He gave half of it to Taban and kept half for himself.

"I'll keep the money in my half for safety. That way if anyone grabs you, you won't have any money with you."

"I'm not afraid. But how will we pay this Bagarra?"

"If she answers all three questions, look in my direction and nod. I'll be leaning on that wall over there, with the newspaper in my arm."

"Ok. What do I do now?"

"Hang around right here and wait for a skinny older Bagarra and a young Dinka girl to approach you. And practice asking the questions."

"I won't forget them. I'm ready."

At 2 minutes after one, two mean looking Arab men walking closely on each side of a young tall thin black woman in a Muslim dress came into view. They walked slowly, scanning the crowd. The woman was looking down at the ground. One looked in Taban's direction and then said something to his counterpart. They approached Taban. Jerome was only 20 yards away. The girl he almost instantly knew was Yandeng's sister. She looked so much like her, had the same skin color, slender yet strong build, and a face that even though wasn't as soft or glowing as Yandeng's, looked very similar. He couldn't hear their voices but could tell they were talking. He saw Alual's lips move.

"She must be answering the first question, 'What was your mother's name?'"

There was more talk. The men were trying to pressure Taban. He seemed to be arguing. Then he spoke to Alual again. Her lips moved again. She must have now told him her father's name. Then he saw Taban show her the color print of the photo. He must be asking her who was in the picture. Alual seemed to choke, then she closed her eyes and put down her head. She started to cry. Taban looked over to Jerome and nodded his head. Jerome looked around for Ali. Sure enough, he was in the crowd about 50 feet away glaring at Jerome. One of the men took Taban's newspaper and handed it to the other. Taban said something to him and then motioned in Jerome's direction. They all looked over at him. He tapped his newspaper with his finger, then he set it on top of a low wall beside him. The two men looked at each other and then one walked menacingly over and leaned against the wall beside Jerome, letting his hand fall hard as he snatched the paper off the window sill.

"It's all there, 67,000 dinars," Jerome said in a low voice while looking straight ahead.

"It better all be here," the thug growled, as he started thumbing through the money all the while keeping it covered by the newspaper. He counted it several times, and finally said, "It's a good thing it's all here." Ali, Alual, Taban, and the other Arab man were all watching. The thug looked up, nodded, then walked in Ali's direction. The other thug let go of Alual's arm and also walked in Ali's direction. When Ali got the newspaper in his hands, he turned and the three quickly vanished into the crowd.

Taban was talking to Alual and motioning towards Jerome. They weren't arguing, but he could tell they weren't agreeing either. He motioned for her to come with him over to Jerome. Jerome wanted to run over and hug her but he knew that would be a mistake for a number of reasons. She finally took a few steps, very slowly, then a few more, and made her way over to him. She stared at him with a look that showed both defiance and suspicion. He couldn't blame her. He could only guess what she had been through. He felt very bashful all of a sudden, looking into her face. It was a face that betrayed a lot of suffering, yet was still proud. Whatever she had been through, it hadn't broken her spirit. She reminded him so much of Yandeng. Yet she lacked Yandeng's warmth and joy.

"Alual, I am very happy to meet you. Your sister Yandeng has asked me to help you get to Bentiu where she can see you again and take care of you."

Alual was silent. She continued to stare at him.

"Alual, do you understand English better, or Arabic? I'm sorry, I don't know Dinka."

She didn't say anything for about 15 seconds and Jerome was about to ask Taban to ask her the same question in Dinka when she answered, "I understand both. Who are you?"

"I'm sorry, my name is Jerome."

"How do you know my sister?"

"She is a friend. I work with her?"

"She works? Where?"

"We work for an oil company. We work at a camp in Mayom County."

"I don't believe you."

"Taban, hand me the picture."

Jerome unfolded it and handed it to Alual.

Alual scrutinized it. She seemed to be noticing every detail. It was first of all a shock to learn that Yandeng was still alive. And yet here she was, older, wearing a new dress, smiling and leaning towards Jerome. She was very much a young woman. And working now too! And there was a computer monitor on a desk behind them. Did she know how to work with a computer? Things had certainly changed since that horrible day when they had last seen each other."

"Where are my parents?" she asked abruptly, looking up from the picture and staring at Jerome.

This time Jerome fell silent. The silence became more and more awkward as he searched for an explanation. Should he be the one to bear the bad news? Taban finally broke the silence, "Jerome, do you know where her parents are?"

"Well, Yandeng has mentioned them to me."

"Tell me! Tell me what you know!"

Jerome spoke slowly, deliberately. "I don't want to tell you because I have bad news to share. But I will tell you because if I were in your position, I'd want to know."

He let another long pause elapse to help prepare her for the worst.

"I only know what Yandeng has told me. She said the day you were taken, her village was destroyed and her parents were... killed."

"I knew as much," Alual said without emotion. "I know the murahaleen take captives, but leave no survivors. So how did Yandeng survive?"

"She has never told me her story. She doesn't like to talk about it. I would love to hear it."

"Yes, she is like me. I do not talk about it either."

She handed the picture back to Jerome.

"Keep it if you want it," he said.

She took it, holding it as if it were a valuable possession. It was then Jerome realized she had no other possessions.

"Ah yes, let's talk about your trip, and arrangements."

"Where am I going?"

"To Bentiu. I have an address where Yandeng has a friend who will care for you until she can get there."

"Where is she?"

"Well, she works at a camp a few hours from Bentiu. Unfortunately, she won't be in Bentiu again until a week from tomorrow."

"What will I do in Bentiu by myself? I have never been there."

Jerome handed her a piece of paper with the name of the church and Gatwech written in both English and Arabic.

"Can you read this?"

She looked at it and then slowly pronounced the words.

"Yes, that's right. You ask for the Good Shepherd Anglican Church. She said it is a 15-minute walk south of the bus station. When you get to the church, ask for Gatwech. He is a friend of your sister and will find you a place to stay and take care of you until Yandeng gets back. Does that seem clear?"

"How do I get to Bentiu?"

"By bus."

"I don't have money for a bus."

"I'm so sorry. Here is a little something for your trip. You will find enough there to by a bus ticket, some food, some clothes if you like, and whatever else you should need in the next week."

He handed her a wad of bills wrapped up in another piece of newspaper. It was nearly all his remaining cash, 30,000 dinars or about $150. He figured he could get more out of the bank later for himself. She peeled back the newspaper and glanced in. She quickly leafed through the bills and then gave Jerome another hard and suspicious look.

"Why are you doing this?"

"Listen, you mean the world to Yandeng. I told you, we're friends."

She shook her head like she wanted to say that she didn't understand. But then she quickly rewrapped the money.

Thirty minutes later she rolled out of the bus lot in front of a cloud of red dust and choking black exhaust.

# Chapter 49

Jerome felt really good to think he had helped set a human being free from slavery and had helped Yandeng at the same time. He felt giddy he was so happy. It seemed nothing could wreck the high he now felt as they walked back to the dojo. Taban interrupted his thoughts.

"Why do you work for this oil company?"

"The oil company? Well it's my job."

"Well that's why these things have happened. My people have always been taken as slaves by northerners, but never in the numbers since the oil companies have come."

"But we're not involved in any of that."

Taban stopped walking and stared at Jerome. "What do you mean you're not involved?" he asked.

"We're just exploring for oil, drilling it, and piping it out. Your country is getting revenue from it."

"No, the country is not getting money from it, the government is. It is the government who is responsible for the slave trade, and it is your employer who is funding them. So, it's great that you bought back one slave, but how many has your company helped the government to enslave?"

Jerome felt like he had just taken an unblocked kick to the stomach. He was indignant and offended that Taban would group him with the likes of slave traders, but he knew that from his perspective, he was aiding and abetting the enemy. He marveled at the government, at his company, and at the world in general that would allow human life to be valued so lightly. He marveled at himself. How did he get into all this? The last he remembered, he was off for an adventure. He was going to learn a trade, see the world, maybe even help some undeveloped country to develop, all while having exciting experiences leading to self-realization and personal growth. Now here he was, working for an organization that was taking sides in an evil war in which lives were being ruined. And these weren't faceless, nameless lives. They had recognizable faces, one of which he was quite fond of. His mood had definitely changed. He was now not feeling giddy at all.

He took leave of Taban and went back to the apartment. It felt cathartic to write to Herb, even if he was mad.

"Well Herb. The deed is done. I paid the ransom price to a human dealer who somehow in all the teeming crowds in Khartoum found Yandeng's sister. So, in conclusion, if there is no slavery is this country, then there isn't any oil either, and no Nile River, and no damned war going on, and I'm a damned idiot. I know people are saying it didn't take place. Hell, I could say I'm a concert pianist. You said the shareholders were raising a stink. Well, where the hell did they get the idea that they ought to raise a stink? Somebody has heard things all the way back in Canada that caused them to raise a stink. I'm mad Herb. I no longer feel real good about helping the Sudanese government find more oil."

Herb was apparently in the office and sent a reply within 15 minutes.

"Jerome, give me a call. I'm in the office."

He opened Skype, found Herb's number and clicked the green call button.

"Yeah?"

"Herb, it's Jerome."

"Yeah buddy, what's up?"

"You asked me to call you."

"Yeah, I know. You sounded upset in your email. Are you Ok?"

"Well no! I don't like taking sides in a civil war. Especially when people I know have been hurt by it."

"Woa. Hang on Jerome. Who's taking sides? Last I heard, we were staying out of it."

"It's pretty hard to stay out of it Herb. You're either for the government or against them. If you're for them, you're taking part in what they're doing."

"Well, I wouldn't put it that way. That's a bit extreme."

"Herb, clearing land by destroying villages and killing families, and taking slaves so we can drill oil for them... that's extreme. I'm not liking this."

"Listen, I know our VP in Khartoum is trying to stay neutral. Don't start letting people know you're taking sides."

"I think the word is already out about me. But I don't understand why Tallman is sticking its head in the sand. Even the shareholders are apparently getting wind of what's going on here."

"Hmm. Listen, this is confidential. I've been told the Canadian government is sending over a private team to do an investigation. Tallman has always maintained that no villages have been touched in our blocks by the government. They have even passed around pictures in our blocks taken back in the 1970's and again today that contain villages and show no change."

"Are you joking? Our blocks are gigantic. If I get a chance, I'll send you some picture of at least one village that was there a year ago and today is toast, and the inhabitants are toast too, and they're still laying in their huts."

"Are you sure it's in our block?"

"Yep. Block 4. I can give you the gps coordinates."

"Hmm. This is getting risky. But send me the coordinates. And, try to get pictures. But Jerome... don't get caught. I don't like this business. It could get us both in trouble, but especially you."

"Ok, but what if I do get caught? What will happen to me?"

"Just don't! But, Jerome, listen, I like you. I've liked you from the start. I'm trying to watch your back. In fact, I've been thinking about finding another position for you and getting you the hell out of there."

"Thanks Herb. I appreciate it. But I'm not looking to leave yet."

"Ok. Hey, I got another call. Keep me in the loop." His screen showed that the call had ended.

Jerome was still brooding when his satellite phone rang. It was Yandeng.

"Well Jerome! What news do you have?"

"Good news Yandeng! Alual is on a bus heading to Bentiu."

"Oh Jerome, that is such news! Thank God! Thank you Jesus!"

"You can thank me too," Jerome said a little sheepishly.

"Yes, of course. Thank you Jerome! I am so happy. When will she arrive?"

"Maybe tomorrow night, maybe the next morning. They couldn't say. She has to change buses in Malakal and no one knows if the road from Malakal to Bentiu will be open."

"Oh, but I need to be here when she arrives."

"Yandeng, you have to be at the camp tomorrow."

"I know, but I just can't. I have to see her. I'll just call the camp and tell them my sister is coming."

"Hmmm. Yandeng, I don't think it's a good idea to tell people at the camp about your sister. I think it could cause you trouble."

"I don't care. I need to see her!"

There was a long pause. Then an awkward good-bye. Jerome felt like, all things considered, he should be extremely happy, but he wasn't. Things just didn't seem quite right. He turned off his computer, walked around the city for a while, avoiding the dojo, then went to bed. The next day he joined Mikhail and flew down to Leghig camp. They landed before lunchtime. The landing provided a surprise, if not a shock. There was a military helicopter sitting to the side of the runway.

"Those bastards are here again," Mikhail muttered.

"When have you seen them before?" Jerome asked

"I've seen them 2 or 3 times in the past few months. They take our fuel, eat at the cafeteria, and move on."

"Where do they go?"

"I see them fly south. They must have missions down in the Nuer territory, down towards Bentiu."

"Missions! You mean they're shooting up villages."

"Yeah, I assume so."

"I thought they pushed home-made bombs out the back of Antonovs?"

"It looks like they're starting to get their hands on the oil money now and can buy real weapons."

"I thought we had agreements, as a matter of fact UN-sanctioned agreements, that the military wouldn't use our airstrip!"

"Those agreements are shit."

Jerome took the camera out of his backpack and snapped a few pictures, getting a panorama of the camp in the background with the gunship centered in the foreground.

"Careful, Jerome. Don't let anyone know you're taking pictures. I won't talk, but others will."

"Ok, it's a promise."

# Chapter 50

The land rover caravan arrived just before lunch with the next shift aboard. When Yandeng stepped out of one of the vehicles Jerome almost shouted for joy.

"What are you doing here?" Jerome asked as he reached her and the others unpacking their bags from the roof rack.

"I called Fatima and told her about my sister and said I wouldn't be here this week. She told me to call her back. When I did, she said she had called Khartoum and they said that if I didn't return to camp this week, I'd be fired."

Jerome's concern rose. She would now be known in the Khartoum office as a war refugee, which was not a good thing. If she mentioned her sister was returning from Khartoum, he may also be suspected of being involved in securing her release, which definitely was a bad thing. He tried not to let this ruin the moment.

"So, Alual is on the way. She's probably halfway between Khartoum and Bentiu right now."

"Yes. I am so happy. I could hardly sleep last night. I prayed all night thanking God. I must have slept though because I had a dream."

She was handed a small bag of belongings from the unloaded baggage. Jerome wondered what was in it, but didn't dare ask her.

"Can I carry your bag for you?"

"Of course not. It is light. But oh thank you so, so much Jerome. I will never forget that you have done this for us. I thank you so much."

"Oh, well... I'm so happy for you. I'd do it again."

"Well I better go to the office and talk to Fatima and see what needs done. I'll see you at lunch."

She gave Jerome a very sweet smile that seemed to melt his heart. He instantly forgot his foul mood, turned and walked to the mess hall. He assembled his team and organized the now standard lunch turnaround meeting, each man sitting with his counterpart. He learned that their survey team would need to leave early in the morning.

Jerome noticed there were 2 extra military men in the cafeteria. They were sitting with the 2 regulars who accompanied them on their survey trips. He figured they must be the helicopter pilots. They were talking loudly in Arabic. Yandeng walked in with Fatima. The soldiers took notice of them and one of the soldiers yelled something at them and the others started laughing.

Fatima ignored them but it seemed to upset Yandeng. This caused the soldier to yell something else and there was more laughter. All conversation in the room stopped. This was not standard behavior at camp. The soldiers were usually quiet spectators on the fringes of camp life.

Yandeng and Fatima joined the women's table and tried their best to ignore the periodic cat calls made from the military table. As the soldiers finished their lunch, they got up in unison. Leaving their trays at the table they walked out past the women's table and stopped. The most vocal soldier greeted the women in a saccharine-sweet voice, then put his hand on Yandeng's shoulder. She startled at his touch.

"What is the 'abida' doing tonight?" he asked in Arabic, in a voice loud enough for the whole room to hear.

Time seemed to stand still. No one in the room spoke, or moved, or even seemed to breathe, except for the soldiers who were having a good laugh at this comment. Jerome wanted to move but he felt like his arms and legs were glued down. He also had a tightness in the pit of his stomach that seemed to prevent him from even breathing. Finally, Osman stood, and walked over to the table. The eyes of all were on him. He approached one of the regular camp soldiers and whispered something in his ear. Then the soldier laughed loudly and they all turned and left. There was an uneasy silence in the cafeteria. Jerome's tenseness relaxed but he felt his pulse still pounding. He was angry and also ashamed. Why hadn't he jumped to his feet? Should he have? What would have happened? It didn't matter. It would have been better to take a stand. He was furious at himself for about 30 seconds. Then he calmed down and said to himself, "Ok, I took the first punch to my stomach. I'm still standing. Next punch I block and return one of my own."

Right after lunch, Jerome heard the helicopter gunship leave.

"Good riddance!" he thought to himself. "I wonder what unfortunate souls will meet you today?"

The afternoon was spent preparing for the following day's trip. The equipment was checked and tested. Repairs were made.

Just before dinner the helicopter returned, causing a large cloud of dust to rise over the whole camp. At dinner Jerome sat with the guys. Osman for some reason sat with the military guys at their table. Yandeng sat at the women's table. Jerome glanced over at her several times. He wanted to talk with her, to find out how she was doing and make sure arrangements had been made for her sister's arrival. In actual fact, he really wanted to just be with her. He'd leave in the morning and wouldn't see her again for a week, at which time she'd leave for Bentiu. Then when she got back from Bentiu, he'd be in Khartoum. He had never wanted to be with a girl before as much as he wanted to be with her. He had never been in love or even seriously attracted to a girl. There was Nastia on Sakhalin Island. But she wasn't exactly attracted to him in the same way he was to her. Most of the girls he had found attractive back home didn't seem to notice he existed, or if they did, were openly hostile. Yandeng was different. She seemed to like him. She respected him, which he liked. He found her very attractive. Her dark skin, thin strong body, and face that seemed to shine from a light from another world attracted him. If he let himself, he figured he could look at her for hours. She also had a faith in God was scary yet attractive at the same time. In truth, he wanted her and everything she had. But they were worlds apart. She had grown up in a grass-roofed hut somewhere not far away, isolated from the modern world. She had also apparently suffered terribly, although she didn't speak of it. He had never really suffered. He seemed so plain and colorless in comparison with her. He had so much, and yet seemed so needy. She had so little and yet seemed to have so much. He made his mind up to try to talk with her after dinner. He'd even look for an opportunity to tell her how he felt about her. What did he have to lose? He saw her get up from her seat to go to the dessert table. He quickly followed.

"Are you going back over to the office after dinner?"

"Yes. I left instructions for my sister to call whenever she arrives. I don't know if she'll be to Bentiu yet, but I want to be in the office in case she does call."

"How will she call?"

"Gatwech knows a shop owner who has a telephone. That's where I've started calling from too."

"Oh, that's great. Maybe I'll come over and wait with you."

Yandeng fell silent, then smiled and said, "That would be nice Jerome."

Did he read more into her response than she meant? Did African girls fall in love? Were they attracted to guys like him?

After dessert, Yandeng got up and left. Jerome waited what seemed like an appropriate amount of time, excused himself from the movie viewing and left.

He found her at her desk looking through her stack of paper scraps.

"Sure you don't mind if I wait with you?"

"Of course not. I have you to thank that she is returning. I just can't hardly believe it now that it is happening. Tell me how it happened. Tell me everything."

So Jerome began to recount the events of the last day and not in near enough detail for Yandeng, so he had to retell and answer many questions, such as what Alual was wearing and if she smiled a lot and how tall she seemed in comparison to her.

They had been talking about a half hour when the office door opened. The two new military men entered the office. One of the guys had a smirk on his face. He surveyed the two of them and then said in poor English, "You, Canadian, leave. We have business with abida."

# Chapter 51

The soldiers let out sickening laughs as they stared at Jerome. Jerome glanced over at Yandeng. She seemed frozen with fear. He looked back at the soldiers. Their laughter now stopped and the older soldier shouted, "I say you, get out!"

Anger began to rise inside of Jerome. Still he remained silent. The younger of the two soldiers, who seemed to carry the rank took his automatic rifle off his shoulder and pointed it at Jerome and shouted again, "Move Canadian."

Jerome, with adrenalin now running in his veins stood and said very resolutely, "I'm staying right here."

"I will shoot you!"

"You will have to," he said, unbudging.

Yandeng tugged his arm and whispered, "Jerome, please! Don't. He will kill you."

He could tell her hand was trembling, as was her voice. He stared hard in the soldier's eyes, but didn't move.

The officer hesitated, then delegated. He snarled to his colleague in English for Jerome's benefit, "If he give trouble, shoot him!"

He then stomped over to the far side of Yandeng and yanked her to her feet by her arm. Jerome lunged at him but he hit him with the butt of his rifle, knocking him to the floor. Then he put the gun to his chest and said, "You no move. I will pull trigger."

Then he again grabbed Yandeng by the arm and shoved her across the office and into a side room. Before he slammed the door between the two rooms he shouted back to his underling in Arabic, "If he gives you trouble, kill him, but not in the office. No blood in here. Understand?"

His colleague grunted his approval as the door slammed shut between them.

Jerome jumped to his feet and moved toward the remaining soldier. He pointed his automatic weapon at Jerome undoing the release with a clear clicking sound.

"Not in here!" Jerome repeated in Arabic. "You heard him. No blood in the office. You'd be in big trouble for killing an oil employee."

This gave the soldier pause, if only for a brief second. Jerome quickly stepped forward, grabbed the barrel of the gun and twisted and yanked it from his hands, tossing it behind him as he had practiced many times in the dojo. The soldier then lunged forward at Jerome, swinging wildly. This was easier than sparring in Khartoum. He stepped to the side, blocked the punches with a side chop and punched hard to the side of his head, knocking him off balance. He then stepped in and for the first time kicked with all his might. His foot snapped against his ribs. He fell, gasping for air. Jerome had never been in this position before. His opponent was on the floor writhing in pain. He needed to get to the other room but he knew his current opponent's situation was temporary. He spotted some gray tape on the desk, quickly unrolled some and wrapped his opponent's hands behind his back and put a quick wrap around his feet too. He then got up and charged into the adjoining room. His first sight was the bare buttocks of the officer. He had pulled down his pants, had his bare cheeks in the air as he fought on his hands and knees to get Yandeng's dress up. Jerome gave a swift front kick to the exposed bare back side, sending him head first into the wall in front of him. The officer seemed to bounce off the wall and was on his feet immediately, albeit with his pants down around his ankles and trying to lunge at Jerome. If the situation had been different, Jerome would have laughed at the sight. The targets were so exposed he didn't know where to strike first. He decided for the obvious, the exposed crotch. He decided to try a front kick and for the second time kicked with all his might. The officer fell in a heap to the floor, right beside his automatic rifle. Jerome was quick to scoop up the rifle and put the nozzle to the back of the officer's skull. Jerome had never fired a weapon before, but assumed he could figure it out.

"I don't care about blood in my office. I'll clean up when I'm done. Ready to meet Allah?" he said.

He put his hand on the trigger and slowly started to squeeze. Out of the corner of his eye he saw movement and then he felt and saw long thin black trembling fingers move on top of his own and he heard a trembling but familiar voice say, "No Jerome. Don't do it."

He paused. "What do you mean don't do it. He tried to rape you and to kill me. He deserves to die."

Her voice was still trembling when she repeated, "Don't Jerome!"

"Why not!" he shouted.

"If you do what they do, you become what they are."

This hit Jerome hard. He so much wanted to do to them as they had done to others yet he hated what they were. His mind raced.

"So what if I'm like them for a minute?"

"No Jerome. I couldn't look at you if you do it. Jesus forgave those who hurt him!"

"I'm not Jesus!"

"But you know him, don't you?"

"Know him? What do you mean do I know him?"

This conversation seemed out of place.

"Look Yandeng, if I don't kill him, he'll kill us."

"If you do kill him, others will come after us and they'll have good reason to kill us. If we allow him to live, at least we won't be guilty of taking a life. I don't want to do to them what they've done to us."

"Well, we're stuck then. If we let him live, they chase us. If we kill him, they chase us."

At this point the man in the other room began to shout loudly for help. Jerome wondered if they could hear him outside.

"We have to move quickly. Get the roll of gray tape from the other room, please. I have an idea. And put some in that guy's mouth as soon as possible!"

While Yandeng went and got the tape and quieted the other soldier, Jerome spoke to the officer, but with the rifle still pointed at him.

"OK officer, you wanted your pants down, now take them off, boots too, shirt, and everything else."

The officer gave Jerome a hateful glare and shook his head no. Jerome gave him another hard kick.

"The girl saved your life. She's not here now and I'm losing my patience again."

He undressed until he was completely naked. The shouting in the other room stopped and then Yandeng appeared in the doorway.

"What is going on?" she gasped.

"I found you a new outfit. Try these on."

He pushed the clothing in her direction with his foot while still keeping the rifle fixed on the officer.

"Now, you, lay on your stomach."

Jerome taped his feet, his hands behind his back, and put a few wraps through his mouth and around his head.

Just then they heard the front office door open. Jerome hurried into the other room to find Osman standing there, surveying the other soldier on the floor and taped up tight.

"What is going on Jerome? You will pay for this!"

Jerome still had the rifle in his hands.

"I don't plan to pay for this one, Osman. You should be the one who pays. I think you arranged it if I'm not mistaken."

Osman started towards him. Jerome pointed the rifle at his chest.

"I know you Jerome. You're a coward. You wouldn't shoot me."

And he continued toward Jerome. Jerome knew there was part of him that could easily pull the trigger. Instead, he slid the gun on the floor toward Yandeng who was now standing in the back doorway. Then he turned in time to block Osman's awkward attack. Jerome sidestepped an all-out lunge in his direction while punching hard to the side of Osman's head. This stunned him and he turned and lunged again. Jerome repeated his sidestep and punch. Osman, much more slowly this time came back at Jerome. This time he tried a kick, holding nothing back, right at Osman's chest, who fell, sucking for air.

"Come on, Osman. That was too easy. Get up!"

Osman struggled to his feet. He took a step forward, then warily backed up. He was undecided on whether to attack or run and seemed to freeze. Jerome took another kick, this time at Osman's knee. He fell again, this time writhing in pain making no effort to get up.

"Yandeng, could I please have the tape?"

He taped Osman like he had taped the others. Then he returned to the still clothed soldier, took off his boots, untaped his legs, pulled off his pants, then retaped his legs. Then he removed his shirt the same way. He left this soldier in his underwear.

"Ok Yandeng. Let's put our uniforms on."

Jerome quickly changed clothing and wrapped his civilian clothes up in a roll. Yandeng simply put the uniform on over her dress. They had to laugh as they looked at each other.

"You don't look bad in a uniform," he said. "Oh, do you have the keys to the land rover?" he asked.

She checked her pockets, found them, and handed them to Jerome.

"You look pretty good too," she said, smiling sweetly.

Jerome opened the front door and peeked out.

"Wait here," he said.

He hurried over to the military landrover, hopped in, started it up and pulled it around to the office door. Yandeng jumped in. Then he went back into the office, found his backpack with laptop, camera, and passport, shut out the lights and shut and locked the front door. He jumped in the driver's seat and headed south towards Bentiu on the only road in the region.

"We should have until about 6 AM before the soldiers are discovered and they start looking for us."

# Chapter 52

Yandeng was quiet for a while. Then she spoke, "Why did you do it?"

"Do what?"

"You know what I'm asking. Why didn't you leave the office when the soldiers told you to leave?"

"Yandeng... I wouldn't... How could I... ? I'd never sit by and let that happen."

"You almost got killed. You almost got us both killed."

"Well, I'm sorry if I put us in danger, you were already in danger. Right?"

"Yes, we were both in danger. I appreciate it Jerome. No one has ever done anything like that for me before."

"Well, I've never done anything like that for anyone before."

"Really? Why did you do it for me?"

"Well, because...."

"Because why?"

"Well because I think a lot about you Yandeng. I don't know that I've ever thought, or felt, about anyone the way I feel about you."

"Really?"

"Really! But, I have a question for you. Why didn't you let me pull the trigger? I think it would have been justified self-defense. You continue to surprise me."

"Well, to be honest, I surprised myself. Or maybe God surprised me."

"God surprised you?! What are you talking about?"

"I've actually been really angry inside with Arab men, for this very reason. I have sometimes fantasized about the day when I would get my revenge. Then tonight it happened. I had my chance. I could have killed them, or let you kill them. But revenge is a heavy burden. I know God doesn't want me to carry it. And when I had the chance to let you pull the trigger I realized something."

"What's that?"

"I realized I no longer wanted to carry the heaviness of hate with me anymore. I don't want to be like them."

"Yeah, you said that. You said that if you do what they do, you become what they are."

"A dear friend told me that. I think you'll get a chance to meet him soon."

"Yeah, well, I'm not so into forgiveness. It seems unnatural to me."

"It is unnatural. I think tonight when I asked you not to pull the trigger, I really forgave them, not only the two soldiers and Osman, but the soldiers who destroyed my village, and the murahaleen, and the government. I really feel like I let go of my anger. I felt like God took it from me. Forgiveness is not really … natural. I feel like I touched God tonight."

Just then they came under light rifle fire. A few bullets hit the back of the vehicle. Jerome hit the gas. They sped down the road leaving dust and darkness behind them. "Must be the SPLA. They think we're military. We have to be careful," Jerome said.

They sped as fast as he dared for the next 15 minutes. No vehicles appeared to be following. Jerome kept a constant watch in his rear view mirror as he drove. Their conversation, although not finished, was definitely put on hold.

At about midnight Jerome pulled the hand-held GPS from his backpack. They were close to the burned out village. He slowed down and watched for it. He found it and pulled the landrover near the tukul with the dead bodies.

"Why are we stopping here?"

"I want to get some pictures."

"Of what? The village is destroyed."

"Well, I want pictures of a destroyed village."

Jerome got out, went to the tukul he had been to twice before. He took out his camera, made sure the flash was turned on, and stepped inside. He couldn't see anything. He found his flashlight in the backpack and turned it on. Nothing had changed. He started snapping pictures. He heard movement and realized Yandeng was standing somewhere close behind him. After 30 or 40 shots he put the camera back in the pack and turned to leave.

"We can't leave them like this," she said in a choking voice.

"What can we do?"

"We should try our best to bury them."

Jerome didn't know how to respond. He wanted to keep moving, but he wanted to show the utmost respect at this moment. He knew it meant something very personal to Yandeng. She could have been related to the people whose charred bodies now lay decomposed.

"Where? How?"

"Anywhere is better than this."

They looked around outside the tukul. They found a ditch not far away. They worked together to carry the bodies out and lay them in the ditch. Then Jerome found a shovel in the landrover and covered the bodies with a foot or two of dirt. Then they carried rocks and lay them over the graves.

"May they find rest in God's presence," Yandeng said solemnly.

Jerome could think of nothing to say, so he stood silently. Then they turned together and left. They drove on until almost dawn. Jerome looked at his GPS. He feared driving on the road after dawn so he drove off a few miles to the east of the road into the bush and looked for what appeared to be a level and unobstructed horizon and turned south to continue towards Bentiu.

"They'll soon be looking for us on the road," he said.

The route was now slow because they had to maneuver around and through dry river beds, rocks, and trees of various sizes. Later in the morning they came into the Bentiu area. They could see the outskirts of the city in the distance. Jerome found a section of thick trees and brush. He drove in under a canopy. They left the uniforms in the back seat. He pulled branches off nearby trees and covered the landrover so nothing was visible from any distance. They then left on foot in their civilian gear. Within an hour they were in town.

"Do you know where to go?" Jerome asked.

"Yes, follow me."

Within 30 more minutes they were at the church.

"I'm so excited," Yandeng said.

Gatwech was walking out when he saw her and ran up and hugged her.

"What are you doing here? We weren't expecting you. Oh, someone is waiting to see you."

They entered the unlit church from the bright sunlight and everything seemed dark. He heard Yandeng scream, then another scream and then crying. They had found each other. After some minutes they let go of each other and Alual looked at Jerome.

"Thank you," she said. "I never did thank you."

Yandeng took him by the arm and pulled him close.

"He has helped me too. He is a very good friend."

Gatwech was also by their side.

"What are you doing here? I thought you couldn't leave the camp until next week."

"Yes, but we had … a problem. We are now in trouble. We are running from the army."

"Why, what did you do?" he asked.

"Well, for one I stole their land rover," Jerome said.

"And he beat up two soldiers who were trying to hurt me and tied them up," Yandeng added enthusiastically.

Alual and Gatwech looked at Jerome in near disbelief. He could tell they were surveying his physical stature and wondering how her statement could be true.

"It's true," she said. "He's a good fighter."

"Well, then you are in danger here," Gatwech concluded. "What will you do?"

"We have to leave the country," Jerome said, his statement causing shocked silence.

"But how?" Gatwech finally answered. "It is too far to walk. Many thousands have died walking out."

. "I have a land rover,"

"Ok. That will help, but the road is dangerous. There are SPLA soldiers all over who will take the land rover if they see it. There are Sudanese army soldiers always moving about, and there are thieves. But oh, I need to tell you something Yandeng. I have already told your sister."

"Yes?"

"A man came by after you left for camp and before Alual got here. His name is Bodogou…"

At this Yandeng squealed with joy.

"He said he saw your note at the post office, which led him here. He said your brother had been captured and forced into the SPLA army, but recently escaped. He's staying in a village a day or two from here. He said he'd let your brother know and that he'd probably be here soon."

Yandeng and Alual cried and hugged again.

"Oh this is one of the happiest days of my life," Yandeng said. "Did Bodogou say anything else?"

"He asked about you. He seemed very concerned for you and said he'd been praying for you."

"Yes, I knew he was. He is like a father to me, a spiritual father," she said.

"What is a spiritual father?" Jerome asked.

"Without him, I would not have come to know God."

"You have become like Lual," Alual stated dryly. "How did that happen?"

Jerome was glad she asked because he wanted to know too. He had assumed Yandeng had been a strong believer all her life. That day he learned her story. They sat on the hard dirt floor in the tukul church, very much like the tukul the 2 girls had grown up in. He was horrified, amazed, and in utter admiration of this girl he had been growing to love. Alual had the same questions he had.

"How can you be so confident that Jesus is helping you, or that he even exists?"

"I've invited him into my life, and I know he's come in."

"But how do you know? Have you seen him?"

"Only in a dream. But I hear him, sort of."

"What do you mean you hear him?"

"I sometimes hear him say things to me."

"You hear voices?"

"Not exactly. I hear him, but not with my ears."

"What else would you hear with?"

"I have ears deep inside me. I think we all have them. The only way to hear him is with those ears."

"Hmm. I don't understand you. But what does he say to you?"

"Lots of things. He told me he'd find you and bring us back together. He told me he loves me and will take care of me."

"He hasn't taken care of me," Alual said coldly.

"Well he hasn't abandoned you. And if you ask him, I'm sure he'll take care of you like he does of me."

Alual stared at Yandeng for a long time, her cold skepticism confronting Yandeng's childlike faith.

"Even if he does exist, he wouldn't take me."

"Why? Of course he would."

"I'm polluted. I've been used like an animal, and enslaved and I can't even talk about what I've been through. I'm not the type of person God likes."

"No, Alual. No. I'm not good at convincing people. But you don't know him, that's why you say that. If you met him, even just for a minute, like I met him, you wouldn't say that about yourself. One look in his eyes and you'd see yourself differently."

"How would you know? You haven't been where I've been. How could he accept me?"

Yandeng reached out and squeezed her hand and with tears in her eyes said, "Alual, I accept you, and I'm not better than God."

Alual looked to the floor, unable to meet Yandeng's tearful gaze.

"What about your white friend?" she asked, changing the subject. "I assume he believes too. This is their religion isn't it?"

This both amused and offended Jerome. He didn't like being typecast, and he had never seen Jesus Christ as the white man's heritage and wondered why she did.

"Yes Jerome, you have met Jesus haven't you? You mentioned that you prayed. Surely you know him too."

Now he was on the spot. He wanted so much to be able to please, but this wasn't an area where he could, or would, fake.

"Actually Yandeng, I was raised not to believe in God, and especially in Jesus. There is something in me though that goes against the way I was raised and wants to know God. I have prayed to him, recently, when I asked that we'd find Alual. You could say I've seen him answer prayer. But I can't say I've ever heard him speak with ears that are somewhere inside of me or that I've ever seen his eyes, or that I know him."

Yandeng seemed deeply pained by this confession. He wished it weren't so, but there he had summed up honestly all he knew or had ever experienced on the topic of God.

"But would you at least like to know him? Both of you?"

"Yes, of course," Jerome said without hesitation.

"... I guess so," Alual said reluctantly.

"Will you talk to him, directly to him."

"Hmm. I guess… You mean, like pray to him?"

"Yes."

"Well, I guess I could. Not out loud though, right?" Jerome asked.

"Why not out loud?" Yandeng asked.

"Sure, what does it matter?" Alual said, almost defiantly.

"But how should we pray?" Jerome asked.

"Say something like this. Ok? … Jesus, I don't know you but I want to know you."

Jerome and Alual repeated out loud.

"I invite you into my tukul. You know where I live. My door is open. Come in. Live with me. Be my friend, my protector, my Father, my Lord."

Jerome was waiting for more. This seemed so… brief and simple, yet it expressed a true desire. There wasn't even an Amen. In any case, he agreed with the prayer. The prayer and conversation seemed to have ended. There was no epiphany or a bright light of revelation, but it seemed significant. He was definitely sincere. He didn't know what he needed to do next, if anything. It seemed though like the conversation had not ended. He hoped not.

# Chapter 53

After praying, Jerome realized he was dead tired since he hadn't slept the night before. He knew Yandeng was tired and Alual must be too. The girls announced they would rest. He badly wanted to sleep but first needed to find a way to send some emails, notably one with the pictures he'd taken over the past day of the helicopters and the burned tukul. He asked Gatwech if there were an internet café in town. It didn't seem by his answer that that even knew what an internet café might be. Jerome tried to explain, but got blank looks, even from Yandeng. So he sat and thought.

"Yandeng, you've received emails at the camp from the office here in Bentiu, haven't you?"

"Yes?"

"Well they must have internet connection via satellite, like ours at the camp. And they probably have a wireless router too."

"I don't know what you mean Jerome, but they do send emails."

At least she now said they "sent" emails. She was learning.

"Where is their office?"

"About a half hour walk from here. Gatwech knows where."

Jerome downloaded, reviewed, and compressed the pictures from his camera. He then attached them to an email and addressed it to Herb and added the message:

Herb: Last night Osman Allaoui, the Tallman seismic crew leader, conspired with 2 military personnel to rape Yandeng. They also attempted to kill me. Thank God I stopped them. I then had to tie them up or they would have harmed, if not killed us both. I then had no choice but to make a run for it. So, I'm no longer at the camp. Yandeng and I are fugitives. I need to try to get out of the country. I have no idea how. Yandeng is a Sudanese national and has no passport. It would compromise her safety to try to obtain one at this point. I think Tallman owes her one. Can you help us? You said you had my back Herb. I need a favor now. I won't forget it. We need some way to get out of the Sudan and somewhere to go. I'll try to contact you within 24 hours although email access is not a guarantee.

Oh, here's the pictures, and the GPS coordinates. If you check, you'll see the village is well within Tallman's block. It looks like it took place within the last 12 months. The bodies were not totally decomposed. We did our best to bury them. Jerome."

He then composed another email:

"To Whom It May Concern:

Last night at 6 PM E Africa time, two military personnel from the Army of Sudan attacked two Tallman employees, myself, Jerome Schultz and Yandeng Nyeal. The attack took place in the offices of the Ligheg Drilling Camp. The attack was organized by Tallman employee Osman Allaoui. The military personnel attempted to rape Miss Nyeal and kill me. Both attempts were thwarted. I could have taken all their lives in self-defense, but did not. We detained them temporarily with tape. We now have no choice but to flee for our lives. We ask for your support and understanding as this event was not of our choosing.

Sincerely,

Jerome Schultz"

He addressed the message to a group address, "All Tallman Employees" and hit the send button. He figured this might buy him some support somewhere along the line.

He then found Gatwech and they walked together to the employment office. When they got nearby Jerome pulled the computer out of his backpack, turned it on, and searched for a wireless network. He was not disappointed. The name of the Tallman wireless network showed on his screen. He clicked "Connect" and waited. Fifteen seconds later he was in. Thirty minutes later they were back at the church. Yandeng and Alual were asleep on a mat, side by side, holding hands. They looked so much alike, and yet so different. One had a look of utter contentment and joy, while the other had a face drawn tight by torment and pain. Jerome found an unused mat, slid it near the girls, lay down, and was asleep within minutes. They didn't wake until the bread was delivered to the front door.

"Great idea. I'm hungry," Jerome said.

Everyone else agreed too. They saw new people who had showed up while they slept. There were at least 25 others. Jerome figured that when everyone spread out and lay down, the floor would be completely covered. They were introduced to the group, although Yandeng seemed to know most of them. Then they sat in small groups, and ate.

"Save some for breakfast," Yandeng said.

"Why?" asked Jerome. "Why not buy more in the morning?"

"Why? Because the bread only comes once a day."

The reality sunk in. Jerome had noticed many of the people were extremely emaciated. A few looked like they were in the early stages of starvation. He was sharing bread with people who were literally dying of hunger. He felt ashamed for having been so well fed all his life, although he didn't know if this was something should feel ashamed about.

After they ate, a few candles were lit inside the tukul as the outside light was now completely gone. Gatwech joined Yandeng, Alual, and Jerome and they talked for a few hours, mostly about Alual's captivity in Khartoum. She was very reluctant to talk about it, but with all the questions, began to open up and spill the secrets of her journey, often in tears.

"The day the murahaleen destroyed Palwung, they tied me in a line with 25 or so other women and children from the village and began marching us north. After 2 days we were tied together with people captured from other villages and made to walk long marches. The women were raped regularly."

At this she looked down and couldn't continue for a minute. Jerome thought she wouldn't continue, but she regained her composure and went on.

"The young boys were sodomized. If anyone refused to cooperate they were hacked to death in front of everyone. Food was scarce and some died of starvation on the march. Others got sick or injured from the harsh conditions and were shot or left to die. It took us over a month to reach Khartoum. At that point we were split up and sold off. I was sold to an old Arab man who sells cloth in Omdurman. He was harsh and always angry. Fortunately, he had 3 wives, and he wasn't home much so he didn't bother me often. But the other wives were merciless. They made me cook their meals and wash their clothes and they constantly jeered me. I was known only as 'el abida' (the slave). They never asked my name." I was so alone. I wished I would die. I lacked the courage to take my own life."

Yandeng held her hand tightly, tears coming to her eyes.

"I wish I could have found you earlier," Yandeng sobbed. "I just didn't know how. I was so occupied with my own problems. Forgive me."

"But how did you find me?"

"I was given the name of a Bagarra whom I was told might be able to locate you. I contacted him. Then Jerome went to Khartoum and he did the rest."

Alual looked at Jerome with a softer look than she had yet given him. She seemed so hardened and suspicious of motives, and especially cold towards men, although, now he could understand why.

"Thank you," she whispered.

"You're quite welcome, Alual."

"How much did he ask for me?" Alual asked, betraying a slight sense of humor.

"Not near as much as you're worth, fortunately," Jerome replied.

Alual's hardness softened yet a little more.

"What will you do now?"

"Well, I'm working on finding something new. I'm asking around for a job for Yandeng too."

"Me? How? Where?"

"Somewhere else, outside the Sudan."

"Jerome, I could never leave the Sudan. This is my home."

"Yandeng, if the government finds us, all I owe them is a vehicle. They'd probably torture me for a few weeks then expel me. But you... there is no telling what they'd do."

Jerome had put words to what they all knew was true but didn't want to mention.

It was late, and they all still felt tired, and so with little discussion, they took to their mats, blew out the candle and slept.

The next morning Jerome awoke when he heard the early risers moving about. Gatwech was up and was over near the church alter and appeared to be praying or meditating. Jerome waited until he was done and approached him. He asked if he could buy everyone breakfast, preferably something more than just bread. Gatwech seemed pleased and the two of them went out to some nearby shops and bought bread, yoghurt, and cheese for 30 people. It caused a little stir when they returned and everyone smiled widely at Jerome.

"What are the plans for today?" Gatwech asked.

"Well, I guess we wait for Lual," Jerome said. "He was apparently told where we are, so we can only wait until he finds us. And oh, can you walk with me to the employment office again? I need to check my email."

So after breakfast they made an email run. There were messages from people within the company who didn't even know him. Some were asking if it was true or just a joke while others were extending their sympathy. There was also a message from Herb.

"Jerome:

How are you? God, what a mess you're in! I don't know how the hell I'm going to get you out of there? But I'm working on it. I think I have a job lined up for you. The tricky part is getting you out of the Sudan. I checked with our staff in Khartoum and they say you're a wanted man. That girl is too. And oh, by the way, the job I'm working on for you will only allow professional staff plus spouse, ie. you, but no foreign nationals from the Sudan. I wish I could help the girl, but I can't. Keep a low profile and make yourself scarce until I can put a plan together.

Herb"

Jerome sat silent.

"What news did you get Jerome?" Yandeng asked.

"Not much news yet."

"I am praying for good news. For you and Alual, and Lual, and me too. God will take care of us. You'll see."

Jerome was touched. But he was fighting not to slip into despondency. He guessed she had seen far worse. But this was as bad a predicament as he'd ever known.

## Chapter 54

One of the women who stayed with them at the church ran in from the outside. She looked at Jerome and Yandeng, then quickly ran to Gatwech and whispered in his ear. He looked over at them, then hurried out of the church with her. Then his head appeared again in the doorway and he shouted, "Yandeng, stay inside the church until I return. Don't go anywhere!"

Fifteen minutes later he returned.

"Yandeng, Jerome, army officers have posted pictures of you both at the post office. They say you are wanted for an assault on government personnel and property. I found the note you posted on the wall, only a few feet from your pictures. I tore it down. We wouldn't want to announce to them where you're staying."

"What should we do?" Jerome asked. "Should we run?"

"No!" Yandeng almost shouted. "We will wait for Lual. He will come for us. He will come as quickly as he can."

"I think we should leave and move south. The government is less likely to find us there."

"No! Then my brother would not find us either. I am going to wait here until he comes. If you need to leave, I understand."

Jerome could tell by her tone that she was determined. He knew he'd stay with her, come what may. His angst grew the more the day wore on. The church seemed smaller and smaller and he had an urge to run south and not stop running until he got to the Uganda border. He gave Gatwech some more money to go out and buy food. He brought back fruit and yoghurt and bread. They ate and napped and chatted until evening. The crowd started to return and the evening bread was delivered.

"Gatwech, do you think we should make an announcement, asking people not to turn us in?" Jerome asked.

"No, my son. I think it is better not to call attention to your predicament. I would suggest though that you treat everyone to breakfast again in the morning. Allegiances in this country nearly always go to those who feed you."

This sounded fine to Jerome. He'd gladly feed the hungry anyway.

They broke bread together in small groups, sitting on mats. Everyone had stories to share, stories of destruction of homes, separation from loved ones, and hardship. Even though the stories were hard, everyone seemed to have a sense that they were the lucky ones because they were still alive. Jerome realized he was now part of their story and drama. He too was a victim who had experienced loss at the hands of those stronger than him. He felt a sudden affinity for these poor, thin, suffering Africans. He may look like he didn't belong, but he felt as though he was now part and parcel with them. He finally felt like he understood Yandeng. And now that he understood her, he knew that he loved her. He would do anything for her. He also knew their predicament was serious, even life threatening. He had never felt so in love nor so ill at ease in all his life.

That night Jerome lay on his cardboard mat and tossed and turned. It wasn't just the discomfort of lying on a hard floor, he was scared. Sleep would not come. He was sweating profusely and kept rolling over. Yandeng was lying beside him. At one point he heard her whisper in the darkness.

"Jesus, help Jerome. Help him see you, and see your angels surrounding him so he won't be afraid."

"Do you see angels, Yandeng?" he whispered back.

"I sense them. I've sensed them all day, since even before Gatwech told us about our pictures."

"Why are they here?"

"I think they may always be here. But I sense there are more than usual. They're watching us. Don't be afraid."

"I don't know Jesus like you do."

"Do you want to?"

"Yes. I really do."

"Then ask him. Tell him you want to open that door and let him come in."

"I already did when we prayed together."

"That's good. Tell him again, yourself, in your own words. He likes it when we talk to him with our own words."

"How do you know?"

"I can tell he likes it when I talk to him."

"Ok. I'll try."

Jerome prayed silently.

"God, I know she's right. I need to talk to you directly… There's two things going on here. One, I've never known you. Truth be told, I didn't want to know you. I thought I was enough all by myself. I know I've been wrong. Forgive me. I need you. Come in through the door Yandeng talks about. I'm not real sure what that means but I know I want it. I guess I feel about you sort of like I do about Yandeng. I know I want you. I also know I'm stepping into the unknown and there is part of me that is scared. But I want you anyway. Second, I'm scared about my situation. I'm in deep shit… or I mean do-do. No, I mean shit. I'm sure you've heard the word before. Anyway, I need help. I figure you're the only one that can help me, and Yandeng, and her family too. So I'm asking you to watch my back. Herb is nice and all, but he's only Herb. I need your kind of help… Help me to connect with you like Yandeng does, so I know you're listening, and even enjoying listening. Anyway, that's my situation in a nutshell. I'll leave it with you. Thanks."

He felt calmed and began to relax. Within minutes he was asleep. As he slept he had a dream. He saw a big door, it was thick and heavy and was hung on old rusty hinges. It was open only a crack. Someone was knocking on it from the outside.

"Why doesn't someone answer that door?" he wondered.

The knocking continued and continued. He didn't know whose house or whose door it was, but he was tired of the knocking. He went over to the door and began to pull on it, but it wouldn't budge. The knocking continued.

"What? Come in already," he shouted to the person on the other side of the door.

He pulled again and this time felt someone pushing from the other direction and the door opened. He didn't see anyone, but bright sunlight flooded the room. He felt a tremendous sense of relief that the knocking had stopped and that the door was opened.

He awoke some time thereafter feeling like he had been sparring and had won. He felt like something had been resolved. He knew in his heart that he too, like Yandeng, had opened the door. Jesus was now no longer a theory, or a religion, but part of his experience.

He quickly found Gatwech and did as he had suggested. He pulled out 4000 dinars and asked if he'd buy breakfast for the group again.

"I'd go with you to help carry the food, but I think in light of my recently won reputation I probably should stay here."

"By all means Mr. Jerome. I would insist that you not leave the church. Spend time with us as our guest. We will take care of you."

Gatwech quickly left to get bread and yoghurt. The word somehow had gotten out and people began getting up and watching the front door. He was noticing occasional grateful smiles and nods coming in his direction.

"Amazing what a reaction $20 spent in the right circumstance will produce," he thought. "I should make a habit of this."

Gatwech was quickly surrounded in ten minutes by a happy throng. Jerome, Yandeng, and Alual ate last. Gatwech made sure to save some for them. Jerome had an urge to pray before his meal and thank God for not only the meal, but for the fact that his fear had all but left him and that he felt more like he was eating with family than he could ever remember. It was a special moment.

"Your pictures are still displayed at the post office," Gatwech said solemnly.

"Are the pictures very good ones?" Jerome asked, simply wondering how recognizable they would be from the pictures.

"Oh yes. You both look wonderful!" Gatwech said enthusiastically.

This caused Jerome to laugh, and then continue to laugh, until he couldn't stop. This then caused Yandeng to laugh, and then Gatwech, and then the whole room was laughing, although most had no idea why, except that it looked terribly funny to see the little white guy so out of control. Even Alual laughed. When they finally stopped laughing, he gained his composure, took Yandeng's hand and said, "I'm glad they have good pictures of us."

The day was spent sitting and talking. Alual asked Yandeng what happened the day Palwung was destroyed. All laughing was long past when she described how she had seen what happened to Alual but was too afraid to move.

"You did the right thing. If you had cried out, they would have taken you too. Then who would have found me and brought us back together."

They hugged again. Yandeng then started describing her journey. It took her 2 hours. She finished by saying, "Yet in the end, God worked something good out of something bad. Within a few days of leaving the camp, I not only found a new home here at the church, but also a job. And I met Jerome too!"

She turned and smiled at Jerome. Alual pondered the story. She too smiled briefly at Jerome but said, "I don't think God could ever work something good out of my bad experience."

"I didn't think so either. But it happened. We're together again."

They hugged again. Jerome wanted to hear more but the story seemed to be over. Jerome now knew Yandeng's life story, or at least the most important parts, most of which were traumatic and difficult. He resolved anew that he would do whatever was in his power to defend and protect her.

# Chapter 55

Jerome lay in the dark, his thoughts keeping him from sleep. He knew they needed to leave as soon as possible. The longer they stayed at the church, the greater the chances they'd be caught. He knew Yandeng wouldn't leave until her brother arrived. As he lay there he prayed.

"God, Father, you're my father now, so I hope it's Ok to call you that. I've heard other people call you Father, but I really want you to be my father. Anyway, I know you already know this, but I'll say it again, just to clarify. We're really in trouble here. I want to take care of Yandeng and her sister but if we're caught, I'm just a little guy against a big army. I'm not going to cut and run. I'm going to fight this time, just like I did back in the office. And oh, by the way, I hope you didn't mind what I did there. I mean, as I look back on it, it seemed like it was you helping me and all, so I'm assuming you didn't mind. I realize that Yandeng was right though, about not killing that guy. I was angry enough to have killed him. I can sense you would not have liked that. I'm sorry. Anyway, what I'm saying is, I'm in way over my head, but as I now understand who you are, it's not way over yours. So, help us out here. Could you please get her brother here and help us get to somewhere safe? I'm starting to get really scared. Thanks … Dad."

Sleep again came with peaceful dreams. Jerome woke early and through Gatwech treated the church to breakfast again.

After breakfast Jerome showed Gatwech how to power on his computer, find a wireless network connection, and download email. Gatwech then went off with Jerome's backpack and gear. He returned an hour later.

"I did the things you requested Mr. Jerome, and I read a sentence that said I was successful. How does it know that?"

"Ah, well… it just does. Thanks Gatwech."

Jerome opened his email and found a new message from Herb.

"Good job Gatwech. Let me tell you too. You were successful!"

Gatwech seemed very pleased. He had never touched a computer before.

The message from Herb read:

"Jerome:

I just learned that the Canadian government sent an independent investigation team to Khartoum and they're due to arrive today. I sent your pictures and gps coordinates on to them anonymously, and told them about you. I don't know how long they're staying. Is there any way you could get to Khartoum? I'm almost positive they could get you out of there. Let me know what's up. I'm worried about you. It's not safe there.

Herb."

Jerome powered down the computer to save the battery and thought about possible responses to Herb.

There seemed nothing to do now but wait. Jerome noticed Gatwech reading a Bible. When he saw Gatwech close it he asked if he could borrow it for an hour or so.

"Why of course you can borrow it. I am very fortunate to have my own copy. I consider it belonging to anyone who needs it."

Jerome then read the Bible on his own for the first time. Gatwech had recommended he start with the gospel of Matthew, the first book in the New Testament. In a few hours he read the whole book. Jerome found it amazing that Jesus knew he was going to die, yet didn't try to run. He could have escaped, but didn't.

"Read to us from the Bible," Yandeng said. "You have been reading for 2 hours. You have read more than I have!"

"I'll read you the last paragraph in the book," Jerome offered.

"Ok, read it. Alual, do you want to hear a verse from the Bible?"

"Yeah, I guess. I don't think I've ever heard one before."

"Well, here it is...

*When they saw him, they worshiped him; but some doubted. Then Jesus came to them and said, 'All authority in heaven and on earth has been given to me. Therefore, go and make disciples of all nations, baptizing them in the name of the Father and of the Son and of the Holy Spirit, and teaching them to obey everything I have commanded you. And surely I am with you always, to the very end of the age.'"*

They sat and thought together and Jerome asked, "How could some of them doubt? How could they doubt after he had just risen from the dead?"

"I don't know," said Yandeng. "I doubt sometimes too."

"You doubt!" said Jerome, completely surprised.

"Sure, I've doubted that he is always with me. But at this point, even though I know we're in trouble, I know he is with me... I mean us."

"Yeah, I've doubted all my life, until just the other day. I also believe he is with me until the end. And I don't believe the end is close. I believe we're going to get out of this. We sure need his help."

Yandeng shook her head in agreement, but Alual just knitted her brows and fell deep in thought.

That afternoon as they sat in the heat and made conversation, the door darkened and a tall young man walked in. Yandeng squealed and jumped to her feet. Alual followed. They hugged and spoke unintelligible Dinka words. Tears flowed as the surviving members of the Nyeal family of Mayom County were at last reunited.

After a time, they introduced Jerome as a dear friend who had beat up two soldiers to save Yandeng and had negotiated with a slave trader to redeem Alual, but who was now a wanted man.

"Yes, I have seen your picture," Lual said respectfully. "I am in debt to you. I am sorry I was not there to help," he said.

"Well Lual, your help is still needed. We need to make plans to get from here to a safer place."

"It seems unfortunately no part of the country is safe. But we will talk of plans as soon as we can."

He then turned to his sisters and they began to catch up on each other's story. They spoke in English as much as they could for Jerome's sake, but often lapsed into Dinka. It seems that the day Yandeng hurt her leg and was put onto a bus to Bentiu, the SPLA soldiers caught up to the traveling band that she had been part of. They were angry that she had gotten away, but happy to get Lual. They insisted he come with them, either by his own will, or by the barrel of a gun. And so, he never made it to Nimne to find food. Instead he found himself running from one outpost to another carrying out raids on government troops.

"We got into some skirmishes. I saw many killed. It was horrible. The worst part though was raiding our own people. We had no food of our own and so we were dependent on the food of others. Sometimes we raided government food supplies, but most often we raided the food of our own starving people. I am ashamed, but I had no choice. They would have killed me if I hadn't helped steal food. I finally found an opportunity and escaped from them. I hope they will not find me."

"So where did you go?"

"I only escaped recently. I went to a newly created village of refugees south of here where I heard rumors that Bodogou had gone. I was hoping I would find you there with him. I was very disappointed that you were not there Yandeng. I would have come to Bentiu to look for you, but when I found Bodogou, he told me he was making a trip here to look for his brother. He said he would check around for you too."

"What is the village like?" Jerome asked.

"What village?" Lual asked.

"The village you went to? Are there government troops around?"

"No, it is in a region mostly controlled by the SPLA."

"Can we go there? All of us? Me too, and stay there unnoticed."

"I suppose. Bodogou has 2 tukuls. We could even build another. Yes, that would be possible."

"How far away is it?"

"Well I had to walk about an hour to get to the road that leads from Waw to Bentiu. I waited 2 hours, then flagged down a bus. The bus took about 6 hours."

"What if we had our own vehicle? Would you know how to get there?"

"Yes, of course. I could find it. We could probably make it in 5 hours, or less."

"Well we have a vehicle. I propose we leave tonight, after dark."

"Tonight?" they all said, almost in unison. "Why so soon?"

"Soon? Yandeng, our pictures have been posted all over town for days. It is only a matter of time before someone who walks through these church doors mentions to a friend who mentions to another friend who mentions to a soldier that we're here. We're free now. If we want to stay free we need to leave.

Lual shook his head in agreement.

"Good. Let's leave after everyone is asleep. We'll let Gatwech know, but no one else. I think if we can, we should try to rest now, because we'll be up all night."

That night after the bread had been distributed, the three lay down and waited. No one could sleep. Jerome waited until 9 PM. At this hour the streets were nearly empty. It seemed as though everyone in the church was asleep. The poor and destitute seemed to sleep early and rise early in the Sudan. He nudged Lual and then whispered to the girls to follow in a minute or two and to keep them in sight. He and Lual slipped out the front door. Gatwech followed. He was very emotional and far too loud for Jerome's liking. They hugged and said good-bye. Jerome was very grateful to him for all he had done, especially for Yandeng. He gave Gatwech about $100 in cash. He wanted to give him more, but he had no idea how much more he'd need. He had about $400 in dinars left. He and Lual then started out. Jerome had put a towel over his head, in a turban effect, so his white face would not be too obvious. He heard loud sobbing behind him as Yandeng and Alual hugged Gatwech. They walked north until they found the vehicle. Jerome got out his hand held GPS and turned it on.

"I don't know if it is safe to take the road?" he said. "But if we don't, we may not find the village."

"I know the road near Bentiu is watched by soldiers," Lual said.

"Hmm. Let's bypass the road until we're well outside of town."

They drove west slowly, over rough terrain, until town was well behind them. Then they turned south for about 10 miles looking for the road leading to Waw. They had made a large arc to bypass Bentiu. They eventually found the road. It was also a dirt road, but in good condition. After 4 hours, Lual spotted a large tree to the side of the road.

"This is the tree beside the trail I followed."

## Chapter 56

Jerome drove off the road and along a river bed at least a quarter mile from the road when they came to a small patch of low trees.

"This is a good place to hide the land rover," Jerome said.

He pushed the vehicle into the small grove. They got out and covered it as best they could with branches. Then they found the path. They arrived at the village just at dawn. A few morning fires were already lit and the smell of roast sorghum was already in the air.

Lual quickly led them to a group of tukuls and called Bodogou's name. A big man with a weathered, but kind face stepped quickly out and gave Lual a hug, then turned to the girls and let out a loud laugh and reached forward. Yandeng instantly wept for joy in his arms. After a moment, in his big, deep voice he asked, "Who is this?" smiling and pointing at Alual.

"This is our dear sister Alual."

"But... I thought she had been taken away to the north... as a slave?" he said incredulously.

"She was. But thank God, she is now here with us."

"God be praised. But how does one get free from slavery?"

Yandeng spoke up. "God helped us. And our friend Jerome worked very hard until she was free. We could not have done it without his help."

Bodogou now looked Jerome over. He had a surprised expression on his face to be sure.

"I have seen your picture, Mr. Jerome. And yours too, Yandeng. You are wanted by the government. The report I read claims you attacked government troops and stole government property." At this Bodogou smiled and looked Jerome over again.

"You two must have some stories to tell! But come, sit down, you must be hungry and breakfast is almost ready."

There was a good laugh about attacking government troops and Yandeng filled Bodogou in on their story.

"Hmm," Bodogou said, looking respectfully at Jerome. "So you have rescued both of the Nyeal girls." Then he winked at Jerome and burst into loud laughter again.

"Yes he has!" Yandeng said laughing. Alual nodded her head and smiled at Jerome. Lual smiled too.

They all laughed again and Bodogou slapped him on the back and said, "You are welcome in my tukul."

"I am honored," Jerome said. "But I fear my presence may put you in danger," he added.

"In danger? From whom?"

"From the government army."

"Oh, they won't come here. This area is controlled by the SPLA. It is the Nyeals who are not safe here."

"Why is that?" Jerome asked.

"If soldiers come through, they will conscript Lual again, and if they see his sisters, they may take them, as the government soldiers tried to do."

"So, I have come to safety, only to bring the rest of you into danger. I had no idea." This discovery completely deflated Jerome.

"Don't be silly," Bodogou said. "We are at war. No one is safe. If you think you are safe, you are deceived. It is God who protects us. If you think differently, you are again deceived. When you are in the desert, you ask him to protect you from the cobra, when you are in the bush, you ask him to protect you from the jackal. It is only the danger that has changed."

Yandeng and Lual shook their heads in agreement.

"A few weeks ago, I would not have believed that God was protecting me," Jerome confessed, "but I have begun to believe it."

"Good, because we can count on no other protection here."

They ate breakfast, a sort of pasty gruel, along with a local variety of tea. Jerome was relieved to no longer be captive to the small, dimly lit church in Bentiu. He was tired, as were the rest, but there were morning chores and the Nyeals seemed to understand it was time to begin. Yandeng and Alual ground grain with a large pestle. Jerome helped Lual find firewood. They had to walk over a mile from camp. They made 2 trips, then got some fishing gear and went to a nearby river and fished until noon.

"What are your plans?" Jerome asked Lual. "Are you concerned about being conscripted again?"

"Of course I am. But I have nowhere else to go."

"Where would you like to go?"

"I'd like to move further south, further away from the fighting. But I have no land there, and no animals to barter with. The family's herd is gone now."

"How much money would you need to start over?"

"I'd need a fortune."

"How much is a fortune?"

"A fortune of 500,000 dinars would be needed to buy a small herd and buy favor with the elders in a new village."

Jerome did the math in his head. It was a sum of about $2500. A small price it seemed to start a new life.

They caught two fish and brought them back to the village. The heat by now was reaching well over 100 degrees in the shade. No afternoon activities were planned. They quickly cooked the fish, ate, then found a place on the tukul floor and slept soundly until late afternoon.

That night after a dinner of sorghum gruel, Bodogou led them to the center of the village area where all the villagers gathered. This was an unusual village, Bodogou explained to them. There were Nuer, Shillick, Dinka, and even some Nubans present. Never in the history of Sudan had peoples mixed like this. Hard times had brought unusual circumstances.

The drums began, and then the dancing. Men danced with men, then women with women. Bodogou interpreted for them what was taking place.

"They are celebrating their tribes' histories."

Then men began to jump and dance in front of certain younger women. A few men came and jumped vigorously in front of Yandeng and Alual. Jerome felt Yandeng lean towards him when this happened.

"These are courtship dances," Bodogou explained. "The young men are trying to attract women that they want to marry."

Then some young men knelt down in the center of the dance area and thinly clad girls began to dance around them. After a time, one of the girls draped her bare leg over the man's shoulder. The crowd whistled and shouted. Then the man looked to see who it was. He then stood and danced with the girl.

"If he dances with her, it means that their courtship is sealed. They are then engaged to be married," Bodogou explained.

On the way back to the tukul that night Bodogou lamented, "We still have our dances, but most of the traditions are disappearing."

"What do you mean?" asked Jerome.

"Dances are one thing, but traditions are another altogether. The dance is only the beginning of courtship. After the dance comes the family discussions over the dowry. But men no longer own cattle as in the past, so there is no dowry to give."

"So what happens?"

"Some suitors give promises of cattle. No one knows if they'll ever be able to fulfill their promises. Some offer nothing. Some fathers refuse to give their daughters in marriage under such circumstances. Many daughters have no father to speak for them. Our traditions are being lost."

At the tukul Jerome stayed outside, alone. He sat by the coals of the earlier fire, put more wood on, and stirred them back to life. This helped keep the mosquitos away. But his thoughts were not on the mosquitos. His thoughts were on Yandeng. He was definitely in love with her. He was tormented that he had now put her life in grave danger. Where could she go? The government or the SPLA could pursue her to any corner of the Sudan and she had no possibility of leaving the country. Although he had kept her from being raped, if they caught up with her, her fate would be worse. Would she have been better off if he had never intervened? He saw one way out but couldn't believe she would agree. His thoughts were disturbed by a thin black hand on his shoulder.

"What are you doing out here? Aren't you tired?"

"Yes, I'm tired. I was just thinking."

"About what?"

"Hmmm. About the future and things."

"What things?"

"Hmmm. Things it is hard for me to express in words."

"I find that hard to believe. You're good with words, like the Dinka are with sorghum."

"The Dinka with sorghum?"

"Yes, we can make 1000 different meals from it, and serve it at any time for any type of guest."

"Hmmm. Well, let me try to serve up my thoughts."

"Good. I'm hungry."

"Well, what I was wondering was… if I knew how to dance and jump, would you be happy if I danced in front of you?"

"Really? That is what you were thinking?"

"Yes. Or if I were kneeling in the middle of the crowd, would you dance over to me and hang your leg over my shoulder?"

"I don't know. Go over there and kneel."

"I'm serious Yandeng!"

"So am I. Go over there and kneel."

Jerome slowly started to move.

"Go ahead. What are you waiting for? Those Shillick boys weren't bashful."

Jerome moved away from the fire and knelt down.

## Chapter 57

As Jerome knelt by the fire, he heard rustling and movement. He waited and was tempted to look and say this whole thing seemed silly, when he felt a thin, strong, sweaty bare leg drape over his shoulder. He looked up and in the moonlight he saw her bright eyes and skin shining. She had taken her dress off, leaving only her panties and had put on a tight sleeveless t-shirt. She smiled but seemed to be trembling, as was he. He put his hand on her calve and moved it slowly up past her knee then onto her thin hip, then stood and they embraced, tightly in each other's arms. He kissed her forehead, then her cheek, then their lips locked. They stayed embraced in the moonlight for a long time.

"I don't want to leave you," Jerome said at last.

"I don't want you to leave me," Yandeng answered.

"What I mean is, I want to marry you," Jerome said at last.

"I want you to marry me," Yandeng answered.

They kissed again.

"I think we need to marry soon, and then leave."

"Leave? Why?"

"I don't think we can stay. What if the army comes and tries to take you? Or Lual or Alual?"

"But I can't leave them."

"I think I can help Lual resettle in the south. He can take Alual with him. It will be safer there."

"Where will we go?"

"I'll get work in another country. We can come back and visit when this war is over."

"I don't know."

They embraced again, knowing that their love would involve great personal sacrifice which could destroy the small family, or maybe ultimately save it.

After a long silence, wrapped in each other's arms, they went into the tukul and lay beside each other, holding onto each other and trying to make out each other's face for a long time. When Jerome awoke, he was alone in the tukul. He wondered if the previous night's experience had been a dream or had really happened. When he got up and walked out of the tukul all eyes were on him. He could sense from the expressions on their faces that not only had the previous night's experience certainly taken place, but that everyone looking at him also knew about it. Yandeng seemed to have more of a glow than usual. She smiled brightly at him.

"Good morning everyone," Jerome said. "Sorry. I slept in."

"It is Ok young man. You had an important evening last night," Bodogou said.

The others laughed. Yandeng laughed too. So, Jerome decided to laugh.

"Yandeng told us you asked her a question last night," Bodogou said, sounding like he had rehearsed the phrase.

"Yes. I did. I asked her to marry me. And to my surprise, she accepted."

The all laughed and slapped Jerome on the back. Bodogou reached out his hand and gave a formal hand shake. Then Lual did the same.

"What arrangements have you made? When will this take place?" Bodogou asked.

"Well, by arrangements, you may be referring to a dowry."

"Oh no, I wasn't referring to that," he answered.

"Well, let me speak of that first. I don't have any cattle to give to Lual and Alual. But I can give them money. They can then buy cattle, or whatever they want."

"Do you have money with you?"

"No. It is in a bank. But I can have it wired to Lual."

"Really? What does that mean?"

"Well, Lual, I think you can go to Juba, or Waw, or some place where there is a bank. I will give you a little cash, maybe 5000 dinars. This will allow you to open an account. Then you can call me and tell me the number of the account. My bank will wire money to the account and you can withdraw it."

There were blank stares around the breakfast fire.

"Do you understand what I mean?" Jerome asked.

"Not exactly," Lual said. "Especially the part about the wire. 5000 dinars is nice. But I can't buy a cow with 5000 dinars."

"Yes I know that. No, the 5000 dinars aren't to buy cattle, but to open a bank account. It's like being a member of a village, but instead you're a member of a bank. You have to give them a little money to allow you to be a member."

"I see, so they ask for 5000 dinars to allow me to be a member. I understand."

"Well sort of. They don't keep the 5000 dinars. You put them in the bank so they allow you to accept more money. I plan to send you a lot more dinars. I want to send you a million dinars, but if you don't let them hold your 5000 dinars, they won't allow me to send you a million more. Understand?"

There was dead silence.

Yandeng spoke. "Jerome, do you really have a million dinars?"

"Sure," he answered. He realized that even though it was only $5000 it must seem like a fortune to them.

"Ok," Lual said at last. "I trust you. You have saved my sisters. I believe you will do this thing you're telling us about."

"I'll explain it again later in more detail. And, you'll need this." Jerome handed him his satellite cell phone. This is how we'll talk to each other when we leave. Yandeng can talk to all of you when she wants to."

"I have seen people talk into these. You must explain how it works."

"Yes, I will explain it to you Lual. And I will get another one, and then we can call each other."

"When will you get married?" Bodogou asked.

Jerome looked at Yandeng. She smiled and shrugged her shoulders.

"I think we should do so as soon as possible," Jerome said.

"How soon is that?"

"How about tomorrow?"

"Tomorrow? Why so soon?" Bodogou asked.

"As you said Bodogou, you are all at risk here. The sooner you can resettle further south, the better. Also, Yandeng and I are going to have a hard time getting out of the country. If we move quickly, we may be able to get out, but we must be married."

"What do you mean?" Yandeng asked. "What is your plan?"

"Herb, my boss in Canada, told me there is a government team from Canada that flew into the Sudan in a private airplane. He said if I can get back to Khartoum I could leave with them on their plane. But they won't let you leave with me unless we are married. And unless we leave on that plane, I don't know of any other way for us to get out of the Sudan. You don't have a passport, and I don't think it would be a good idea for you to walk into a government office and apply for one, with your picture being posted all over the country by them and all."

There was a long silence. Yandeng and Alual stared into the breakfast fire. Lual stared at the ground. Bodogou stared off above everyone's head. Finally, he spoke.

"Jerome's plan is a good one. May God give him success. You should marry tomorrow. We must make plans."

Jerome couldn't believe that he had proposed and had now convinced them all to follow his advice. He wasn't very sure his plan had a high chance of success. Yandeng was looking at him with concern in her eyes and yet there was that look that said, "I trust you."

No girl had ever given him that look before, and now it was a girl whom he loved and admired deeply. He knew she was no ordinary girl, not even for a Dinka. He knew she was the girl he would risk his life for. And now, she was risking her life to follow him.

Bodogou went off to a neighboring village to find a notary, and the Nyeals all seemed to know what to do. They started scrambling around, took nearly all Jerome's remaining money for food, and began shopping and enlisting others in the village to cook. The day was spent organizing and delegating. The whole village got involved. By lunchtime there was not a soul in the village who didn't not only know that Jerome and Yandeng were getting married, but had some small role to play.

This was the first wedding in this new makeshift village. It seemed to have a unifying effect on everyone. People of different tribes were working together to celebrate the union of a Dinka girl and a white man. Love and war both had unpredictable results.

Cooking began at 8 AM the next morning. Along with the smell of sorghum roasting on wood fires came dancing and the thumping of drums. Bull horns and songs also filled the air. Young men ran and leaped. Women sang, chanted, and ululated. Jerome pulled Lual off to the side and gave him a quick course on cell phones, banking, and international wire transfers. He knew they wouldn't be able to stay long after the wedding.

Later in the afternoon, he was taken to the groom's tukul in another section of the village. He was given a formal Dinka costume, which needed considerable altering. Dinka men were usually at least 6 feet tall. Jerome was several inches short of the Dinka standard. Then he was taken to a tukul where he was joined by Bodogou, Lual, and a few other men. Traditionally, this was the time when the male members of both sides of the family got together to finalize the dowry agreement and sign formal wedding papers. Lual was the ranking male of the Nyeal family and since Jerome had no family, Bodogou filled in. Such exceptions to accepted tradition were no longer unusual in southern Sudan. The justice of the peace witnessed and documented the shaking of hands. This was the formal or civil wedding. Jerome, in the presence of Lual, Bodogou, and a complete stranger, was pronounced married.

They left the tukul area and returned to the center of the camp where everyone living in a 5-mile radius had gathered. There was more singing, ululating, and drumming. The young men were now worked up into a jumping frenzy, jumping backwards as high and far as they could, which they explained to Jerome had a mesmerizing effect on the young women. He decided to reserve judgement, and simply enjoy it. It was, after all, partly in his honor. Two seats were placed facing the main dance area. Yandeng was escorted to one of them and sat down. She had a new dress on, and her hair was done up in colorful braids. He skin was radiant. She shone brighter than he had ever seen her. And she smiled at him. Everyone laughed and told him to sit next to his wife. Jerome took his seat and different people stood up and gave speeches, advice, and pronounced blessings. Finally, Bodogou stood. He was the recognized elder of this village with no history. He spoke with authority and Jerome could tell he had the attention of every ear.

"My fellow Dinka, Nuer, Shillick, and Nubans, we gather this day to celebrate together, not as many peoples, but as one people. We celebrate the union of a white man and a black woman, no longer two, but one. Their story is an unusual one. It is the story of us all. These two young people have been brought together in the midst of war as we have all been. Out of difficulty, unity is born, from death comes new life. Their marriage is a symbol of what God offers us. As difficulty has caused them to come together and unite and start a new life, so God offers us the opportunity in our difficulty to come to him and unite with him and find new life. They have both asked for and received this new life from God which is the foundation of their union. I can only hope you, like Jerome and Yandeng, may also find salvation from God and new lives as they have. I pray God's blessing on Jerome and Yandeng, as I pray it for all of you who have come here to celebrate with them. Let us now celebrate their new life and be thankful each one, for the new life offered to us in the name of Jesus."

Not everyone believed like Bodogou, but they respected his words which caused more shouting, singing, and ululating. Food was then served as night fell and lanterns and fires were lit. The dancing and singing went on for hours. Jerome wondered from where all these emaciated people drew their energy. Many had been jumping and dancing since the morning.

Jerome hugged and shook hands with hundreds of people from all over the south of Sudan who came over to wish him and Yandeng well. Jerome wished the well-wishing and drumming and ululating would end, but Yandeng assured him it would be dawn before it would end.

And at about dawn the party thinned out and people started to head back to their tukuls. Jerome gathered his new family to make plans. It was then that he heard the sound of a jeep engine. Vehicles were rare in these parts, and it usually meant trouble. Two landrovers came into view a few hundred yards away.

"It's the SPLA," someone shouted.

# Chapter 58

Two landrovers filled to overflowing with SPLA soldiers pulled just outside the village and in their rag tag uniforms started spilling out and into the open area, which had been filled with dancers only a short time before.

The commander of the group stepped forward and shouted, "Everyone out of their tukuls."

He gave Jerome a long hard look.

"Who is in charge here?" he barked.

"I am," said Bodogou.

"Well then, get my men something to eat! And explain to me what a white man is doing here sitting beside this young Dinka."

"We have married them. He is now a Dinka."

"A Dinka!" he sputtered. "Then he must serve with us to defend the Dinka lands."

"He has already fought," Bodogou quickly answered. "He is wanted by the government army. They have hung pictures of him and are looking for him."

"Oh, so it's you. I have seen your picture!"

Then he turned and barked orders to an underling to pull everyone out of their tukuls and line them up.

"We need soldiers! We also need some women to accompany us."

The mood suddenly grew tense. Jerome reached over and took Yandeng's hand. He then stood in front of her facing the soldier, still holding her hand. The message was clear.

"Relax white man," the soldier shouted. "I am a decent man. I would not take a woman away from her man on her wedding day. You have helped our cause, and we will reward you."

People were being forced out of their tukuls and lined up, either willingly or unwillingly, and marched towards the dance area. Jerome, Yandeng, and Bodogou scanned the faces. Lual and Alual were nowhere to be seen. The soldiers put the young men into one group and the young women into another. The commander raised his voice.

"Men and women of southern Sudan, you must join the struggle for freedom. You are called to do your duty to your people and your lands. You should have joined us earlier, but we'll take you now without punishment."

He then walked slowly past the young people inspecting them.

"You women can return in a day or so. You men will be with us until our struggle is over."

He motioned to have them sit down by the landrovers to wait. He then called for food and his men quickly ate every remaining bit of sorghum, fig cakes, fruit, and bread. Then they got up and started towards the landrovers. Everyone watched in horror. An older man watching his son being taken away stepped forward and protested. He was knocked to the ground with a harsh swat. Jerome stepped forward and almost shouted.

"No! No sir. You must not do this!"

All grew quiet and every eye was on Jerome. People had been killed for less.

"What are you trying to do? Do you want to die, today of all days?"

"No sir, but you must not do this. We will feed you for as long as you want to stay. We will give you whatever clothing and tools we can spare. But don't take these young girls. They could be your daughters and nieces. Let them and the young men serve the army by starting a new village, and planting crops, and raising herds. As you see, the land is wasted. It needs its people to return and start their lives again. Help them, Commander. You can be remembered as the one who made it possible."

The commander stood still as a statue for 15 seconds. Jerome and all present knew that his life hung in a delicate balance. Finally, the commander spoke.

"This white man has fought with us. The government wants to find him, as it wants to find us. We will honor his wedding day. Let the women return to their tukuls. Let the young boys return as well. Keep only those boys 16 years of age and older."

The soldiers started pushing the girls back towards the main group. They pulled the young boys out and shoved them back towards the group as well. In the end 5 boys were taken. They then climbed into and on top of the landrovers and left quickly. The horrified group, now 5 members smaller, watched and wept as the vehicles drove out of sight. What had been a scene of uncontrolled celebration only hours before had now turned to sorrow.

Bodogou spoke. "Let us be thankful for those who were not taken. Let us pray for those who were. We don't know the road we will walk. But we can choose who will walk it with us. I urge you not to walk alone. God will walk with those who invite him."

He then asked all who wanted to pray with him. He prayed for the five boys who were taken. He prayed for the families who were left. And he prayed God's blessing on the union of Jerome and Yandeng.

"For we know Father that all life passes quickly. We will all pass. But you allow new life to follow us, as a sign that you are the giver of life in this life and in the next. So we pray life would come from this union that will last into eternity."

There were nods and tears and "Amens" from the crowd, and they slowly departed to their tukuls and a new day.

"I am sorry, but I think we must leave," Jerome said to Bodogou.

"I know. Lual and Alual have already left. Thank God. He has witnessed this scene before."

Yandeng started to weep and she fell into Bodogou's arms.

"I don't know how to thank you," she repeated over and over.

He held her for about five minutes, then kissed her on top of her head and nodded to Jerome that it was time.

"Try to keep in touch my children," he said as they picked their few belongings out of the tukul and left.

"We will do our best Bodogou," Jerome promised.

They walked silently, hand in hand, for the next hour. There was a deep connect. It seemed no words could communicate the feelings. They only spoke when they came to the landrover. They drove off the road, using the GPS to guide them.

"It's funny, but I never felt like I had a family so much as I do today. And today we're leaving everyone behind. I promise, when we can, we'll return."

"I promise I will make you keep your promise."

"Ok. It's a promise."

They bypassed Bentiu and headed north until the afternoon.

"The survey crew should be nearby, probably within 10 miles of us, but probably on the east side of the dirt road. We can't make contact with them, but I need to get close enough to get in range of their wireless router."

"How close?"

"I think within eyesight."

Jerome did some mental calculations and figured they would be about 5 miles further north of their current position. He turned east and drove more slowly. They passed a few empty tukuls. No signs of fire or devastation were seen, just empty tukuls. Within 10 minutes he came over a rise and saw the dirt road off ahead. He stopped and backed down a bit to stay out of sight and turned the engine off. It was about 3 in the afternoon.

"We can't go any further until dark or we'll risk being seen. We should be able to spot the lights from camp. If we start right at dark, they'll be watching videos and won't hear our engine."

"Ok. What do we do until then?" Yandeng asked, with a hint of a smile on her face.

"Hmm. This is our honeymoon. I can think of something."

"Hmm. What?"

Jerome turned the landrover around and drove back towards the empty tukuls.

"Where are you going?" Yandeng asked mischievously.

"I was told that the bride and groom always spent their first night together in a new tukul."

They had three hours until dark. By dark they were asleep in each other's arms, their energies sapped, and their love consummated.

# Chapter 59

Jerome startled out of his sleep at 9 PM, well after dark.
"Oh no. We overslept!"
They quickly pulled on their clothes.
Jerome started the landrover, retraced their route and eased over the rise where they had stopped earlier, keeping the headlights off. They saw not 2 miles to the north the light of the camp. Jerome turned the engine off and rolled downhill until he got to the road. He started the engine, and drove very slowly. As they neared the camp he pulled off to the west side of the road.

"I think you should stay here Yandeng. If I get caught, I don't want them to find you too."

"And what would I do without you? I can't drive. I'm coming with you."

Jerome put on his backpack and took Yandeng's hand. About 15 minutes later they could see artificial light illuminating the skyline ahead.

"We're within ¼ mile. Let me try now."

He took out his computer and booted up. He did a search for wireless networks and found a weak signal.

"I think we need to get closer."

They walked still closer and came to a clearing. At the far side of the clearing he could see two people walking around.

He did a new search and this time got a strong signal. He opened his email account and clicked the send/receive button. Within 30 seconds it finished. He saw 2 messages from Herb. The first one read:

"Jerome:

The Canadian government crew will be in Khartoum until Thursday the 5th. Can you get there? I told them you may show up, so they're looking for you. They said they'd consider taking you with them if you were not involved in any war crimes. Did you steal a government vehicle? That may be problematic. God, Jerome, you're in a mess. I'm doing what I can. Talk to me.

Herb"

By Their Fruit

There was a second message sent just 5 hours earlier.
"Jerome:
Where the hell are you? Talk to me! The government plane
leaves Khartoum tomorrow. I can't hold them. Help me out here.
Herb"
Jerome quickly banged out a response.
"Herb,
Hold that plane. I'm going to make it. I'm about 5 hours south
of the camp. I plan to drive there now and then get a flight back to
Khartoum on the Thursday morning camp shuttle. Yes I have a
government vehicle. I only borrowed it. I'll return it tomorrow. So
tell them to hold 2 seats on the plane. You did say I could bring a
spouse didn't you? Yes, I'm married. Can't wait til you meet the
bride. You'll love her. Anyway, I have a long way to go. Talk
soon.
Jerome"
He hit the send button and logged off. 15 minutes later they
were heading north on the dirt road. At about 3 AM they got within
range of the Ligheg camp.
"This could be tricky now. I know there is still a military guard
at the camp. They are supposed to stay up all night and watch. I bet
they don't."
He drove as quietly as possible, lights off. He drove off the road
and onto the air strip. Then he drove into the bush and thicket just
east of the landing strip. He drove into as much cover as he could
find and turned the engine off.
"Anyone tired?"
"Oh yes. I've been trying to stay awake to keep you awake."
They climbed into the back of the landrover and wrapped in each
other's arms. They made love again and fell asleep. They were
awakened by the drone of the Tallman airplane landing on the
nearby strip.
"Hey, wake up! Time to travel again."
They pushed through the brush to the edge of the runway. The
plane was parked and Jerome could see Mikhail unloading packages.
He knew he'd check in at the office, come back, and take off as
quickly as possible. They made their way to the plane staying in the
brush. Mikhail was not around. Jerome opened the door and helped

Yandeng inside. There were four seats, including the pilot's seat. He helped Yandeng into a seat in the back and sat beside her. They slid down in their seats so as not to be seen from the outside. Jerome took advantage of the situation and turned on his computer. He downloaded email again and found a new message from Herb.

"Jerome:

I'm so glad to hear from you. It sounds risky, but go ahead and try to make it. You're lucky. I was just on my way out when I got your message. I just emailed someone on the investigation team in Khartoum. It's the middle of the night there. What are you doing awake? Anyway, I asked them to be looking for you. And I mentioned your wife! I don't think they'll take her if you don't have some papers. See what you can do. Oh, I think I have a job for you. I'll tell you more later.

Herb"

They heard voices outside. Jerome peaked out the window. One of the soldiers was talking with Mikhail. Mikhail handed him a bag and the soldier handed him some money.

"Hmm. Looks like my Russian friend has a small business on the side," he said.

The soldier left and they heard Mikhail loading gear in the hold behind them. Then he opened the door and climbed in. When he saw his passengers he froze. Jerome spoke to him in Russian.

"I'd like to ask a favor."

"Let me guess, you want to hijack my plane."

"No, I just want a lift to Khartoum."

"You're crazy. You know they're looking for you."

"They have no reason to look for me. I haven't done anything wrong."

"You beat up two soldiers, a Tallman employee, and stole an army vehicle. Nice job!"

"It was self-defense, and I just returned the vehicle."

"You could get me in a lot of trouble Jerome. What is in it for me?"

"I'll be forever grateful."

"Ha! You know I'm thinking about dollars, or dinars at the very least."

"Hmm. Don't have either of those. Can you take a promise of payment?"

"I don't take promises."

"Oh. Well I was also going to promise I wouldn't tell anyone about your little business with the soldiers."

"What business?"

"The business where you hand them a bag and they hand you money."

"You're nuts. It's only alcohol."

"Like I said, I was going to promise not to tell anyone."

Mikhail thought, then stared at Jerome, then spoke.

"The only reason I'm doing this is because I like you. And I don't know why I like you. And what's up with the girl?"

"She's my wife. Be careful what you say about her."

"Shit. You're really crazy! Let's go." And he squeezed into his seat, put on his earphones, flicked switches and in no time they were lifting off over the African bush.

Yandeng squeezed Jerome's hand hard. She was peeking out of the window, her body rigid as a board.

"I didn't know it was this scary. What if we fall?"

She didn't let go of Jerome's hand until they landed. They could see a private jet marked Canada Air on the air strip. As soon as the plan stopped, they climbed out and ran to it. The pilot and co-pilot were hanging around below the aircraft.

"When are you taking off?" Jerome asked.

"We head for Paris as soon as the passengers get here. Why?"

"Did anyone mention the possibility of us coming on board? And why Paris?"

"Yes, the team lead did mention there may be two more flying out with us. Why Paris? Because we can't fly non-stop to Calgary from here. You do have paperwork?"

"What kind of paperwork?"

"Well, like a passport."

"Hmm. I have a passport, and this is my wife. But she doesn't have a passport."

"Well she needs something or she doesn't fly with us."

"But if she stays here, her life is in danger."

By Their Fruit

"I can't help any of that. I'm just telling you what I can and can't do."

"Hmm. Could you delay the flight until we get back?"

"That depends on when you get back. The group was due an hour ago. As soon as they get here, they are going to want to leave. I can let them know you are here, but I can't guarantee they'll wait."

Jerome jotted down the pilot's cell phone number and grabbed Yandeng's hand.

# Chapter 60

Jerome and Yandeng ran hand in hand towards the commercial terminal and caught a taxi out front.

"To the closest bank with a cash machine," Jerome barked to the driver.

Within minutes Jerome was inserting his card into an ATM machine and praying for success. This time, it allowed him to withdraw the equivalent of two hundred dollars, enough dinars to satisfy the taxi driver and take care of any embassy fees they might encounter. Within minutes he was back in the taxi.

When they arrived at the embassy they saw hundreds of people standing glumly in the hot sun waiting in a line.

Jerome pushed passed the line and up to the tinted window by the front gate. He couldn't tell if anyone was there.

"Excuse me. I'm in trouble with the Sudanese government. I need to see someone immediately."

A voice from behind the window said in a very businesslike, unhurried voice, "Passport please."

Jerome handed his passport through the opening at the bottom of the window. A marine appeared at the gate next to the window.

"Mr. Schultz, come in, quickly please."

Jerome took Yandeng by the arm and ushered her in front of him. The marine put his hand up and said, "Where is her passport?"

"That is why we're here. She is my wife. I want to start paperwork for her."

"Yes sir. This way Mr. and Mrs. Schultz."

They were led to an office marked "Consul" and ushered in. A man behind a big desk was on the phone and motioned for them to come in.

"I see," he was saying, "they are still wanted for theft of a vehicle. Ok. I'll address it."

When he hung up, Jerome spoke first.

"Sir, it is true we borrowed a vehicle, but it was needed to flee in peril of our lives."

"In peril of your lives? Very poetic. Why?"

"Two soldiers at the camp where we work were attempting to rape my friend, I mean my wife, I mean, we were only friends at the time, but we're married now, which brings me to the reason for my visit and we are very short on time."

"Woa! Back up about a paragraph young man. We're still not past the stolen vehicle. Ok. You've established motive, but a theft was still committed, and committed against the host government. This is awkward, very awkward."

"If it helps, Sir, we've returned the landrover."

"You've returned it!"

"Yes sir. We'll sort of. It's back at the camp and the keys are in it."

"Does the GOS know the vehicle is parked at the camp with the keys in it?"

"Well, that is a good point sir. They probably do not. But if you would allow me to send an email, they can reclaim it within the hour."

The Consul gave a hard stare at the two of them, then opened his web browser and backed away from his desk while looking closely over Jerome's shoulder. Jerome sent a message from the consul's email account to the office.

"Whoever is at the office:

This is Jerome. I am asking you on behalf of the GOS, Tallman, and myself, to send someone to the airstrip immediately and walk back about 20 yards into the brush on the east side. They will find a white GOS landrover. The keys are on the floor. Have them drive it to the office and alert the guard on duty. Then, email back to this address. It is very important. There are government people waiting for your response.

Thank you.

Jerome"

He hit the send button and returned to his seat.

"Ok, we'll wait for a response," the consul said.

"While we're waiting, I'd like to ask a huge favor," Jerome said. "Yandeng Nyeal, this young lady, and I recently married. I have paperwork here from a notary as evidence. I want to leave the country and I want to leave with my wife. I may be treated mercifully if apprehended by the GOS, especially since I've returned their landrover, but I am nearly certain she will face harsh consequences, if not death."

The consul had a look of doubt on his face, but he didn't argue, so Jerome continued.

"Since we're married and she is a political refugee, I thought you could help us."

"Wow. A political refugee! That may be pushing it. But then again, we could argue that everyone from Southern Sudan is a political refugee. Hmm. So what do you want?"

"I would like you to start her paperwork so she can not only leave the country with me, but more importantly get into another country, such as France."

"We need to do a little reality check Mr. Schultz. It would be a stretch for us to clear just your name so you can leave this country. This young lady wouldn't stand a prayer of a chance to just walk through customs, get her papers stamped, even if she had some, and walk or fly out of this country."

"Well, we have reserved seats on a private flight, which leaves in less than an hour by the way."

With that remark the consul gave a loud hoot and a laugh.

"What have you been smoking down at that oil camp, young man?"

"It's true sir. We're on the Canada Air flight that was chartered by the Canadian government investigation team that is looking into Tallman's involvement in the war. And they're holding seats for us if we get back to the airport before they leave. So, please, I'd appreciate it if you could do a huge favor for us quickly."

The consul gave Jerome a long, piercing stare. He didn't know if he could believe him or not. He figured Jerome must be on the level. After all, he did work for Tallman and he had become high-profile in the last week. He would be very happy to see him leave the country. He sighed, got up, and walked out the office door and returned with a Sudanese national.

"Please, Mr. and Mrs. Schultz, follow Naima. She'll take care of you. And Naima, please push it along as fast as you can. They have a flight to catch."

"Yes sir. Follow me please," she said.

They followed her into an office and took seats. Jerome showed his marriage certificate and passport. Yandeng had no birth certificate.

In 25 minutes Yandeng had temporary US paperwork, which she was told, would help her get into France, where she could get more paperwork. Naima then called the US embassy in France and notified them that Jerome and Yandeng would be visiting within days. She emailed their records on to them. The consul stuck his head in the door to see how things were going.

"They found your landrover Mr. Schultz. I asked the sergeant down at the camp to forward the news to his commander. Your name should be cleared from the government list shortly. How's it going, Naima?"

"Well, that's all I can do for now," she answered.

Jerome didn't know what that meant.

"Well, you'd better hurry. You have a flight to catch don't you?" the consul asked.

"Oh! Ok. Thank you both. Oh, and sir, could I ask one last favor?"

"Such as?"

"Could you please call this number and tell the pilot we're on the way."

"I thought they were holding the flight for you."

"Well, a call from you might ensure that. Sorry, I gave my cell phone away."

They shook hands and Jerome and Yandeng ran for the taxi.

They rushed through the city, dodging pedestrians and bicycles. When they got to the private terminal they saw that the stairs were still pushed up to the airplane. They got to the bottom and looked up to see the pilot standing there with his arms folded.

"I'm so glad you're still here," Jerome huffed, short of breath.

"Well it was the American consul who asked us to hold the flight for you, right?"

"Yes, it was," Jerome said as he shook the pilot's hand and showed his new paperwork to the flight attendant. There were only about 10 people on the flight. All eyes were on them as they entered the cabin.

"Hi," Jerome said sheepishly. "Mind if we join you?"

"You must be Mr. Schultz. We've heard about you and would actually like to thank you for some information that helped our team over the past week. We're glad we can help. There's lots of seats left, so sit anywhere you like."

"I hope you don't mind if we sit in the back," Jerome said. "We're on our honeymoon," he added after a pause. There were smiles and congratulations as they walked past the small crowd.

"How can this big thing fly?" Yandeng asked. She seemed incredulous.

"You'll see. And we may even see a movie, and have a meal."

"Don't tease me!" she said.

"See," Jerome said, as they served the meal. "I wasn't teasing."

They greedily finished their meal and asked for another. Then as the movie was coming on, they fell asleep in each other's arms. They didn't wake until they were landing in Paris. Yandeng went into a sort of cross between absolute delight and shock at seeing the large terminal building and all the airplanes and people and buses. Then they took a train, the first in her life, to the Gare du Nord. There they found a dark little hotel room near the Gare and made love until they surrendered to sleep. In the morning Jerome discovered wifi in the room and hooked up. He found another email from Herb.

"Jerome:

What's up? Give me news. Did you make it out of the Sudan? I heard unofficially that you were on the flight. Tell me it's true. I finally got a job worked out for you. It's in the oil business and it's in Africa. It's not with Tallman. I'm sorry. I hate to lose you, but I understand your situation. I hope you like it. I have a few reservations about it, but I'm sure you'll do Ok. It's in Algeria. I'm told it's pretty safe there. They've been having a bit of a civil war there though. Call me.

Herb"

Made in the USA
Charleston, SC
09 March 2017